Wheelbase

Dark dealings in the classic car world

Michael Kliebenstein

First published in December 2024

Published by Porter Press International Ltd
Hilltop Farm, Knighton-on-Teme, Tenbury Wells, WR15 8LY, UK
www.porterpress.co.uk

Printed by Gomer Press Ltd

ISBN 978-1-913089-51-1

A new classic car motoring thriller that offers a striking inside view into the world of dealers and collectors.

ABOUT PORTER PRESS INTERNATIONAL

Porter Press International was founded in 2005 by acclaimed automotive author Philip Porter. The company established its reputation as a leading publisher of top-quality motoring books with the segment-defining 'Great Cars' series, which has won numerous awards.

The flagship 'Ultimate' series covers major motoring subjects in exceptional depth. Beautifully designed and lavishly illustrated, these genuinely definitive histories are written by highly respected authors chosen for their superior knowledge and experience.

Alongside these series, Porter Press offers a very popular Land-Rover collection and numerous individual titles covering a wide range of topics from an ex-Colin McRae Subaru Impreza and the world's oldest Jaguar E-type to an extraordinary collection of pioneering motoring photographs.

The unrivalled Porter Press production team includes James Page, former editor of *Classic & Sports Car*; Steve Rendle, former senior commissioning editor for Haynes Publishing and chief design contributor Martin Port, former art director of *Classic & Sports Car*.

Authors include Doug Nye, Ian Wagstaff, Keith Bluemel, Mick Walsh, Chas Parker, Rinsey Mills, Richard Heseltine, Mark Cole, James Page, Serge Vanbockryck, Martin Port, J. Mac Hulbert, Gordon Bruce, Michael Kliebenstein and Philip Porter, several of whom have won the Guild of Motoring Writers' Montagu of Beaulieu Trophy. Porter Press is proud to have worked closely with motoring icons including Murray Walker, Martin Brundle, Derek Bell, Gordon Murray and Stirling Moss.

The dedicated Porter Press in-house team are based in a restored thatched 16th century barn at Philip and Julie's rural home in Worcestershire, England where Philip has lived for more than 40 years. Many of the office team, and those based remotely, have worked with the Porters for more than 10 years. All take enormous pride in their work.

Our list of published titles is expanding all the time with additions to the established series and exciting new individual titles. Each volume confirms Porter Press International as the publisher of choice for discerning motoring enthusiasts.

NEWEST TITLES

Spy Octane: The Vehicles of James Bond – Volume 1 by Matthew Field and Ajay Chowdhury

Prodrive: 40 Years of Success by Ian Wagstaff

Great Cars: Brawn BGP001/02 by David Tremayne

Great Cars: Subaru Impreza P8 WRC by Ian Wagstaff

JaguarSport XJR15 by Peter Steves

Ferrari 166MM Uovo by James Page

Three Men in a Land Rover by 'Waxy' Wainwright, Mike Palmer and Chris Wall

The Last Eye Witness by Doug Nye

Design & Desire by Keith Helfet

The Austin Pedal Car Story by David Wryly

MORE BOOKS BY PORTER PRESS INTERNATIONAL

ULTIMATE SERIES

Ultimate Works Porsche 962 by Serge Vanbockryck

Ultimate Ferrari 250 GTO by James Page

Ultimate McLaren F1 GTR by Mark Cole

Ultimate Works Porsche 956 by Serge Vanbockryck

Ultimate John Fitzpatrick Group C Porsches by Mark Cole

GREAT CARS SERIES

TWR-Porsche WSC95 by Serge Vanbockryck

Audi R8-405 by Ian Wagstaff

Jaguar Lightweight E-type 4 WPD by Philip Porter

Porsche 917-023 by Ian Wagstaff

Jaguar D-type XKD 504 by Philip Porter & Chas Parker

Ferrari 250 GT Short Wheelbase 2119 GT by Doug Nye

Maserati 250F 2528 by Ian Wagstaff

ERA R4D by J. Mac Hulbert

Jaguar Lightweight E-type 49 FXN by Philip Porter & James Page

Ferrari 250 GTO 4153 by Keith Bluemel

Jaguar C-type XKC 051 by Chas Parker & Philip Porter

Lotus 18 '912' by Ian Wagstaff

Alfa Romeo Monza 2211130 by Mick Walsh

Ford GT40 1075 by Ray Hutton

Bugatti Type 50 by Mark Morris and Julius Kruta

Shelby Cobra CSX2300 by Rinsey Mills

For more information, to place an order, or to join the free
Porter Press book club for offers and updates
please visit www.porterpress.co.uk

ACKNOWLEDGEMENTS

This book would not exist without the help of my publisher, Philip Porter of Porter Press International. I have entertained the idea of writing such a book for many years, and he eventually made me realise that the moment had come to put it all down on paper.

I would like to thank my structural editor Lewis Kingston for his generous help and patience in providing me with guidance in finding the correct words, phrases and descriptions to express my thoughts and emotions, to make this book possible. Even though I was writing in English, not my native tongue, his input and steerage gave me the confidence and capability to press on, and to deliver the story I wanted.

I would also like to thank Christian Hercher and the Hercher family for their enormous friendship, contribution and help, and much more besides.

Many special thanks go to Julie Porter, Andrew Noakes, Keith Bluemel, Hermann Layher, Jürgen Lewandowski, Thomas Sommer, Corrado Cupellini, Robert Fink, Franz Wittner, Uwe Klatt, James Page, Peer Steffensen, Richard Biddulph and Bruno Jarach for their inspiration, opportunity of comprehensive research, contribution of contacts and support. They are the most wonderful people.

I am most grateful to my family – my wife Annette, and my son Christopher – who have always provided support, humour and love. I dedicate this book to them.

CHAPTER 1

Mike Chapman glanced at his battered Rolex Daytona as the aircraft started to bank, the cash pressed against his heart shifting slightly. He caught a glimpse of the grey-blue Thames Estuary sweeping around Canvey Island through his window, checked the brown-faded dial of his watch again, and shook his head. The flight to London had departed late, and they hadn't made up the time; it was coming up on nine, and he figured it would be almost ten by the time he was through passport control, unpleasantly compressing his schedule.

In his tight-fitting chest sling was a neatly arranged and sealed brick of Euro notes that totalled fifty thousand. It was commission, from the sale of a stunning Bugatti, but it paled in comparison with what was stowed in the slender briefcase beneath his seat. Mike looked around cautiously, then reached down and patted the case, a vintage Louis Vuitton piece, reassuring himself that it was still present and correct. He permitted himself a small smile as he felt the familiar world-worn dark green leather and gilt metal lock beneath his fingers, a new high point in his career as a high-level classic car broker just within reach, soothing his ragged nerves.

He looked out of the window of the Airbus at the silvery strake of the Thames sliding past beneath him, and reflected on the Bugatti, his most recent deal. The car was a 1936 Type 57C, with a lovely Vanvooren body, and he'd managed to find an appreciative gentleman from Vienna to buy it. All told, it had been two days of sun, the best Sauvignon Blanc, slow drives through the region, and a smooth transaction. The perfect mix of employment and enjoyment. The rest of the time away had been challenging but that, that had been a pleasure.

A chime rang through the cabin. Mike again looked down at his wrist and clocked minute and hour hand alike, then quickly totted up the remaining time, steps and miles in the day, his mind working to avoid delays, to avoid disappointment; he clenched his fists, snuck another glimpse out of the window, and closed his eyes, letting work flood back in and take over completely.

Meet the representative from the Bugatti seller's legal team, give them their commission for helping broker the sale, dot the i's and cross the t's, done, he thought. That's the immediate sorted, and then the real hard business begins.

Not many knew much, if anything, about his professional life. For the most part, it was tremendously secretive. For starters, he had quickly come to understand that wealthy people, the truly wealthy, wanted nothing but discretion. If there was business to be carried out, it was to be done out of sight, with no attention. And he had found himself adopting a similar style; if there was work to be done, he didn't want to be seen, didn't want to be watched, didn't want anything to be noted, by anyone not directly involved. His clients were often tremendously sensitive about their physical assets, and their money doubly so.

For the uninitiated, this could make his line of work crippling. But he knew his way around the cars, around the market, and he didn't need to rely on gossip or reports to have a handle on values. After all, those who knew what was good for them did not talk publicly about completed deals. Those who did, for their sins, could find themselves on the sharp end of something unpleasant. Given the hidden microcosm of high-society types in which he operated, and factoring in the seemingly endless pool of criminals that pursued them all, privacy was essential.

Not always pretty, not always easy, but you have to swim with the sharks. That's what Rick always said, anyway. Just stay away from the biggest ones.

The aircraft heaved as it settled into its approach, and Mike's train of thought skipped onto the next track. Secure in his briefcase was a diligently negotiated options contract, the makings of a historic deal, which would give him permission to sell a collection of six significant Ferraris. The cars were part of an estate sale, being handled by the family of the deceased, who wanted a no-fuss solution; he had suggested the options route, which would allow him to sell the cars in whichever way he preferred, for whatever figure, provided he ultimately delivered £70 million back to the family.

Whatever was made above that mark was his to keep or, at least, his company's. There were tall hurdles still to tackle, though; firstly, they needed to swiftly raise the retainer required to get the deal signed and finalised, so they could access the cars. And, once that had been done, they couldn't sit on them, because the family wanted the money sooner rather than later. The cars would have to go out as almost as quickly as they came in anyway, to keep the money flowing the right way, to avoid the business getting tied up and overcommitted, and they'd ideally go to one buyer. That would be no mean feat but if Mike could play his cards, his contacts, and his opportunities right, he figured they could make the thick end of £10 million in a single shot, after costs.

But the money wasn't his sole concern or objective. Competition was rife and every car, every collection, was constantly being hunted by rival dealers, brokers, investors, and more. The deal he'd started in Italy, and was flying back to the UK to advance, would help elevate his business, unlocking access to even more potential clients, transactions and caches of desirable classics.

Mike heard someone approaching him and his head jerked upwards, his eyes open wide. But it was just a flight attendant, marching down the aisle towards him, checking that the passengers were all in order. He exhaled slowly, settling himself, and looked again at the older gentleman to his left; the man was still fast asleep, his safety belt fastened and visible, but his tray table was down, the remnants of the in-flight meal and insipid black coffee atop it. Carefully, Mike gathered up the debris, folded the table, and caught the eye of the hostess with a polite upwards nod. She stopped by their row, looked at the sleeping older gentleman, smiled warmly at Mike, and took the plate and cup.

He turned his attention back to his work, his eyes falling on the back of the seat in front of him. In the pocket was the in-flight travel magazine, an article about the best places to visit in Austria splashed across its cover.

The Austrian Collection, he thought, a wry smile spreading across his face, that's what we'll call it.

The truth was, the cars had all been found in a private collection in Andora, but the name would keep those curious off-track. The sales themselves could then be routed through Austria, adding some credibility to the name, while the finance and legal side would be handled by teams in the UK. There was still much to be done, and not much time to do it, but it was there for the taking.

And the world is changing, getting more complicated, more confusing, more challenging. We need this. I need it.

His fingers made small motions in the air as he played out the next steps in his head repeatedly, trying to ensure he would be where he needed to be, at the right time, with the right thing to say. But what lay beyond, the complication and difficulty of what was coming next, drove an unshakeable sense of restlessness through him, like a dark cloud looming on the horizon.

The hostess, making her way back up the cabin, spotted his pensive expression.

'Everything alright, sir?' she said quietly, leaning over the sleeping man a little.

Mike's head dipped. 'Thank you. Just the usual work stuff. Deadlines, deals, debts, doubts.'

'Well, you know what they say: you can't get anywhere unless you're willing to take a risk.'

'I hope that's not how you advertise this airline,' he responded, flashing a grin at her. 'But I hope you're right. If I get this wrong, we'll be out of cash, out of work, out of respect, and possibly out of the entire game. Just a light bit of pressure.'

'I'm sure you'll do just fine, sir,' she said, without missing a beat. 'But the best of luck to you, in any case.'

The hostess nodded once more, turned, and resumed her checks. Mike watched her for a minute, admiring the precision of her process, his thumb brushing the collar of his shirt.

Maybe she's right. Maybe I can land this. And it will plug a few holes if it comes to fruition. But you can't sell the bear's fur before you've shot the bear.

He looked at his Daytona again, his eyes locking momentarily on the inexorable onwards march of its second hand, as the world rushed towards him.

———————— • ————————

The damp conspired to amplify his aches and pains. Weeks of travelling, viewings, meetings, mostly poor hotels, and overly air-conditioned rooms, all felt like they were catching up with him at the same time. Mike sluggishly circled the company's 2009 Rolls-Royce Phantom in the airport car park, gritting his teeth while massaging his shoulder with his spare hand, and worked his way into the driver's seat. He tossed his case onto the passenger seat, watched the instruments of the Phantom come to life as he thumbed the starter button, and took a moment to gather his senses.

Been burning the candle at both ends for too long. But we're in tough waters. And there are plenty of sharks, just like Rick said.

Rick Sunderland was the other half of Chapman & Sunderland Vintage Motors, their classic car business, which based in Buckingham.

Things had been good until recently, but it seemed like the market had now fallen out of bed, and times were hard. They had to keep moving or fail; finding and grabbing opportunities was now mandatory, not optional.

Another heavy shower erupted outside Heathrow as the Phantom surged away from the airport, the rain thrashing against its windscreen. Mike's stern gaze slipped from the road ahead to the Spirit of Ecstasy at the tip of the Phantom, its prominence and solidity giving him a momentary boost of confidence, briefly mesmerising him. He'd always liked Rolls-Royces, but the fleeting distraction wasn't enough to shift his ongoing sense of unease, one that kept surging up, despite him repeatedly tucking it away, deep into the back of his mind.

A feeling like today is the tomorrow you always feared yesterday.

The downpour intensified, seemingly agreeing with him, and he shook his head at the gathered clouds. There were more urgent matters to tackle; once the Bugatti commission was dealt with, the juggernaut that was the acquisition and sale of the Austrian Collection would need painstakingly putting together. He'd already earmarked some financiers and potential clients to talk to in London, but needed to collar those that could move quickly. Secondly, Rick was busy chasing down an auctioneer named James Ratlick in the Docklands. Mike and Rick had entrusted him with the sale of a grey 1960 Mercedes-Benz 300SL Roadster, which had subsequently netted £1.1 million, but the car's former owner had received no payment.

The Phantom carved through heavy traffic, its Pirellis pushing the standing water aside with ease. The radio piped up with *London's Calling*, brightening Mike's mood, transporting him back to easier, more gentle times. The hectic and tiny roads around Heathrow disappeared behind the Rolls-Royce as it surged down the slip road onto the M25, its V12 murmuring peacefully, and Mike felt some weight slipping from his shoulders. His thumb rolled over the Rolls' finely hewn switchgear, effortlessly selecting and dialling Rick's number. As he expected, Rick answered almost immediately.

'Welcome back,' said Rick snappily. 'How are you?'

'Thank you. I'm on the M25, so I could be better but, yes, I'm okay,' said Mike. 'Just on my way to hand over the legal team's commission, for the Bugatti sale.'

'That panned out alright?'

'Yes, they managed to swing things our way. They wanted Euros, cash, something tangible, something they could keep fully off the record.'

'Wouldn't want to make it easy for us, would they?' said Rick gruffly.

'No, but I managed to get it out before heading back, so we're not going to have to wait on a bank here to arrange that Euro withdrawal. The sooner we get this sorted, the better.'

'Don't waste your time chatting me up, then.'

'Chance would be a fine thing.'

A single gritty, mocking laugh cracked its way out of the Phantom's speakers.

'In all seriousness, I'm putting the hammer down,' said Mike. 'But I just wanted to find out the latest from your end.'

'I'm in the Docklands still, working on this Mercedes issue. But look, we've a new curveball or two to deal with.'

Mike raised an eyebrow and involuntarily tightened his grip on the wheel of the Rolls-Royce.

'I know you're loaded to the nines but, once you've dropped off the cash, drive straight to the Goring Hotel, get yourself a room, and get ready for a morning meeting with the hedge fund people from Hadfords. The investment guys. They're interested in buying our new collection.'

'The Austrian Collection?'

'Ah, so that's what we're going to call it. Yes, that one. They're not car people, but I think they understand the potential and want to buy the collection.'

'They're not car people,' said Mike curtly, the muscles in his neck still twinging. 'They're an arrogant bunch of tossers, that's what they are. I know them.'

'Focus on their money, not their character. Don't lead with that,' said Rick, a hint of irritation flitting into his voice. 'Make a great first impression, lay the groundwork, and call me after.'

Mike's eyes flashed over to his suitcase, a leftover from his much-loved Derby Bentley with a green Vanden Plas body; the memories of easier-going trips blunted his frustrations, putting a thin smile on his face, while the thoughts of the potential success within helped bring his focus sharply back into line.

'Alright, alright. I'll get a conference room set up and I'll go from there,' he said, conviction filling his voice. 'As you say, selling is the focus. That aside, what's the story with the 300SL Roadster?'

He heard Rick huff in annoyance. 'Ratlick says that the liquidity from the auction is all gone, so he's offering a yellow Lamborghini Miura P400 as payment for the Mercedes instead.'

Mike shook his head. 'Getting all too common, that. What's the difficulty with putting the bloody money in an escrow account and keeping it for your clients?'

'I know, Mike, I know. I think he's got some kind of Ponzi scheme going, pulling money from new other pots into others, or his own. And I bet you he's stashed some of the cars away for himself.'

'But that never works, in the long run.'

'I didn't say he was being smart about it, Mike. And now there's a lot of heat on him.'

'So, too much cash, too much temptation, and his head's got too big.'

'Can't have got that big, Mike,' said Rick. 'It still fits up his ass, apparently.'

A smirk flashed across Mike's face as he nudged the Phantom into the next lane, passing a line of trucks pegged against their limiters. 'Alright, well, the Miura is probably worth as much, even if it's not an S, but I'm not sure what good that does Bayerwald.'

'He's been waiting for the money from the Mercedes for a while, and he's not in any rush,' said Rick. 'He knows, at least, that we're good for it.'

'Okay, so we take on the Miura, we sell that, Bayerwald gets his cheque, and everyone's happy. I think we can manage that.'

'I know we can do it. We won't have any trouble shifting a low-mileage Miura in a desirable colour; I've dealt with a few recently and I've got a good bead on the cars and the clients,' said Rick confidently. 'We'll need to get it picked up, though, because it's at the ExCel Centre, with papers and keys.'

A relieved smile flashed across Mike's face. 'That's a plan, then. And we do have proof of ownership, right?'

'He's got a V5C in his name, which I know isn't proof, but he's also got all the documentation and a contract of sale, too. No one seems to be missing one, either.'

'Right,' said Mike, feeling more content. 'I am sincerely looking forward to getting that sorted.'

'Yeah. But listen,' said Rick ominously. 'One more thing. Before you end up at the Goring, swing by our garage in Bathurst Mews, will you? Got something to show you.'

'Important?'

'Important, but I don't want to discuss it right now.'

'Right,' said Mike, the contentment fleeing from his body as the call ended. He felt an overwhelming sense of tiredness wash over him, the rainfall swelling and obscuring the view ahead, until the Rolls-Royce's wipers cut cleanly through it; he blinked, paused for a moment, then scrolled through his phone book and dialled the Goring hotel. The manager greeted him by name, wished him well, and set aside one of the few remaining rooms and a conference room for seven in the morning. Mike thanked him, hung up, and dialled Simon, the showroom manager for Chapman & Sunderland. The phone rang out, and the voicemail picked up.

'Short order, I know, Simon, but can you pick up a yellow Miura from the ExCel Centre as soon as possible? Documents, keys, the works, should all be present,' said Mike. 'And no payment required. It's in car park five, and the ticket's in the glove box. Call me back if there are any gripes.'

He pressed the end-call button again. Ahead, a truck started to indicate; he dabbed the Phantom's brake pedal, flashed its mains a few times, and watched the eighteen-wheeler slide sideways, starting a tiny-speed-differential drag race with another on the inside lane. He indicated, pulled clear, and sailed past, the trucks rapidly disappearing behind him as he pushed the Phantom's accelerator further towards the plush carpet below.

'And, hopefully, the Hadfords people are interested in the collection,' he muttered to himself. They were a tough bunch, only really engaged when a massive profit was on the cards, and he suspected any deal would be a nightmare to flesh out.

'Big money people, not car people,' he murmured. 'Another uphill battle, for sure.'

Nevertheless, as the Phantom swept into South Kensington, it represented an opportunity.

And we must take it.

CHAPTER 2

The Phantom rolled slowly through a narrow, tan-bricked archway into a small courtyard, enclosed by elegant three-storey townhouses. On the right was a series of wide double-doored garages, two of which sported small glass plaques with C&S etched into them. The door to one was open, and Rick stepped out and waved as the Phantom approached. He gestured for Mike to park the Phantom across the doors, then disappeared inside.

The Rolls-Royce fell silent as Mike stepped out onto the damp cobbles. He took a moment to straighten his long coat, rolled his head left then right, brushed his hair back, then flexed his fingers, testing his tired joints. He looked around inquisitively, saw no one, and revelled fleetingly in the peaceful, cool ambiance of the courtyard.

'I haven't got all day,' proclaimed Rick from inside, his voice firm but friendly.

Mike smirked and stepped inside, his eyes falling immediately onto a red 1960 Ferrari 250 GT SWB. It was sitting square in the middle of the garage, resplendent and unmissable on an all-white background, the soft light from the warm halogens overhead flowing over it like a waterfall, exaggerating its beautiful curves.

'Alright, Mike,' said Rick, slapping his wide palm down on Mike's shoulder. The force of the welcoming gesture made Mike stagger sideways; he grunted in surprise, took a moment to compose himself, and coughed assertively, clearing his throat.

'Good to see you too, Rick.'

'Now we've the pleasantries out of the way, I don't suppose you happen to remember this Ferrari?'

'Couldn't forget it,' said Mike, tossing his coat neatly onto a hook on the wall. 'We sold this about three months ago to a collector in Malta, right?'

'Yes and no,' said Rick, a grimace materialising on his face. 'The owner has returned it.'

'For what damned reason?' said Mike. 'This car was as straight as a die, from nose to tail.'

Rick tipped his head and waved a hand in the Ferrari's direction. 'He thinks it's not the same car. He says, and I quote, "It's a bloody fake."'

Mike's eyes bulged. 'What? Not possible. We had it checked by all the relevant specialists, and it's in every single book about the type. The best people have been over this with a fine-tooth comb.'

Rick nodded, then pointed towards the Ferrari's engine bay. 'See for yourself. Look at the chassis number.'

Mike marched over to a gloss-white workbench and extricated a magnifying glass, a jeweller's loupe, and a torch, from the top drawer. Rick watched attentively as Mike leant over the Ferrari's exposed and immaculate engine, the beam from the torch prying deep into the depths.

'Good car?' said Rick.

'Wonderful,' said Mike, one hand covering his belt buckle and trouser buttons, to avoid marring the car's paint. 'And the number is correct.'

'But?'

'It is the correct chassis number, for sure, but the digits look slightly odd, yes. The style isn't quite right, like they weren't struck with original tools, and the strikes are too light, too. And I don't like the spacing. This isn't original.'

'So, you agree. It's not the car. It's a car, but not the car we sold.'

'There's no pitting on the unpainted surfaces between the numbers,' said Mike, his voice straining as he leant further into the engine bay. 'This is all new, and amateurish. What else have you clocked?'

'You know the fine details better than I,' said Rick, turning his palms upwards. 'The engine number looks good, but the carburettors look new to me. Ditto the leads, filters, cam cover gaskets, that kind of thing.'

'The engine number's not bad, agreed, but it could be a new casting. And these inner panels are too shiny, too new. I can see some kind of regular scratching on the inside, possibly from an English wheel. That means they were not made in the Italy of the sixties, that's for sure.'

'How can you tell?' said Rick, puzzled.

'The Italians at Carrozzeria Scaglietti, in those days, especially under master craftsman Giancarlo Guerra, worked purely by hand. They worked with hand-crafting tools like hammers and other hand beating equipment for panelling. You'd see traces of that work, but you wouldn't see regular, consistent marks, like that from an English wheel.'

'The whole thing is a fake, then?' said Rick, his tone a mix of intrigue and frustration.

'It would appear the body was made recently in England, or at least somewhere in the Northern hemisphere of Europe. It's certainly not a hammered body.'

'Bollocks. My suspicions confirmed, then,' said Rick, his voice dull. 'And now the client wants his money back.'

'From us, or from the seller?'

'He doesn't care. We were the brokers. All he cares about is that he gets eight million sterling right back into his account. The real car back, or the cash back, we choose, as soon as possible.'

'But how could this happen?' said Mike, anger creeping into edges of his voice. 'I mean the original car was delivered by us on a covered truck to Malta. Did the buyer exchange it?'

Rick shook his head slowly as Mike started inspecting the car's interior, his fingers tracing over the panelling, stitching, and instrumentation.

'No, I trust the buyer, but someone evidently has, and they evidently thought the buyer wouldn't realise,' said Rick. 'He found out very quickly though, when he drove it. It's miserable, apparently. Said it just feels like a collection of random parts motoring along in loose formation.'

'Shame. Some effort's gone in here,' said Mike. 'Cream leather, as it should be, but artificially patinated with some kind of varnish. This is no mean feat, you know, Rick. This is the exact same specification as the car we sent out. Colour, interior, even the same Heuer-model stopwatch. Someone has got to have put at least £500,000 into this.'

'Can't get the smell right, though, can they?'

'No,' said Mike. 'That originality, that history, that's practically impossible to emulate.'

Rick sat down on a small wooden chair, the wood creaking beneath his stocky frame, and stared out into the mews. 'I don't think there was enough time for them to build something outright, to get in on this deal, so they must have found an existing replica, reworked it, and exchanged it on the truck.'

'What about the delivery driver?'

'He's disappeared.'

'Great. Along with our car, and our payday for eight million,' said Mike, exasperated. 'We've got to find out where this thing came from,' he added, pointing at the Ferrari. 'This deal happened quickly; it must have been bought recently from somewhere, from someone.'

'Pretty bloody impressive,' said Rick, looking at Mike sternly.

'I'll give you that,' said Mike. 'It's remarkable. We sold one of the most original Ferrari 250 GT SWBs in the world. And here it is, back again, but as a total bloody fake.'

Rick extracted a flask from his pocket, took a swig, and gestured towards the faux Ferrari. 'Someone knew exactly what we were doing here, Mike. Someone close to us.'

'But what good's the real thing to whoever's got it now? Its identity is known to all, and it's useless to the new buyer once it's registered as stolen.'

'Maybe the new owner doesn't care. It could just end up stashed away in some warehouse in the States, or in a garage in a mansion in Vietnam, or maybe even on display in a luxury suite in China. A buyer going down this route probably isn't going to care about heritage or paperwork.'

'You figure?'

'Maybe the Emirates, maybe out there. The buyer won't care, if it's the real deal,' said Rick. He slowly screwed the cap back onto his flask, the scratching of the threads cutting through the silence of the workshop, then cracked the knuckles on one hand, then on the other.

'Right,' said Mike, shaking his head in disbelief. 'Alright, then. Insurance?'

'We're not covered for anything like this. We've got to find the real car, and get it back, otherwise we're up the proverbial creek, without the proverbial paddle. Hopefully, it's still in Europe.'

'And if it's not?'

'We won't even have a fucking canoe. If we keep our heads above the water, it'll be a miracle.'

Mike stepped back from the Ferrari and brushed himself down. One hand went up to his face, his index finger tapping on his nose. Slowly, his posture softened, his breathing slowed. Rick could see him murmuring to himself, his eyes sweeping back and forth across the cloned car.

'Okay,' said Mike in a calm, controlled voice. 'Well, we best hope it's still in Europe, then.'

'What's our course of action?'

'You're going to have to handle this. I've got to go to the Goring to set up everything for the meeting with Hadfords. We've got to push on with that, in case that deal ends up having to offset the damage from this mess.'

'Sound. You focus on the Austrian Collection for now. I'll start making some enquiries and keep things subtle until we've some idea of what's going on. Now, it just looks like we delivered a fake car, and that's far from ideal.'

'To say the least,' said Mike gruffly. 'The last thing we want is the buyer spreading that kind of story.'

'No, it's not a good spot to be in at all, Mike. This could put us out of business, and whoever's done this, well, they're no joke.'

Sharks.

'Sharks,' said Mike under his breath, as they closed the garage.

CHAPTER 3

Mike leaned back in his chair and tapped his pen against his pad. Seventy million hanging in the air for the Austrian Collection. Eight million in the form of a vanished Ferrari. One million in outstanding trades elsewhere. A financial and literal nightmare, leveraged against everything he and Rick owned.

A contact was highlighted on Rick's phone, glowing dimly, undialed. Mike's eyes kept swinging back to it, despite his best efforts.

And more, he thought, agitated. *There's Harriston.*

Chapman & Sunderland had done well so far, but it had not yet been able to drum up the finances required to capitalise on some of the larger opportunities that had come its way. As a result, and driven by a need and desire to expand, Mike and Rick had gone seeking investment. After several false starts and dead ends, Mike had been introduced to Lord Harriston at a local vintage racing event. He transpired to be quite the shark himself; he had an extensive business network, stacks of capital behind him, and made decisions like a flash of lightning.

He was also generally accepted as being a brutal man to do business with, leading many to give him a wide berth. *But you can't always choose your partners*, thought Mike, flicking through the paperwork on his desk. *They're all dangerous animals.*

Mike idly typed Harriston's name into the search engine, to see if there was anything new he needed to know, anything that might give him some edge or insight. There was nothing that leapt out, just an article compiling the latest details: Richard Charles Harriston, born in 1948, former House of Lords, estimated fortune of £5.7 billion, son of famous property developers, educated at the Columbia business school, made a fortune developing US businesses and selling them on, keen interest in racing.

Although I'd not say he's a true car person.

The pages flipped by as Mike scanned for anything else of interest. One article detailed some of Harriston's less evocative exploits, including a part share in a wind-farm project with a European consortium, which had secured funding totalling £2.3 billion from major banks. The story's footnote also detailed Harriston's recent investment in mining facilities for lithium, cobalt, nickel, graphite, anything that was rising in demand.

'Harriston is reputed to have ties to the communist party of China and, through his work as an industrial advisor to the European Parliament in Brussels, supports its aims,' said Mike, reading the remainder out loud. 'He was also a devout backer of Brexit, voting in favour of it in 2016.'

Bastard.

'But what can you do?' he murmured. 'Even the most perfect of partners can end up stabbing you in the back. At least we've our guard up.'

He idly flicked through a website slideshow displaying some of Harriston's cars. He nodded approvingly as a Porsche 917, Lola T70, Ferrari 312P and Jaguar D-type slipped past on his screen.

Real showstoppers. Steeped in motorsport history. But all just Top Trumps-style stuff. The most expensive toys.

He rapped his fingers on his desk, and the display on his phone timed out. But the memory of Harriston remained sharp and vivid.

Probably, mused Mike, *because I've got to talk to him about money again*.

The Austrian Collection stood to be a prime money-maker. It consisted of some sublime cars, including a 1964 Ferrari 250 LM, and a 1963 250 P that had later been upgraded to a 330 P, but the centrepiece was a stellar 1962 250 GTO. Alone, it stood to net north of thirty million pounds. But, predictably, it wasn't the kind of collection that you could just offer to sell, with no security. You had to put a business card in the door jamb, and then hammer it home with a serious chunk of change, something that really demonstrated your intent, your security, your confidence.

In this instance, what was needed to secure the deal, to grant access to the cars to begin selling, was £2 million. The kind of cash that a sharp-minded businessman, with plenty of resources and an awareness of the market, might be willing to gamble on a classic car company that was seeking to expand, to up its game, provided it knew what it was talking about.

Harriston.

Mike breathed in slowly, exhaled, and picked up his phone.

———————— • ————————

The conference room in the Goring was exactly what Mike wanted: spacious, with warm wood panelling, a neutral light carpet, plush padded reclining office chairs, and plenty of tea, coffee and fresh water on hand. He'd even been easily able to connect his laptop to the large monitor on the wall, which suggested to him that it truly was going to be a good day. Mike nodded, checked the time on his Daytona, and hovered near the door. He could hear the large clock in the hotel's foyer striking the hour, *one, two, three,* but before its count finished the door to the conference room swung open.

Edward Hadford, a beanpole of a man, strode into the room, making a beeline for Mike. He shook his hand firmly, didn't say a word, and then wandered straight over to the coffee machine, punching the button for a double espresso.

Feels about right, thought Mike. *Typical brash hedge-fund type.*

'Now, look,' said Hadford, his voice deeper and more assertive than his frame would suggest. 'You know we typically go for artwork, not cars. The former I'm not fussed about, myself, but that's considerably more interest than I express in the latter.'

Well, at least he's honest.

'So, Michael, you've got to win me over with these potential assets,' said Hadford. 'And here's fifteen minutes in which to do it.'

'How many years have you been in the hedge-fund trade, Mr Hadford?' said Mike, trying to sound unfazed.

'Thirty-five years, virtually all of it in the arts sector. But you know this,' said Hadford, rolling his eyes.

'So, you know your way around, and you know priceless works when you see them. The kind of pieces that make you immediately reach for your prime contacts book.'

'Yes.'

'Well, Mr Hadford, I've been in the classic car market for forty-five years. And, yes, I've seen, and dealt with, countless priceless works. The most fantastic of designs. The most remarkable pieces of engineering. Character and soul that can charm and captivate.'

Hadford's head tipped to the side a little.

'But I know that's not the real interest here,' said Mike, putting up a picture on the screen. 'This is a Ferrari GTO. Ten years ago, you could pick one up for £25 million.'

'Sounds like £25 million too much,' said Hadford wryly.

'Two months ago, this same car changed hands for £62 million.'

Hadford blinked, stirred his coffee, and remained silent.

Damned good poker face.

The picture on the screen changed.

'This is the ultra-rare Uhlenhaut Mercedes-Benz 300SLR. Only two exist. One sold recently for £125 million. A single trade, worth £125 million. And all that had to be handled was a car.'

Hadford's head tipped to the other side.

'And that means a car is automatically comparable to a piece of art?' said Hadford, smiling maliciously. 'I don't think a few high points automatically entail a huge amount of potential. Property, now that's more interesting. London, Bangkok, Paris, New York, we've plenty going on there.'

'All markets with flourishing classic markets, and there are many other regions where investment and acquisition of notable classics is expanding at a rapid rate,' responded Mike assertively. 'Take China, for example; more and more millionaires and billionaires, all seeking ways to invest and enjoy their riches.'

'And what about security? This is evidently just a market, and markets can go down as well as up.'

Rich, coming from someone who's tanked accounts totalling $15 billion in the past, and walked away with nary a scratch.

'This is true. But there's no reason to look down on classic cars. The customers are demanding and knowledgeable. And many are viewed as assets, not just collectables. Their rarity, for one thing, helps secure their value. And some, their design and prestige alone makes them comparable and accepted as art.'

Hadford just stirred his coffee again.

'As a case in point, we've recently brokered deals between owners and art collectors, with the cars either going on display in galleries or private collections, amid other high-end artworks. If someone spends, say, twenty million on an Aston Martin DBR1 or Mercedes W196, it does not look out of place alongside a Monet, a van Gogh, a Baishi.'

'But cars, well, they're just a bit passé now, no?' said Hadford. 'You've seen how the world is changing. Technology is leaving the traditional appreciation of the car in the dust, and those keen on them, well, you could just classify them as a dying breed. I only hear young types talking about Tesla these days, or those unpronounceable Chinese brands that are springing up left, right and centre.'

'That might appear to be the case, if you only look at the surface. In my direct experience, and on the contrary, we've seen plenty of new and younger customers approaching us in the past few years. Many of them have come to us through their involvement in art; they consider a car as a sculpture that's capable of motion, evoking countless different sensations and reactions.'

Hadford let out a chuckle, shook his head, then put his hands on the table, arms wide. 'Last week, I had a client acquire a prominent painting by Roy Lichtenstein, and he spent $750,000 building a climate-controlled viewing room for it,' said Hadford, making it sound like someone was just paying a small bill. 'Its own plot, its own standalone building, just for that one sole piece of work. That is the importance, and the merit, with which art is treated. Can you give me an example of anything like that in the classic world?'

'Countless,' said Mike confidently. 'Collectors have them in their houses, garages, and sometimes even their offices and living rooms. Just like paintings. We recently delivered a 1962 Ferrari GT Lusso to a client in New York. She had the car lifted into her Manhattan lobby on the 25th floor. They had to take all the windows out, and use a helicopter, to get it up there. You should have seen the insurance paperwork and costs. And she did that solely to place it by her desk, so she could admire it, along with some Calder pieces she'd also collected.'

'How old was this client?'

Ah.

'Yes, fair, she was a… mature client. But, on the flip side, we've seen many younger collectors starting to show similar motives. In the Asian market, for example, a good Ferrari is now being treated like an haute couture modernist sculpture that can be enjoyed in both dynamic and static forms. And you know the kind of money that's swimming around in that market.'

'I'm still not convinced that you can class cars as art,' said Hadford, seeming dissatisfied. 'But maybe we'll have to agree to disagree.'

The spoon made its little dance in his cup again.

'Tell me about what you're offering,' said Hadford casually.

Mike nodded and pushed a box of documents towards him. 'I have an off-market collection, in which there are six very significant cars that I would offer to you in a package deal.'

'How much?'

'The package will cost you £97.5 million, including delivery and storage in a Swiss bonded warehouse, in which the cars can remain until resale.'

'And my return?'

'Based on recent auction sales, and historic trends, I can see you reselling the cars, individually, for a total of at least £180 million. Perhaps more, if you can store them and bide your time.'

'And what am I buying, exactly?'

'A 1962 Ferrari GTO, a 1964 Ferrari 250 LM, a 1960 250 GT SWB Berlinetta Competizione, a 1957 Ferrari 250 GT Tour de France-winning car, a 1963 Ferrari 250 P upgraded to 330 P specification, and a 1959 Ferrari 250 GT Interim Berlinetta, all alloy.'

'I'll ask my last question again.'

'It's like someone turning up on your doorstep with a crate full of unseen, never-on-the-market Monets. And the GTO, well, that alone might as well be the Mona Lisa.'

Hadford nodded, then made a little spiralling gesture with his hand.

'These are the greatest examples of pure technical craftsmanship, outstanding design, distinctive personality, and buyer taste,' continued Mike. 'They are universally recognised by investors, collectors, and drivers alike. The people who made these cars were artisans, commanding nothing but authority and admiration in their periods of work. Especially in the decades that these cars were built. And the ownership of any guarantees a client access to countless opportunities to display and show off their priceless works.'

A flash of something resembling enthusiasm rippled across Hadford's face.

'And buying collectable, desirable, and storied cars that are new onto the market, that's a smart move. These cars often haven't been seen for years, decades, and many may not realise they still exist, which makes them even more noteworthy, even more likely to grab the attention of buyers. But you must check them thoroughly, and that's exactly what I do, for every single car.'

'Right,' said Hadford. 'Including, presumably, for these?'

'Yes. I have here the documentation on every car,' said Mike. 'Pictures, details, a historic background, even the Foglio Montaggios in little bound booklets, all of which will help you and your customers understand the nature and value of these cars. Every car has also been carefully verified and comes with all its original papers and certificates.'

'I'd prefer them to end up in Lichtenstein,' said Hadford, firmly pressing his index finger against the top of the wooden conference desk. 'We've a place there to store our paintings and valuables. They've not handled cars before, but I suspect they'll find them easier to move.'

'I'm sure they'll find them easier to sell, too.'

'Very well,' said Hadford. 'Give me ten days to discuss it with my partners and clients. I'd like to see if I can disperse the cars quickly, rather than sitting on them in storage. We've a client in Riyadh who likes this kind of thing. We sold his shares in Saudi Aramco to the Americans in December, and they'd like to invest some of that elsewhere.'

Hadford pushed his coffee aside, stood up, and shook Mike's hand firmly.

'You'll be hearing from me shortly. Good day.'

'Right,' said Mike, as Hadford strode out of the room. 'Same to you.'

Blimey, thought Mike, as he listened to Hadford's receding footsteps. *Another one to swim with*.

CHAPTER 4

The Phantom accelerated away from the hotel, its twelve cylinders soothing Mike's mood a little. The meeting had felt like an assault but, in just seven minutes, he appeared to have the answer he wanted, and a much-needed buyer in the works. He hurriedly flipped through his contacts list to dial Rick.

'It was quick and dirty, Rick. But Hadford's got someone on the hook. I think it's Abdul Ben Ali.'

'The son of that Saudi Prince who was in the news recently?'

'The very same. I used to know him, you know?'

'Small world, eh?' said Rick.

'I haven't spoken to him for longer than I can remember, though. The fortune he left behind was, what, fifteen billion? And the shares in those companies, to boot.'

'So, a few hundred million or so on a bit of flash shouldn't be a problem for him.'

'Not in the slightest. I read that he recently picked up the Estrela de Fura ruby, the star of all rubies, and that was $34 million.'

'For a single gemstone?' said Rick incredulously.

'Yeah. Admittedly 55.2 carats, and cut from a 101-carat stone, but still, just a single stone.'

'Well, at least we know who Hadfords is considering, and that they're not toytown. Bit of a slip-up on their behalf. Might give us an advantage.'

'Maybe. Maybe not. But I'll take it, either way.'

The central screen in the Rolls-Royce lit up, a new readout showing another incoming call.

Harriston.

'Rick, I have to go. Harriston's calling me.'

'Good luck,' said Rick quickly, as Mike accepted the new call.

'How are proceedings with the Ferrari collection?' said Harriston, his deep, smooth voice filling the Rolls-Royce. 'I'm keen to hear how you're progressing.'

'The options contract, for £70 million, runs until Friday next week. There's a big margin at hand and we've got everything we need, barring the initial deposit we spoke about,' said Mike, a tinge of hopefulness creeping into this voice. 'The one we discussed again recently.'

'I see,' said Harriston nonchalantly. 'And after that?'

'We'll get the cars into the country as quickly as possible. We're already working on finding buyers, so we're hoping that we can disperse the collection quickly.'

'You've told me that before,' said Harriston a little less nonchalantly. 'What I want to know is exactly how long it will take.'

'Once we have the investment from your good self, for the deposit, and the paperwork is signed, we'll probably have the cars here in a matter of days. Beyond that, I don't think it'll take long to move them on. It really depends on who steps forward, and how we choose to sell them.'

Harriston grunted. No response was forthcoming. Silence invaded the cabin of the Phantom and squatted on Mike's shoulders oppressively. He squinted and shook his head in annoyance, then took a moment to calm himself, envisioning the cars rolling over the block, the money rolling in.

'Time is a factor,' said Mike politely.

'Come and see me at Silverstone at three today. Take the south entrance, come to box 34. We'll catch up there.'

He says 'jump,' I say…

'It would be my pleasure. I will make my way there, and I look forward to seeing you.'

Harriston said nothing more and hung up, leaving Mike listening to the dull thrum of the road passing beneath the Phantom. He pointed it north, on the M1, and started towards Buckinghamshire, its prow parting the traffic like Moses the Red Sea.

Upon reaching Silverstone, he guided the Rolls-Royce carefully around the outer roads, looking for the south entrance, only stumbling on it after taking some half-heard instructions from a track marshal. It felt like a distinctly hidden and private entrance to the far end of the track, one that avoided all the congestion of the main entrance over the bridge.

Mike abandoned the Phantom somewhere where it looked like it was supposed to be, then quizzed a guard about where to find box 34. A series of tunnels led him to the pitlane, where there were at least 25 cars idling noisily. He weaved his way through the crowd of team members, press and public, covering his ears occasionally as the cars intermittently delved into their engine warm-up routine.

'GT3 timed training starts in ten,' a crisp, clipped voice announced over the Tannoy, somehow cutting through the din. Porsches, Ferraris, McLarens and more began to make their way past Mike as he walked down the pitlane, his hands reaching up to the sides of his head every time one rolled past, the blare of the exhausts spearing through his skin and bones.

A set of ear defenders would be great, right about now. This is just intolerable.

The numbers on the doors of the pits continued to ascend, finally reaching 34. He wandered inside, and up the stairs, into an empty viewing area. He heard footsteps behind him; a pit crew engineer was marching up the stairs, approaching him.

'Chapman, yes?' asked the man, sizing him up.

'Yes. I'm here to see–'

'Yes, Harriston is downstairs. Come with me,' he said, pointing back down the stairs. 'Come far today?'

'Just from London. You?'

'Me? I was in Shanghai the day before yesterday, along with several of the other engineers. We just got here yesterday.'

He guided Mike swiftly into the pit area, and handed over a helmet, pair of gloves, shoes, ear plugs, and a racing suit.

'Get dressed. You're going out.'

I'm doing what?

'Sorry, what?'

'Harriston's car,' said the engineer, sticking his hand up and pointing his thumb over his shoulder. Behind him, an aggressive-looking bright-green Lamborghini Huracan GT3 hovered a few inches off the ground, its air jacks deployed as the team slung a set of fresh wheels and pre-heated tyres onto it. 'Crew or co-drivers can go out as passengers in these sessions. You get to be ballast.'

Mike frantically donned his protective equipment as another one of the engineers removed the passenger door for easier access. *East Asian, I think. Small red flag, gold stars, on his sleeve. Chinese. Must be part of the same bunch.*

The engineer waved to him, grabbed him firmly by the shoulders, and guided him into the tight-fitting passenger seat. Mike felt braces slapping over his body and buckles being fastened, then the engineer braced himself against Mike's chest and heaved on the straps, making sure they were boa-constrictor tight. He gave Mike a thumbs-up, which Mike tried to return in a confident, cool fashion, failing miserably. The engineer smirked as he refitted the door, casting Mike into darkness.

A clatter of harness fittings against carbon fibre signified the arrival of Lord Harriston. Mike tried to turn to face him, but the neck protector and restrictive straps meant Harriston was just on the periphery of Mike's vision. Harriston didn't appear to acknowledge him; he just strapped in, settled down, and started hitting switches.

This thing's like a Hawker Siddeley Harrier, thought Mike, trying to qualm his nerves. *Stark, no frills, just battle-ready functionality. No curves, no subtlety, not like the stuff I like.*

The Lamborghini snarled into life, its ten cylinders thrashing away over Mike's shoulder, and its transmission screamed angrily as Harriston pulled the car out of the pit garage. Already tight-chested from the harnesses, Mike found his breathing becoming even harder as eye-watering fumes filled the cabin of the crawling Lamborghini; unburnt hydrocarbons, fuel vapours and hot composites made for a heady, unpleasant mix.

Every gear change, as the Lamborghini made its way out from the pits onto the circuit, felt like a hammer blow to Mike's back. Harriston glimpsed at him, a mocking smile on his face, and pushed the Lamborghini's accelerator to the floor. The race car leapt forwards, the cacophony of its engine deafening Mike, the force pushing his helmet firmly against the seat.

This isn't fast, thought Mike fleetingly. *This is something else altogether*.

A small display in front of Mike read 270, the numbers suddenly diving along with the nose of the car. He felt his body try to tear forwards, through the harnesses, as a braking-point marker flashed past the edges of his view. The process repeated, over and over, Mike becoming increasingly uncomfortable and fatigued.

And I don't think we've even done a lap yet.

Harriston laughed out loud, pressing deeper into the corners, letting the Lamborghini run wide-open for longer, as the heat permeated its tyres, brakes, powertrain and fluids. A Ferrari 488 GT3 was just ahead, its exhaust emitting what felt like a solid wall of noise, and Harriston was honing in on it; every time it slowed for a corner, Harriston drew closer and closer, until the front splitter of the Lamborghini was rubbing against the 488's bumper. Ahead, the next target, two Porsche 911s.

The Ferrari caved under the pressure at the next bend, running wide and letting Harriston's Lamborghini blast past, straight onto the heels of the Porsches. The Huracan's deeper V10 voice overwhelmed the noise of the Ferrari behind as Harriston held its throttles wide, taking tighter lines, guiding the Lamborghini up and over the kerbs, the thumping of the suspension sounding like the most violent drums Mike had ever heard.

And yet the Lamborghini took it in its stride, the 911s getting closer to its nose, like a lion pursuing its prey across the plains. One Porsche misjudged its corner approach, braked too hard, got on the power too early, its rear-mounted engine dragging its tail wide, spinning the car out into the gravel trap. The next, now with more room to breathe, pressed on, intent on keeping the Huracan in its mirrors. But the Lamborghini had more in reserve, the gap closing on every straight.

Bloody hell, thought Mike, just about hearing his own thoughts. *He's going to get that one too.*

He saw the familiar peak of Silverstone's main building, alongside the finishing straight, coming into view, the Lamborghini giving it everything it had, Harriston's foot looking like it was trying to practically push the accelerator pedal through the floor. Ahead, a chequered flag was being waved from a gantry. The Porsche was still out in front, heat pluming from its cooling packs and exhaust, but only just. The flag flashed past overhead, and Mike felt the V10's note change, relax, and the car settle down.

Almost. But not this time.

Harriston smoothly guided the Lamborghini back to the pits and shut it down, its brakes and exhaust ticking noisily as they cooled. He pulled himself effortlessly out of the car, as the pit crew lifted Mike out inelegantly, and took off his helmet.

'I think that was a pretty good run,' he said, looking unfazed. 'But your weight tweaked the balance of the car a little bit. I was having to brake a bit earlier, be a bit gentler. A bit tricky.'

Mike put his hands over his ears for a moment, rubbed his temples, and leant against the side of the Lamborghini. He shook his head as he gathered his senses.

'It's that sensitive?' he said, finally looking up at Harriston. He was as Mike remembered: a tall, powerful-looking man, with a closely trimmed jet-black beard and a crew cut, his imposing stature tainted only by a heavy midriff and a slight limp.

A hallmark of indulgence. Or stress. Or both.

'Oh yes. It's very close, in terms of performance, to the LMP3 cars. Maybe three, four seconds a lap behind.'

'That's impressive, all things considered.'

'It is,' said Harriston, accepting a cup of tea from one of the crew. 'One moment.'

Harriston stepped away and collared another of the crew, then pointed at something towards the rear of the car. Mike couldn't make out the exchange, but he could hear an increasing volume of crosstalk; Harriston's voice was getting more audible, more angry, by the moment. The mechanic looked flustered, then embarrassed, then scared. Harriston waved him away and he scurried off, returning seconds later with tools and parts on a tray.

'Right,' said Harriston, stepping back towards Mike, his voice calm again. 'Don't mind that. They didn't make the changes I asked for. Small details, but I end up paying the price.'

Mike nodded at him. He could sense the sweat seeping through his clothes, and the bruises from the harnesses starting to make themselves evident beneath. The sensations made it difficult to focus.

'You wanted some money, I believe,' said Harriston patiently.

'Yes, but only with a view to making you more,' said Mike cautiously, his mind working overtime to keep his speech sane, clear, and sensibly paced, amid the torrent of adrenaline and stress that was raging around his system. 'It's a great opportunity.'

'I'll instruct my legal team to make the transfer, then,' said Harriston casually. 'You can then go and sort out the option. I take it that a notary or lawyer will be involved somewhere?'

'That's correct,' said Mike, still waiting for his heart rate to drop. 'Once the deposit reaches the escrow account, we'll meet up with the family's side in Salzburg, in the notary's office, to sign the options contract and any other required documentation. Our associate, Joseph, will be aiding us with a lot of this.'

'And you think we're doing the right thing here?' said Harriston, tossing his gloves on the table next to him.

'Absolutely,' said Mike, feeling confident for a moment. 'It's probably the best Ferrari collection available today, and it's still unknown and off the market.'

'Good,' said Harriston. 'And the cars all check out, including the 1962 GTO?'

'It's exactly what it says on the tin,' said Mike, nodding. 'All good and proper. I've been over that one myself. And that car, and some of the others, has been red-booked by Ferrari. The others have racing history. Blue chips, all of them.'

'Fine,' said Harriston, at the same time tapping out a message. 'The deposit will be on its way to you in short order. And tell me when we meet the notary.'

'You want to come to Salzburg?' said Mike, sounding surprised. 'There's really no need, in terms of paperwork, because the only signatures required are ours.'

'If I'm committing to a deal totalling seventy million quid, I'd prefer to be there myself.'

'As you know, the deposit is only two million, and we'll sell the cars freely after that. You won't be putting up seventy, and you'll get twenty-five per cent of whatever we make.'

'Still, this is a substantial trade. I want to be involved, to see how you work,' said Harriston, massaging his neck. 'Just keep me posted. Get the paperwork done and send me the date and address for the signing.'

'Of course. And thank you,' said Mike, offering out his hand.

Harriston raised an eyebrow at him. There was no warmth, sympathy, or interest in his green-grey eyes. He regarded Mike for a second, then slowly reached out and shook his hand. His grip was firm, tightening. Mike just smiled courteously.

'Well, get to it,' said Harriston, his thumb flashing over his phone.

'Of course,' said Mike, carefully maintaining a pleasant and agreeable tone. 'The official buyers in the deal will be Chapman & Sunderland Vintage Motors, and we'll handle the cars exclusively as discussed. Ideally, we'll arrange a facility agreement to that extent, to document the terms of your backing, just to provide peace of mind for both of us.'

'You've got your money,' said Harriston, uninterested.

'Do speak to Rick about that, if you can, as he'll be in the office more than I am. And thank you again.'

'I'll try to remember to do that,' said Harriston. 'Anyway, I'm going. Messages and shipments from overseas coming in. Back to the real work.'

Mike put his hand up to wave, but Harriston didn't respond. He just turned around and walked away, his eyes focused on his phone.

———————— • ————————

The warm, quiet interior of the Phantom provided some solace from the tornado Mike felt he had just walked through. His mind wandered to more comforting places, familiar and stable, to settle his nerves.

The back of my dad's Ford Anglia, in the heady heat of summer, on the way to a picnic in the Lakes. Safe, happy. Better times.

It was one of the reasons, he reflected, that people ended up spending vast amounts of money on classic and vintage cars: nostalgia. The sensations, the smells, the associations. All those memories, wrapped up in a car, could transport someone to a bygone age. The age of their parents, grandparents, heroes of their youth, or elsewhere.

A memorable car also offered a form of escapism, from unpleasant times, appreciated by many. Which, in turn, would drive up its value over time. And if a car was collectable, rare, desirable, well, the hikes in value could subsequently be tremendous.

Like that DBS I bought for £7,000 in the eighties. That's a £100,000 car now.

Some of the lives that many cars have lived were amazing, too, and for them merely to survive was a feat. The 1960 Ferrari 250 GT SWB Competizione that had been discovered by Mike's Italian friend in the seventies was a prime example. After having been found, under the mayor's house in Lima, Peru, it was shipped, not in the protection of a container, but on the deck of an oil tanker for a two-month voyage back to Italy. It was then delivered by rail from Genoa to Monaco, covered in salt, dirt and surface rust. It wasn't cleaned, but it was reputedly put somewhere safe.

That safe location turned out to be a rooftop behind the Monaco-Monte-Carlo train station, where the car stayed for almost two months because the new owner was too busy to collect it. Apparently, the owner wished to go sailing for a few weeks in the Mediterranean before taking the car home.

Today, that would be unthinkable. But then it had no value in 1973.

'And now it's probably among the priciest Ferraris out there,' said Mike out loud as he casually scrolled through his messages. 'That car's probably worth, what, £15 million now.'

It wasn't just the outright classics that had their longevity. Mike had learned, over the years, that old race cars also seemed to have their own natural energy. *Pre-war racers pulled out of scrap yards in the mid-1970s, he recalled, soon back on track directly after their rescues.*

The pictures of the first club races in England revealed a fascinating line-up of these long-standing pre-war racers, tiptoeing around the grid on their wobbly wire wheels, their engines barking and revving hard on methanol, exhausts smoking and flaming like chimneys. Enchanting to see, and exciting. Before long, these pre-war veterans were soon all over Europe, and being exhumed from their places of rest in Argentina, Uruguay and Madagascar.

Restoration wasn't something associated with them at the time, though. For the most part, those vintage racers were just cleaned, fettled, fiddled with, and flung back onto the circuits. In some cases, many of the original factory team mechanics were still alive. And, after a few weeks' work, the racers were back on track as if nothing had ever happened to them.

Timeless, both in design and disposition. And yet they still felt durable, well built, dependable, even the Maseratis, the Ferraris, the ERAs, and, above all, the Alfas.

'Ah, the 8C Alfas,' he said softly, sensing his heart rate finally slowing. 'Incredible machines.'

In the dim and distant past, Mike had spent a lot of time with a 1932 Alfa Romeo Tipo B Monoposto, a P3. It was another long-abandoned racer, but it had still been on its original engine, untouched internally since being overhauled prior to the war. *It still had all its pre-war lead seals in place. And it never let me down.*

Not that running it was without effort. Mike's nose twitched at the memory of methanol, acetone and toluene, the volatile mix that the Alfa deemed suitable as fuel. Five hundred litres, for every event, in big barrels that, when handled, made you feel like you were dealing with high explosives.

Flames from methanol aren't visible. The first thing that hits you is the heat. A risky thing to deal with.

'No smoking, please,' he said, smirking.

As risky as the classic car business itself, his mind added, as he started up the Phantom.

The Rolls-Royce had just passed through Bletchley when Mike's phone rang loudly, reeling his mind back to the present day. He stabbed the answer button, then knocked the cruise control speed down by ten miles per hour, focusing his thoughts.

'What did Harriston want with you?' said Rick, the sounds of a garage in the background drifting quietly over the line.

'I'm not sure if he wanted to impress or intimidate me.'

'Maybe it was both,' said Rick, snorting quietly. 'I did warn you, and we've heard the stories. He's a walking piece of work. But did we get what we need?'

'He says that he's willing to go ahead and is sending the deposit, so we should be good to go.'

'Well, now I'm warming to him a bit. That's something.'

'I get the feeling that he's most keen on that 250 GTO,' said Mike thoughtfully. 'I know he's not much one for classic stuff, but he's shown more interest in it than the rest.'

'Can't fault him for that,' said Rick. 'Not many like those that come along. But that's the crown jewel, the linchpin of the package. Pull that and the lot's less interesting, and harder to sell.'

'Yeah,' said Mike slowly. 'Hell, if he was that keen, surely he could just buy all of them and shed the rest later.'

'Maybe he's not got that kind of disposable. I'd say he could wait for another to come up and buy that, but it's a once-in-a-blue-moon car, to be fair,' said Rick. 'But I'm sure the profits will soothe any ruffles there.'

'Quite. Money, I get the distinct feeling, is his driving motivation.'

'Always the case with these types. And at least he's playing ball with us.'

'Perhaps,' said Mike. 'But I'm not sure he's playing it in our field.'

'Don't worry about it. Any more on Hadfords?'

'I'm still not sure that they're willing to proceed,' said Mike. 'They want some time to think about it.'

'In my experience, they've probably already made a decision.'

'I don't see what's going to change. They don't appear keen on cars, so I'm already not a huge fan of theirs, either.'

Rick laughed, a hefty *floomf* suggesting he'd just collapsed into one of the ancient leather recliners in the offices of Chapman & Sunderland Vintage Motors.

'Could they really sell the lot to that buyer they mentioned?' he said, the sound of pen on paper making itself heard.

'Abdul Ben Ali? Maybe. Last I heard from him was years ago. Strange that he pops up in these discussions, of all places.'

'Do you think you could get in touch with him?'

'You're the one that's supposed to have the network of handy types to contact about finding people, or getting things done, not me,' said Mike, smirking.

'It's always easier if it comes from a familiar voice.'

'True. I'll see what I can do. I wonder what this lot are doing getting looped in with him, though?'

'You could put down what I know about investments and hedge funds on the back of a matchbox,' said Rick bluntly. 'I've got no idea, and the money they throw around, sometimes like they're just playing roulette, baffles me. Not my world.'

'Definitely not my shot of whiskey either,' said Mike, weaving the Phantom neatly through the five o'clock traffic. 'But Hadfords does deal with some serious assets, and they've got the warehousing and facilities to deal with the scale of sale we're talking about.'

'And I hear their bonded storage facilities in Switzerland and Lichtenstein are free from tax and all very legal,' said Rick, clicking his tongue.

'Yes. They're meticulous in their sales and storage processes, too. I'd hazard that, if they get hold of the cars, no one will ever see or drive them. They'll just be stored, as a commodity.'

'Shame. I've been in one of those huge, bonded warehouses once. Thousands of pieces of art, tonnes of gold, from all sorts, all stored in little rooms. God knows what else might be in there, or who it belongs to.'

'Or who it used to belong to.'

'Indeed,' said Rick quietly. 'Skeletons, meet closets.'

'Or that whatever's in there even exists,' said Mike. 'I had that with a client from Italy. The family didn't know that their relatives had a collection of art and cars. The children all thought they were going to be poor and then, *poof*, a few million in assets landed in their laps. Sensible to keep it off the table.'

'Especially in this day and age. Otherwise, you'll have all manner of knuckleheads turning up at your door and, *poof*, you'll be scammed of the lot in no time.'

'Precisely,' said Mike dispassionately. 'Trust isn't exactly in wide circulation now.'

'Nope. But we've got to play the game. Anyway, maybe Hadfords will just buy the Ferraris, and then it'll cease to be our problem. You said you knew this Abdul Ben Ali character they're considering?'

Mike pulled the Phantom into a service station, let it idle for a moment, and then shut it down. He nodded. 'Yeah. I knew him when we were students in London, and then he turned up on some of the shoots we worked on. He was jetting around as a professional diver, back then. Underwater shoots, that kind of thing.'

'Got any kind of an in with him, you think?'

'I'm sure he'd remember me. He went by Benny at the time. I had this tatty Submariner. Suffering a bit of salt-water ingress, the works. Benny loved it. He ended up being recalled to Riyadh and I gifted it to him. I've only seen him a few times since, though.'

'You never know. What goes around comes around, that kind of thing.'

'We can dream,' said Mike thoughtfully. 'Catch you later.'

CHAPTER 5

Vintage cars, Mike believed, were often alive, in some shape or form, and had a soul of their own. He knew he was not alone in thinking that; most collectors, if asked, would be quick to furnish various emotional tales about their cars. They weren't just adornments in a garage for them. They had personalities, traits, moments, histories. People built relationships with them.

In some way, it's a form of escape, thought Mike. *Or a way to develop a different perspective.*

A collector once told him that, in his lowest moments, the cars gave him strength and support. The gentleman had said that, dispatching with the purely rational side of the vintage car business, it was an emotional thing to care for old cars. No one really needed them. They were bought for other reasons, often not monetary ones. A car from an old wedding, a childhood romance, something that belonged to an old family member; whatever it was had become inextricably woven into the fabric of an owner's past, and revisiting it would offer comfort, that warm glow of days gone.

And many collectors see themselves as custodians of history. And the stories they can tell.

The wicker of the chair rustled as Mike shifted around, making himself more comfortable outside a small but cozy Vienna-style café near Park Lane. He pulled out his laptop, set his phone alongside it, and ordered an espresso. A lengthy list of unanswered emails popped up on his computer, demanding his attention. He glanced at his phone, checking the time, and set to work. The hours ticked by, the list shrinking by the minute, when a text message snagged his attention: *Still on for lunch?*

He checked the phone and smiled. *Julie*. He sent a quick response, letting her know where he was, and leant back in his chair.

She must be in her thirties now, he thought. *I wonder if she's still driving that 1954 R-Type Continental Fastback?*

The sound of a substantial straight-six, some twenty minutes later, answered his question. The light-grey Bentley didn't so much as pull up alongside the kerb as it did dock at it, given its size and weight. And its scale was at complete odds with Julie; she stepped out, all five-foot-nothing of petiteness, dressed entirely in Chanel. Her eyes and curls were jet-black, her manner sharp and alive.

'Ogni ricciolo un capriccio,' said Mike, cheerily, waving at her.

'Mike!' she responded, her eyes lighting up. 'Yes, every one of these curls has its own whim!'

She grabbed a chair and pulled it over to his tiny table. 'Nice place.'

'You're welcome. It's been a while. Drink?'

Mike gestured at the waiter behind the glass.

'Si, grazie,' she said, nodding, 'San Pellegrino, a glass.'

'I hear you've been working as a dentist with your mother?'

'Yes, that's right. I was thinking of going back to Sicily after graduating, but she's drowning in work at her centre, so she asked if I'd join her.'

'Sounds like a good arrangement to me.'

'It is, yes. I do like London, so the opportunity to stay here for a while is appreciated.'

'Permanently, maybe?' said Mike inquisitively.

'Nothing's set in stone like that, Mike, you know. But for a while, yes. And how about you?

'Well, Rick and I went into business in the vintage and classic car field, in earnest, recently.'

'Old habits die hard,' she responded, her smile illuminating the street. 'My mother always goes on about your cars.'

'Well, she knows her way around them as well. Lord knows she's got plenty of interesting ones. Has the Contessa added anything new to her collection?'

'What's it been, four years? There's a neat little Triumph TR4A IRS, a left-hand-drive one. Not what you might expect.'

'Imported?'

Julie nodded, sipping her drink. 'Yes, from America. I understand that you could get it with a solid back axle there, but the original owner paid a premium for the independent rear. But anyway, it still has those Michelotti lines. I think that's why she likes it.'

Mike raised an eyebrow.

'That's a bit more than you might have said on the matter a few years ago,' he said, grinning.

Julie tipped her head towards the Bentley. 'That was my father's car. I've had to get up to speed a bit to live with this treasure, for one thing. And, well, mum's fascination with them has rubbed off a little.'

'I'd always wondered if it would, but I'd concluded that it wasn't your scene.'

'When I was younger, they were just old things,' she said, looking out into the street. 'And now, well…'

'I know what you mean,' he said, his chin dropping a fraction.

'I have to say,' she said, her voice sounding brighter, 'that the Bentley isn't really my thing, though. I prefer Alfas, and a few of the Ferraris.'

'Not falling too far from the tree, then,' said Mike, beaming. 'You might almost say it's stereotypical. Especially for someone whose full name is Giulietta.'

She hissed at him jokingly. 'But what of you?' she added. 'Anything interesting in the works?'

'It's a bit rough and tumble, to be honest. We sold a Bugatti and a Mercedes-Benz for good coin recently, but we've unexpectedly ended up with a Miura as payment for the latter.'

'I think I'd be happy with that outcome,' said Julie, smirking at him.

'Heh. It's not the only Italian car we've had strife with recently. But we do have a Ferrari collection coming up that could swing things around a little. Hopefully, it'll all pan out. And what about your mother?'

'She's good. I'd like to go back to Sicily with her, but she says it's troppo pericoloso. I'd still prefer to be there than here, though.'

'Sicilians have been leaving their country for centuries. Many settled here in London.'

'That's true. We have more relatives in the UK than we do in Italy.'

She flicked her hand into the air and the waiter appeared almost instantaneously, taking her order for another San Pellegrino, along with some wiener schnitzel with bratkartoffeln and preiselbeere.

I wish I could command that much attention, thought Mike. *Faring far better than I did, at that age.*

'And you, for lunch?' she said, her foot tapping Mike's under the table. 'Unless you asked me here for other reasons, you scoundrel.'

Mike cleared his throat and ordered sole meuniere with potatoes, along with Aperol spritz for the pair of them.

'So, you've been immersing yourself more into the world of cars, then,' said Mike. 'Much caught your attention?'

'I've been doing some reading about an Alfa Romeo P3 that Tazio Nuvolari used to race. I understand he drove in the Targa Florio, near home, and mum's always talking about him.'

'That car sure was something, as was he. What was it, eight German cars he beat at the Nürburgring in 1934?'

'I've just got to that,' said Julie, grinning. 'It was 1935. Four Auto Union and five Mercedes-Benz racers, all Silver Arrows, all left trailing an old Alfa.'

'Pretty sure the Germans weren't impressed.'

'Pretty sure the Italians were.'

'That car is still around, you know?'

'Really?' said Julie, sitting up.

'Yeah. Another survivor. It turned up near Buenos Aires in the seventies.'

'What a find. Nuvolari has always been a hero to our family. And I still remember my mother teaching me the word for single-seat race cars, "monoposto", when I was little. I can't say it was my first word, but you know how these odd moments stick in the memory.'

'I've got a lot of time for those pre-war Italian racers myself, but it's the real oddballs that fascinate me. Like the luxury cars that were modified into trucks or utility vehicles. Very hard to come by these days.'

'Utility?'

'I found one Maybach Zeppelin, for example, which had been turned into a mobile bandsaw, of all things,' said Mike, smiling. 'It would have had a V12 engine when it was new, but here it was, with a two-cylinder diesel, thudding along like an old tractor.'

'Do you deal in anything older?'

'No, but the cars that predate World War One, those, those are often something else. And so many have crazy stories to tell.'

'Such as?' she said, tucking into her schnitzel.

'My favourite's probably the one about a 1912 Rolls-Royce Silver Ghost. It was owned by an officer who drove it out to the Somme in 1914 but, unfortunately, he didn't last long out there. But the car survived and reappeared in Belgium as an ambulance.'

'A Rolls-Royce ambulance?'

'Yeah,' said Mike. 'And, after the war, it ended up back in the UK, and then served as an armoured vehicle in Northern Ireland, and then became a wooden-bodied safari car for the Prince of Wales. It went out to Kenya for that.'

'Caspita,' she said. 'And it survived all of that?'

'Oh, its story didn't end there. It ended up as a school bus in Africa, and then served as a military command car in World War Two.

They used to drive it around with baskets of homing pigeons on the roof!'

'And then?!'

'It ended up returning to England, along with its pigeon baskets, and ended up being used at a school. They still used the pigeons, too, but to relay match scores, not artillery coordinates. The body got discarded in the fifties, we think, and the chassis was raffled off to build a school chapel.'

'That's crazy. Did it get scrapped in the end?'

'Surprisingly, no. It got new bodywork eventually and is still being used to this day on big continental tours. Beautiful Roi-des-Belges coachwork. I know the owner, he's in the club. I don't think the engine's ever been apart.'

'Not a bad career for a bus, I have to say. If we get as many chances as it did in life, I'd consider us very lucky.'

'This is true. We could do with some of that luck now.'

'Really not too happy about work, then?'

'The market's in the toilet but we're surviving. People are interested in things but closing deals is getting a bit harder, especially with Europeans.'

'Is that a fault of the market, though, or success? My mother said you'd rubbed up a few the wrong way, by being successful when others were not.'

'There is a bit of envy, perhaps. We've grown quickly, and, yes, we're certainly making markets for pre-war cars, especially early Lagondas, Astons, Bentleys, Rolls. But the best margins are still in the ultra-rare race cars and such, like some of the Ferraris we're handling now.'

'I'm sure the new owners will appreciate the speed you sell them at, and the price,' said Julie. 'And your partner, Rick, right? How is he?'

'Sharp as barbed wire and utterly reliable, as always. I'm surprised at how creative he is with the business, too. Got quite the digital edge, which I didn't expect.'

'You two are like *The Persuaders!*, I swear, if not quite as well dressed,' said Julie, cheerily. 'Is he easy to work with?'

'It's like being in a foxhole with a Royal Marine,' said Mike, laughing. 'But, seriously, he's great.'

'One tough, one soft. A good combination for a business.'

'That's true. Closing these deals requires the right mix of force and finesse. And we're both trustworthy and honest. At least, we like to think so. It makes a world of difference when you're dealing with these cars, collectors, and collections.'

'I've heard you've added wings to the business, too?' said Julie, neatly arranging her cutlery on her empty plate.

'No, that's Rick's baby. He's got an old Boeing and a Transall that he uses to shunt stuff around. I only fly single-engine stuff, small fry.'

'Helps to diversify, though. You never know what's around the corner.'

'Amen to that. And it's helped us keep ahead in the vintage world. It's always useful to be able to expedite transport on our own terms, and not wait for carriers to get things in order.'

'On that note,' said Julie, 'I must go. We've got some conferences coming up, so time for fresh attire, and maybe a more appropriate choice of car.'

Mike stood and shook her hand. She leant forward into him, then hugged him lightly.

'Take care, Julie. My best to your mother.'

'And my best to Rick. Be seeing you soon, hopefully!'

He watched as she bounded over and into the Bentley, listened to its big six turn over, and waited until it had cruised out of sight. He sat down at the table, poked his food disinterestedly, and sighed.

Wish I had someone like that to push me along. Still, some company is better than none.

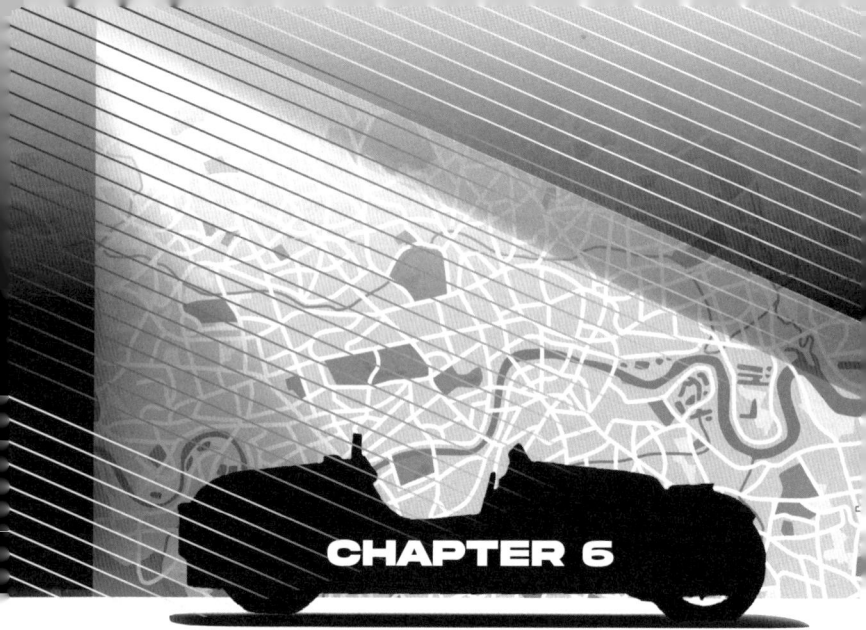

CHAPTER 6

The cool, calming ambience of the café had settled Mike's mind, while the company had energised it. He stood up, feeling refreshed, and started towards his car, mentally charting what he needed to do next. He had not so much as gone a single step when his phone buzzed noisily in his pocket.

'Can I speak to Mike Chapman, please?' said the voice.

'Speaking,' said Mike welcomingly. 'How can I help you?'

'I'm calling about the Morgan you have, the red three-wheeler.'

'Ah, yes. That's a car I'd like to own myself.'

'Can you tell me more about it?'

Well, it is all in the advert, thought Mike. *But maybe they haven't seen it. Stow the sarcasm.*

'Of course,' said Mike, sitting back down on his still-warm chair outside the café. 'It's a 1934 Super Sports with a Matchless engine, a real fine example of the breed.'

'What's it like to drive?'

'It's excellent, and in top order. Docile around town, fast on smooth B-roads, and it's got a delightful bark to it. Great little car.'

'What about the engine?'

'It's just been rebuilt and runs like a top. The rest of the running gear is in great shape, too.'

'And the chassis, any rattles or noises?'

'A Morgan could never be called quiet, but this one's free from anything unwanted. It's quite stiff, compared to some others. The steering's light, it's well balanced, and great fun to drive. Just don't try to avoid potholes in the usual way; you'll probably miss them with the front wheels, then clout them with the rear one.'

'I see,' said the voice. 'You do seem to like it.'

Alright.

'Apologies, who am I speaking with?' said Mike.

'Ah, Philip. I saw a post online about the Morgan, but there wasn't much otherwise on it.'

Rick at it again. My mistake.

'I see. Yes, well, we recently found the Morgan in an estate sale. It's always been well maintained. It's an absolute hoot to drive. Proper bugs-in-the-teeth vintage motoring. Like flying a Tiger Moth, just without wings or a prop.'

'And is it ready to go?'

'It needs nothing. We try to sell our cars, when feasible, as turn-key affairs.'

'What can we do on the price?'

'It's £38,000, but that does include delivery. It's also just been serviced, valeted, and polished from nose to tail. It's a show-standard car.'

'No movement?'

'You may find some around for less, but I can guarantee that you'll put more into them than you would just buying this one outright, and you still won't have as nice an example.'

'What about part-exchanging something against it?'

'That's not a problem,' said Mike warily, 'but it very much depends on what's involved.'

'I have a TVR Tasmin 280i. It's in good condition but it hasn't moved for a few years. I just ran my course with it and, well, you know what time's like. One week parked became two, then a month, and here we are now.'

Mike leaned back in his chair, then looked to the sky for a moment. 'I've not dealt with a Tasmin for a long time,' he said slowly. 'Interesting cars, though. What's the body and paint like?'

The momentary pause told him everything he needed to know.

'It's an old TVR,' said Philip cautiously. 'It's got its marks, its cracks in the fibreglass, that kind of thing. But, mechanically, it's very sound.'

'For us, the problem would be that we would want to present the car in the best possible light,' said Mike amiably. 'And, for us, it sounds like that might involve a lot of cosmetic work.'

'I think that might be the case, yes.'

'Unfortunately, that kind of work is very expensive and time-consuming. Which would mean that we probably wouldn't be able to offer an appealing trade-in value for your TVR.'

'Because you'd have to do too much to it.'

'Potentially, yes. Of course, that might change if we see the car, and you can always send us some more details.'

The line went quiet for a moment. Mike waited, his eyes falling back to the street, watching the people amble back and forth.

'I do really like the look of the Morgan,' said Philip emphatically.

'What we could do, if you were interested, would be to help you sell the TVR through an auction, or privately,' said Mike. 'We could certainly help you put together a listing, and get it photographed. If it's a sound car, which it sounds like it is, it would make a great project for someone.'

'Really?'

'Of course,' said Mike warmly. 'And that, at the very least, would help get it out from under your feet.'

'I like the sound of that,' said Philip enthusiastically. 'I've also been considering a Plus 4, from the sixties. Could you recommend that as an alternative?'

'Those are very different, but similarly interesting, cars. Personally, I'd vote for the three-wheeler, as it's more exhilarating. You'll certainly draw more of a crowd with it. It's just that bit more exciting, that bit more special.'

'Fab. Okay. I'll take the Morgan,' said Philip confidently. 'Can you deliver it to Wales this week?'

'That'll take a bit of doing, but if you can send me some contact details, then I can put my colleague Simon on the case. I'm sure we can get it to you in that timeframe, though, if we can sort the paperwork and funds promptly.'

'Excellent,' said Philip, sounding cheerful. 'I'll get in touch with you by email now and we can go from there.'

'That sounds grand. We can get you an invoice then, and we'll deliver the car to your doorstep, then we can pick up on the TVR front afterwards.'

'Thank you, Mike. I'll speak to you soon.'

'Certainly, sir. Obliged!'

Mike put the phone back in his pocket and smiled broadly. He noticed the waiter still hadn't collected his £10 tip from the table. Mike looked at it for a moment, picked it up, and put £20 back in its place.

Well, I'm having a good day. Let's pass it on.

He stood up, neatly tucked his chair under the table, and wandered back towards the Rolls-Royce. There was a ticket machine nearby; Mike wandered over and fed his parking stub into it, watched the charge pop up on the screen, and slipped his credit card onto the scanner. The ticket machine graunched as it decided whether it was going to give Mike his parking stub back or not. He patted the side of it in frustration, its screen remaining unhelpful, when his phone started vibrating again.

Video call. Not ideal.

Mike looked at his background. Busy shops and the café to his back, a fence and hedgerows to his front, the Phantom a short walk away.

That'll have to do.

'Mike, it's Steve. I understand you've got a '48 Land Rover in at the moment.'

'Hello, Steve, how are you? And, yes, we do.'

'Fine, on both counts. We've not got any in at W&H at the moment, and I've a customer who's scouting around for one.'

'Well, we're always up for helping out.'

'Excellent,' he said cheerily. 'Do you mind talking to him now?'

'Not at all.'

The camera panned slightly, revealing a gentleman sitting on the other side of a broad wooden desk.

'Mike, this is Harry Weckam. He's interested in your Land Rover and has a few questions.'

'Mr Weckam, a pleasure. What would you like to know?'

'Hello, Mike, thanks. I've just a few questions. My dad had an early one, and I want something like that. I'm looking for the best example around, basically.'

'That's definitely our 80-inch Land Rover, for sure,' said Mike confidently.

'Okay,' said Weckam, sounding unconvinced. 'Why is it so expensive, then, compared to all the other freshly restored ones I've looked at? Does it have special history, something along those lines?'

'There are two distinct reasons for its price. As you say, history, that's a key one. It's one of the earliest factory show cars, from April of 1948, and it's one of the two actual show cars that were present at the Amsterdam Motor Show in 1948.'

'That's a neat bit of history,' said Weckam, nodding at the camera. 'I'm not hugely into Land Rovers, to be honest, but I just like that it's similar to my father's. But has it ever been restored?'

'Thankfully not,' said Mike. 'It's still got its original paint, and trim, and its numbers match throughout.'

'I'll be honest, it just looks pretty scruffy, at least to me.'

'It's certainly got its patina, that's for sure,' said Mike understandingly. 'But that's the second reason as to why it's so valuable: it has never been restored. It's completely as Land Rover envisioned it. And there's a big chunk of cachet associated to that, and a big chunk of charm, character and appeal.'

'So, you'd not want to disturb that look,' said Weckam.

'Only if you wanted to cleave its value in half.'

'I see. But it still appears quite expensive, especially considering its mileage and condition.'

'It is certainly more expensive than others, but its history and original condition are unrepeatable. And it's now been properly preserved, and mechanically refreshed, so it'll continue on for decades to come.'

'I quite like the sound of that. Something usable. But why aren't we treating Lamborghinis in the same way, then?'

'To some extent, we do. An original, untouched car is going to be viewed in a different light to a restored, or overly restored, example. But the Land Rover is synonymous with outdoor life and activity, while simultaneously being associated with the upper classes, with royalty, old British heritage and money. An original car like this, in untouched condition, is a very valuable and desirable piece of history. An icon. Consider it in the same class as Harris Tweed. It's an amplifier of class, standing and history.'

'Not something that would be exhibited at, say, Hampton Court, then?'

'You could exhibit a stunningly restored one, yes, but the original would draw bigger crowds. It's a survivor. And eligible for, and deserving of, just as much attention, if not more.'

'I see,' said Weckam, still not looking or sounding entirely reassured.

'What's worth remembering is that this car has lived a life,' said Mike engagingly, sweeping his free hand across the camera's view, and on outwards. 'From being worked on by those developing the prototypes and production cars, through to being used as a working vehicle, for all those decades, it's all about the hands it has been touched by, and the memories that have been created. In a restored car, that's all but gone, for the most part, cast away to the wind. But this, this is still here. It's still the same car as it was decades ago. Aside from its important heritage, it's only original once. And this, remarkably, still is, hence its value.'

'Only original once,' said Weckam, smiling at the camera. 'Well, would it be possible to have it trailered down to Kent, once you've received payment?'

Mike tried hard to conceal his surprised expression.

'Okay, sure, that would be absolutely no problem. We can get an invoice to you very quickly.'

'Excellent.'

'It's a very good car,' said Mike. 'It represents a sense of longevity and quiet, understated class that goes hand in hand with old money. If you were ever to sell it, I'd like to be the first to know about it.'

'Thank you. Transport included, I presume?'

'Of course, Mr Weckam.'

'I look forward to it,' said Weckam, as he leant forward to end the call.

I'll take that, thought Mike, as he opened a messenger app.

'Drinks are on me next time, Steve,' he said, recording a voice note. 'Maybe even lunch.'

He pocketed his phone and turned his attention back to the malfunctioning ticket machine, and briefly wondered whether it was worth feeding it with coins instead. He shook his head, still pleasingly bewildered by the onslaught of calls and sales, looked towards the Rolls-Royce, glanced at the tempting and inviting café again, and was then distracted by a loud, insistent beeping. He turned back to the parking ticket machine, to find his ticket processed and cleared.

'This day's really going somewhere, and I need to get moving as well,' he said, shaking his head again in disbelief. 'I wonder what else will get pulled out of the hat today.'

He barely had a moment to gather his senses before his phone rang again.

'Did you get that Landy deal?' said Rick breathlessly. 'Our dealer friend called earlier, but I didn't know quite what to say about that car.'

'It's all done and dusted. Hopefully, we can return the favour to Steve at some point.'

'Agreed. What's next?'

'We need to get an invoice over to the buyer, then once the money is in, we'll deliver it to Kent.'

'How much?'

'Full asking. It's a great earner for us.'

'A great earner? More like ringing the damned bell! We paid, what, £38,000 for that at the estate sale?'

'That's true. But then it cost us, what, £110,000 alone to start spreading our wings. That wasn't long ago. And we've a lot of other overheads.'

'Don't sweat it,' said Rick firmly. 'We've got to spend, and spend hard, to get ahead. It'll come back, and then some.'

'You're right. Not going to happen as if by magic. And, hey, we've sold the Morgan as well. Full asking, again.'

'Didn't think that would take much effort.'

'Well, the seller found us through one of your online ads. But, please, can you make sure they've all got the relevant details in them,' said Mike adamantly. 'He didn't have anything to go on, and it took me more than a hot minute to work out he wasn't just wasting my time or trying to scam me. And a few pictures and a number isn't the most professional of looks.'

Mike heard something being unscrewed, something sloshing, something wet, then Rick drew breath through his teeth.

'Alright. That one's on me. I might have missed one. Consider me still learning some ropes. But don't lose focus on the Austrian Collection. We really need to dial that deal in, especially given how far south things have gone with our other prancing horse.'

Mike murmured quietly in agreement.

'Keep at it, and hit the ball out of the court,' said Rick. 'I'll be checking the accounts and make sure we've got the money from Harriston. I'll let you know once it's in, then we can set about transferring the deposit and securing the deal.'

'You planning to be there in person?'

'At the signing? I wouldn't miss it for the world,' said Rick.

'Me neither. You check on Harriston's funds, and get that all in line, and I'll keep wheeling things along. If we're lucky, I think we can get this all knocked out in a few weeks.'

'Happy days,' said Rick. 'Oh, and before you go, that yellow Miura turned up. Simon says it's good. It'll be in the showroom soon, so swing by and check it out for yourself.'

'Brilliant. Speak to you later, Rick. Thanks again.'

CHAPTER 7

Mike found himself in a reflective mood as he cautiously piloted the Phantom out of inner London. He sometimes felt a little insecure, both in terms of what they were doing and what they were capable of, but Rick less so. It figured: he was tougher, sterner. He rarely spoke about his upbringing, but Mike knew he was orphaned, weaving his strange way through life until he became, of all things, a stunt driver.

And that was how the two met, in Switzerland. Mike had some involvement in the film business, supplying cars from time to time, and had crossed paths with Rick. He would put in a word for Mike on shoots, leading to him supplying more cars, and Mike would return the favour as and when he could. Before long, the two were dealing with bikes, planes, cars, boats, anything that could be filmed, crashed, rolled, bought or sold.

The increase in work and income gave Rick some security, and Mike coerced him to start anew in London. Soon after, they started a small classic car dealership and Rick, still passionate about flying, established a shipping company at Bournemouth Airport. It was, as he continued to maintain, more his kind of gig. The car business went through a few changes, becoming Chapman & Sunderland Vintage Motors as it grew, while the cargo company remained, to this day, Cargo Air B.

It didn't stand out in the listings, and that was intentional, thought Mike, a little nervously.

Their first classic and shipping deals were done out of a little wooden garden shed in St Albans. Everything was spread out on old work benches, from tools to telexes. When it rained, they had to prop up car covers to shield themselves while they worked underneath. Even the dog would have to seek cover, such was the tatty nature of the roof.

Occasionally hilarious, more often frustrating, but necessary.

The first cars to roll in and out of their workshops were old Shadows, Clouds, Mark IIs and XJ6s, the kind of thing they could pick up cheaply, titivate, and turn around. As their cashflow ramped up, they introduced Ferrari 308s and 328s to the mix, getting ahead of the curve and making bank while the market caught up. Mike and Rick would also pick up the occasional Derby Bentley or Phantom II, often sought-after by film companies, the speed at which they sold often astounding them both. Business boomed and didn't seem like it would ever slow down.

Slowly, they began to handle more and more pre-war cars. And, to Mike's surprise, he liked them. Especially the early Silver Ghosts, like the Alpine Eagle chassis and the open-drive limousines.

And by that point we had a good set-up, a cheap one, and things were easy to deal with.

Mike's role was straightforward, albeit multifaceted. Historian, car finder, negotiator, and assessor, he was responsible for both European and US markets. Rick, on the other hand, had found good success and enjoyment dealing with the Asian and UK markets, and he was a fine hand at keeping tabs on the finances and listings. Between the two, they also covered the Emirates and India, later broadening out into Thailand and Malaysia.

More cars entailed more space, and the two moved into a complex of Nissen huts outside Medmenham. The place had been an old chicken farm, and the smell never went. While it wasn't ideal, the quality of their offerings continued to improve. WO Bentleys, Lagondas, Invictas, immaculate Rolls-Royces, and more, trickled in and out of the barn.

But the Bugattis were the breakthrough, thought Mike, his memory still able to recall the exact feel of their curves beneath his hands. Two Type 57Cs, from a deceased owner's collection in France. The widow wanted quick cash, and Rick and Mike were there to offer it, snagging a once-in-a-lifetime deal on a Galibier Sports Limousine and a breathtaking Coupé by Gangloff.

Overnight, their image went from boys playing on the block to a serious pair of classic car traders. But there was a flipside to that; to maintain that stature, and to continue their upwards trajectory, good cars were now essential, not optional.

A further step up came a year later with the sale of two Kompressor Mercedes from a Korean collection. One was a Castagna 710 SS, the other a unique Erdmann & Rossi S 680 tourer. Mike found the cars hidden away in Sweden and, after some shrewd negotiating from Rick, the pair netted a million in profit alone.

Immediately, they moved to a better location in Buckingham. Out went the overpowering scent of the old chicken farm and its unpainted concrete floors, and in came clean, white, new-build units, replete with sealed floors and proper lighting.

The next thing Mike knew, Rick was buying a Boeing 737-800 BCF from a broke Saudi arms dealer to start an air cargo business. He knew it had been on the cards for a while but didn't expect Rick to jump straight in at the deep end. On the flip side, Rick's boldness should have told him otherwise. It didn't surprise him, however, to find out that somehow Rick had managed to negotiate getting a functional, albeit tatty, ageing C-160 Transall thrown in as part of the deal. It wasn't pretty, but it was a whole lot of fun.

And it'd always get you where you needed to go.

The planes, paid for in cash, were flown from Riyadh to Bournemouth. The Transall was good to go but the 737, well, it wasn't as expected. It had been described as a cargo variant but, when it turned up, it was outfitted as a luxury airliner. Out went the gold basins, plush seats, beds, and bars, all of which put some cash back in Rick's pocket, and in went a modified main deck, pallet-securing and handling systems, window plugs, while the function of the cargo door was reinstated.

Rick then began the process of bidding for contracts. He lowballed practically everyone to get his foot in the door, and his network of contacts helped him be more flexible, more willing, than some others. Anything you needed to move, well, he could probably move it for you.

But maybe he should sometimes ask a few more questions about his cargo, thought Mike, a little restlessly. *There's risk, then there's recklessness.*

'But then what's the difference, sometimes,' said Mike, pointing the Phantom towards Chapman & Sunderland. 'I think he's got a better handle on that than I ever did.'

———————— • ————————

The sun was getting low but, as Mike slewed the Phantom into a service station for a coffee and a break, his phone rang noisily.
This is a bit relentless, he thought, the aches and bruises still poking at his core, *even by my standards.*

'Simon,' he said loudly, answering the phone. 'What's up?'

'Hello, Mike. I've got someone here who wants to charter some flights. I can't raise Rick, so I was wondering if you could talk to him now.'

'Go for it. I know my way around well enough.'

A new voice flowed from the Phantom's speakers.

'Henry Kroeze. From Amsterdam. Understand you have two carriers?'

'That's right, Mr Kroeze,' said Mike. 'They're based in Bournemouth. What are you looking to move?'

'Freight. Mostly around Eastern Europe.'

'How much?'

'Enough to engage both aircraft, I believe.'

'Passengers?'

'No more than two or three per flight.'

'Good. Our Boeing's only outfitted for four passengers, crew aside.'

'Lifting and loading?'

'You'll need to provide that, I'm afraid.'

'And the Transall, still suitable for vehicles?'

'Correct, yes. It's got reinforced treadways, so it can deal with vehicles of up to 5,000kg. All in, it'll handle up to 16,000kg of cargo alone.'

'Vehicle capacity?'

'If you've got, say, four cars, no more than 4.5 metres in length each, you can load four.'

'Close enough,' said Kroeze. 'Let me relay that and I will come back within the hour.'

'Appreciated, Mr Kroeze. I can handle your initial enquiries, but you'll otherwise be dealing with my partner. If you send me some details, I will make an introduction in short order. I believe he may be flying at this moment.'

'Please,' said Kroeze. 'I will await it.'

Kroeze's voice was replaced by Simon's.

'All good, Mike?'

'I could do with a massage, and a break from these calls,' said Mike jokingly.

'Well,' said Simon. 'I don't think we're close enough for me to offer you the former, but I can certainly divert your calls for the rest of the day.'

Mike laughed. 'Appreciated, but no. We're in the groove, so let's try and stay in it.'

CHAPTER 8

The sky over Chapman & Sunderland was grey and leaden, the clouds moving sluggishly and erratically. Mike closed the door of the Phantom gently, so as not to further anger the skies, and cast his eyes over their storage and sales units, their off-white cladding stretching upwards, away from the neatly laid Tarmac of the car park and access road, over the wrought-iron railings that surrounded the perimeter. Beyond, quiet woodland and fields, imposing a sense of peace, at odds with the skies above.

But all was not peaceful inside. The sound of a distant argument drifted up and over, from behind the unit, and Mike could hear angry bangs and thuds, things being thrown around, the sound of feet on polished concrete floors squeaking hurriedly back and forth. Rick's voice slashed through the silence, barking at someone, and Mike's good mood started to evaporate. He steeled himself, took a restful breath, and stepped through the office door.

'Mike, Ratlick fucked up,' shouted Rick, banging a folder full of papers down on the desk.

'What?!' said Mike, reeling from a mix of anger and confusion.

'There are people here reclaiming the Miura,' said Rick, waving in the direction of the showroom floor behind him. 'Apparently, he faked its documentation. They were supposed to collect it, to take it home.'

'You're kidding me!' said Mike bitterly. 'It wasn't his to move on.'

'Not in the slightest,' said Rick, his voice seething. 'He's just painted another target on our heads.'

'Have you spoken to him?'

'You think you can raise someone who's just pulled a stunt like that? Of course I haven't fucking spoken to him.'

Mike put his hand on Rick's shoulder. 'Okay, okay. What about the Mercedes? Can we intercept that before it reaches its client?'

'Let's not put us in the same boat. The 300SL's owner's paid, the car's his.'

'Fair point,' said Mike. 'Outside of a harshly worded letter, what can we do? We've got to put some pressure on him.'

Rick hissed and pulled his flask out of his jacket pocket. He stared at it for a few seconds, his head dipped, his thumb rolling across the flask's cap, then he looked back up at Mike, a deep frown stretching across his forehead.

'Wasn't the guy selling the Mercedes, Bayerwald, the one that got pissy at Ratlick a few years back?'

Mike nodded, catching a glimpse over Rick's shoulder of the yellow Lamborghini being shunted around on dollies by a distinctly unfriendly looking crew of workers.

'He was polite and held off saying anything for a long time,' said Mike. 'But, yes, he ended up suing Ratlick. Nothing ever came of it, though, and Ratlick's not been to Germany since.'

'What if Ratlick did go to Germany? Would the police want to have a word with him?'

'Perhaps the owner might think it worth the police having a word with him. I'm sure a word in his ear would make him spread the word to the relevant people. Some of these types, well, they can hold a pretty brutal grudge.'

Rick slipped the flask back into his pocket, then patted it a few times, and clapped his hands together. To Mike, it sounded like a thunderclap.

'Here's what we're going to do,' said Rick, his voice settled, solid. 'We set up a great car collection as bait. Doesn't need to exist. We pose as the owners. Rope Ratlick in to value it. Get him on the ground, bang.'

The corner of his mouth climbed upwards and he rubbed his hands together, a pleased look settling on his previously darkened face.

'Yeah,' he added, his voice low and slow. 'That'd do nicely.'

Mike nodded in agreement, the gears inside his head spinning. 'That might work, you know. He's greedy. We can pretend to not know much about the cars. Maybe we'll be broke.'

'And he'll look down his nose at us, like the twat he is, and think we're perfect victims.'

A truck fired up in the background, its coarse idle penetrating the insulated walls of the office.

'There goes the Miura, in comes our new plan,' said Rick. 'I'll speak to a few people, see what I can sort out.'

'We didn't need another new problem, so let's get this sorted swiftly,' said Mike, rapping his knuckles on the desk. 'I'm sure we can drum up the requisite sticks and carrots to sort this out pronto. Let's lure this fish into shallow waters with a floating worm.'

'Right,' said Rick authoritatively. 'On it.'

Rick turned and marched out of the room and closed the door firmly behind him, the frame rattling in protest. The noise of the truck faded, the workshop fell silent, and Mike sensed the moment's storm passing, its intensity subsiding. He sighed heavily, put the kettle on, and tried to establish some normality by setting about going through the month's turnovers, margins, and mail. A little peace floated back into the office as he delved through the pile of work, successful work, which had put money in the bank.

Mike stared briefly at a stub detailing two deposits for £30,000, neither of which tallied with anything in the live accounts, his index fingers tapping against his thumbs as his mind went to work.

The supercharged Mercedes, I think.

He scrolled through the inbox and found an unread email from a prospective buyer.

'Further to our discussion … resending the two 30,000 GBP deposits, by express,' said Mike out loud, reading the email. 'Balance of 7.5 million GBP to follow, for pair of Mercedes, Kompressors. Contracts required.'

Mike picked up a pen and twirled it between his fingers, thinking for a moment. He drafted a quick response, asking for the full buyer's name, proof of identification, and shipping details, and sent it on its way.

Got to dot the i's and cross the t's first, my friend.

Rick blazed back into the office with a coffee and started digging through the drawers in his desk, paper scattering this way and that.

'Remember that buyer for the Mercedes from a few weeks back?' said Mike.

'Owes us two deposits, £30,000 apiece, still no sign.'

'That's the one. What do you make of him?'

'If money hits the bank, we'll know pretty quickly. Sure as hell not arranging, or assuming, anything else before then.'

'True. Let's draft up some contracts to lock him in. If real money gets involved, he might disappear.'

'Shame we can't just make these things non-refundable,' said Rick, pulling a small black book from amid his files. 'That'd sort the wheat from the chaff, pronto.'

'Yes, but also make a lot of buyers nervous. Could put a dent in our operations.'

'Still,' said Rick irritably, 'those deposits should have been in days ago.'

'I'll send him a reminder now.'

'Make it a final one.'

———————— • ————————

The clock in the office struck eight, and the automatic security lights sprang to life outside. Mike's eyes rolled over to his screen.

The email he was looking for wasn't there.

Think our mystery Mercedes buyer is a dud, he thought. *I just don't get what they get out of the experience.*

He wandered over to the fridge and opened it. Inside were the usual stack of long-life milks, still and sparkling water, a few overly sugary drinks, and, confusingly, a small bottle of Merlot.

'As you do,' he said, amused. 'A sip will do.'

Mike extricated a dusty crystal glass from a shelf, blew the debris out of it, and decanted the entire bottle into the glass. He slumped back into his office chair, the hours of the day suddenly catching up to him, as the wine started to warm him. He idly pushed around a few papers atop his desk, looked out into the showroom, and clattered his fingers on his computer's keyboard for a moment.

Sod it. I need a break.

He walked through the showroom and into the service area beyond, where a 1929 Alfa Romeo 1750 Testa Fissa was resting between the lifts. It wasn't ready for sale yet, but it was getting there. Mike wandered over to a box on the wall and flipped a switch, rolling up a stamped steel shutter at the end of the workshop. It opened into a small section of what had once been the tail end of an airfield, its concrete surface coarse but continuous.

I got into this because I loved cars. Just need a reminder.

Mike carefully lowered himself into the Alfa's seat, trying to avoid marring its finely patinated seat trim. He ran his hands around the perimeter of its wheel, admired its hand-finished gauges, and worked the pedals and gear lever, listening to the sounds of the mechanisms beyond.

Ever since a young age, even on his daily journey to school in the seventies, he'd choose routes based on where the most interesting cars were parked in the streets. Back then, the cars that fascinated him most were mainly Lamborghini Miuras, Maserati Ghiblis, Jaguar E-types and Ferrari 275 GTBs or Daytonas. Cars that simply screamed speed, performance, prestige, exactly the kind of thing that might appeal to someone in their formative years. The pinnacle of performance and appeal.

In those days, many of these now highly prized cars were owned by colourful characters who drove them daily, despite not having the financial means to properly maintain them. It wasn't uncommon to discover dented, dusty and weeping thoroughbreds that had been sat in the same spot for months, their tyres sinking and cracking as time went by. Sometimes he'd repeatedly loop around the same areas, just to see if the cars had moved, or if anyone had shown any sign of care for them. Sometimes they would have gone, but he'd later find they'd only made it as far as the back row on the used car dealer's lot just around the corner.

The dealers were always a friendly sort, though, and not adverse to letting this curious kid poke around their more exotic stock. He'd peer into the interiors, study the panel work, marvel at their engines, and relish the aroma of ageing Connolly leather. And the history of each, even then, proved fascinating to him. The artefacts left behind allowed him to extrapolate, or simply imagine, what kind of past, glorious or otherwise, the car he was looking at had experienced. Hotel brochures, *Playboy* magazines, fashion boutique invoices, half-spent packs of expensive cigarettes, and foreign currency, all told a tale.

And they still do. Like that Halston perfume bottle I found in that abandoned Miura a while back, he thought, smirking. *The one that was parked next to a crashed Ferrari 250 GT Tour de France.*

Finding such a car, and its associated artefacts, was like finding treasure, even then. The faded paintwork, the tired but ever-glorious instrumentation, what remained of the finishes on the air boxes, the ageing fabrics and leathers, the wear patterns on the controls, the heavy smells of the interior, everything told its story, and fascinated him.

And I feel like some of these cars can talk, really talk, but only to those willing to listen, to look, to pay them the time and attention they deserve.

He took another sip of wine and mulled how his appreciation had grown in later years, going beyond the obvious. The technical wonders, the manifestations of remarkable design and luxury, the showcases of pure power, the masterpieces of style, elegance and glamour.

But not just the cars, he realised. In the early eighties, he had discovered the world of racing cars. Living near the Nürburgring at the time, he took every chance he could to go to the Oldtimer Grand Prix. Not having the money for the expensive tickets, he climbed fences or hid in the boot of some race driver's support vehicle. He also once managed to get into Brands Hatch to watch the Grand Prix by hiding deep in the cockpit of a Ferrari P4, buried under helmets and race gear, smuggled in by a British privateer. Mike just adored all the aircraft-inspired cockpits of the cars, such as the Jaguar D-type, 250 SWB and GTO, Maserati 450 or 300 S and, of course, the incredible Birdcage. But he admired the mighty Lister Jaguars even more.

All blended a heady mix of fashion, early aerodynamics, raw power and elegance that he still found fascinating. And as his career progressed, he began discovering many of these cars in barns and underground collections, all over Europe.

Like that cache of neglected Miuras and a DB4 in France, he thought, taking another small sip of the wine. *You could have had the lot for $10,000*.

'Not that I could afford it at the time,' he said to the Alfa, patting it. 'I'd managed to pick up a pretty good 250 GTE for some five grand.'

He looked over into the corner of the workshop and tipped his glass in the Ferrari's direction.

To tomorrow.

———————— ◆ ————————

Mike made a beeline for the workshop in the morning, feeling reinvigorated, and lowered himself once again into the driver's seat of the Alfa. He pulled its key from under the mat, hit the main power switch, inserted the key, puffed three shots of fuel into the intake with the Ki-Gass primer, then retarded the ignition timing. He stabbed the starter button and the Alfa barked to life almost instantly, its oil pressure climbing.

'Easy as that,' he said over the sound of the exhaust. 'Perfect.'

The supercharged engine whirred musically from in front of him, and a tap of the central throttle pedal revealed a crisp, lively response.

Just like a modern superbike, he thought. *Low weight, low drag, snappy*.

He knew the car's history like the back of his hand. It was an ex-Fred Stiles Alfa, one that placed third in the 1930 Tourist Trophy with Achille Varzi at the wheel. Nuvolari was in a similar car and placed first. The second-placed car was another 1750 Alfa, driven by Campari. A rare, memorable, one-two-three podium finish.

Mike gently manoeuvred the supercharged Alfa, as sympathetically as one could, out onto the B-roads around the dealership, letting the drivetrain and tyres warm. The process of simply getting the car to move smoothly down the road was a demanding one, and one that required his focus, a process that boosted his attention and sharpness considerably.

Like a good shot of caffeine, he thought, deftly working the clutch as he shifted up to second gear, the speedometer needle already touching 65km/h. *All part of the experience. Living history and pure emotion*.

Not that Mike could pick one particular driving experience as a favourite; all offered something memorable, and anyone who had spent time in any similar machinery, be it a Vincent Black Lightning, a Supermarine Spitfire, an A1 locomotive, or even a humble classic Mini or Land Rover, would understand.

A day driving a Ghibli, a 917 Kurzheck, a Phantom I, a Traction Avant 15CV Six, a Daytona 365 GTB/4, an E-type roadster … I don't know which I'd pick to experience again.

Did he prefer Italian elegance, German rationality or down-to-earth, laid-back French charm? He couldn't decide and chuckled at the thought. As different as the cars were, they shared countless traits: a special spot in automotive history, and a multitude of sensations and feelings. A Citroën 2CV was just as admirable, and often just as enjoyable, if not more, than a Lamborghini Miura.

But I like them both. And then there's the travelling, and the socialising.

The Alfa Romeo coughed as he squeezed its accelerator, then cleared its throat and pulled cleanly, the needle of the small Jaeger tachometer jittering towards the red.

Then there are the owners, the stashes, the finds, the places, those special drives. When it all comes together, magic.

'Just like now,' he said, opening up the Alfa again, letting it spear towards the horizon. He let it sing all the way out in fourth gear, stretching the legs of its newly rebuilt engine, and felt like he was driving the fastest car on the road.

The skies began to darken, so Mike turned the sonorous straight-six Alfa around and beat a hasty retreat to the workshop, feeling a little more in tune with both the car and the world around him.

Rick was standing at the entrance to the workshop, waiting for him, a satisfied look on his face. Mike parked the Alfa neatly, let it idle for a few moments, and then shut it off.

'I'd buy that if I had the money,' said Mike, smiling.

'You might well soon have,' said Rick, returning the smile. 'Two million, from Harriston, confirmed in the accounts this morning.'

'Well, that's fantastic news!'

'Yup. I need you to take care of the Austrian side of things and get the legal side sorted, and then we can shunt the money around.'

'Of course,' said Mike, cheer flushing through his body. 'Harriston wants to be in Salzburg, too, when we make the deal, by the way. So, it seems a done thing.'

'Oh, really? Well, make sure all and any contracts are just between us and the sellers, as planned. He's a pivotal part of this deal, but let's not make him integral to the legal side of things. The cars are ours.'

'Agreed,' said Mike. 'I did tell him that it wasn't necessary, but he wants to be present.'

Rick shrugged. 'I suppose I'd want to be there, too, if I was dumping a fortune into a bit of a gamble. Just for peace of mind.'

'Let's not call it a gamble. We know what we've got. And I'm sure Harriston has plenty of ways to ensure peace of mind, anyway. Most of them not peaceful for whoever's on the receiving end.'

'He's been on the receiving end of a few bits, so I've heard recently,' said Rick. 'Got wrapped up in a fairly lairy evening with a lot of left-leaning politicians, some drugs, and lord knows what else a few years back.'

'And your mysterious source came about this info how?' said Mike suspiciously.

'They were there. There was a bit of a sting, money flying around, a few photos that went missing, followed by a few people. That kind of gig.'

'I think I'll stick to the local Indian and a beer, thanks.'

Rick snorted, then tapped the bonnet of the Alfa.

'Speaking of hot Italians, you need to head over to Milton Keynes,' said Rick. 'A certain contessa is having troubles with her Superfast. I'll ping you the location now.'

'Not Contessa D'Avossa, surely?'

'The one and same.'

Julie's mother.

'Not one I'd ever want to piss off,' said Rick, grinning. 'And definitely a bit more age-appropriate, Mike.'

'She's well north of thirty, Rick, and anyway, it's not like that,' said Mike snappily, albeit not entirely convincingly. 'But I do know her, and that car, well.'

'See if you can call her now and see what's up. She was on her way to Milan, would you believe. Mad, but admirable.'

'Sounds about right,' said Mike. 'Sounds about right.'

CHAPTER 9

Chiara Angelina, the Contessa D'Avossa, was anything but subtle. Mike first met her in Monza, during the old Ferrari Challenge days, when she had come screaming into the pits in a 1935 Maserati 8CM Monoposto.

Just like it was yesterday, he thought, as the Phantom loped down the road towards Milton Keynes. He closed his eyes for a fraction of a second and smelt race fuel, heard the angry crackle of exhausts, and felt the heat of the circuit beneath him.

An Italian lady was shouting something inaudible at him as he stood watching the racing, and was gesturing wildly at a helmet sat atop of spare tyres. Her just-parked Maserati was spitting and snarling, smoke pluming from its brakes.

The lady cut the engine for a moment, and her voice cut clear through Mike's skull. 'Andiamo, andiamo, veloce, now! Get a helmet on!'

Mike shrugged at her, uncertain, but moved closer. She restarted the engine, blipping the throttle to keep the 8CM running. 'Veloce, veloce. I need a break, you drive.'

He couldn't believe what was happening. 'I don't have a licence, or a helmet!' he shouted back, over the deafening noise of the Maserati.

A helmet suddenly appeared in his hands, passed over by his friend Robert, whose 1932 Alfa Romeo P3 Tipo B was parked in the next pit.

'That's D'Avossa,' said Robert, stifling a grin. 'Don't argue, just do.'

D'Avossa nodded at Robert, jumped out of the car, pushed Mike in its direction, and disappeared in the direction of the bathroom.

Fortune favours the bold, he thought. I hope.

He lowered himself into the small leather seat of the precious Maserati, familiarised himself with the controls, and launched the Monoposto away from the pits. It screamed, smoke pluming from its tyres, dashing away before anyone could recognise him.

This car feels great, he thought, as he rejoined the circuit amid a Maserati 26B, a fast 250F and a 4CLT from the Netherlands. It was evidently running on methanol, because it stank like a crude refinery. Its exhaust had a strange, crisp note to it, and the smell alone was almost causing him to faint.

Acetone. Bet there's acetone in there.

He managed to pass the obnoxious 4CLT, the Maserati responding willingly to his inputs, a glorious 159 Alfetta Monoposto appearing in front of him. It remained in front, though, its power and gearing giving it the legs over the 8CM.

She must know of me through Robert, otherwise why the hell would she let me drive?!

A few more laps passed, and Mike slipped into a routine in the 8CM, just keeping pace with the 159 without pushing the car too hard. He had almost forgotten it wasn't his until he spotted the Contessa waving wildly from the pit wall. He brought the car back in, leapt out, and before he knew what had happened, she disappeared in a cloud of smoke, sound, and rubber.

It always amazed me how quick she was. How easily she handed that big eight-cylinder single seater.

Something in the Rolls-Royce beeped and he felt himself yanked back to the real world, nothing but a disappointingly dull section of Tarmac stretching away in front of him, the Phantom sitting squarely in the middle of its lane.

'One of those autopilot moments,' he said quietly. 'You've been driving, but you just can't remember it. Often the way with these modern cars.'

At least I caught up with her later, in person, at least.

It had been at dinner, after the race. Contessa D'Avossa, as he had assumed from her driving, was confident and experienced, as well as cultured. At a dinner hosted locally she told him about growing up in a castle in Sicily, where her uncle taught her to hunt, shoot, ride and drive. He had a penchant for Targa Florio racers, something he evidently passed down.

'He raised me like a boy,' she said, recalled Mike. Later, her family had moved closer to Palermo, into the cooler hills near the village of San Cipirello, but violent times ensued, and they found themselves forced to move. Eventually, they decided to leave Sicily for good and went to Trieste, in Friuli, the very north of Italy, to put as much distance as possible between themselves and Palermo.

Unfortunately, in the Sicily of the eighties, the syndicates took over public life. There was no future, no security, for anyone who wanted to run a business. Those who could left the island, either to the US, UK, or Germany. Chiara's family had ended up heading to London, starting entirely new lives for themselves. Chiara settled there, too, training as a dentist, and married a retired General from the Italian army.

I remember her saying the family didn't approve. Too many links between crime and anyone remotely political.

They had a daughter, Giulietta, but the General would die a few years later, taking his own life by running his car in a closed garage. A letter was in the glovebox, explaining his reasons why.

But no one believed it then. I doubt any do now.

———————————— • ————————————

The black 1966 Ferrari 500 Superfast was almost impossible to see in the gloom, only the dull overhead lights of the service station barely revealing its surface. The only thing that stood out, and what caught

Mike's eye, were the neat chrome bumpers at each corner, silver flashes in the dark.

Chiara was standing next to it, the bonnet up, the door open, revealing its sensational turquoise leather interior. He smiled at the sight of it; everybody in the classic car racing world knew that car, and its owner. She regularly drove to the European races in it, fully loaded with tools, parts, clothes, presents, handbags, shoes, everything stowed on the seats and in the trunk.

It was a priceless machine, too, and it was truly admirable that she continued to use it. Only 12 of the very couture cars had been built, with a five-speed gearbox in place of the earlier four-speed unit with overdrive. The 12-cylinder engine put out north of 400 horsepower, giving the Ferrari serious pace, and it was all wrapped up in a subtle, elegant body. A very significant, desirable Ferrari, one that had been gifted to her as a present when her daughter was born.

Collected from Enzo himself, if I recall correctly. And an engine straight out of the racing department.

Chiara dashed towards the Phantom, battering on its door before Mike had even shut it off. He hopped out and she embraced him, kissing him three times on both cheeks, the smell of Jo Malone Pomegranate lingering in his nostrils.

'Michele, ma come estai? Tu sei bellissimo,' she said musically.

'I'm good, thank you,' he said, smiling broadly. 'Good to see you. What's the story here, then?'

'Ah, la Ferrari. Sempre una prima donna,' she said, holding up her hands. 'It's running too rich, fouling the plugs. I had it set up earlier, but something must have changed. And my tools are in the Ghibli.'

'Well, let me see if I can help,' said Mike. 'Does it still start?'

'Certo! Que male.'

Mike turned the Ferrari over and it caught, but it sounded distinctly out of sorts. Ugly black smoke drifted intermittently from one side of its exhaust system, and the tachometer needle dipped and wavered continually. He turned the key off and the engine continued to run unevenly for a few moments, then shut off.

'Look at the tailpipes on that side,' he said. 'Loaded with carbon. It must just be one bank.'

Chiara nodded at him. 'Do you have a toolkit? I will pull the plugs. Maybe something in one of the carburettors has come adrift.'

'Yup, I brought everything we might need, and the rest, just in case,' said Mike, pointing at the Phantom's boot. 'Did you happen to fill up recently, by any chance?

'Si, one hundred kilometres or so ago.'

'Do you recall what you put in it?'

'No super, they only had 95. It had to do.'

'It won't have liked that, either. Let's tackle that afterwards.'

'Si, va bene, I do the right side. You do the left. Six plugs each.'

'Good idea. I'll get the tools. I've got a small soft-tipped mallet; we can use that to free the floats off, if they're stuck.'

Chiara nodded and started pulling HT leads off the plugs. Mike gathered the tools and started pulling the plugs on his bank, one by one, inspecting them and cleaning the tips with a cigarette lighter and brush. Chiara followed, and they chatted about life, work, and, of course, cars. But rain started to fall, forcing them to focus on the task at hand.

'It looks like the float in the rearmost Weber was stuck,' said Mike, tapping it with his soft rubber mallet to free it off. 'It'll probably run much more cleanly now.'

The engine restarted and ran cleanly, singing as sweetly and as smoothly as only a V12 could. Mike brought the idle up a little, the engine responding happily and seeming more content.

'Maybe a bit too low before,' he said, pointing at the tacho. 'Probably loading it up a bit.'

'I prefer it to be sharper. This is better,' said Chiara, nodding approvingly.

'Brim it with super now, if you can, or at least soon. That'll help keep it on form.'

'I really appreciate it, Mike. I'm sure I'll be able to repay the favour at some point.'

'If I ever need fashion advice, I know who to call.'

She laughed as she closed the Ferrari's bonnet and checked around it. 'And I understand you caught up with Julie recently?'

'I did. Glad to find she's getting on in London. She's certainly not one to be messed with, either. Full of energy, just like you.'

'A family trait, I think. She keeps making noise about going back to Trieste or Sicily but, well, you know.'

'Troppo pericoloso, so you say.'

'Exactly.' She wagged a finger at him. 'And you be careful, too. Nothing but good intentions, Mr Chapman!'

Mike imitated doffing a cap. 'As always, of course, Mia signora!'

'Come sempre infatti. Anyway, I must go, I'm afraid. Must catch the boat.'

He shrugged. 'I understand. Still, great to see you, even if it's just for a moment.'

She smiled softly at him, shook his hand gently, and slipped back into the Ferrari. It roared away, leaving him again in a cloud of dust, rubber, sound and fumes, heading roughly in the direction of Milan.

'Don't make them like that these days,' he said to the empty forecourt.

CHAPTER 10

Mike watched as the travellers came and went from the departure lounge at Düsseldorf Airport. The flight had been delayed and his coffee was cold, but he could still see the smartly dressed Dr Bayerwald, and his son, sitting at a table at the café opposite. Just behind them, concealed by a pillar, was a young police officer and a stern-looking lawyer.

The police officer was tapping his fingers against the holster of his pistol, and Mike caught himself subconsciously rapping his fingers on the table, echoing the officer's restless nature. They had been waiting for over an hour. But still nothing. The lawyer caught his eye, shrugged at him, then went back to staring into his phone. Mike glanced at the departure board and felt his heart skip a beat.

It's here. They should be here any moment now.

Bayerwald looked up and over at him, a pensive look on his face. His son tapped his hand quickly and pointed over Bayerwald's shoulder. Bayerwald turned, looking, and then coughed loudly. The officer and the lawyer straightened up but stayed where they were, out of sight.

A wiry-looking man, dressed in a blue suit, a diamond-studded fake Rolex occasionally peeking out from beneath the cuff of his jacket, was striding through the crowd. His thinning hair was combed over, poorly dyed, his teeth far whiter than they should be.

Ratlick, thought Mike, one corner of his mouth turning upwards, *you bastard*.

Bayerwald stood up, turned around, and marched towards Ratlick. There was a vague flicker of recollection on the auctioneer's face, followed by a flash of confusion and concern.

'Mr Ratlick,' said Bayerwald confidently. 'It is odd to encounter you here.'

Ratlick stuttered for a moment. 'And, and you too, Mr… Bayerwald, right?'

'That's right. You sold my Mercedes-Benz 300SL recently.'

'Yes, that's right. I hope things are, uh, proceeding as expected.'

'Not in a fashion that I would like,' said Bayerwald. 'And I know that many involved in the transaction are also finding the proceedings far from expected.'

Ratlick stepped backwards, his head shaking slightly.

'I'm… I'm afraid I don't know what you mean.'

Bayerwald stuck a finger in the air and waved it. The police officer and lawyer strode over to him, bracketing Ratlick.

'I understand this gentleman, and my lawyer, need to have a lengthy conversation with you,' said Bayerwald. 'It is, as you may have correctly assumed, about the 300SL, the money, the Miura, and the questionable operation you are running.'

Ratlick took another step backwards, and started to turn, but the police officer grabbed his arm, effortlessly holding him in place. Ratlick's shoes squeaked on the polished floor of the airport for a moment.

'I'm sure, I'm sure, I'm sure this is just some kind of misunderstanding,' he said, voice rising in pitch. 'Let me go!'

The police officer smirked and shook his head.

'You'll find we're quite efficient, as always, when it comes to things such as this,' said Bayerwald, casually inspecting his cuff links and neatly pressed shirt.

'But what does it matter to you?!' shouted Ratlick. 'You'll get your money!'

'But he won't,' said Bayerwald, looking up, his finger pointing at Mike. 'This is not proper business and none of us like it.'

Mike waved cheerily at Ratlick, from across the corridor, and raised his coffee cup to him.

'You bastard, Chapman,' shouted Ratlick. 'You …'

'Don't have a leg to stand on,' said Bayerwald dismissively. 'Game's over.'

The lawyer stepped forward, proffering a thick folder of documentation.

'You can read this while you're on the way to the station,' he said flatly. 'If you pay us nine hundred and fifty thousand Euros, plus costs, we may be able to settle this. You'll only have a short stay inside.'

Ratlick shook his head violently.

'Or you can choose to not read it, and not pay, and we can make your stay considerably longer.'

Ratlick shook his head more violently, sweat beading on his forehead.

'Take him away,' said the lawyer. 'And think about it, won't you,' he added with disdain, his lips pursed.

Bayerwald huffed, his shoulders slumping, as the police officer walked off with Ratlick in tow. Mike wandered over, shaking his head.

'Quite the show,' he said. 'Thanks for that, Dr Bayerwald. I appreciate your time and effort.'

'You're welcome,' said Bayerwald. 'This wasn't what I hoped for, you understand.'

'It wasn't what we hoped for, either, and I hope it does not tarnish your view of us. Do you think he'll pay up?'

'I think the threat of incarceration will make the funds mysteriously materialise, yes. What happens beyond that point, I don't know.'

'Probably the end of that auction house, though.'

'Oh, certainly,' said Bayerwald. 'But I doubt he'll change.'

'We live in hope,' said Mike.

Bayerwald nodded genially as his phone beeped. He looked down at it, his focus falling entirely on the screen. Mike couldn't help but recognise the web page that had popped up: it was the catalogue page for an upcoming auction.

'So, looking to add anything new to the collection?' said Mike inquisitively. 'A Ferrari, perhaps?'

———————— • ————————

Mike stayed overnight in Cologne. The next day, he rented a Piper Cherokee PA-28 from Tenberg Aero Charter to fly to Salzburg. He had to meet Joseph, his middleman for the Austrian Collection deal, to talk over the legal side in person.

Since Rick and Mike had received the initial down payment from Lord Harriston into their escrow account, they could now move forward. This entailed Joseph preparing a meeting with the Austrian lawyers and a notary, establishing the documentation and signing processes that were required to secure and close the deal.

'They have a lot of bureaucracy in Austria,' grumbled Mike, as he pulled his hire car into a parking area at Cologne Airport. 'I hate this part of the business.'

Mike was also conscious that he was going to have to deal with Harriston directly, again, to finalise their facility agreement about his investment and the handling of the cars. *More bloody paperwork*, he thought, as he walked through security.

The Cherokee from Tenberg turned out to be a lovely old thing from the eighties, finished in white and blue, with a plush blue velour interior, analogue instruments, and only a few modern additions.

Perfect. Just like the ones I saw when I got my private licence here.

Once ground checked, Mike settled into the left seat and went through the dog-eared checklist that he found lying between the seats. He fastened the seat belt, feeling for the rudder pedals with his feet. The wheel brakes came on and felt good. He flipped the main switch, toggled both magnetos on, set the mixture to rich, pushed the throttle forward a quarter, and pressed the starter.

Mike listened to the engine crank then catch, and watched the needles come alive, checking the pressures and readings carefully. He then checked all the frequencies and map points, making sure his radio and flightpath were in order, and asked the tower for clearance to taxi.

Satisfied and cleared, he released the Cherokee's brakes and rolled towards the taxiway. He held short of the runway, gazing through the blades whirring past in front of him, eyes making their way to the skies above. The airport was quiet and his request for clearance was quickly approved, and the Cherokee murmured merrily as it passed over the threshold and onto the runway.

Mike checked that he was good to go, pushed the throttle to its stop, and the Cherokee accelerated down the runway. It pushed its way through the 15-knot headwind and clattered noisily into the sky, the engine becoming more subdued as Mike pulled the power and settled into steady flight. At about 1,000 feet he squeezed the left rudder pedal, and pushed gently on the stick between his knees, pointing the plane down the Rhine valley.

At 3,000 feet, Mike levelled out the little Piper and took in his surroundings. It was a beautiful day over the Rhine, the sun blasting through intermittent clouds. *Good visibility, though,* he thought. He took a 180-degree heading, towards Frankfurt, the weather slowly shifting to rain and wind as the miles passed, getting worse over Koblenz. *Knew my luck wouldn't hold.*

The weather and landscape continued to change, with more wind rolling in near Aschaffenburg. *Turbulent, like the classic car market,* thought Mike, cycling the controls gently to keep the Piper pointing in the right direction. *A changing landscape.*

Historically, classic car values rose almost every six months, and dealers were willing to purchase inventory and hold it for a year or more until sold. However, Mike had noticed two things in recent years that had changed the status quo. Many dealers were now avoiding inventory altogether and were working on either a consignment basis, or purely on a commission for brokering arrangements between buyer and seller. No longer were they keen to invest, acquire, and sit on classics.

He'd also clocked that auction houses had increasingly become retailers, a process that had led to them taking over most of the classic car market in the process. Their scale and leverage meant they could more easily deal in the ultra-rare and highly desirable cars, generating record sale prices that stole the show and limelight from dealers.

Spectacle and theatre. That's how.

The big auction houses had cleverly poured money into marketing and brand awareness, leaving many classic car dealers behind, even the established ones. And their ability to put on huge sales, broadcast live around the world, with every glass being routinely refilled with champagne, every sale turned into an event, left a lot of buyers simply overlooking dealers. Who, in turn, ended up fighting for a diminishing market share of the hugely competitive midstream, or low-margin bottom end.

Only a few dealers had managed to buck the trend, becoming more recognised brands with wider appeal, and several – including Chapman & Sunderland – were working on plans to that end.

The rest, well, they're not adapting. And that'll be the death of them.

The millennial generation, which was transpiring to be a strong new customer base for classic supercars, were completely at ease with the idea of online auctions. They were happy to bid, buy, and have delivered, without even seeing the car in person. That had its pitfalls, of course, but it was a tremendous win for anyone who could offer the right cars through the right methods.

I was in marketing for, what, thirty years? But it doesn't take that experience to know that you just cannot overlook those opportunities.

Shifts in collectors' tastes had also caught some out, with younger cars becoming more desirable, as buyer profile, desires and ages changed. A Ferrari F40 might have set you back six hundred thousand dollars several years ago, and now you could easily pay north of three million for one, if you could find a good one.

And the aging profile of some buyers has just left some eras for dead.

Pre-war brands such as Invicta, Alvis, Delahaye, Lagonda and Amilcar were no longer appealing to many. The pool of buyers interested in such cars was getting older and smaller, at a rapid rate, compounded by a lack of promotional efforts. Some brands were now almost dead, in terms of appeal, and very hard to move on.

Even the best pre-war cars from Bentley, Bugatti and Mercedes had suddenly found themselves competing with youngsters such as the McLaren F1, Pagani Zonda, Bugatti Veyron, or the smart Ferrari supercars of the eighties and nineties.

Which is why you'll see many auctions putting those cars close together, thought Mike, as he checked the Cherokee's mixture setting. *Very smart.*

Ultimately, for classic car dealers of the future, there was only one way to go. They needed to develop a better understanding of their core customers. The customers were seeking pleasure, relaxation, sound advice, and appreciated service and creativity. They were confident, knowledgeable people, with their own styles and tastes. Personal relationships were going to be at the core of any successful business, in the future. You needed to be considered a friend, rather than a dealer, and share stories, work and advice, in a truly authentic and honest manner.

Like the collections I manage. A privilege to care for them but also to know the people, visit their homes, their families. All about going that extra mile.

As a result, many long-standing dealers were at imminent risk of getting stuck with a showroom full of the most beautiful exotica you could own. A Bentley S1 Continental, a Bugatti Type 57, Mercedes-Benz 500K, Delahaye 135M Figoni et Falaschi; all phenomenal machines, but requiring substantial effort and energy to move, and not what a lot of the market was looking for.

It does help that many of these aren't just cars, but tickets into another world. Pebble Beach, Mille Miglia, Villa d'Este. Long may they continue.

'And then there's the paperwork and the bureaucracy,' he said gruffly to the Piper's cabin, face contorting.

Service and export demands had risen dramatically in the past years, but many companies with tight margins couldn't absorb the cost of the work or transport. That made them even less desirable to clients. And anyone who had tried to bring an untaxed car on a trailer into Belgium, Switzerland or Germany had found the implications to be huge when they got caught out. In fact, the receiving client might be fined for not being able to produce a carnet or T1 document at customs in their homeland when they wanted to register the car. To dealers who didn't know this, it could be a death knell.

The parts business had also been badly hit, even for EU-based distributors who desperately needed UK parts. For some, the situation had become untenable. There were hundreds of classic cars in the EU and overseas blocking workshop lifts and workshop space, waiting for parts, sometimes for months. Owners were rightly getting angry, all of which was directed squarely at the dealers.

Thanks, Brexit. Now we've the perfect storm.

Smart dealers were moving quickly with the trends, responding to increasingly knowledgeable buyers, market price corrections, and inventory, acquiring cars such as Ferrari F50s and Porsche GT2s.

But there are still oddities. Like why a 1962 Jaguar E-type 3.8 Roadster is worth one-tenth of a Ferrari 250 GT Cabriolet. Madness.

'Sometimes the market can be wrong too,' said Mike, as the Alps behind Salzburg came into sight.

CHAPTER 11

The Cherokee's tyres chirped as it touched down at Salzburg Mozart Airport. Even in the worst-case scenario, it would never need all 2.7 kilometres of runway 033; the headwind Mike had battled had drained most of its fuel, and the wind was still up, so the tiny aircraft stopped practically on a dime.

Joseph, the middleman for the Austrian deal, was waiting for him outside a wide, low hanger. He was dressed casually, in a white shirt and dark blue jeans, his sunglasses perched on his head. Mike taxied to the apron alongside the hanger, shut down the Piper, and leapt out. Joseph waved, leant back against the wall, and watched as Mike chocked and secured the plane.

Mike couldn't help but notice a highly polished Lockheed P-38 Lightning and North American B-25J Mitchell in the hanger, a few rays of sun striking their spectacular silver surfaces.

'Part of a display and VIP affair,' said Joseph, spotting his gaze as Mike walked towards him. 'A bit more serious than what you've bumbled over in.'

Mike laughed and shook his hand, the smell of flowers in the surrounding fields, hot concrete and aviation fuel strangely welcoming.

'How are you doing,' he said, smiling broadly.

'All good,' said Joseph. 'Almost done with the work on my house at Lake Garda. You're welcome any time.'

'I'll take any opportunity to visit Salo,' said Mike cheerily.

'And how about the financing, did you sort that out?'

'It's all okay, so far,' said Mike. 'We've got two million for the deposit, ready to hit your account. Make sure that figure is in the paperwork.'

'Pounds or Euros?' said Joseph.

'Pounds.'

'And you do realise this will be non-refundable? If this goes south, that's it.'

Mike swallowed and nodded.

'Yeah, I know. It's a risk that Rick and I are willing to take. Everything's in order, though, so I can't foresee any complications.'

'Alright,' said Joseph, tapping on the screen of his phone. 'I'll send a draft of the remaining documentation to you now, and we'll update everything else to suit.'

'Any other changes I need to know about?'

'No, it's still the same as before. The family's looking for full payment in no later than three months. The notary will be in Salzburg for ten days, from the 29th, to sign the options contract and other papers. You must be there.'

'Of course.'

'Once we've the deposit and the signatures, you can have the Ferrari in the UK on commission, but they need to be stored securely and tracked. You cannot move them around without consent.'

'Fine by us,' said Mike. 'Sensible.'

'Have you made any arrangements yet?'

'We have a shipping company in Buckingham, with secure storage that looks like a showroom, which will be taking the cars in. It'll make viewings and selling easier.'

'Excellent,' said Joseph, sticking his thumb up. 'Apart from that, there is a commission contract for my side, too. It'll be, once you've sold the cars, for seven hundred and fifty thousand Euros.'

Mike squinted at him, then shook his head regretfully.

'That's too much. We're taking the risk; your party is just shunting numbers and contacts around.'

Joseph shook his head smartly in response. 'We also kept the auction houses away, the collection secret, and more. We had plenty of interested parties.'

'Five hundred.'

'Too low.'

'Please, try to bring that figure down closer to five hundred. That's a big return on their time and effort.'

Joseph rocked his head noncommittally, but the gears were obviously turning.

'We'll strike a middle ground, perhaps.'

'Close enough,' said Mike, relieved.

'Do you have any potential clients in mind already?'

'Yes,' said Mike confidently. 'There's a hedge fund already engaged. It'll need a little time, but it's a good option.'

Joseph studied Mike for a moment. 'You want to give me a little more on that front? It might help me settle some nerves elsewhere.'

'Off the record, or to be passed on?'

'Only I need to know,' said Joseph.

'The hedge fund's called Hadfords. They usually move on art but, well, I think the values in this field are turning their heads.'

'I know the Hadford name, but that's about it. Do they have a client in mind?'

'A Saudi Prince. Abdul Ben Ali.'

Joseph nodded, then smiled broadly. 'Okay. That's certainly useful to know.'

'We're hoping to hear back from them within a week or so.'

'The sooner the better,' said Joseph eagerly. 'But okay, we will proceed as planned.'

The two shook hands as the mechanics wheeled the P-38 out of the hanger, its triple-bladed propellers sparkling in the sunlight.

'And you're sure you've got a handle on Harriston?' added Joseph. 'I've heard rumours that he's been pushing into lots of sectors recently. Anything involving motors, batteries, electric cars. Chemicals, raw materials, the works. I'm surprised you can pin him down.'

Mike shook his head in agreement. 'Yeah, so I've read, along those lines. He definitely has some interest in automotive, historical and modern, but I'm not sure he's really a car person. And brutal, with the most intimidating glare I've encountered, but straightforward.'

'Straightforward we can deal with. He stands to do well out of this, with minimal effort, as do we.'

Joseph turned to inspect the Cherokee, which had caught the attention of some of the mechanics. They, too, were admiring its bright blue interior.

'What are your plans now?' said Joseph. 'I'm going to assume you're not about to leave in that.'

'Italy, for me,' said Mike happily. 'A collection there to check out, hopefully a few cars that'll come our way. After that, a few meetings, then to Geneva to engage a new client.'

'Another collection in Italy?'

'Yes, mostly pre-war stuff. The owners are being a bit tight-lipped about it, but I understand they've got an Isotta Fraschini 8B by Castagna, a Lagonda LG45 Coupé, and a few other bits.'

'Not my cup of tea,' said Joseph. 'But let me know if there are any early Alfas in there.'

'Consider that noted,' said Mike, grinning. 'I think I need a car more than you do right now, though.'

'Not flying over?' said Joseph, pointing at the Cherokee.

'No, unfortunately not. It's chartered and stays here, so I've got to get my hands on a car.'

'Any preferences?'

'As long as it moves and is legal, that'll be fine,' said Mike. 'I could just hire something, but where's the fun in that?'

Joseph tipped his head back, glanced around as if worried about being watched, then leant forwards.

'You could take my car, if you want,' he said.

'Take?'

'Well, buy.'

'What is it?'

'It's a 1940 Cadillac Series 62 Convertible Sedan. Drives beautifully. And original, and reliable.'

'Flathead?'

'Exactly. My wife quite likes it, but I'd rather get back into something Italian.'

'Where is it?' said Mike, intrigued.

'Near the terminal. You buy it, and I'll just get a taxi home.'

'I'm guessing this isn't going to represent a cheap ride, though.'

'You know what these things are worth.'

How long's a piece of string, thought Mike. *It could be a basket case.*

'I tell you what,' said Joseph, rubbing his hands together. 'You take the car, drive it, and if we do the big deal, you give me one hundred thousand Euros for it.'

'And if the deal falls through?'

'If the deal falls apart, or if you decide it's not for you, just get it back to me and tip something in my favour next time,' said Joseph. 'We've known each other long enough, and I'm sure we'll cross paths again.'

No, I'd be mad to do that. But then, well, we're only going to go around this circuit once. Why not? Why not!

'Deal. Let's do it,' said Mike, his voice wavering a little.

'Perfect, here are the keys. Papers are in the glove box. There are a few spares and some oil in the back, as you might expect.'

'Thanks, I think,' said Mike. 'It might stay in Bergamo with a friend, once I'm done with Italy. Or maybe I'll just run it all the way to Geneva. Let's find out.'

'Good luck,' said Joseph. 'I'll email you soon.'

———————— • ————————

The Cadillac was better than he hoped. Its grey paint and metalwork appeared pristine, its tyres recent and glossy. Its light-blue interior, which was slightly worn and appealingly original, paired beautifully with bright switchgear, blue Bakelite finishes, and chrome detailing. The deep, rich smell of the seats rolled into his nostrils, triggering countless memories of old. He smiled, slipped the small key into the ignition barrel and pressed the starter button, the big flathead V8 turning over lazily. It coughed, caught, and settled into a smooth burble.

Magic, he thought, as he familiarised himself with the three-on-the-tree manual shifter. He continued to inspect the controls and interior as the Cadillac warmed but, having studied the sky for a moment, he decided to lower the long roof.

When in Rome, or words to that effect.

The happy-sounding flathead throbbed as the Cadillac took to the road, motoring south, heading for the Tauern Autobahn. The road, one of Mike's favourites, ran from Salzburg to Venice. The Cadillac steered easily, rode beautifully, and ate up the miles as the scenic roadway slipped past; first Salzburg, then Villach, the sun going out as the car plunged into the long Tauern tunnel. Snow-capped mountains soon greeted it, along with waterfalls and breathtaking valleys, as it wandered amid the Alps.

Far better than the Brenner, from Innsbruck to Bolzano, thought Mike. *A hundred passes, in countless cars, and I'd still always pick this route.*

The Cadillac, unsurprisingly, preferred a more casual pace, and Mike appreciated the time it gave him to take in the sights. No technology, no pressure, no rush. No constant bombardment from infotainment systems, safety systems, driver assistance features, or connected communications.

Just peace.

He flicked the old valve radio on, Tchaikovsky's *1812 Overture* just about making itself heard through the tiny and ageing single speaker, and pointed the long bonnet of the Cadillac towards Villach.

I wish she could see this again.

The remaining miles passed without fuss and, to Mike's relief, the Cadillac managed to squeeze into the underground garage of the Holiday Inn Hotel, in the middle of Villach. It was always a good place to stay, offering spectacular views over the river Drau, and cosy rooms.

Mike ambled up to the reception, travel bag in hand, and rang the bell. The manager appeared from a side room, smiling at him.

'Evening, Mr Chapman. It's been a little while,' he said as he shuffled some papers behind the desk. 'For two?'

Mike shook his head and grimaced for a moment. 'Just the one, please.'

The manager cocked his head but didn't say anything as his fingers flashed over a keyboard. 'We can do that, of course. And the Luganer and a chicken salad, to your room?'

'That would be fine, thanks. It'll be an early night for me.'

———————— • ————————

The food was up to its usual standard and the room was compact but neatly furnished, a mixture of warm woods and soft fabrics. He'd stayed in countless similar rooms at the Holiday Inn, and realised his life was starting to feel like one without any fixed abode. All rented rooms, hotels, abandoned warehouses, estates, barns, underground garages. All removed from the public eye, all intensely private and secretive.

Lonely, he thought, as the sun settled beneath the horizon. *I'm not sure I enjoy it as much as I used to.*

The room brightened, an intense white glare from his phone shattering the darkness.

Rick. Well, it's something.

'You're just in time,' he said, sounding a little groggy. 'Just drawing to a close here.'

'I've just had one of those moments, Mike,' he said, his voice flustered and stressed.

'You what?' said Mike, sitting upright.

'You know, one of those fractions of a second when you think, "Yeah, this is it, I'm done for."'

'I'm not following you.'

'I mean, you know that I don't ride those things to get myself killed.'

'I'm still not with you, Rick.'

'But, you know, I get the buzz.'

'Rick.'

'Yes?'

'What's going on?!'

'I mean, we've been racing bikes and cars for 30 years now, but I've never had anything like this.'

'Rick,' said Mike, pleadingly 'What are you talking about?'

'I was doing 140mph on the M1, I know, I know, and this BMW M5 damned near killed me. Just brushed me, but that was all it took.'

'You what?!'

'I know, I was pushing my luck, and they obviously wanted in on the game, but I perhaps backed off a bit, and they misjudged the gap a bit, and…'

'And?'

'Well, the Kawasaki's gone. And the BMW didn't stop.'

'What about you?'

'I went on what felt like an unending slip 'n' slide, all the way over to the hard shoulder.'

'It was raining?' said Mike, aghast.

'Well, yeah.'

'Jesus, Rick. Jesus. You're lucky to be able to call me now, let alone still be breathing.'

'It was a bit hairy. Yeah, I'm banged up a bit, but nothing's broken. At least, not significantly. I think.'

'You better take it a bit easier. Maybe time to leave the bikes alone for a bit. We're not getting any younger, at any rate.'

'Speak for yourself,' said Rick, laughing dryly. 'I'll catch you later.'

CHAPTER 12

Bright and early in the morning, Mike went straight down to the garage to pre-flight the Cadillac. Its water, oil levels, tyre pressures, and everything else obvious Mike could inspect, all appeared perfect. He dug out a torch and shone it underneath the car, looking for anything on the floor.

Not a drop, he thought. *Impressive.*

'Maybe this isn't such a bad deal, after all,' he said, feeling cheerier. He made himself comfortable, pressed the starter, and listened to the engine idle. He took a moment to message Rick, making sure he was still upright and breathing, and marvelled in the box-fresh feel of the Cadillac.

His phone suggested the route ahead was clear; it was about four hours to Vicenza, where he'd exit at Vicenza North for a meeting. He'd done a lot of business there, because the junction was right next to a motorway toll station.

Never understood why Italians like doing business by motorways, but there we are.

The Cadillac effortlessly burbled clear of the hotel, and out onto the motorway. After crossing the Italian border and wafting down towards Udine and Padova, Mike pulled over and dialled a few numbers, filling in a few blanks at work. There wasn't much to see, otherwise; the wide-open countryside of Friuli and the Veneto that was passing by was free from much of note and took a long time to traverse. He kept a cautious eye on the gauges, and paid particular note to the fuel gauge, topping up as and when.

Not going to trust it too much. Not after last time, in that Alfa. I don't want to block another intersection.

Mike knew most of the villages on the route well, having explored them for classic car finds, and he'd also spent much private time in the region. He subsequently knew there weren't many fuel stations, and baking in the sun was not something he had in mind.

A signpost for Vicenza passed by, its bright white background catching Mike's attention, his mind instantly changing tack and focusing on a stark, unyielding memory.

And there it is, he thought, shuddering. *There it is.*

He gripped the steering wheel, his knuckles slowly turning white, the Cadillac becoming jerky and restless in response, unable to follow its desired line.

Right in the centre. Near the Basilica Palladiana.

Mike closed his eyes for the moment, listening to the thrum of the road and the flathead, trying to tear his mind away from his memories. The road continued to march by, relentless, the remaining distance shrinking, the pressure rising inexorably in Mike's head and heart.

'Nope,' he said out loud, as he swerved the Cadillac into a layby. 'Not today. Not ever.'

He peeled his fingers from the wheel and dialled his client, the steady vibrations from the Cadillac's engine reaching up through his feet, helping to settle his heart a fraction.

'Mr Arnando,' he said, a quiver in his voice. 'I'm sorry to say that I can't make it to Vicenza today. My sincere apologies.'

'Mike, we've talked about this before,' said a relaxed, friendly voice. 'You shouldn't have tried in the first place.'

'I know, but there has to come a point, surely.'

'Grief like that, my friend, rarely passes. You just get used to living with it.'

Mike said nothing and stared at the floorboard of the Cadillac.

'Let me just send you an email instead,' said Arnando. 'We'll sort it out remotely.'

'Are you sure?'

'You'd offer the same, if I was in a similar spot. I know you would.'

'Appreciated.'

'You take it easy, friend. Don't beat yourself up.'

'I'll try,' said Mike, as he tipped his head up to stare into the Italian skies, the sun beating down on him.

It's the right thing to do, he thought, sensing a vast weight easing from his shoulders. *Maybe next time.*

The big Cadillac happily hummed away to itself as Mike rejoined the road, all eight cylinders firing cleanly. Near Verona, he realised the sun was burning his forehead, so he stopped again to put up the immense canvas roof but left the windows down. The natural warm airflow was calming, comforting, the Cadillac's chrome-framed quarterlights guiding fresh air into the interior, with no draughts.

'Much more like it,' he mumbled to himself. 'No poxy air conditioning needed.'

———————•———————

Mike cautiously leant against the Cadillac, a perilously stacked gelato in one hand, an espresso in the other. The small village he'd pulled into was exactly as hoped; beautiful stone-lined streets, ancient cafés and bars, dotted with rich green trees, immaculate borders, and a quiet, pleasant thrum of activity. If someone had snapped a picture of him in black and white at that moment, it would have resembled something from a charming yet classy fifties motoring advertisement, one designed to entice people to the region, to merrily explore in their cars.

His phone buzzed, breaking the momentary peace and forcing him to balance his espresso on the Cadillac's imposing bonnet.

Rick again. Now what?!

'Mike, I'm at the showroom with the owner of, well, what was a 250 GT SWB.'

'Okay,' said Mike calmly. 'How are things going?'

'Friendly enough so far, but we're definitely going to have to come up with some kind of resolution.'

'Any clues as to what happened, or when, yet?' said Mike hopefully.

'I'm sorry to say that I've come up with nothing yet. The owner wants his money back as soon as possible, understandably.'

Mike heard some movement, the sound of feet along a hallway, a door being closed.

'Look, Mike,' said Rick quietly, 'we're in a hot spot with this.'

'I know, Rick. We don't have the funds on hand to solve that problem right now, unless you've something tucked away that we can liquidate.'

'I wish that were the case.'

'Look, we've dealt with this guy for a while now. See if you can offer something to placate him; a car from the showroom on loan, or anything like that, as a distraction.'

'But what about the actual problem?'

'Tell him we're working on it, that we must establish what's happened first, so we can go about things the right way. It'll take some time, but we will make sure he is accounted for.'

'Alright,' said Rick begrudgingly. 'You'll have to wish me luck.'

'Good luck,' said Mike. 'I'm going to carry on hunting down some other cars, though, just in case. Got to keep the wheels turning, prop up the accounts if need be.'

Rick murmured in agreement. 'Oh, there was one other thing.'

Here we go, thought Mike, rolling his eyes.

'Simon gave this replica, clone, knock-off, whatever, a once-over, and found some Krone driven right down into the seat cushions.'

Denmark?

'They're marked 2022,' said Rick. 'Our original car, anyone we originally engaged, nothing or no one came anywhere near to Denmark.'

'Do we know anyone in that region involved with Ferraris in any way?'

'Not unless you count Harriston's wife, but then she's got as much interest in Ferraris as I have in Taylor Swift's music,' said Rick.

'She's Danish?'

'Yeah, they've got an old estate out there. Barely used these days, mind. Just another bit of property on an ever-expanding roster.'

'At least that gives us something to go on,' said Mike. 'Maybe someone's trying to get us to point the finger at them, so our deposit and the Austrian Collection goes up in smoke.'

'Could be, Mike, could be. There's enough riding on it, for sure.'

'Make some calls, will you?'

'I'll make some calls,' said Rick determinedly.

CHAPTER 13

Joseph's voice broke up as the Cadillac barrelled into a tunnel, his voice becoming over-processed and erratic.

'–ow's the Ca–'

'Sorry,' said Mike, touching his Bluetooth earpiece as the Cadillac blasted into fresh air. 'Sorry, can you hear me? What was that, Joseph?'

'Ah, there you are. How's the Cadillac? Treating you okay, I hope?'

'You'll be relieved, I'm sure, to hear it is. Great character, a proper soul. Poetry in motion, as they say.'

'No wonder,' said Joseph. 'That car is over 80 years old, and it's seen a lot of action.'

'And it's still quicker than most Italian trucks out here, on the way to Bergamo,' said Mike, smiling. 'But I have to ask: what's with those old metal French plates in the boot?'

'Ah,' said Joseph again, lingering on the *haitch* for a long time. 'Well, originally, it appears the car was delivered to San Francisco.'

'I saw the delivery note in the file, yes,' said Mike.

'My assumption is that it ended up in Normandy for military purposes, hence that grey finish. Maybe it saw the liberation of Paris, maybe even Berlin.'

'I did wonder. Navy, maybe, or Air Force?'

'I wouldn't know. I just enjoyed the car.'

'Makes sense, though,' said Mike thoughtfully. 'It wasn't just Jeeps, Dodges and Shermans that made their way into Europe. There were all those staff cars, through Omaha and Cherbourg.'

'Like the Cadillac, perhaps?'

'Yes, Series 62, Series 75 Sedans, even a few Convertible Sedans, like this one.'

'Remarkable. Yours was found near Salzburg,' said Joseph. 'I always wanted to try an early one but never had the opportunity, at least until I spotted this one.'

'I dread to ask, but did it set you back much?'

'Well, let's say it was up for a fair price. You know how it goes. I did have to put my 1957 Beetle into the deal.'

'Not that cheap, then,' said Mike, feeling a little relieved. 'And speaking of deals, what's the latest on our business side of things?'

'The documentation is almost all drawn up, and we're set to have it over to you soon,' said Joseph. 'As before, it'll just be the signatures and the deposit, after that, and the cars will be yours.'

'And the commission?'

'I have managed to coerce them down to six hundred thousand Euros.'

Mike watched the digits on the Cadillac's odometer spinning for a moment, then tapped the top of the dashboard thankfully, then swept his hand across it with a flourish.

'Great. We can work with that.'

'Thank you, Mike. Anyway, I will let you go. I understand you'll be in Bergamo tomorrow?'

'That's the plan, provided this Cadillac carries on ticking.'

'Go over to the notary's office and prepare all the contracts. He'll probably have a bill for you, too. You know how they are.'

'Great,' said Mike hesitantly.

More expenditure. This deal better pay off.

'I've sent you the layout for the remainder of the paperwork, including the facility agreement you wanted to draw up between yourselves and Harriston,' said Joseph. 'It should all be in order, and just clarifies that you've received £2 million, you'll deal with the cars, and he'll get his return. It's no different from what you've documented already, effectively, anyway.'

'Thanks. Still, best to cover the bases. Let's get this thing over the line.'

'Drinks on me, in Salo, when we're done.'

'I look forward to it,' said Mike. 'I truly do.'

———————— • ————————

Mike perched on the running board of the Cadillac, looking out over the rolling fields, and took a much-needed break from staring through a windscreen. He sipped on some sparkling water, listened to the birds and the distant roar of passing motorway traffic, and delved into his travel bag.

'A deal is all well and good, so you keep telling me,' Mike said to himself, 'but you always need a backup.'

He nodded, agreeing with the distant memory, and pulled out a slim leather-bound notebook. He opened it up on the bookmarked page, the itinerary for his trip, and started tracing an index finger down the planned dates, times, and places. Beneath each stopover was a short list of contacts, followed by cars.

Despite the optimism and progress made on the Austrian Collection, there had to be an alternative strategy in place in case it didn't make it over the line. Mike checked his location, and then worked through the details of the cars of interest, potential purchases, which were going to be along his route.

A Plan B, he thought. Let's give the Isotta a whirl.

He'd heard about the car a few years ago, while at the Concorso d'Eleganza Villa d'Este. Reputedly, the Isotta Fraschini, a 1931 Tipo 8B Landaulette-de-Ville Imperial by Castagna, had been the original Milan, London and New York motor show star. It was a storied car, with much history, and an ideal acquisition for a classic connoisseur.

Email after email had eventually led him to the owners, who had subsequently extended him an invite to view if he were ever in the area.

A bit of a long shot, but nothing ventured…

Mike texted the number they had sent him, expressing his interest and location, and slipped back into the driver's seat of the Cadillac, unwinding in the quiet. He felt the miles catching up with him again and allowed his eyes to close for a minute. A minute became ten, became twenty, thirty, the clouds ahead continuing to motor past.

His phone rang, waking him from his slumber.

'Parli Italiano?' said the voice.

'Un po,' said Mike, cautiously. 'But not enough for complex stuff.'

'Ah, no worries, no worries. My name is Sergio. You texted me about the car.'

'The Isotta, yes. Is it still available for viewing?'

'It is, as is the rest of the collection.'

'The rest?' said Mike, confused.

'I'm the one looking after the family's collection. It's time, it's all to be sold.'

Jackpot. Perhaps.

'I'm a few hours away. Is there any chance we could do anything today?'

'Yes. I'm here most days now, because I'm dealing with the other assets here. I will text you a location, you come there, and I will guide you onwards.'

'Grazie. Arrivederci!' said Mike happily.

I bet you it's a toll or service station. I bet you he wants to meet me alongside the motorway. Again.

It made good sense, of course; giving out the address of a collection potentially worth millions, to all and sundry who asked for it, was just begging for trouble. But, on many an occasion, the drive from the meeting point to the cars had often proven to be an hour, rather than ten minutes.

Mike drove on for a while until the toll station Sergio had directed him to loomed into view. He pulled over, parked up, and waited, the Cadillac burbling impatiently. No one was around, and nothing that caught his eye was parked up and waiting, just a few of the usual battered Puntos and Pandas.

His ears twitched as a familiar sound drifted down the road, its tone cutting cleanly through the humdrum noise of the cars and trucks passing by. The coarse, hollow bark of a naturally aspirated flat-six engine on song.

A 911. Has to be.

A white 1974 Porsche 911 Coupé with blue Carrera lettering on its flanks screamed up to the toll, screeched to a halt, the driver waving in Mike's direction. He sprinted over to the car, the window dropping as he approached.

'Mike?'

'Yes,' he shouted over the clatter of the engine. 'Sergio?'

'Si! Okay to follow me?'

'Yes,' said Mike, nodding enthusiastically. 'Might struggle to keep up, though,' he added, tipping his head in the direction of the Cadillac.

'Ah, you'll have no problem. Twenty minutes, no problem. Let's go!'

Mike gave him a thumbs-up, marched back to the Cadillac, and dropped it into first. It didn't come as a surprise to him when Sergio floored the Porsche, popped its clutch, and tore off up the road, leaving two narrow, slick lines of rubber on the floor. The Cadillac rose up, teetering on its tall bias-ply tyres, and heaved off in pursuit, with Mike sawing away at its big steering wheel.

An exhausting hour later, much of it spent avoiding huge potholes in the road, Mike felt completely lost, and only caught the occasional glimpse of the 911 spearing off in another direction. His GPS was unhelpful, showing a weak signal.

Bloody technology.

'Twenty minutes my ass,' he muttered, testing the Cadillac's strained brakes gingerly as another corner approached. 'I must be right out in the boondocks now.'

The Porsche appeared at a junction further down the road, with Sergio waving wildly from its window, and then took off again.

Mike heaved on the Cadillac's brakes, spun the steering wheel, and hauled the Cadillac into the junction, only to find the Porsche stopped square in front of him.

'Shit,' he yelped, as he swung off the road, over the grass, before swerving back onto the Tarmac, the Cadillac's tyres squealing in protest. The big car screeched to a halt, thudding softly as it settled on its suspension.

'Jesus, Sergio,' grumbled Mike. 'This doesn't have stopping power like that.'

Sergio grinned as he stepped out of the Porsche. 'Sorry,' he hollered. 'Forgot, pre-war, eh? Come, this way.'

He guided Mike through a dusty reception area and into a semi-derelict storage unit that was littered with containers and cars under cover, of all shapes and sizes. Some of them were evidently of a fine pedigree, others more conventional Lancias and Fiats. In one far corner, there was a small table with five people sitting around it. Sergio waved at them, and they waved back in response.

'They are the family, Mike. All staying here at the moment, sorting this out. Espresso?'

'Please,' said Mike. 'Do they speak any English?'

'They are more interested in just watching and listening today. They are, how you say, discreet. Simplicity and privacy, that's what they want.'

'I see,' said Mike quietly. 'So, what's the story here?'

Sergio gestured to the vast hall of cars. 'These have been handed down through generations, and the family is now not really sure what they have. I have kept the cars serviceable, and documented them as best I can, but they are interested in knowing more, seeing them run, and getting an authoritative opinion.'

'I see. Hence asking me.'

'There is also the matter of the collection's future. You had a good reputation, and the family may decide to engage your services to disperse it.'

Mike nodded. 'That's very kind of them. Please let them know I appreciate their interest and for letting me view the cars.'

Sergio waved the family over, and then waved Mike in the direction of the cars. 'Come, tell us what you know, and they will shadow us. I will translate for them.'

'May I?' said Mike, pointing at the sheet covering one car close to them, one with a profile that had caught his eye.

One of the family members nodded, and Sergio nodded as well.

Mike carefully pulled the sheet from the car, revealing a big 1931 Isotta Fraschini Tipo 8B. Its long, imposing bonnet and wide front wings swept away from him, towards a tall, square cabin, its upright windscreen topped by a light tan soft top, the paint a deep blue. Its vast grille was polished to a mirror finish, reflecting its surroundings with such clarity that it almost appeared invisible from the right angle.

It really is here. And it really is a B, not an A.

'I can assure you that not many people have ever seen one of these before,' said Mike, speaking loudly and clearly. 'Cars of this calibre rarely come out into the open, and the Tipo 8B is akin to a crown jewel, in terms of automotive heritage. It's as rare as a good Rembrandt portrait, a van Gogh landscape, or a Pieter Bruegel winter scene.'

The Tipo 8B was flanked by a totally original Tipo 8A Sedanca and an assortment of Alfas. One particularly fine 6C Alfa Romeo 1750, with a body by Gangloff, also caught his eye.

'I'm not exactly sure how many 8Bs are left, but certainly not more than two or three,' he added.

'There has been some research done and we agree,' said Sergio. 'It seems the luxury car company got caught out by the big Wall Street crash in 1929 and soon had to stop production of this hugely expensive model. Many orders were cancelled. It's still unknown how many Tipo 8Bs were built but, based on what we have seen, only two survive.'

'I'll let you know if that turns out to be otherwise,' said Mike. 'The only other one I might have seen was on the lawn at Pebble Beach, but none is as important as this one. This is the best Isotta I have ever seen. I understand it has some British history, too?'

'That's right,' said Sergio. 'This Tipo 8B was the star of the 1931 Salone dell'Automobile di Milano in April and was then shipped to New York for the Auto Show shortly afterwards. According to a testimony by Carlo Castagna, it was destined for press magnate William Hearst, already the owner of a Tipo 8A with body by Castagna. However, Castagna recalled that the deal was not completed, and that the car was sent back to Europe. A new, solvent client had to be found immediately. In England.'

'That must have been pretty bad news for Castagna,' said Mike, inspecting the 8B's tyres, the tops of which came almost up to his waist. Their vast sidewalls were intact, with no cracking or decay evident, and the polished wheel centres, each topped with large knock-off hubs, appeared almost as if new.

'Yes, with the help of the famous Isotta Fraschini importer Anthony Lago, the car apparently was a last-minute exhibit at the London Olympia Motor Show in 1931,' said Sergio. 'The car was very well received, and was bought by a trusted client of Anthony Lago, a Mrs Vera Twyford of Lowndes Square, London, and registered on 1 September 1931.'

'She was well known for her extravagant cars,' said Mike. 'I've seen her name against several interesting and desirable models.'

'From our research, it was the third Isotta Fraschini owned by the Twyfords, the previous ones having been bought in 1927 and 1929. They didn't use the car much, and it survived World War Two unscathed in one of their country houses.'

'I believe there is a link between the Twyford family and the American Twyford car company,' said Mike. 'But I'm not sure if that's correct.'

'I can only speak to research that's been done previously,' said Sergio. 'In 1956, the car was given to a noted British collector and they kept it until 1961, when the engine block became frost damaged. In 1985, after long negotiations, the car was purchased by my father, who found a brand-new engine, and returned the car to Italy.'

'Can I open the bonnet?' said Mike.

'Of course,' said Sergio, handing him a pair of thin gloves. 'Some work was done by Maitre Lecocq in Paris, my father knew him well. The original engine is still here right behind the car.'

Mike looked past the Isotta, to a large workbench beyond. Atop its thick wooden boards was a crated engine, standing several feet tall, a thin sheet draped over it.

'That's quite the sight,' said Mike, whistling. 'Looks like a work of art.'

Sergio opened the driver's door and waved a hand around its interior. 'The Isotta Fraschini Tipo 8B is very luxuriously appointed, as a unique Landaulette-de-Ville Imperial, and features very precious fabrics and trimmings, occasional seats in the rear, original scent and perfume bottles, cigar lighters, and a unique electric signalling system to the chauffeur.'

'I can see there are even blinds in the windows and courtesy lights to the running boards,' said Mike, appreciatively. 'The interior is palatial, much in the fashion of a good Rolls-Royce Phantom or a grand Bentley 8 Litre limousine, but a bit more luxurious I would say, and more refined, with Italian style and elegance.'

Sergio nodded. 'I think the same. It has full Grebel lighting all around. The best of the best.'

'The epitome of luxury in the days of the grand Hollywood stars and high society, eh?' said Mike. 'As much as I love Rolls-Royce Phantoms, or big Bentleys and grand Bugattis, they clearly came second to the Isotta Fraschini 8B. A Bugatti Royale is austere in comparison.'

He heard the family whispering among themselves in the background, their feet occasionally scuffing on the hard flooring as they hovered behind Mike and Sergio. He said something in rapid-fire Italian to them, and then turned back to Mike.

'Our Landaulette Imperial has also covered only a minuscule mileage. It's around, uh, 19,000 miles or so, and the car is in truly outstanding original condition. My father only used it occasionally.'

'It really is majestic,' said Mike.

'Intimidating might be a better word to describe it. There's a lot of history here, too. As kids we used to play Prince and Princess in the back. It's like a little palace of its own.'

'Do you think it would be okay to start it up?'

'Ah, yes,' said Sergio. 'I think… yes, you can view and start it if you please.'

The family were nodding. Mike lifted the bonnet, checked the fuel and water, and investigated the oil filler cap for any signs of moisture or off-white foam. All appeared good, a sense of solidity and readiness emanating from the ancient machine. He carefully removed the large cam cover and poured a litre of fresh engine oil over the top of the valve gear and the cylinder head. The engine being cold and more than a metre high, it would take at least two minutes for the oil to pump up to the valve gallery, causing excess wear and tear.

And I do not want to trash this, he thought, catching a glimpse of the watching family members out of the corner of his eye.

'This is how you used to do it,' he said to them, hoping they were finding the process interesting. 'You didn't call the AA, back then; you just got your toolbox out and started taking the engine apart, wherever you had broken down.'

He heard pleasant-sounding chatter behind him as Sergio passed him a booster pack. Ensuring the ignition was off, Mike cranked the engine over, bringing up the oil pressure. He smelt fuel, meaning the carburettor float chamber was full, and then lifted the main valve needle to make sure it was free; ignition to late, mixture to rich, he hit the starter. It turned over, lazily, coughed, then caught, settling into a deep, steady 500rpm idle, the oil pressure gauge pegging at its maximum.

'Runs like a champ,' said Mike, giving the spectating family a thumbs-up. 'Reminds me of a Phantom II or a six-cylinder Bentley, but deeper and more purposeful. Like a big Hispano. Pretty serious!'

'It's been a while,' said Sergio, watching the engine intently. 'But it is a thoroughbred.'

Mike nodded as he checked the radiator, making sure it was warming uniformly, ensuring good flow, and then pulled the radiator shutters open. He stuck his head underneath the car, just in case, checking for anything obvious amiss.

'Looks like it's ready to roll,' he said. 'Can we go for a ride?'

'If you can handle such a huge car, yes,' said Sergio. 'It's certainly not easy to drive.'

Everybody clambered into the Isotta, then Mike slowly pulled the burbling beast out of the factory building, onto the roads around the complex.

'It does feel heavy,' said Mike, over the noise of the engine. 'But it's a controllable weight, and I like it. And look at these beautiful art-deco instruments. It's lovely.'

Despite being cold, the gearbox was willing and ready to serve up the next gear, and the engine happily propelled the majestic machine down the road.

'I always thought the steering remarkable,' said Sergio. 'When I drove it a long time ago, it was amazing how light it was once moving.'

'Agreed,' said Mike. 'This must be a three-ton car. And how well it accelerates!'

'I always struggled a bit with the clutch, though.'

'I can see why; it's weighty, and just feels like you're standing on a wooden block!'

They completed a few loops, letting the Isotta warm thoroughly, and loped back to the unit, Sergio keeping a cautious eye on the gauges.

'I could keep driving this around forever,' said Mike cheerily.

'Well, until we run out of fuel,' said Sergio. 'We don't know how much is in it. We best shut it down.'

'Agreed. And, from the smell, I'd say it's at least five or so years old. Some fresh high-octane will make a world of difference.'

Mike listened to the engine idling for a moment; a well-orchestrated concerto of valves and helical gears emanated from beneath its covers, and the lack of smoke or leaks further indicated that it was in fine tune. He cut the ignition and the engine stopped immediately, with no running-on or coughing.

'I'm glad we gave it a bit of fresh air,' said Sergio. 'I think they appreciated it.'

Mike turned around, to find the family all smiling.

'Grazie, tantissimo,' he said to them. 'It is a privilege to experience this, and I now understand what that marvellous Isotta Fraschini Tipo 8B legend was all about.'

Sergio tapped him on the shoulder. 'Is there anything else we should know about this car?'

'I know that the Tipo 8B included a great many improvements over the Tipo 8A,' said Mike. It had an all-new 7,300cc straight-eight engine, with 5:1 compression. A new nickel-steel block, pistons and rods from the same. The valve gear was very light, which is one of the reasons it revs so readily. And it had two separate exhaust manifolds, like a race car, for improved extraction. A unique engine, really.'

'That's useful,' said Sergio. 'I wasn't sure if it was that different from the earlier one.'

'There were lots of upgrades that made it more tractable, more enjoyable, more durable. It'll rev easily to about three thousand, thanks to a stiffer crank and nine main bearings, and a Bosch coil-based ignition system that replaces the magneto. It got a four-speed synchromesh gearbox with helical gears, too.'

'Ah,' said Sergio, knowingly. 'That'll be why the other Isotta is so much louder.'

'Yes. The chassis was stronger and stiffer, too, with deeper side members and two extra crossmembers. Its power output was about 150hp, so the same as a Tipo 8SS, which was enough to get it to almost 100mph, if you were bold enough. Like an 8 Litre Bentley, basically.'

'A shame they didn't build more of them,' said Sergio.

'Well, the economics of the time led to all of that coming to a close,' said Mike sadly. 'This was the swansong of Isotta Fraschini. The Wall Street crash, and new competitors such as the V12 Hispano-Suiza, and Rolls-Royce Phantom II and III, all conspired to bring down Isotta.'

'Italy would have done well to save that car company,' said Sergio, a hint of frustration in his voice.

'Did you know it was in part because Mussolini hated Isotta? He preferred Alfas. Isotta Fraschini production was already winding down in 1933, and the last chassis rolled off the line in 1935. Very few Tipo 8Bs were made at all.'

'A luxury in a time where such things were not as desired or viable,' said Sergio.

'Quite. After 1935, the company only made maritime engines and commercial diesel, first for the Italo-Ethiopian War and then for World War Two. Some of the unsold chassis became ambulances. I'd love to find one, one day.'

Mike gently patted the Tipo's wing and shook Sergio's hand. 'Thank you again. This is a real automotive treasure, a rolling display of art, passion and genius. I love it.'

'Don't go getting any ideas,' said Sergio, grinning. 'I guess you've already clocked that it's still registered in the UK.'

'We'd love to have it back, that's for sure. Maybe I'll have to speak to the Prime Minister.'

'You may be under the impression that the family doesn't want to sell it, and that may be the case,' added Sergio, his voice a little quieter. 'But we would be interested in options, and what it may be valued at. If anything, for insurance purposes.'

'Entirely understandable. And the other cars here?'

'I will ask them. It may be that the entire collection goes as a package. Would that be of interest?'

'I'm sure we could put something together,' said Mike, rubbing his hands together. 'Yes, I'm sure we could put something together.'

CHAPTER 14

As Mike nudged the Cadillac onto the motorway, heading towards Milan, rain started to fall. Just a gentle smattering, at first, which slowly turned into a shower. Mike eased off the Cadillac's throttle a fraction, settling into a more relaxed cruise, then found a jazz station broadcasting on a frequency the car's ancient valve radio could still receive. Memories of Paris, and a past girlfriend, flashed through his mind as the tuneful music trickled from the Cadillac's speaker. They had only three albums in their apartment near the Etoile, but they defined jazz for him: John Coltrane's *A Love Supreme*, the Bill Evans Trio's *Explorations*, and Miles Davis's *Kind of Blue*. That was Paris to him. And the perfect soundtrack for driving in Italy.

The shower became a storm, as the Cadillac rolled along, the drops getting bigger and heavier as every metre passed. Mike flipped the Cadillac's lights on, and its wipers, the rain starting to sheet off its flat glass, and then instinctively turned its radio down. A crack of thunder boomed through its cabin, and the sky darkened further. Mike caught a glimpse of something white, something that wasn't rain, hammering towards him.

Hailstones!

The hard ice drummed across the bonnet of the Cadillac and beat like a drum on its canvas roof. The modern cars around him swerved a little, their thin panels and plastic trims being dented and cracked by the hailstones. Windscreens and sunroofs started to splinter, and roof panels were pounded inwards, as the stone-like ice rocks pounded downwards.

But the Cadillac just shrugged. Its American steel was too thick, too resilient, to get dented by the storm. The ice merely slammed into its panels and was pulverised, and the wind couldn't shift it from its course. A grin spread across Mike's face as the Cadillac pushed onwards, unstoppable, as a sign for Bergamo flashed by.

As the weather eased off, and the miles and minutes continued to tick by, Mike's eye caught the needle of the fuel gauge start to waver, its point dipping unnervingly low as the Cadillac rose and fell over bumps. He swung into the next services, braked to a halt, and waited for the big car to stop swaying gently on its soft springs. The fuel pump at the service station clicked noisily as he refilled the Cadillac, the pump's relentless ticking becoming audible over the sound of the receding storm. Mike watched the digits on the pump roll ever upwards, the Cadillac vacuuming up some 75 litres of fuel with ease.

About ten litres left, he thought. So, the gauge isn't far off.

He ambled into the service station, grabbed a black coffee and a sandwich, and shunted the Cadillac into a parking bay. He sat, one leg out of the open driver's door, and flicked through his phone. Julie had been messaging him; he scrolled through her texts and pictures, every word and image helping him shed some of the cold of the hailstorm, and he sent a few messages in response.

We should catch up again soon! came the quick reply. He swooned a little at the mere mention of the opportunity and chided himself.

'You're a grown man,' he muttered. 'You can have a conversation with her without falling apart.'

I don't know about that. I think she's more than a match for me. But then there's what's been.

'Maybe in London. Maybe we can just catch up then, something casual, see how it goes.'

He straightened up and reached for the Cadillac's keys. He twirled the keys around his index finger for a moment, then his phone flashed again.

Maybe it's her!

Mike grabbed the phone and stabbed its buttons: it wasn't Julie, it was Rick. His heart fell.

'Hello, Rick,' said Mike ponderously.

'Mike, Harriston's starting to piss me off,' said Rick, his voice dripping with discontent.

'That took longer than I expected,' said Mike sarcastically.

'No, seriously. His legal team's giving me the run-around on the facility agreement, and he's even trying to muscle in on some of the discussions around the storage and sale of the collection. He's a spanner in my works and making progressing with the collection a royal pain in the ass.'

'It'll happen, one way or another,' said Mike reassuringly. 'He's just trying to put a foot on our necks. You know how he is.'

'He'll have a foot somewhere unpleasant, if he's not careful,' said Rick gruffly. 'I don't like having my hands tied. He needs to remember he has partners.'

'Harriston knows who and what's involved, and what's at stake, I have no doubt. We'll just have to wait until we're in front of him, with the notary, to sort that all out.'

Rick mumbled something unpleasant, but reluctantly agreed.

'Look, I'll drop him a line, see if I can settle the water.'

'Don't say anything I might say,' muttered Rick. 'But it's not all bad news today, admittedly,' he added, the dissatisfaction sloughing from his voice as he continued. 'On the upside, Ratlick's paid up.'

'Really?!' said Mike quizzically.

'Yup. Nine hundred grand, released today. It doesn't make me happy that we're fifty down, but it's better than being down nine hundred and fifty.'

'A fifty grand loss. That's not easy to swallow, but you're right.'

'You win some, you lose some,' said Rick. 'Look at it this way: it was a small price to pay to see him cornered, like a deer in the headlights. And his true colours have shone through. A liar, and a coward to boot, and now everyone knows it.'

'That's true,' said Mike. He smiled, the look of confusion and terror on Ratlick's face in the airport popping into his mind. 'Still, I can't imagine he's learned his lesson.'

'Crooks like that never do. He'll be back at it, somewhere else, before long.'

'Another shark, back in the water.'

'Exactly,' said Rick. 'Fortunately, we're getting pretty good at hunting them.'

———————— • ————————

Despite the Cadillac's refined and relaxing ride, Mike felt a rising sense of restlessness. Rick's complications with Harriston had cast a shadow over his imminent meeting, making him doubt the solidity of the Austrian Collection sale.

But we'll be okay, one way or another, he thought, calming himself. *There's always a solution.*

'And, hell, maybe everything will just be alright,' he said to the Cadillac's cabin. 'Harriston's probably achieving exactly what he wants, which is to put us on edge.'

His headset beeped, announcing another incoming call. Mike slowed the Cadillac to a sedate 55mph, glanced around quickly, and pressed the answer button.

'Mike, it's Steven,' said a bright English voice. 'How are you doing?'

'Not too bad, thanks. I'm in Italy now, viewing some more cars. How's business?'

'Plenty of interesting cars delivered here recently. Feel like I'm clogging up Nottingham with them!'

'And now you've just got to get rid of them,' said Mike, laughing.

'Yeah, well, I bet you're having just another boring day in the office as well, with prosecco and spaghetti al mare every few hours.'

'Something like that,' retorted Mike. 'It's been raining bloody cats and dogs, though. Typical. Anyway, what can I do for you?'

'Listen, I want to buy a 1962 E-type Series 1 Coupé. Got to be a '62, got to be totally original and reliable. Preferably unrestored. Know of any?'

'That's a tall order, a very tall order,' said Mike. 'Really good, original, 3.8-litre E-types are hard to find. Most are left-hand drive, from the US, or have been butchered and badly restored somewhere in Eastern Europe. Those cars always drive like wooden blocks.'

'Yeah, that's what I've found so far, which is why I've come to you. These cars are on the same level as a Ferrari 250 GT, as far as I'm concerned, and I'm willing to pay for it.'

'Don't tell that to the Italians,' said Mike, subconsciously checking the Cadillac's mirrors for any sign of the Carabinieri. 'But you're right. But you do need one with the long rear axle and a good setup to do so.'

'And that takes bloody ages,' said Steven. 'And most owners and restorers never get it done, and even those that do it rarely understand it or get it right.'

'Agreed. Everything needs to be in harmony, properly synchronised. And then the car just flows.'

'I'm sure you're just as sick of the botched ones as I am.'

'They're all too common now,' said Mike, sadly. 'I did once have a good, original, low-miler E-type Coupé, though.'

'Is it still around?'

Mike laughed. 'I admire your optimism, Steven. It's been 35 years, at least. It was metallic blue, a '62, from Sicily. I bought it and kept it for five years.'

'I like the sound of a metallic blue one.'

'It had original grey leather, too. A beautiful combination. Unusual bonnet side louvres and plexiglass windows, too. Bit of an odd combo. No radio, heater, or ashtray, either.'

'And you bought it for next to nothing, right?'

'Ah, well, you know E-types, or even Astons, had no value back then. I didn't have the money for it, though, I had to borrow for it, and then transported it out of Italy on a battered Fiat Ducato flatbed. Not the most stress-free of trips.'

'Restoration?'

'Barely. Just a few days of fiddling and fettling, and it was soon up and running. That car gave me years of pleasure.'

'Why did you part with it, then?' said Steven, quizzically.

'It drove beautifully, and I loved it, and it provided a good in, as I was working in the film business at the time. But, well, one day, someone rang my doorbell…'

'And offered you a price you couldn't resist?'

'She said she wanted to buy it as a birthday present for her husband. The cash she was waving at me made it hard to say no.'

'Damn. Well, if I find a blue '62 Coupé with grey leather and those few other bits you mentioned, chances are it's the same car. Think the club might know of its whereabouts?'

'You could check with them,' said Mike.

'That's exactly what I'm going to do now,' said Steven, sounding satisfied. 'Lunch on me, next time.'

'You keep telling me that,' said Mike, grinning.

'If I find it, you'll be the first to know. Safe travels, mate.'

———————— ● ————————

Mike felt sluggish as he checked in at the Hotel Excelsior San Marco in the lower part of Bergamo, the Città Bassa. He'd used the hotel for at least fifteen years, and his usual room on the fourth floor had a great view of the Città Alta. It was an ancient and striking old city, situated in the hills, and a grand sight.

An early night for me, he thought, as he worked his way up to the room. *Busy day tomorrow*.

The room was in order and as expected, so he checked through his itinerary while downing an ice-cold beer. The next day,

Mike would meet with his collector friend Signore Argento, at his golf club for lunch, in the Bergamo hills. Ten minutes, by car, no more. He showered, felt a little steadier and settled about the situation, and went to bed.

After a good night's sleep, and a cold shower, he welcomed the new day. Having missed breakfast, Mike ambled out of the hotel to the café next door and ordered a cappuccino and a cornetto with marmalade. They didn't have one, but gave him a plain croissant instead, which he deemed close enough. The Cadillac was parked in front of the hotel, secured and cordoned off, the centre of attention. Mike smiled at it warmly, and hoped it was enjoying its time in the limelight.

I'll probably take a taxi today, though, he thought. *Steep and narrow in the hills. I don't want to get jammed in.*

Mike picked up the newspaper lying on the table next to his and glanced at the headline. A German wind energy pioneer had been murdered, near his home in Peschiera del Garda.

Mathias Fechtel was shot in broad daylight with a rifle, in traffic on the lakeside promenade not far from his house. He was pronounced dead at the scene.

Furrows appeared in Mike's forehead.

Reports say his attackers came on a motorbike and used a Kalashnikov rifle, which was later found in the lake. At least seven rounds were fired into Mr Fechtel's car. Fechtel…

'Jesus,' said Mike out loud. 'I knew that guy.'

'You did?' said an inquisitive voice from behind him. 'Sorry to read the news.'

Mike turned in the direction of the voice; a burly American had sat down behind him, and a woman promptly joined him.

'Ah, not needed. He had some nice cars and I'd dealt with him a few times, that's all, but it's a shame nonetheless.'

'You have to wonder what it's all about, don't you?' said the American, putting his own copy of the paper down on the table.

'Yeah, that's true. I only got introduced to him by chance, by a gentleman I knew called Bentmann, a few years back. He was working on an offshore wind farm project with him, something out in the North Sea.'

The man offered his hand, and Mike shook it. 'Phil,' he said, his voice deep and pleasant. 'My wife,' he added, nodding, 'Jeanie.'

'Politics, probably,' she said chirpily.

'What?' said Mike and John simultaneously.

'You know, politics, criminals, money,' said Jeanie. 'Clean energy, right? I bet plenty of people would want to axe that.'

Mike smirked. 'You have a point. I don't remember him being that involved, though. I thought he was an engineer, just doing regular advising and management. Not exactly the kind of guy you'd hit.'

'Well, to my mind, a lot of those clean energy companies are rotten. Taking funds left, right and centre from who knows, from radical and bought-out politicians alike, and then they just disappear, pop, and no one questions them.'

Mike nodded, a glum look washing over his face. 'It does feel like fraud involving government funds is high on the roster these days. And then come the syndicates, putting a gun to your head if you so much as suggest another course of action.'

'I've been around Europe a bit,' said Phil casually. 'There are plenty of sophisticated gangs around, knocking off anyone who's threatening to tighten up their laws, or clamp down on fraud.'

Jeanie winked at Mike and made a finger gun, firing it a few times wildly into the street.

'It's the same in the US now,' he added. 'Cartels, criminals, politically involved and protected. Just rotten.'

Jeanie nodded her head in agreement. 'And then you've the Chinese government,' she said loudly, making Mike wince a little. 'Billions spent on lobbying, controlling everything, buying out and capitalising anything that's on the up. Renewables, electric cars, you name it!'

Phil grunted, seemingly in agreement, and Mike nodded slowly. 'There does seem to be some link between Europe's increasingly convoluted and strict energy laws and the surge in alternative - and renewable-derived kit arriving from China. Cars, power generation, heat pumps, the works.'

'And a lot of it is just churned out, and thrown away at short notice,' said Jeanie. 'It's depressing. All that waste, all that equipment, all those cars that get built, used, and dispatched in no time at all.'

'And if the market does get flooded with cheap Chinese electric vehicles, none of the long-standing brands will be able to compete,' said Mike warily. 'And then, poof, just like that, all those brands, that history, will up and vanish.'

'And how many see that threat?' said Jeanie. 'It'll happen, before you know it, mark my words.'

'Well, my Mustang's not going anywhere,' said Phil proudly. 'Fifty-two years old and still going strong. How's that for cradle-to-grave emissions?'

Mike tipped his head appreciatively at him. 'Fair comment,' he said. 'A classic that lasts fifty years or a new car that is binned after five. Which is better? I think I know which I would vote for.'

'And just wait until the legislators in this place start really hating on individual property,' said Phil. 'They'll get hold of the banking system and, voila, your money will be gone. You guys are too naïve, you know?'

'Well, I get the feeling it's not much better in the US these days,' said Mike warmly.

'Truth,' said Phil and Jeanie at the same time.

Mike finished his cappuccino and bid them farewell. He flagged down a taxi and, as it cruised up the hills towards the golf club, he idly wondered about his own future. The increasing amount of legislation, political nonsense, endless noise about emissions, green targets, seemingly unreachable goals and illogical thinking, was making the future look dim, in his eyes.

And one day it'll finally trash the economy, and millions will be out of work, he thought, making a fist with one hand. *And then European liberty, equality and fraternity will be in the toilet. Just like that.*

'And anyone looking to be trueful, or honest, will be up against the wall in no time. Maybe that's what happened to Fechtel,' said Mike, gritting his teeth. 'Dead, just like that.'

The taxi driver glanced up at him in his mirror, then cocked his head. 'Are you alright, sir?'

'I'm not sure,' said Mike, a hint of uncertainty in his voice.

CHAPTER 15

Mike brushed himself off as he stepped out of the taxi and admired the intricate marble pillars at the entrance to the golf club. A concierge stepped out from the foyer and directed him inside, towards the restaurant. Signore Carlo Argento was sitting at the back of the restaurant, watching people come and go, waiting for him.

'Ciao Michael. Here you are. How was your journey?' he said, as he poured some wine into the glasses on the table. He then stood up, kissed Mike on both cheeks, and patted him heartily on the shoulders.

'I'm not bad, Carlo, not bad. It's been a fair trip, though; I came by car from Austria.'

'A cabriolet, judging by the sunburn,' he said, laughing.

'Correct. A 1940s Cadillac.'

'A nice car, I'm sure,' he said, seemingly uninterested. 'No Ferrari, though, or even a Jaguar.'

'That much is true. But it's a pleasant way to travel.'

'Anyway, Michael, two things' he said, voice getting quieter by the word. 'Firstly, I have found a lot of incredible paperwork, original. Would you like to see it?'

His foot tapped an ancient black suitcase that was tucked under the edge of the table. He watched Mike's face carefully, rejoicing as he saw a smile spread.

'You know I like original documentation,' said Mike, unconsciously reaching for the briefcase. 'May I?'

He nodded, pushing the case towards Mike with his foot. 'You know these people, and how to handle them,' he said cooly. 'It's all for sale.'

'What have we got in here, then?'

'On the top, those are original papers for a 1961 Aston Martin DB4 GT lightweight Zagato,' said Carlo. 'They got left behind when the car was sold and shipped to the United States.'

'Amazing,' said Mike, handling the delicate documents carefully.

'The next binder is a complete set of Italian papers, including the original number plate, for the ex-Luigi Castelbarco Maserati 6CM Monoposto, chassis number 1535. You wouldn't think that number plates existed for a Monoposto racer, but they did, as you'd often see them displayed during street races and hill-climbs in Italy.'

'I think that car still exists. That's worth some coin, to the right person.'

'Then there are absolute curiosities like a genuine full Chinese registration set for a 1961 Alfa Romeo Giulietta SZ,' said Carlo. 'The car was first registered in China but later an Italian owner used them in the 1970s to avoid parking tickets. A clever guy.'

'Not a bad idea, that,' said Mike, grinning.

Carlo nodded. 'The black folder, at the bottom, that's the top-shelf item. It's the original foglio complementare and correspondence for an Alfa Romeo T33 Stradale with Varese number plate, VA 242413. It's the only Stradale delivered in Royal Blue paintwork and its lucky first owner was Count Corrado Agusta of MV Agusta motorcycles and Agusta helicopters. He sold the car shortly after fitting it out with custom-made helicopter seats.'

Mike whistled quietly. 'That car's in Switzerland,' he said. 'It reappeared after what must have been an extensive restoration. The new owner would be very keen to have this.'

'I'm not in a rush to sell. You make me an offer, when you're ready. I have the time.'

Mike nodded appreciatively, then paused for a moment to take a drink from his glass. The white wine was crisp, with a warm, clean aftertaste.

'These are significant documents and have a lot of historical value, even the ones for lost cars,' said Mike earnestly. 'The older handwritten logbooks, the French carte grise or Italian foglio complementare, those are really something. We're picking up as many as we can these days, and I'd love to have these.'

Carlo smiled. 'You just let me know when. Consider them yours, in the meantime.'

'What's the other thing?' said Mike, as he carefully put the paperwork back in its folders and slipped them into the case.

'Ah,' said Carlo, winking. 'I've another collection that might be of interest to you.'

'Paperwork?'

'Cars,' said Carlo, leaning forwards. 'A very special collection.'

Mike cocked his head and tried to not look that interested.

'Known or unknown?' he said, still inspecting the paperwork.

'That's the thing,' said Carlo, even quieter than before. 'It's secret. They're all walled up in the first floor of a 19th-century villa.'

'You're kidding me,' said Mike loudly.

Carlo raised an eyebrow, tipped his wine glass to the side, and shrugged.

'It's about two hours away, near Bellagio,' said Carlo. 'You want to see it today?'

'Certo. If that's possible, yes, I'd love to. The usual finder's fee?'

'A bit more, for this,' said Carlo. Mike held up a few fingers in response and Carlo nodded, seemingly satisfied. 'It's worth it, trust me.'

'Great,' said Mike, chin bobbing up and down. 'I've a few other things to finish but, after this, I'll aim to come back here in autumn, and catch up with you some more.'

'Certo. Shall we go now? My car is outside, if you have a jacket.'

'I don't,' said Mike, pointing at the sun outside. 'Didn't plan on bad weather.'

'You'll need one. Get the concierge to give you one. It's good now, but it's going to rain later, for sure.'

'Another convertible?'

'Something a bit more serious,' said Carlo, smiling broadly. 'My Blower Bentley.'

Mike followed the direction Carlo was pointing in, to a gravelled parking area just beyond the restaurant, his gaze falling upon a beautiful 1929 Bentley parked under a tree. It was heavily patinated, proudly wearing its original paint, trim, the works. He followed Carlo out to the car and admired its interior while he clambered aboard, the concierge handing him a black down jacket as he settled into his seat.

'Simple and authentic,' he said to himself.

'That's right,' said Carlo, as he dressed himself for the occasion. 'It's a 1929 Bentley 4½ Litre Blower, a most famous race car of the Bentley Boys era. I bought it for £100,000, some 35 years ago, which was a lot for a Blower back then. Today, it's worth five million or so. But I don't care about that.'

'These things were never meant to be objects of visual appeal,' said Mike. 'Just functional, efficient, pragmatic. But now, well, they're just art.'

Carlo nodded as he slipped into a large jacket, put on a pilot's helmet, cast his view up at the darkening skies overhead, and beckoned Mike out of the car.

'I've been driving fast all my life, Mike. Today, it's your turn.'

'Are you sure?' said Mike, taken aback. 'I haven't driven a Blower for years.'

'You'll be fine,' said Carlo confidently, pushing Mike in the direction of the driver's seat. 'Let's get going. We drive via Lecco. The cars are close to Como in an old villa. I want to beat the traffic.'

Mike nodded as he made himself comfortable. He knew from experience that driving a genuine Blower in normal traffic over a large distance is all about taking a deep breath, syncing up your movements to the mechanical precision that the car demands, and hoping not to make a fool of yourself. Just doing it brings reward, but doing it well takes the experience to another level. And doing it through narrow streets, overtaking trucks, and tackling roundabouts, is another ball game altogether.

And this car's one hell of a responsibility, thought Mike, as Carlo checked everything over. *And it looks like it's on its original engine and supercharger.*

'Could we perhaps take the motorway towards Milan, then head up to Como, and drive back via Lecco later? We'll still avoid the traffic, using the A51 and A4,' said Mike.

'As you wish,' said Carlo. 'The rain's coming, so let's go!'

Mike cranked the engine and felt the Blower vibrate every bone in his body. It was going to be at least a two-hour drive, in what looked like to be appalling weather. He'd driven Bentleys in the wet, but never in rain as hard as the ever-darkening clouds suggested.

They motored out onto the A51, the Bentley unfazed at an 85mph cruise, as the rain started to fall. It got heavier and heavier, until water was flowing out over the instruments, down their faces, and filling the pockets of their coat.

If this continues, I'll drown, thought Mike, turning his head to check on Carlo. He was just grinning. *It's either steamy and hot here, or raining cats and dogs!*

The rain was stinging his face and the weight of the controls was testing his muscles, but he knew Bentley Boys were supposed to be made of sterner stuff. Carlo still seemed untroubled, looking happy and evidently enjoying the ride, so he clenched his fingers, gritted his teeth, and pushed on.

'Are you okay, Mike?' he heard Carlo shout. 'I'm only eighty-three years old, but I can take this easily. Don't slow down on my behalf!'

Grin and bear it!

The quivering hands of the wet and foggy dials were almost unreadable beneath the stream of water, but Mike could make out that the compressor pressure gauge was showing a little over one pound per square inch, which seemed acceptable. The water temperature, however, had dropped to a very low sixty-five degrees centigrade, which was bad news with a Blower Bentley.

Too cool, too wet, too lean, he thought. Might write off a piston or two.

'It's too easy to one run one of these lean, in cold rain,' shouted Mike. 'I'm going to richen it up a bit!'

Carlo nodded at him, watching as Mike eased off, slowing to 60mph and adjusting the mixture. The engine's tone deepened, relaxed, and Mike nodded happily.

Trucks in front of them were kicking up a huge amount of spray, and Mike carefully nudged the Bentley over the centreline, looking at the road ahead. A fountain of water poured into the cockpit, drenching their trousers and shoes. He could barely see through the Brooklands screen but, for a moment, he glimpsed what he needed: a clear, straight stretch. He squeezed the centre throttle pedal and the Bentley surged ahead, its speedometer needle flicking past ninety, water pouring off every one of its surfaces and its occupants.

The instruments danced wildly as Mike lifted off, pulling in ahead of the slow-moving trucks, and he allowed the two oil feeders for the compressor bearings a few more drops per minute.

Just two half turns, he thought, as he scanned the instruments. *Jesus, this thing's deafening.*

After forty minutes Mike's brain said *Enough!* but he had no time to listen to it as the huge Milan pay station appeared ahead. He slowed the heavy Bentley to a crawl but managing and driving it was still back-breaking work, and the effort of mingling with the smaller cars and jostling for position at the toll gates was tiring him out.

Mike dug through his pockets for change, his fingers numb from the cold. 'What the hell are we paying for again?' he said to Carlo, as he tossed a Euro and fifty cents into the machine.

As the Bentley rolled through the gate, Mike pulled on the outside handbrake, clearing some of the water from the Bentley's drums, and then carefully accelerated away, trying not to push the limits of the Blower's adhesion in the rain. He glanced down at the gauges and realised the water temperature had climbed up to a healthier 85 degrees.

'Perfect,' he shouted, pointing at the gauge. 'It's fine!'

Carlo nodded appreciatively, then pointed Mike north. The Bentley smashed through the rain, thundering towards Como, passing Seregno and Giussano, the urban backgrounds slowly giving way to less densely packed and greener surroundings. Carlo tapped Mike on the shoulder, guiding him off the main route into a province called Lurago d'Erba, and a highway that led through to Como. Turn after turn followed, the lake roads shrinking around the Bentley as they got further and further off the beaten track, until they eventually arrived in front of the villa Carlo had mentioned.

Finally, thought Mike, as he pulled into the villa's drive. *I'm saturated.*

Carlo smirked at him as Mike clambered ungracefully out of the Bentley.

'Well?' he said, shaking water out of his coat.

'That,' said Mike, clearing his throat, 'was quite the drive.'

'A thrill, isn't it, even in the pouring rain.'

'To drive that for so long, in these conditions, is something else. But you're right, thrilling.'

I won't be forgetting this quickly. Or the wet. Or the cold.

Mike looked at the villa. Paint was flaking off its walls, followed by decaying brick and concrete in places, and the remaining ochre paint was heavily stained and faded. He wondered, for a moment, if the whole thing was a hoax, having heard countless similar tales over the years, but Carlo wasn't one for wasting his time. The path beyond the drive was heavily overgrown, thick brambles and vines preventing them from easily approaching, and Mike could see large, rusted padlocks on anything that might otherwise be opened.

'One moment, Mike,' said Carlo, pulling out his phone. He stepped to the side and chatted with someone on the other end of the line.

'It's the owner, Mike. He says he'll be another twenty minutes.'

'I'm not rushing. So, what do you think we might be able to see today?

'It's an Aston Martin DB3, I think the first prototype, among many other things,' said Carlo, quietly. 'Una machina molto, molto importante!'

I'd heard rumours, thought Mike, unconsciously crossing his fingers. *Eric Forrest-Greene supposedly squirred a few cars like that away.*

'It was among some brought in by a post-war importer,' said Carlo, his hand roughly tracing the outline of the villa in front of him. 'A dealer in Argentina, he liked the British cars.'

'Greene?' said Mike tentatively.

'Ah, si, Forrest-Greene, I think.'

He had DB3s, that much I know.

Twenty minutes passed. They waited patiently in their wet clothes, sitting quietly in the old Bentley war horse. Another twenty minutes passed, the rain subsiding, and then another five.

'The true Italian experience,' said Mike quietly.

'Eh, it's normal,' said Carlo, shrugging. 'But at least it's not raining now.'

'Do you know much about the first DB3, chassis DB3/1?' said Mike, wishing he had something hot to drink.

'Astons aren't really my thing,' said Carlo. 'Interesting?'

'Well,' said Mike, 'in late 1950, Professor Eberan von Eberhorst, of pre-war Auto Union fame, joined Aston Martin and was tasked with designing a new sports-racing car to replace the old DB2 in international race events. The outcome was the new DB3, which had its first outing in the Tourist Trophy in September 1951. Of the ten cars built, five were to be sold to private teams, and the other five were known as the works team cars.'

The sun split the clouds ahead, the warmth pouring down on the two.

'The first DB3, chassis number 1, was manufactured in 1951, but was not fully finished due to a large-scale strike at Aston's old factory in Feltham, Middlesex,' added Mike. 'An old test driver from Aston told me all about that.'

Carlo laughed. 'British workers on strike? You don't say.'

Mike grinned as the world brightened.

'It all was a real hush-hush affair. For its first race, the car was quietly removed from the factory during the night. Untested, the bare-metal prototype was taken to Ireland where it was entered into the Tourist Trophy at Dundrod. Before the race, the car was quickly painted by brush and some limited testing was carried out, the paint still wet. In the race, driver Lance Macklin was going well in second place behind Stirling Moss in a C-type before a broken exhaust forced him to retire at around the two-hour mark.'

'Impressive,' said Carlo. 'He sounds a bit like me,' he said, playfully elbowing Mike in the ribs.

'That car ended up being a factory prototype and was used for testing between races,' said Mike, thoughtfully. 'In a bid to improve top speed, a hard top was fitted for the race at Le Mans in 1952.'

'Did it end up being a Le Mans car?'

'And then some,' said Mike. 'The car went on to be driven at Silverstone, Goodwood, Isle of Man and Le Mans. It was used as the Mille Miglia practice car, and for testing with an experimental supercharged engine. In 1953, the car was loaned to Dennis Poore, who drove it to victory at Thruxton. Immediately following that race, the car was sold to Eric Forrest-Greene, who was sadly killed in a heavy crash while competing in the 1954 Buenos Aires 1,000km race in Argentina. After that, the car was kept in the family before being sold to Europe.'

'But to where?'

'Exactly,' said Mike, who then pointed at the villa.

'Do you think it could be?'

'We'll soon know, I think,' said Mike, expectantly.

Mike and Carlo heard footsteps on gravel and turned to face the drive. A gentleman, neatly dressed and in his sixties, was approaching them, a small bag across his shoulder.

'Carlo,' he said, happily. 'And this must be Michael?'

'Indeed,' said Mike, shaking his hand.

'I suspect you're probably more interested in the cars than I,' he said. 'But I'm Edoardo. I'll show you in.'

Edoardo motioned them in the direction of the old 19th-century villa. In the courtyard, rife with overgrown plants, trees and hedges, were row upon row of cars in the wilderness, all under heavy plastic sheets.

'You do what you need to. I'll be waiting,' said Edoardo.

Mike moved among the cars, lifting some of the sheets tentatively. Old Maseratis, Fiats and Lancias were all tucked away, hiding from the elements. Some were better than others, but all were suffering, the moisture trapped by the sheets eating through their surfaces and structures, slowly returning them to the earth.

'These are interesting, but they need to be taken away and stored properly,' said Mike to Carlo, quietly. 'I think each would be a major restoration project, too, and you'd have to do some serious clearing to get them out of here.'

'You haven't seen anything yet, my friend,' said Carlo, pointing towards the villa itself.

Carlo waved to Edoardo, who wandered over and led them into and around the house, before taking them into the back garden, in which a ladder was leaning against the rearmost wall of the villa.

'Go have a look,' said Edoardo, as he passed Mike a torch.

Mike, still soaking, slogged his way up the rickety wooden ladder, up to a rough hole in the wall. It looked like water damage had blown the brick and concrete apart, causing a three-foot section of the wall to slough out from the house, down into the grounds below. He gingerly put his foot on the floorboard inside, the wood feeling soft and springy.

The torch's beam was weak, but Mike recognised what he was looking at instantly: an elegant Lancia Dilambda cabriolet, in a sophisticated shade of green, and a battered pre-war Fiat 501 Torpedo. In the distance, lurking in the gloom, he could just make out what looked like a Lancia Aurelia B24 'America' Spider, a thick layer of dust accumulating on its grille and bumpers, like ash around a fire grate. Even in the dark, and despite the dirt and dilapidation, their graceful shapes were still striking and enchanting. Mike peered into the furthest visible reaches and spotted other ageing Fiats and Lancias slumbering in their safehold, away from the prying eyes of the outside world.

This old place is a veritable Aladdin's cave of motoring treasures, he thought, shaking his head. *These need to be saved.*

One car, towards the end of the space, was wrapped in several protective covers. He carefully lifted them, peeling back layer after layer, every motion of every sheet dumping thick clouds of dust into the air. But slowly, a familiar shape came into view.

That's DB3/1. It really is. But it could be ruined, under all this.

He pulled off the last remaining sheets and slowly swung the torch over the leading edge of the Aston's bonnet. The paint was dirty, dulled, but the leading edge of the panel was sharp, clean, free from corrosion. He swept the beam over the rest of the car, half trying to avoid looking at it, in case it was ruined, half desperate to take in every single detail.

'It's beautiful,' he said to the darkness. 'It really is.'

Despite the conditions, despite the countless sheets, the Aston had survived, only flash rust in places and decaying rubber in others, despite the extreme humidity of the lakeside villa. But it was all there, sitting proudly on the ancient floorboards, intact.

Mike pulled up a slew of historical pictures and details on his phone and carefully checked the car over from every angle, looking at the shape of the panels and the details in the interior. The body looked good but had evidently been reworked at the rear, and some parts of the interior were missing, but all the steel framing and welding looked correct.

The chassis number looked good, too. There was no stamped engine number, either, which tallied with the supposed racer lineage of DB3/1. The engine identification plates were only mounted at the front of the engine, and easily exchangeable. The rear axle looked wrong, though.

Maybe from a DB2/4 road car. Maybe an exchange after the accident. But you've got to expect some changes, after time.

He continued to pore over the details and, after an hour, he walked back over the gaping hole in the wall.

'I think it's the real deal,' he shouted down at Carlo, grinning. 'It really could be.'

'Then this is a great find,' he responded, with a hearty thumbs-up. 'You need to see this, too, Mike,' he added.

Mike descended from the heavens and followed Carlo around the side of the building, to where two engines were propped up against the side of the villa, a rapidly growing bush doing its best to obscure them.

'This one,' said Carlo, '250 GT. Very tired.'

Carlo tapped the other with his cane.

'But this one, Aston.'

Mike got down on his hands and knees, studying the numbers and details on the tired-looking block.

'I think that might be the same number. I think that might be its engine,' he said, excitedly. 'That means this really is the original car, if it all matches up perfectly!'

Carlo patted him on the shoulder and, over a much-welcomed lunch in a nearby Trattoria in the next village, Edoardo reappeared with original paperwork in hand. As the sun beamed down, Carlo and Mike carefully discussed the options for the collection, the owner listening intently. Mike sympathetically explained how the way many of the cars had been stored meant they were now ground-up restoration projects, and would have to be valued as such, to which Edoardo nodded in response, forlornly but understandingly. Others, including the fabled Aston, could be revived, carefully renovated, to preserve as much of the remaining originality as possible. But all, in any case, would have to be painstakingly studied and documented, to do them justice, to help them find the right buyer at the right price.

'Let's do it,' said Edoardo confidently. 'You deal with these and sell them for me.'

This could have been a wild goose chase, thought Mike, as he stood to shake the owner's hand. *And now it's one of the biggest Aston finds ever.*

CHAPTER 16

After driving back along the picturesque route, via Lecco, Mike parked up in Bergamo again. In the hotel Excelsior San Marco, he got himself an ice-cold bottle of Valdobbiadene Superiore prosecco, some prosciutto San Daniele with toasted white bread, and worked his way through it. He felt a familiar warm haze descending, for the first time in years, everything softening and lightening slightly.

Even for him, it was still hard to believe what he saw. Some eighteen cars, dotted around the ruins of the house, and nobody had acted on them. Most were walled in, sure, but some were visible, just, from the edges of the property. And that Aston, a truly remarkable find, one worth millions. It never failed to amaze him what was out there, still hidden away, even to this day.

He messaged Rick to let him know what he had seen, and partly to help settle his nerves. He got the distinct impression Rick was still twitchy about the Austrian Collection deal, as he was somewhat himself, but this new find would tip the scales in their favour, regardless. And that, that in itself was comfort enough.

A less convoluted find, he thought. *But, well, we'll see what happens in Salzburg next week. Time, as they say, will tell.*

'Maybe we'll end up dealing with two super finds,' he said, laughing gruffly as he fished out his organiser; the next day was clear, a break for both himself and the car, and the day after he would get up early and drive towards Turin. He would stay overnight and proceed towards Geneva, through the Aosta valley, entering the Gotthard tunnel hopefully not later than four. For some reason, the tunnel was to be closed at five in the evening.

The old Cadillac would have to lift its skirts and hurry up in the morning, that much is for sure.

A few calls trickled in, about current cars and deals, along with the usual barrage of emails, as the hours ticked by. Chapman & Sunderland had between 30 and 40 cars in stock, at any given time, and on a good day during the summer season there might be up to three hundred emails and fifty calls to tackle. It was almost too much to cope with, racking up north of two hundred sales per year, but slowing down didn't seem a viable option.

'Time to let it go for today, because it never stops,' said Mike, closing the laptop, and his organiser, and setting them to the side. 'Enough is enough.'

He let his mind wander, a signpost to Vicenza flashing up in his mind again.

Fate was cruel to me there, he thought, *his fingers clenching. The love of my life, gone, just like that.*

Without thinking, he dialled Rick.

'You alright?' said Rick, sounding a bit woozy. 'Late there, isn't it?'

'Could say the same to you. Still bearing up, after your off?' said Mike.

'Just a few nasty bruises left. And some scrapes. And maybe a chip off the odd bone, here or there. You know what would make me feel better?'

'A replacement for your Kawasaki?'

'Some sliver of hope on the Hadfords front. Any updates? I know it's early doors, but still, it'd make me feel a whole lot better if these cars from the Austrian collection had somewhere to go.'

'You might need to cool your jets,' said Mike. 'There's nothing yet.

If they have got Abdul Ben Ali on the line for the collection, he might not be the easiest to pin down.'

'Jet-setting type?'

'One way to put it,' said Mike. 'He's probably got more business deals going than we've cars in stock.'

'Well, maybe I'll stick my nose in, after all, and see if I can dig anything up. We need to stay on their radar, and we need to get on his.'

'Agreed,' said Mike flatly.

'You never answered my question, you know,' said Rick, concern flitting into his voice. 'You're not one for ringing me in the dead of night, at least not like this. What's really troubling you?'

'Dropped out of that meeting at Vicenza, you know.'

'Ah,' said Rick quietly.

'I mean…'

'We all lose loved ones, Mike. Eventually. And we all grieve.'

'I know that,' he snapped. 'But.'

'But you've never really talked about it.'

'No,' he said, despondently. 'No, I haven't. Not even to you.'

'Being too introverted about these things doesn't do any of us any good, Mike. I'm always here, if you need it.'

'I mean, she died in my arms, Rick,' said Mike, his voice strained. 'Right near the Basilica Palladiana. And it was just a stupid traffic accident.'

'You two were quite the couple, that's for sure.'

'I wanted to spend the rest of my life with her.'

'And you may never love like that again. I've seen it happen to some of the lads I know,' said Rick. 'And that pain won't go away.'

Another name flicked into Mike's head, compounding his stress and confusion: *Julie*.

'But she wouldn't have wanted you to stay on your own, Mike. Not in the slightest. She'd want you to explore, to experience, to live. To find someone to keep pushing you down the line.'

Mike realised he was driving his finger and thumb into his eyes.

He sighed, a staccato rattle at the end sounding momentarily like bitter laughter.

'Yeah, something like that,' said Mike bitterly. 'I just wish this pain would go away.'

'It might not go away, mate, but I think you'll get used to it, eventually. But you won't, if you don't fill that void with something, or someone.'

Mike clicked his tongue, then drew in a long, ragged breath.

'And don't overlook what's in front of you,' added Rick. 'It might not be straightforward, but smooth seas never made a skilled sailor.'

'True. And thanks. I should put this down.'

'The phone, or the bottle?' said Rick knowingly.

'That's supposed to be my line.'

Rick laughed, then let silence fill the space, giving Mike time to think.

'You're right,' said Mike. 'I'll switch it off, go for a walk.'

'You do that. And try to take it a bit easier on yourself over the next few days. We've got some big hurdles ahead but, in a week or so, well, we could be squared away.'

Mike bid Rick farewell, turned off his phone, and made his way out of the hotel. He looked at the Cadillac, slumbering under a streetlight in the warm evening air, in front of the hotel. The cars around it looked like toys, light, disposable, cheap.

'It'll still be around, long after you've all buggered off,' he murmured at them. 'Standing the test of time, like the best of them.'

———————•———————

Sunlight was streaming in through gaps in the hotel room's curtains, the bright light cutting into Mike's aching brain like a knife. He slowly rubbed his temples, opened one eye cautiously, and winced. He sat up and reached for his phone, but its battery was flat.

I know that feeling, he thought, as he fumbled for his charger. The glass and two bottles of prosecco, one empty, the other not faring much better, rattled noisily as he raggedly pushed the charger into the socket behind the bedside table.

He sat heavily on the edge of the bed, the springs of the mattress groaning in protest for a moment, and watched as the phone's screen played an animation of a completely flat battery starting to take on charge. He sighed as he pulled his Daytona from the drawer; to his surprise, it was only just past eight.

'Some consolation,' he said quietly, as he weaved his way to the shower. The tiling in the bathroom was cool, and his stiff muscles and sore head clamoured for warmth and comfort; he ran the shower, stepped inside, and hot water coursed over him. But it failed to imbue Mike with any inner relief or comfort, his thoughts weighing heavy on mind and body alike. He cranked the dial the other direction, unleashing a cascade of icy water. He let out a guttural moan as it ran down him, from head to toe, and clenched his fists a few times. His head tipped back, and he breathed deeply, letting out long, controlled breaths.

A little better.

His shaver buzzed, his brush scrubbed, and he slowly began to feel more human. He pulled a clean pair of trousers and a set of underwear from his case, and a free-breathing light-blue shirt with white cuffs and collar from the cupboard, and stepped back to his nightstand, his phone now showing signs of life. He held down the power button, watched the start-up animation play, and stepped over to his balcony. His room overlooked a wide avenue below, with a belt of green running along its middle, and the city was just starting to come to life. Beyond, he could see the Città Alta, high in the hills, the white- and sand-coloured buildings reaching up from the grey walls of the ancient stronghold, layer upon layer of mesmerising history and intrigue.

A series of chimes played behind him, his phone responding to myriad notifications: several missed calls, unread messages and texts, and a boatload of new emails. He scrolled down the lengthy list, clocking Rick's name a few times, until he landed on the last missed call.

Julie. Half an hour ago.

He felt his heart flutter for a moment, a surge of hope and energy flushing the remnants of alcohol, and the darkness of the night before, from his system. Mike slid the balcony door aside, stepped into the fresh air, and pressed the redial button.

The phone rang, and rang, and then skipped to the answer machine. He drew breath through his teeth and dialled again. This time, an ugly engaged tone played back loudly through his phone. He hung up, waited for a moment, and then dialled again. A pause, and then a click.

'Ciao, sono Julie,' said the soft voice. 'Sto guidando!'

Mike's heart skipped another beat.

'Julie? It's Mike. Is everything okay?'

'Yes! Yes, don't worry – I guess you must have a lot of missed calls and messages.'

'Va bene,' said Mike cheerily. 'But what's going on?'

'Well, a little birdy tells me you're having a rough time of it at the moment, so we decided to cheer you up a little bit.'

'I'm afraid you've lost me,' he said, steadying himself against the balcony's railing.

He could hear Julie laughing, the wind rushing past in the background.

'Sarai felice, I'm on my way to you. You've got a free day, correct?'

'But I'm in Bergamo!'

'So am I! Or, at least, I will be in half an hour or so.'

'You what?!'

'A friend in need, you know – the flight to Verona was only a couple of hours, so I hopped over yesterday evening and stayed with some friends in Monitrone. They've given me a car, so I thought I'd head your way first thing. Have you had breakfast yet?'

Mike felt his stomach grumble, although he couldn't figure whether it was in distress or in demand.

'No, I'm barely out of bed, to be honest.'

'Su, su,' she said melodically. 'Get yourself ready. I'll be there in thirty. Ci vediamo!'

Mike blinked a few times, unable to come up with a response, and then realised the call had already ended. He pulled his eyebrows down from his forehead, shook his head softly, and laughed.

'Some consolation,' he said heartily.

———————— • ————————

The cutlery on the plates rattled aggressively as the waiter wheeled around them, but it didn't grate Mike's tired brain, or irritate him. He was just grinning, watching as Julie chastised the waiter for bringing her a cream-filled croissant that was stale. Or, at least, what she deemed as too stale. She turned her gaze back to Mike, rolled her eyes playfully, rested her chin on one delicate-looking hand, and smiled warmly.

'And, yes, once Rick messaged me, I called him back to see what you were doing and where you were,' said Julie. 'I could move some things around, and, well, there were a few things I could do with doing out here anyway, so it was a pleasure to pop over and see you, too.'

'That all worked out rather well, then,' said Mike, raising his cappuccino to her. 'And it's very much appreciated. It's good to see a familiar face.'

She nodded. 'We can't let it all be work and no play, either.'

'I'm not sure many would consider a lot of this work, in many cases,' he said, grinning at her.

'No, but I'm sure they don't realise the stress. Especially given the money, the assets, and the rest, that's all in play.'

'That's very astute,' he said in a confirming fashion, a frown flashing over his face momentarily. 'We do have a lot in the air at the moment.'

'Rick has told me a little about that. It sounds like yesterday went well for you, though.'

He nodded, a beam replacing the frown. 'It did. Some real finds. And tomorrow, I think we might have more on the table, too.'

'And I understand in a week or so, you'll be through the worst?'

'That's the hope. One serious meeting soon, to sign on the dotted lines, then we'll press on as quickly as we can.'

The waiter reappeared with a fresh croissant, and fette biscottate with jam, and a pot of tea, for Mike. The morning sun beat down on the duo, but even without it, Mike felt revived. Julie nodded curtly at the waiter, pulled a strip of pastry from her croissant experimentally, and made a content, soothing noise as she bit into it.

'Gustare,' she said, passing him a piece.

'This isn't bad either,' he said, returning her a jam-covered toast.

'You see, it's all coming up,' she said cheerfully.

Mike beamed at her, the caffeine and carbohydrates bolstering his sense of vigour.

'So, is London still treating you okay?'

'Si. I can't say I'm much for the climate,' she responded, gesturing to the sky, 'but I like the vibrancy of the place, the colour. And it's so easy to get elsewhere from there. The Tunnel, the ferries, Heathrow, the trains.'

'Useful, given all your European exploits.'

'Si, exactly!' she said, head bobbing up and down vigorously. 'Most of my friends are still in Italy, although some are in France and the Netherlands. I couldn't be doing with not seeing them, so it works for me.'

'What's it like on the work front, though?'

A look of happiness spread across her face. 'Good,' she said enthusiastically. 'Especially in a clinic such as ours. Not that I have much call or time to spend it, given how busy we are.'

'If that's the case, thank you again for making the effort to come out here.'

'We only live once, and I don't want these opportunities to slip past. Time flies otherwise, and we could be left wondering what could have been.'

'Time flies, indeed. A week of work starts and then, voila, a month's gone by. But that reminds me: your mother. Did her trip go well? Last time I saw her, she was fighting an uphill battle with her Superfast.'

'She made it all the way out, and all the way back, with no more fuss. Apparently, a knight in a shining Rolls-Royce helped her out.'

Mike grinned and tried his best to suppress a blush.

'So, it's not all bad,' she added. 'But let's not chat all about family, work; that's not why I'm here. You need some escape, some head clearing!'

'It wouldn't go amiss. And the company would very much be appreciated.'

'I'm only here for today, though; I've got to get going after, and then back to London.'

'That's a shame, but it works for me, too, as I'm back at it tomorrow.'

'No rest for the wicked,' she said, grinning. 'Come on then! I'll get the bill, and let's get going!'

'This is definitely on me,' he said firmly. 'You've come all this way, after all.'

'I won't be having any of that,' she said scoldingly, her eyes narrowing. 'This is my day for you, thank you very much. Silenzio.'

Mike returned the squint but withdrew his hand from his wallet. She tipped her head appreciatively and flashed a hand up to catch the next passing waiter.

'What do you have in mind for today, then?' he said inquisitively.

'There's a sanctuary near here I've always wanted to visit. It's not so much the place itself, but how you get there. A beautiful drive, a beautiful walk, and there's a great restaurant nearby for after.'

'And you've a car?'

'Oh, yes,' she said, raising her eyebrows a few times. 'I've got a car.'

———————————— • ————————————

The battered white Fiat 500 swept through Trevasco San Vito, its peppy engine blatting along merrily. Julie laughed as she tipped it into the first of many switchbacks, up the Strada Provinciale 36 road, beginning the climb towards the sanctuary. Mike pulled his seat belt a little tighter, and quietly wished for more supportive seats. Julie flung the wheel again, her shoulder bumping into his as the Fiat teetered on three wheels around another sharp corner.

'I thought it might be something a bit more exotic,' said Mike, almost being cut short by the engine bouncing off its limiter again, the wind whipping through the wide-open windows.

'But it's perfect for this, no?' said Julie, the Fiat's brakes rumbling as the anti-lock system did its magic, the faint smell of burning brake material seeping into Mike's nose. 'Light, small, eager, and not worth very much!'

'Like you in all but one respect,' said Mike jokingly.

Julie punched his arm, then grabbed the next gear, the 500's engine relishing the moments away from its limiter. The road continued on, upwards, sweeping from left to right, the thick, lush woods hiding the way ahead until the car cleared each bend. Mike watched as Julie expertly and energetically threaded the Fiat from corner to corner; she was letting it run out, letting it sing, but she wasn't letting it get away from her. It was an intense ride, but he didn't feel nervous.

Not to be underestimated, that one, he thought, as he jammed one knee against the centre console, the other in the door card, to stop himself from bouncing around the cabin.

'In giornate come queste, eh?' she said musically, her hair fluttering around the cabin.

A sign flashed past and the Fiat's pace slowed, the road leading into a town called Selvino. Julie squeezed the brakes a little more, settling into a relaxed, well-judged cruise, the roads becoming narrower and rougher as they headed back out of the town, upwards, winding their way towards the sanctuary.

'What is this place we're heading to again?' said Mike.

'Il Santuario della Madonna del Perello. It's from the early 1400s. It's a small place, but I've always wanted to see it.'

'It, or the roads loading to it?'

She grinned at him, the Fiat darting neatly between potholes in the road, the dips in the lush green treeline revealing rolling, rising ranges beyond.

'The sanctuary is one of the oldest in this area, and it's packed full of ancient art and antiques. It's not just that, though, I wanted to see the area, the valley in which it sits.'

'It is verdant up here, that much I'll say,' said Mike, squinting as the sun blazed intermittently through the passing trees. 'Bellissima.'

They rounded another bend and the road drew to a close. Julie parked the Fiat neatly outside a restaurant and stepped out, her orange patterned summer dress swirling around her. She reached behind her seat and pulled out a pair of straw hats. She perched one atop Mike's head, stepped back, and grinned.

'Perfetto,' she said. Mike returned her grin, ran his finger around the brim, and whipped it down to point at her.

'Buon pomeriggio, signora.'

She flashed another smile at him, and stepped towards the sanctuary, its bell tower spearing upwards above them. He looked around, taking in the restaurant, the light tan paving and stonework, the fresh-smelling air, and admired the brilliant contrast between the vibrantly green forest and the intense bright blue of the sky. The birds whistled quietly in the background, and he could hear the odd scuffing of feet atop stone, the odd tourist and local making their way around. His eyes settled back on Julie, watching her weave gently away from him, her head inquisitively tipping this way and that, leaning over the railing and looking into the beyond. She put her hand out behind her and flexed her fingers, beckoning to him. He didn't linger.

———————— • ————————

The two stepped from the restaurant, the cooler evening air washing over them. Julie swept the remainder of her Pirlo around her glass, looked towards the setting sun, and tapped Mike's foot with her own.

'Approvare?' said Julie, tipping her head back towards the restaurant.

'That was, yes, very enjoyable. The tortellini was lovely. And the sanctuary, too. Small, but pleasant.'

'Good. I'm glad.'

'The company's not bad either,' he said, smiling.

She poked a single finger into his chest, stuck her tongue out at him, then finished her drink.

'Relaxed?'

'And refreshed. Thank you.'

'Bene. Andiamo,' said Julie, gesturing towards the Fiat. 'The evening is coming to a close, and we should start back.'

Mike sighed, then nodded. They strode across the square together, squeezed themselves back into the Fiat, and set off down into the valley. Mike watched, in a dreamlike trance, the scenery roll by, his mind refreshed, body content, soul sated. Julie was singing along quietly to herself, the wind making her hair spiral around, her touch on the Fiat's steering wheel light.

I could be very happy with her, he thought. *Maybe a touch intimidated, but happy.*

Julie glanced at him, smiling broadly, her bare feet skipping across the Fiat's pedals, her sandals bouncing around on the rear seats.

'I think you could do with some company more often,' she said. 'You're like a different person now. I can see it in your face, in your posture.'

'The chance would be a fine thing,' said Mike affectionately. 'But fortunately, days like today, well, they top up the battery enough.'

'Don't you ever want more than just enough, though?'

'I'm not sure how I'd find the time,' he said thoughtfully.

'I'm sure you'd make the time, for the right person.'

'Maybe the right person would make me make time for them,' said Mike.

'Maybe you'll find out.'

'And what about you, are you happy as you are?'

'I know what would suit me, what I want. No more immature boys, that's for sure,' said Julie, one finger wagging from atop the Fiat's steering wheel. 'I don't have the time or energy for that, not now.'

'More a partner, a companion?'

'Si, like this, yes.'

She was cut short by the sound of the Fiat's anti-lock-braking system chuntering into life, the tyres tossing pebbles from the road forwards, the cheap tyres squealing in protest.

'Wha–,' exclaimed Mike, as the seatbelt's tensioner ratcheted into life, clamping him in place.

'Look!' said Julie.

Mike's head spun round, but the road ahead was clear.

'What was it?'

Julie dropped the Fiat into reverse, the gears whining as she accelerated backwards. To the right, a small, short unpaved road wound around a corner, and a tired, semi-collapsed shed sat square in the corner of a clearing. Next to it was a sun-scorched excavator, faded black letters HYDROMAC on its boom, amid piles of ancient, long-forgotten gravel, hardcore, scrap and long-defunct machinery.

'Looks like it was some kind of working yard,' said Mike. 'I don't think anything in there has moved for a good few decades. Didn't think you were into heavy equipment, that's for sure.'

'Look closer.'

He scanned from left to right. More old tools, stacks of scrap timber, the odd offcut of granite and stone, a shadow in the shed, a curving piece of metal, hinting at something beyond.

Mike reached for his doorhandle but Julie was already out of the car, bounding towards the shed, her bare feet kicking up dust. She pulled the flimsy metal door of the shed towards her, opening it, and bounced up and down excitedly.

'What is it, Mike?' she said, her hair bobbing up and down.

'I'll be damned,' he said, as he worked to pull the other door open. 'That's a Citroën 15CV Six.'

The elegant four-door saloon was tired, its maroon paint faded with age, but the proud upright grille, with its double chevron, still had some shine, a glint that could catch the eye. Three of the four tyres still even had air in them, but all were heavily cracked.

Mike swept some of the dust off the bonnet; it felt like it was an inch thick in places, a mix of sand, concrete, soil, and debris from the roof above.

'The plates are well out of date,' said Mike. 'I'm guessing this hasn't moved in decades, either. It still looks pretty solid, though. You've a good eye!'

'Don't I just,' said Julie, as she scouted around the back of the Citroën.

'These are very hard to find these days, you know. Has it got a spare wheel on the back?'

'It looks like it!'

'One of my favourites, then, with the spare wheel and the wipers on the top edge of the screen.'

Julie twisted the handle on the rear passenger door. A hollow click rang through the shed, and the door swung open.

'It's unlocked!'

Mike walked over to the driver's door, brushed his hand over the glass. The windows had been left open a fraction, and the interior looked in a terrible state. But the closer he looked, the more he realised it was saveable, sound; the velvet seats were patchy and filthy, but there were no tears, no holes; the black-painted tin dash had lost its lustre, but it looked like a good polish could revive it; the rim of the wheel was also cracked, but still perfectly round, and the instruments were all legible, the white needles and digits peering out from behind an oppressive layer of filth.

'It doesn't smell bad,' said Julie.

'I'm surprised. I'd have thought the mice would have made a home in one of the seats, for sure.'

'You should sit in it!'

Mike looked around him, a slight nervousness coursing up and down his spine.

'Come on, there's no one here. No one probably remembers it even exists,' said Julie loudly. 'We'll be careful!'

Mike steeled himself and opened the door. The smell of the Citroën's interior poured over him, the heat on the fabrics, metal and wood amplifying those ancient and peculiar smells; he found himself transported back to Paris, to younger, easier-going times.

'I used to have one of these,' he said, feeling slightly overcome. 'A Big 15, back in the day. Reminds me of my time in Dijon. The yards, the films, the friends. This thing smells like the France of old.'

He lowered himself carefully into the seat, feeling like he was handling some ancient document in a museum.

'I can't believe it has this velvet trim,' he said quietly. 'It was such an uncommon feature, and the others never smelt the same.'

'It suits you,' said Julie. She popped open the passenger door and slipped onto the bench seat next to him.

'I always wanted another, just like this. Something original.'

'Like a time capsule?'

'It does feel like that. A freeze-frame of that moment in my life, that part of history. Like a photograph, but more tangible, visceral.'

'And something that might move!'

Mike laughed and bumped his shoulder against hers.

'I don't think this thing is going anywhere soon. But I'm sure, with some effort, it could live again.'

He put his arms out and clasped the steering wheel, and then lowered his left hand onto the long, wand-like gear lever. He could see the old avenues in front of him, hear the chatter of people sat outside the cafés, the smell of cigarette smoke and red wine in the air. He pressed the throttle, felt the cable move and the pedal return, moved the steering wheel gently, and felt the front wheels respond.

'We have a small tool kit. And we've some fuel, a battery,' said Julie, pointing in the Fiat's direction. She reached out and put her hand on top of Mike's and pretended to row the gear shift back and forth. 'Come on! Credi in te stesso!'

Mike stared at her hand, the sensation of her warmth and softness overpowering him for a moment.

'I'm not sure,' said Mike, one hand unconsciously flipping the switches on the big Citroën's dashboard. 'We might do more damage than good, given it's been sat so long. The oil probably resembles treacle, for one thing.'

'Andiamo!' she shouted cheerily. 'I think you should try!'

He put his hand on her shoulder. 'Tell you what, I'll make you a deal.'

She looked at him, cocked her head, and nodded.

'I've got this collection to deal with. It's going to take a lot of effort, a lot of work, and we've still lots of other hurdles to cross.'

'You're not the only one with problems to tackle,' said Julie, giggling to herself. 'But I'm listening.'

'How about, after that, we come back here, we find out who owns this, and we buy it.'

'And restore it?'

'I think so. We can try to preserve as much of its patina and originality as possible, so we can capture the memory of this day.'

'Our own time capsule,' said Julie, her eyes scanning around the cabin, and then over Mike. 'We can work on it together. I'd like that.'

'Alright,' he said cooly. 'Let's give it a go.'

CHAPTER 17

Mike arrived in Geneva the next afternoon feeling refreshed, energised and a little more level-headed. The Cadillac had made the trip effortlessly and being behind the wheel, in better conditions, had bolstered his confidence and spirit.

He was set to meet a new client and had chosen the bar of the Hotel Four Seasons des Bergues in which to have their first meeting. He knew the hotel well because it was a convenient place to stay whenever attending vintage watch auctions in Geneva. The bar had a lovely classic style, with courteous and warm staff, and it offered the perfect atmosphere in which to talk business.

A large, plush booth was free, so Mike settled in, ordered an Aperol Spritz and a sandwich, and watched the minute hand roll forwards on his old Daytona. As the hand neared an hour marker, he spotted a tall, silver-haired man approaching him. The man walked up to the table and extended his hand.

'Michael Chapman, correct?' he said, as Mike stood and shook his hand. 'I'm Werner Mathis.'

'A pleasure,' said Mike. 'Thank you for coming. And please, call me Mike. Only a few people call me Michael these days.'

Werner tipped his head and Mike gestured for him to sit, his arm sweeping neatly over the table to the seat on the other side of the booth. Werner nodded and lowered himself slowly onto the bench seat, then put his hands down flat on the table.

'I'm going to hazard a guess that you don't remember me, but we have met before.'

'There was a flutter of a recollection, yes,' said Mike. 'Something familiar, which I can't quite place. It must have been some time ago?'

'We do meet an awful lot of people in this business and, like you say, time takes its toll,' said Werner, waving at a waiter. 'Thank you for picking a convenient spot to meet, though.'

Mike's memory raced. The man was in his late seventies, with a full head of neatly cut light grey hair, and dressed in the conventional Swiss manner; white trousers, a blue and white long-sleeved shirt, a shallow collar, attire in itself that was vaguely familiar. Werner's cuffs depicted the Ferrari Cavallino Rampante motif, and his watch was a sodalite-dial white-gold Daytona, with a contrasting blue leather strap.

Nice watch, thought Mike, approvingly. *And lots of velvet, silk and a Hermes briefcase. Your stereotypical, and very rich, Swiss citizen.*

Werner adjusted his watch as he ordered two drinks. 'The reason that I am seeing you,' he said, voice monotone, 'is that I want to sell all of my cars, on commission.'

Mike's eyebrows raced towards the ceiling.

'There is a catch, though. You must not advertise them openly, nor must you mention my name anywhere. These need to be dealt with quietly, privately and unobtrusively.'

'May I ask as to how significant the collection is that you're looking to sell?'

'I think its total value is probably around thirty million Euros, maybe a little more,' said Werner, without a hint of emotion.

We're amassing a collection of collections. Bloody hell.

'That is a substantial sum,' said Mike. 'Why are you looking to sell, and in such a fashion, if you don't mind me asking?'

Werner shook his head at him. 'I don't mind you asking. I have terminal cancer.'

Mike grimaced, his chin dipping towards the table.

'I'm terribly sorry to hear that, Mr Mathis.'

'Please, call me Werner. You won't be able to, for long.'

Mike hesitated for a moment as the gears in his head spun.

'How quickly would you like the cars to be sold, Werner?'

Werner nodded appreciatively at him, then leant forwards, his elbows resting on the table.

'If you could do it in less than ten months, at the most, that would be appreciated. I just don't want people involved, other than you.'

The waiter reappeared, putting two tall glasses of champagne on the table, and Werner sat back, his face becoming stony and resolute. The waiter nodded politely at them both and left, and Werner leant forward again, his face relaxing.

'The cars in the collection are among the best. I have a Ferrari 250 GT SWB California Spider, a Daytona Plexi Spyder, a Bizzarrini Spyder, a Maserati 150S Barchetta, a Maserati 5000 GT by Frua, a Ferrari 312B, and a few others.'

'Do you have a list that I might see, Werner?'

Werner nodded and handed Mike a crisp, white envelope, sealed with a gold wax stamp.

'I believe I've heard about some of your cars,' said Mike, 'and I'm sure I've seen some at Villa d'Este, Pebble, Goodwood…'

'That's right,' said Werner. 'They're fabulous.'

'I think we'll have quite a lot of interested parties for cars such as that.'

Mike cracked the wax seal on the envelope, extricated a single piece of paper, and looked at the delicately handwritten table it presented. Car, year of build, body style, carrossier, mileage, colour, and a price range were all listed, in tiny, intricate and elegant strokes of pen.

Quite the grand total, Mike thought, mentally tallying the values.

'And this figure, that's what you'd be happy with for each?'

'Ideally, yes. But I would leave that in your court. If you went ahead and deemed the offer good, you could sell.'

'That's some responsibility. But then it's some collection,' said Mike, shaking his head in awe. Werner was studying Mike's face carefully.

'It's a life's achievement, no?' he said. 'And I'd like you to deal with the end of it, if you would.'

'I'll do it,' said Mike immediately. 'It is a grand collection, and it would be an honour to handle it. I only wish it were under different circumstances.'

Werner brightened, sat up, and waved his champagne glass at the waiter.

'It won't be the first time you've handled a Ferrari of mine,' said Werner cheerily.

'Ah,' said Mike, hand smacking his forehead. 'The 250 MM Vignale?'

'That's right,' said Werner. 'I know it was decades ago, but that was quite a beautiful car.'

'Yes, you're right. We bought it from you in Switzerland, but I don't think we spoke in person for more than a minute.'

'A crazy deal, and better times,' he said thoughtfully.

'But a good deal,' said Mike, tipping his glass at him, 'for both of us.'

'Yes. I loved that car. A window, like these others, into a world long since gone, a world where people took a different approach to life in general and cars.'

'That's absolutely true,' said Mike. 'Back then, Ferraris were functional tools, cared for and used. It's only these days that Ferraris from that era are generally treated as no more than tickets into major events, as precious jewellery. Only to be seen on concours lawns or sales exhibitions.'

'I've heard that one is now stashed away in Germany,' said Werner, sounding a little glum. 'That body was unique. It's a shame it's not out there for people to see.'

'And it was a Ferrari that, in the days you had it, and before, was used as intended. Most Ferrari 250 MMs were produced by Pinin Farina, all of them extraordinary cars. But yours was a rare exception.'

'Indeed,' said Werner, accepting a fresh glass of champagne from the waiter. 'The MMs were supercars of their day. However, mine was, to my mind, even more extraordinary and intriguing. To my knowledge, only 13 Vignale 250 MMs were built: 12 Barchettas and only one Berlinetta, ordered by Swiss gentleman and racing driver Karl Lanz.'

'I remember the paperwork, the delivery note detailing its arrival at his home in Bern… spring 1954?'

'Correct. It must have been quite a sight, with that long bonnet and curvaceous rear, even in this rich Swiss city. Not all show, though, as I believe it was later entered into the gruelling Liége-Rome-Liége Rally, with Lanz and Sägesser claiming class victory.'

'A great outing for its first owner,' said Mike. 'And you're right, that Vignale design is striking. The complicated aluminium roof architecture, with two integrated air vents, reminds me of the famous Uhlenhaut-designed Mercedes-Benz 300SLR Coupé.'

'Practically identical,' said Werner.

'I had a conversation about that with a renowned Ferrari historian, years ago, and we both agreed the Vignale design came at least a year before the 300SLR Coupé that was developed in 1955 for the 1956 season, although it never competed; Mercedes-Benz withdrew from racing after the 1955 Le Mans tragedy.'

'And the 300SL, and by that, I mean the W198, first shown in New York, in February 1954, also had twin vents above the rear window, as did the W194,' said Werner.

'It's always interesting to study who got there first, but probably not important. Dealing with heat and ventilation in a race car is always a challenge. Maybe the similarities are purely coincidental, maybe not.'

'But they both worked,' said Werner. 'Elegant, and functional.'

'I used to have a Lightweight E-type with similar vents, on the back of the roof,' said Mike. 'It was definitely an idea that caught on.'

'And Mercedes-Benz won the World Sportscar Championship by two points in 1955, finishing just ahead of Ferrari,' said Werner. 'That rubbed up a few people the wrong way, I should say.'

Mike laughed. 'That rivalry continues today, in the equally competitive world of classic cars. We all know how valuable a 250 GTO is these days, but there are those who say that the 300SLR Uhlenhaut Coupé is worth twice as much as a GTO. But that's another story altogether.'

'After that rally, my Vignale was sold to Ricardo Montebello, via an advertisement in *Automobil Revue*, for ten thousand Swiss Francs,' said Werner. 'Along with a Porsche 356 as a trade-in. I just find this history, these stories, fascinating.'

'He loved the car, didn't he, according to the history? I remember the timing slips for the hill-climbs, the rallies, the slaloms.'

'He did, as did I. He was the one who had it painted bronze, with a black roof.'

'Didn't he become the first official Swiss importer for Ferrari, too?'

Werner snorted. 'Yes, he did, until he fell out with Enzo Ferrari. And that, as they say, was that.'

'What did he do after that?'

'Sold Jensens, among other brands, and later went on to build his own cars,' said Werner. 'My car went to classic car dealer Robert de Buerlein, afterwards, for twenty thousand Francs in 1975. I think he was like you, a talented businessman who had a knack for finding and selling classic automobiles.'

'Too kind,' said Mike. 'I knew him, superficially. Robert apparently disliked Ferraris, even though he'd been selling them for decades. Rare Porsches were more his bag, I think. Especially his 356 Carrera Speedster and RS61.'

'Funny you say that,' said Werner. 'I knew him quite well and, despite that, he spent his life looking for Ferraris and Maseratis, in and around Geneva.'

'Maybe he saw some money in it.'

'He definitely completed a few amazing deals. A real treasure hunter.'

'I have found out some more about my car in recent history,' said Werner.

'Oh, really?'

'When the third owner wanted to dispose of the car, after a few years, he put it up for sale in front of his company with a large "Zu Verkaufen" cardboard sign on the windscreen. It remained outside for a long time, and nobody ever appeared to show any interest. Clearly not an easy car to get rid of. The owner got quite frustrated and angry, and by that point could no longer stand the sight of it.'

'And today, they'd be fending off countless buyers, all waving cheques with plenty of zeroes on them.'

'Exactly. So, after several months, he gave up and ordered his workers to take it to the highest floor of the factory building. Once upstairs he ordered them to build a brick wall around it. The story goes that there was no access to this artificial Pharaoh-like tomb. Time went on, people left the company and the car faded from collective memory.'

'I just found another collection that was bricked up, just like that, in Italy. Must have been de rigueur then. At least ours was only on the first floor. What happened to it after that?'

'Years later, the new factory boss knocked on the door of the director and mentioned that he had found a strange wall in the attic with a hidden space behind it. The director suddenly and painfully remembered the car which he had willingly forgotten.'

'And then it finally got its moment in the sun?'

'Yes. He ordered the wall to be torn down and decided to put an advertisement in *Automobil Revue*. He wasn't up to speed with the values, though, and his estimate was, shall we say, extremely reasonable.'

'Plenty of people, then, but waving cheques with fewer zeroes than they should have had on them.'

'There was quite the furore around it.'

Mike nodded, grinning. 'Robert de Buerlein was a clever, well-connected businessman; I'm sure he got tipped off by a lovely assistant he'd wooed at some point and secured the car before it even went out.'

'Surely,' said Werner seriously, 'this must have been one of the last important Ferraris that many overlooked, and which was unearthed in total ignorance of its meaning and value.'

'Those were the days,' said Mike. 'But, well, there are still plenty of surprises out there.'

Werner looked distracted for a moment. 'We were younger then. I would be grateful if you could sort this all soon. My kids have no interest in cars. And my partner, well, they are not technically minded, or into cars.'

Mike jotted down a few notes in his organiser.

'I can take care of it all for you,' he said positively.

'Can you give me some specifics now?'

'Okay,' said Mike assertively. 'We'll do it on a ten per cent commission basis.'

'Eight,' said Werner firmly, and without hesitation.

'It's going to be a lot of work,' responded Mike, somewhat taken aback.

'It's a lot of cars. And it's a lot of money.'

'That's very true,' said Mike. 'But dealing with a collection of this significance will require considerable effort, from many people, especially in order to return the best results.'

Werner tipped his head back slightly, his eyes watching Mike intently, but said nothing.

'And we also have the contacts that will allow us to place these cars with owners who will appreciate them for what they are,' added Mike. 'Nine per cent.'

A smile spread across Werner's face. He nodded approvingly, and Mike quickly tried to suppress a loud sigh of relief.

'The cars can stay in Switzerland,' continued Mike. 'We'll need to catalogue them, with a few hundred shots each, and we'll document and present the history in booklets. We'll put all of that in front of our five best customers and see which leaps at the opportunity.'

'Excellent,' said Werner, brushing his hands together. He reached out with one, and Mike couldn't help but notice its swollen, soft appearance. He shook it gently, with a light grip, and Werner nodded warmly in response.

'It's a deal,' said Mike enthusiastically. 'Thank you for the opportunity.'

'Thank you for making it easy,' said Werner.

CHAPTER 18

The morning sun poured down on Mike as he wandered along the promenade, outside the hotel. He savoured the bright warming light, the fresh air, and the quiet buzz of the street. He checked his phone briefly, then dialled Rick.

At least it's not raining again.

'It's Mike. I think we've got another collection in the works for us, as well as that walled-up one with the Aston.'

'Well, there's a turn-up for the books,' said Rick. 'You're on a bit of a roll.'

'So it seems. I sat down with that Swiss gent who contacted us a while back, and he's got some beautiful Ferraris, among other fine machinery, that he wants us to handle for him. Like the others, though, we have to keep that close to our chest.'

'Loose lips, eh?'

'Privacy and security, yes. I'll send you the details of the cars but, those aside, everything else needs to stay off the radar.'

'Gotcha. I'll put some feelers out for buyers as soon as I can. Regardless, these are all taking the edge off the Austrian fuss. Things could be a lot worse.'

'Agreed,' said Mike. 'And that's a good point: do you remember Mathias Fechtel?'

'Nope. Should I?'

'Moot now, really. He'd got an interesting private collection of cars. Quiet guy, but very bright. Younger than you or I. Anyway, someone took him out, according to the news, with a rifle.'

'I'm guessing it wasn't an accident,' said Rick.

'No, gunmen on bikes, the works. Last time I met him, he was working on wind farms as a consultant engineer or some such. Not exactly the kind of person you'd expect to get bumped off.'

'Maybe Big Oil did it,' said Rick dryly.

Mike heard Rick shunting paper around on his desk. 'Look,' continued Rick. 'I've done a bit of digging and that Abdul Ben Ali, he's making some moves on some big Ferraris. If Hadfords are involving him, we could stand to be sorted.'

'You could say that. I was thinking about him and the last time I saw him, in Bavaria, his family had just acquired a huge estate, like a village. Underground bunkers, the works.'

'Word is that he's a Captain in the Royal Saudi Air Force these days.'

'He always did like a bit of excitement,' said Mike. 'Shame we don't have some way to raise him. If he picked it up, it would be a swift solution to a complex deal.'

'And it would see us set for a while, which would allow us to make the most of what you're lining up now. No quick flips just to keep our heads above water. We could maximise the return on each and every car. This could be really big for us.'

'Let's not build castles in the sky, Rick,' said Mike firmly. 'We need to get the Austrian Collection pinned down in earnest, so we can make waves with that 250 GTO, and then we can be a bit more footloose and fancy-free.'

'Well, I'll keep nosing around about Ali. And it won't be long before we've got that collection signed away. The meeting in Salzburg's only a few days away now.'

'Exactly.'

'I do have a favour to ask, though,' said Rick. 'I'm trying to keep things moving over here, too, and we've got a couple of deals going with a Lagonda and a pre-war Rolls-Royce. The cars look pretty honest to me, but I want your input on some of the finer points.'

'Sounds interesting.'

'Which is why I'm passing it off to you. I know those things are right up your street.'

Mike smiled wryly. 'Too right. Okay, a quick breakfast, then I'll rattle through that. Send me the details.'

He tucked his phone back into his pocket and looped back towards the hotel, looking for an open café, the Cadillac still just about visible in the distance, hunkered down in the street. He found a small place, its doors not long open, and made himself comfortable on an old leather couch inside.

Caffeine, please. Definitely starting to feel a bit knackered, he thought. All this driving, searching, Milan, Verona, Salzburg, Julie, the Austrian collection, Harriston…

The name made Mike shudder slightly. He shook his head, downed a sharp, fresh espresso, and wolfed down a few pastries, before making his way back to the hotel.

———————●———————

Mike scrolled through the classified listings on his computer, making notes of some of the asking prices, a cooling cappuccino on the table next to him. His phone rang, its screen showing a US phone number.

'Mike Chapman speaking,' he said, leaning back in his hotel room's chair.

'This is Elijah Fletcher, from Alabama,' said a distant-sounding voice. 'I understand you have a Ferrari P3 that might be available?'

All about the Italians at the moment, thought Mike.

'We do. To be more precise, it's a 1963 250 P, which was later upgraded by the factory to 330 P specification, from a collection that we're working on.'

'Can you tell me anything about it at the moment?'

'Of course,' said Mike. 'It's an ex-works team car, and later Maranello Concessionaires. It's a great example. The modifications to make the car a 330 P were common, back in the day, with many works Ferraris going back to the factory at the end of the season and being improved and updated.'

'Does the collection you're looking after have any other sports-prototypes in it?'

Ah, so they do know what they're talking about, thought Mike, somewhat relieved.

'No, just this one. It's taken many podium places, though, and was in all the major races, and driven by many of the greats. Hill, Bonnier, Ireland, Scarfiotti, Parkes.'

'Presumably, most of this is verified.'

'Yes,' said Mike confidently. 'It's a well-known car in Maranello, and it's been through Ferrari's Classiche certification. Its cert number is 037F. And it's one of only three built.'

'Can you tell me a bit more about its race history?' said Fletcher.

'It did Sebring and the Nürburgring, where it didn't finish due to transmission problems. It started at Le Mans in 1964, with Hill and Ireland driving, and came second. It won the Tourist Trophy, the 1,000km de Paris, and an event at Monza.'

'A storied car, then. Anything else that really sets it apart?'

'This was also the last prototype Ferrari to sport Borrani wire wheels,' said Mike.

'That's a neat titbit,' said Fletcher.

Mike thought for a moment and rapped his pencil against the tabletop.

'Of course, being in America, you'd be more interested in what comes after.'

'What do you mean?' said Fletcher, curious.

'It was involved in a nasty incident at Oulton, it was stripped down, sold, and ended up in America. It ended up back on track, and then bought for use as a road car.'

'It has some roots here, then. Interesting.'

'It gets better. The new owner transpired to be a drug trafficker. It got confiscated by the FBI, in the end, and was the property of the service for many years.'

'And you're not just trying to sell me some tall tale, right?'

'I have all the proof and correspondence with a Special Agent Craig Caplinger, at the Federal Bureau of Investigation.'

'Jeez,' said Fletcher, sounding suitably impressed. 'And after that?'

'Sold, for just $250,000, to Campidoglio Motor in Italy. It stayed for a while, and later went to Andorra. Of course, back then, it didn't have as much value as it does now.'

'Could I race it?' said Fletcher, sounding optimistic.

Mike put his pencil down and thought for a few moments.

'That's… doable. It has an old FIA pass, but it'll need papers, testing, x-raying, the works.'

'But it's doable.'

'A lot of people might laugh at the idea,' said Mike politely, 'but it is doable, although at great cost.'

'Can I see the documentation for it all?'

'I can't post it to you, because this kind of material tends to go walkabouts. But you're welcome to come and see the car. We'll hopefully have it in the UK soon.'

'And the million-dollar question: how much is it?'

'Substantially more than that, alas, but we'll happily discuss options once you've seen the car. We're aiming for around the eighteen million mark, US dollars.'

'Serious money,' said Fletcher.

'Serious car.'

'Fair point. Alright, now here's a question for you: can you handle gold and coinage for it?'

Mike hesitated for a moment. 'We can, but there are significant issues with moving those around, especially in regard to the values and quantities that might be at hand here.'

'You're talking about armoured shipping, that kind of thing.'

'That, and there can be some cross-border issues.'

'Right. I might have to look at selling that here, then, and just making this a cash deal.'

'That would make things a lot less complicated,' said Mike.

'Can we set up a three-step payment, or something along those lines, in the interim?'

'That's also an option,' said Mike cautiously, 'but we'll need to draw up some documents for that, and make sure all the parties are happy with, and understanding of, all the terms.'

'Sounds fair,' said Fletcher snappily. 'Someone of mine will talk to you soon.'

———————— ● ————————

'Mike,' said Rick, over an increasingly poor line. 'Get in touch with Saganer before you head to Salzburg.'

'Thomas,' said Mike, surprised. 'What does he want?'

'I fed him some details about the cars you found in Geneva the other day, from the Swiss gent,' said Rick, his voice full of cheer. 'And he's interested in the Daytona, maybe the Bizzarrini, one of the Maseratis, the Frua one, and possibly even the 312.'

'Consider it done,' said Mike. 'And thanks, Rick. Good work.'

'Pleasure. And crank down on him about the Austrian Collection, too. I couldn't get him to bite; you're always better at that, and you might have a bit of leverage.'

We do it. Let's go ahead, thought Mike as he bid Rick goodbye and hung up. *That's what Thomas says when he wants a car. And the money's only moments behind.*

Mike knew that Thomas had collected some six hundred cars in just fifteen years, quickly earning himself the status of most important collector in Europe. He was a fine, friendly man, with an outstanding handshake, and could be trusted on any matter.

As he expected, Mike couldn't raise Thomas by phone or messenger, so he drafted a short email that detailed the basics of the cars available. He received an email in response, moments later, that simply said: *reading*.

A minute later, another followed: *Guarantee originality, handle transport?*

Mike smiled and typed: Yes. He hit send.

The response came quickly: *Euro, 9.7 million.*

That'll do it, thought Mike, wishing he had some champagne within arm's reach.

His fingers flashed across the keyboard: *Perfectly judged. Accepted. Deposit of Euro 100,000 to secure.*

Just thirty seconds, this time: *We do it. Let's go ahead. Money in your account already.*

'You sure are a quick shooter,' said Mike, accessing the company's stock control software and earmarking the cars as sold, and the deposits received.

His phone rang, dragging him from his enjoyment, until he realised the incoming caller was Thomas.

'Thank you,' he said immediately. 'I hope you enjoy them.'

'I intend to,' said Thomas, his voice pleasant and warm. 'Just some housekeeping, quicker than typing. I'll send all the funds within 45 days, once the cars are all checked out.'

'That's quite alright with us,' said Mike. 'We're planning to inspect the cars and service them before they leave the country, too.'

'No need, Mike. I've my own people to tackle that. But if you could transport the cars from Geneva to the Konstanz border, where we do all things required by Swiss and European customs, that would be excellent. I'll handle it from there.'

'That's absolutely fine with me, and it'd be a pleasure,' said Mike. 'I'll start collating the required, so you can prepare everything for customs.'

'Excellent. And come over to Nürnberg soon. I'd like to see you in person and have lunch with you. I have discovered a new white wine, and I want you to taste it. It's from Weingut Luckert.'

'I'll do that,' said Mike. 'We've got some other cars you might be interested in hearing about.'

'Okay. Send me the details.'

The line went quiet but, even though Thomas had only just put down the phone, Mike saw a few follow-up emails drifting into his inbox, confirming the arrangement and specifics.

If only all customers were like that, he thought, smiling. *And five per cent off the top, for us, from Mathis.*

'Pay day,' he said, wondering where the nearest bar was.

CHAPTER 19

The Cadillac's melodic exhaust note reverberated off the walls of Museum AutoBau, in Romanshorn, Switzerland, as Mike drove carefully down the access ramp and into the car park. His good friend Karl waved him in the direction of a parking spot, with a clean polished concrete floor and bright white lights overhead.

'Thanks, Karl,' said Mike, closing the Cadillac's door and handing the keys over. 'I'm not sure what the story with this one is yet, but I'll let you know what's happening with it as soon as I can.'

'Okay if I show anyone around, if they're interested?' he said, taking a few pictures.

'I don't see why not. All the paperwork's in the glovebox.'

Never hurts to have a Plan B.

'And what about you?' said Karl. 'Where are you off to now?'

Mike sighed, a little exasperated.

'I'm going to Salzburg, to try to finalise the acquisition of another collection,' he said, frowning.

'Ah, the Austrian one you mentioned. You made it sound like a done deal.'

'It was. At least, it seemed like it. But it might still come to pass. Lots of the usual to do before then, too.'

Emails. Calls. They never end, he thought, taking one last look over the Cadillac. *At least this was straightforward.*

'And what about Rick, he still surviving?'

'His motorbike and an M5 took a good run at him recently, the Egli Kawasaki, but, yeah, he's okay.'

'Take more than that to put a dent in him, I think. Built like the proverbial brick outhouse, after all.'

'Fair point. He's on his way to Salzburg now, shunting some cargo in that 737 of his, then we'll join up.'

'I still prefer the Transall, out of the two,' said Karl, smiling. 'A bit *Mad Max*, that thing.'

'Isn't that the truth. Hopefully, we never need it for anything quite like that.'

————————— • —————————

The weather in the Altstadt district of Salzburg was beautiful, the warm sunlight amplifying the cosy and rich feel of the historic city centre. The feel in the notary's office, however, was quite the opposite. It was far from luxurious and had that decidedly pre-war ambiance and smell to it; it was slightly decrepit, cool, stale, and in desperate need of modernisation.

Mike watched the notary neatly stack a series of papers on his desk. He was of a very small stature, with neatly combed-over black hair, and very dominant in his behaviour. His motions, his lack of fuss, his coolness, all suggested he had done it all, seen it all. Little would faze him.

Rick shifted in his seat, his ill-fitting suit annoying him. He tapped his own watch, an old 18-karat gold Yacht-Master with a broken ceramic bezel, then shrugged at Mike.

'This guy coming, or what?' said Rick, annoyed. 'There's been too much back-and-forth about this already.'

The notary looked at him blankly. 'Lord Harriston will be here as and when,' he said, no trace of emotion in his voice.

Rick made a strangling gesture at Mike. He stormed over to the coffee pot, seeking a distraction.

'Police say anything about that BMW?' said Mike, staring at the ceiling.

'Nothing,' said Rick. 'I'm not sure they even give a damn. Just leaving me to fend for myself, as always.'

'Well, not exactly got much in the way of resources, these days. Blame that one on the budgets.'

The door opened and a smartly dressed woman marched in. She pulled out a seat at the table, sat down, and placed a small file on the table in front of her.

'Mike, Rick,' she said, followed by a single nod to the notary.

'Nice to see you, Frau Fay,' said Mike. 'It's been a while. How are the family?'

'They are well, thank you. They are looking forward to wrapping this up, so the collection can be moved on.'

'You and us both,' he said, simultaneously nodding and sighing, as Joseph joined them in the room. They all nodded at each other welcomingly.

'Glad to see that the Cadillac got you here,' said Joseph cheerfully. 'Not a meeting you'd want to miss.'

'That's a good car you put me in,' said Mike appreciatively. 'I've been all over in it, no fuss whatsoever.'

'And you're still up for taking it on, for one hundred thousand, once we've got this paperwork signed?'

'It'll be the cherry on the cake,' said Mike. 'We've come a long way, and I'm looking very forward to being done here.'

The notary coughed and started to pass around small A4 binders, each filled with freshly printed documents.

'Before we begin, I suggest you just review these among yourselves. Just a few details that we'll be needing to approve today.'

Rick snatched the papers from the notary and started marching up and down the length of the office, his shoes thudding noisily against the bare floorboards. Mike watched him for a moment, then started reading through the papers thrust under his nose by the notary, the smell of hot laser toner making his nose twitch. Fay raised an eyebrow at him, and Mike shrugged in response.

'This all seems to just be what we've said so far,' said Rick, confused. 'The Austrian Collection, represented by Emma Fay, seventy million quid, deposit of two million, etc, etc. What's the story?'

'I'm trying to get through it myself,' said Mike, his eyes tearing through the text.

'Wait,' said Rick, shouting angrily. 'What's this new facility agreement, the one with the bit about Harriston and controlling the collection? That's not part of the deal!'

Mike's finger tore through the papers, finding two appended sheets at the end. 'Expressively wishes to carry on business exclusively with the collection dubbed "The Austrian Collection" … funds only available if he can transport, store, handle and sell the cars in his own time.'

'He's trying to make you just the finders, not the sellers,' said Joseph frostily. 'He wants to bar you from the cars, the rest of the deal.'

'That absolute bastard,' said Mike loudly. 'He can't just barge in and add caveats to his deposit.'

'A little politeness never goes amiss,' said Harriston, as he pushed the door closed softly. 'But, yes, that's about it. They'll be mine, and I'll do with them as we see fit, if we're to go ahead today.'

'Good thing you wore a nice suit, because I'm about to put you in a coffin,' barked Rick. Mike put his hand out, trying to calm him a little.

'I'm not going to sign this,' snarled Rick, pushing towards Harriston. 'Where has this come from? We found the cars, Mike negotiated the contract, and we're calling the shots.'

Harriston laughed heartily. 'Calling the shots? You can't even afford to get in on this deal, remember. That's why you came to me in the first place. I'm in control here, not you.'

Mike pushed Rick back towards his seat. Joseph just shrugged, as if unsurprised.

'Calm the fuck down,' whispered Mike. 'We can turn this around.'

Rick gritted his teeth. 'Finding the damned cars and getting access to them is one thing, but selling them, that's where we really make the business, the headlines. This is us being fucking sidelined, right here.'

Harriston cleared his throat loudly. 'If you don't sign, you'll lose your commissions as well. That's five per cent of the grand net payable, after everything's sold off.'

Fay's head flicked back and forth between Mike, Rick, Harriston, an expressionless Joseph, and the bored-looking notary.

'I'm sorry,' she said regretfully. 'I thought this was as good as done. But if you've not got the money to proceed, well.'

'It is sorted,' said Rick, rising up again, fists pressed against the table. 'We agreed on this. We store the cars. We sell the cars. You put up the deposit money. You get a stack of cash back.'

'Why are you doing this?' said Mike flatly. 'We have email correspondence, the works, detailing our proposal and agreement.'

'I don't remember signing anything,' said Harriston. 'That just sounds like bullshit, to me,' he added snappily, staring at the notary.

'Don't take the mick,' said Rick scathingly. 'We gave you plenty of opportunity to sort out a facility agreement, and you just threw up wall after wall.'

'And you weren't even fussed in the first place,' added Mike, throwing his hands up.

'We have agreements, and made verbal agreements, to consign and sell the cars, at our premises, on our terms,' continued Rick, punching the table at the end of his sentence. 'We wouldn't have bloody engaged you if you were going to about-face on your agreements.'

Harriston just waved his hand around. 'More nonsense,' he said. 'I'm sorry that you've been dragged along by these two amateurs, Frau Fay.'

She cast him an unpleasant look, and the notary coughed loudly. Joseph stared at the ceiling.

'But at least I remain in a position to take the cars on, and retail them for you,' he added, nodding at her confidently. 'We can proceed, and my lawyers can clean up any remaining mess, if that is acceptable.'

The notary coughed again, louder this time.

'This is ridiculous, even by my standards,' said the notary. 'Carry on like this and I'll double my fees from twenty to forty thousand Euros. We can sign these contracts now, and get this underway, or we can end it now and I'll bill you forty thousand anyway. Make up your minds.'

Rick motioned to Mike, who leaned in towards him. 'Mike, look, the options contract hasn't changed. I bet you, now we've come this far, we can just push on through. We've got Harriston's money, the deposit, already. We'll just pay it back, with interest, as soon as possible.'

'And if we can't sell the cars before then?'

'That's the risk,' said Rick. 'We'll be on the hook for hundreds of thousands.'

'Or millions,' said Mike, unsettled. 'He could tie us up in loops, you know, potentially.'

'Rick's right,' said Joseph, butting in. 'He's no recourse here. He's just trying to put you on edge, make you fold. Don't say I didn't warn you, though.'

'And we know the cars,' continued Rick. 'The family likes us. I'm sure Fay and this guy can lean on Harriston a bit, get him to cool off. What's two million to either of them, anyway? And it's not like he actually needs the cars. You never know, Hadfords might come through. If not, we'll sort it out one way or another.'

'What's two million to us, and the rest,' said Mike, a chill running down his spine. 'That's more the problem.'

'I don't think anyone's going to give a fuck if we rub up Harriston the wrong way,' said Rick churlishly. 'We'll stand by our agreements, and he'll just have to suck it up and stand by his.'

Mike shook his head, baffled.

'I don't get it,' he said to Harriston despondently. 'You can't just walk in, staple an undisclosed facility contract to this deal, after the fact, and expect us to proceed. We have your money already. The deal's as good as done. What more do you want?'

Harriston rolled his eyes. 'I want what you seem so unable to display, Chapman. Control.'

'Baloney,' said Mike loudly. 'You just want the lot for yourself, don't you?!'

Mike pointed at the notary, his outstretched index figure bobbing up and down in anger. 'And what's your part in this?' he said curtly.

'I'm just here to authenticate signatures,' said the notary in a disinterested voice.

Mike turned to Fay, his shoulders dropping, his voice quieter. 'What's your stance on this?'

'As far as I'm concerned, we have an options contract that's ready. The deposit, well, that's more your issue. If you have the money ready to transfer, you can proceed. If there are risks attached to that, which bear no relation to us, those are yours to deal with. If you're able to.'

'Too bloody right we are,' said Rick loudly.

'I hope the family won't view this in a bad light,' said Mike apologetically. 'We were not aware.'

'The family doesn't need to know, although I would have preferred it to be otherwise,' she said smoothly. 'But we know who we'd prefer to deal with, that much is clear.'

'Fuck it,' said Rick, waving at the notary. 'Let me have the agreement. I'll sign it on my own. We're going to do this all ourselves.'

'Bollocks,' said Harriston, interrupting them. 'You can't do that. You've got two million of mine, and those are my cars.'

Rick grabbed the contract folder from the notary, from across the table, and dragged it back to his seat. 'Which one is the right contract? This? I just sign it right here?'

The notary looked exasperated but nodded at Rick. He scratched his name roughly on the marked sections on the pages, the notary's watchful eyes tracing the movements of Rick's pen.

'They were never your cars, Harriston,' said Mike, listening to the satisfying sound of pen on paper. 'That wasn't the point of this deal.'

'I'll destroy you both, and your business, if you complete that form,' shouted Harriston.

'We had a deal, Harriston,' said Rick, voice suddenly cool as ice.

'You'll get your money back, with interest, in 12 months, as discussed, countless fucking times.'

'That just won't fly,' said Harriston, his outstretched finger pointing at the notary, who just shrugged, his eyes flicking to the clock on the wall for a moment.

'Yes, it will,' said Rick adamantly. 'We had an agreement, and everything is neatly lined up. Don't torpedo it now. You put in a deposit, took a risk, and you'll get a benefit.'

'And we will sell the cars,' said Mike, chopping in. 'We'll keep our promises, and you'll get your fair share.'

'But I want exclusivity!' whined Harriston. 'I want the cars. They're my property now. I want to store them. I want to know who they're going to. I want to get them where they need to go! This cannot be allowed, as per that contract!'

'Which we haven't signed,' said Rick, smirking. 'We'll deal with the marketing and sales; you rest your ageing body.'

'Bollocks,' said Harriston, loudly, his face a spectacular shade of red. 'I put up the money for these cars, I should have access to them. I need them!'

Rick passed the contract over to Fay. Harriston tried to snatch it away, but Fay was quicker and drew the documents quickly to her chest, out of his reach. She scribbled on the paper hastily, got up, and passed them to the notary. He was shaking his head and tutting quietly.

'Englishmen,' he said, just loudly enough to be heard.

Rick picked up a copy of Harriston's discarded facility agreement, waved it once to straighten the papers, and then tore it in half. He tossed the remnants towards Harriston, huffed, and shook his head. Harriston stood up and moved towards him, but Mike neatly stepped between the two and firmly grabbed Harriston's hand, forcing it into a shaking gesture.

'Very kind of you,' he said, still smirking.

'That's all in order,' said the notary over the kerfuffle. 'You can all go home now.'

The veins in Harriston's forehead were bulging, his muscles taut, his cheeks turning red with anger.

'Fuck you,' said Harriston. He slammed a palm down on the table, the noise making the windows rattle. 'Fuck you, and you lot as well.'

'Fine,' said the notary unexcitedly. 'We've all the documents and protocols in place. Chapman & Sunderland are now the effective owners of the Austrian Collection and are free to sell the cars on commission.'

Fay smiled thinly as she put her papers back into her briefcase. She nodded respectfully at Joseph, who doffed an imaginary cap to her in return.

The notary looked around, picked up the remaining unused paperwork, and stabbed it all into a shredder by his feet.

'Gentlemen,' he added, trying to keep a calm face. 'This meeting is over. And I'll be billing you forty thousand anyway. Good afternoon.'

Harriston pushed Rick away violently, into the wall, and stepped towards him, a fist raised. He swung, a quick and clean throw, but broadcast for too long. Rick shifted his body to the right smoothly, Harriston's fist contacting nothing but air.

'No you don't,' said Rick, trying to supress a laugh. Mike and Joseph just blinked, unsure what to do. Harriston roared, took a few paces back, and looked like he was going to explode.

'I will fucking destroy you!' he finally shouted, his feet stamping against the floor in frustration. He turned, his beady eyes locking on to Rick, Mike and Joseph in turn, and then he marched out of the room, his footsteps making the walls vibrate.

'I will fucking destroy you!' he shouted again, voice getting increasingly distant. 'It's my bloody car!'

'Interesting way of doing business,' said Fay, her soft voice knocking down the angst in the room several notches. 'Hopefully, the rest will be smoother. I'll speak to you later.'

She took a moment to shake the hand of everyone present, including the notary, and then left.

'Well,' said Mike.

'Drink?' said Joseph.

'Best thing I've heard in the past twenty minutes,' said Rick.

'Can I come?' asked the notary politely.

———————————— ● ————————————

Joseph ordered four large beers and gestured for Mike and Rick to join him at the bar of Café Tommaselli's, in Salzburg's Altstadt.

'Now that we can move the cars legitimately, I'll set about organising transport to the UK in earnest,' he said, quietly. 'But I believe it'd be best to send security with it.'

'What do you have in mind?' said Mike.

'Have someone follow the truck,' said Rick. 'Without the driver knowing.'

'I'd not considered that,' said Joseph.

'Fewer question marks,' said Rick. 'Any possibility of an armed escort?'

'Too many border crossings,' said Joseph. 'There's not that much leeway.'

'What about just surveillance with a hotline to the police, something along those lines,' said Mike, knocking the head off his beer.

'I can organise that,' said Joseph. 'It's a long drive to London and it's a serious amount of metal to be moving. You never know.'

'Okay, get to it, and we'll cover the costs,' said Mike, his index and middle finger on one hand alternately tapping against the tip of his thumb. 'And can you do the border carnets for us? It would be a great help. The cars will go into a bonded warehouse in the UK, so there's no tax involved.'

'Absolutely,' said Joseph, as he started to make his way back to the table.

Rick exhaled slowly and took a sip from his glass.

'Any thoughts about retirement, Mike?' he said, laughing.

'I think this job might kill me first,' said Mike, before downing his pint.

CHAPTER 20

As Mike cruised through London, towards his hotel, he watched the myriad brightly lit storefronts roll past. He wasn't interested in their contents, more just the fact that so much was on display, in the public eye, accessible to all. But when it came to automotive masterpieces, most were locked away. They weren't in the care of museums, or other important public places, and available. Instead, they were bought and sold by a select few, and mostly resided in private car collections around the world.

Most of those people, Mike thought, were unique in many ways. They didn't like to be seen or talked about. There were probably some 110 serious, important collectors out there, who could invest in assets commanding hundreds of millions. And focusing on individual brands, epochs, or styles, had become an increasingly prominent fashion among new collectors.

If the collections grew large enough, as was often the case in the US, they would typically become foundations, and then never be sold again. This, in turn, made some of the rare cars even more inaccessible, ramping up the prices of the ones left in circulation. This bolstered their appeal among the smart money people, because the lack of availability meant that owners could set their prices. If someone wanted one, they'd have to pay the requested rate.

But the last thing any collector wanted was to get screwed over by a classic car dealer or auction house. And if there was any hint of a problem, collectors would up and disappear in a shot. They might not care about the value of their cars, but they hated to lose money.

And they were careful with it, that much I can vouch for, thought Mike, keeping a watchful eye out for errant cyclists and pedestrians. *You never get a free lunch from a billionaire.*

———————— • ————————

He was conscious he was dreaming. The sunshine was that fraction too warm, too penetrating, the waves lapping the shore too perfect in their timing. But still, he couldn't help but love the feel of the white sand underfoot. He wandered over to a light blue boat house and opened the door. Inside, as he suspected, a Ferrari.

A 250 GT, a California Spider, he thought. *A rare Short Wheelbase one with the closed headlights.*

Mike looked at it for a while, taking in its curves, its resplendent deep-blue finish, and impeccable brightwork. He recognised the car; its aristocratic first owner was killed in a crash in it in the 1960s. It had only 5,000 miles on the clock and was secretly taken into custody by the old cook at the owner's mansion, who was obviously quite taken with it.

The car had been hidden for decades, the cook slowly piecing it back together. Once it was running, he would drive it at night along the sandy beaches nearby, sometimes getting stuck in the dunes. He never registered the car, and no one wanted it back. Slowly, the memory of it, for most, disappeared into the mists of time.

Mike reached instinctively for his phone, to ring some clients to view the car, when a helicopter appeared out of thin air, the scene around him shifting to the old mansion. A team of smartly dressed auctioneers flooded out from the helicopter, charging towards the beach. He tried to stop them, to hold them back, but paperwork and money was flowing around him, documents and details changing hands, everyone turning a blind eye to him.

He was sweating, he realised, his shirt soaked through.

How?! he thought, panicked. *How have they discovered my find?*

Mike tried to grab someone's attention. In the distance, he spotted a familiar face, lurking by a corner. An expert, someone he trusted, who had asked him obscure questions about the internal engine number of this long-forgotten Ferrari.

You! It was you! You bastard!

A hammer fell and Mike saw millions of dollars floating past his eyes, untouchable. But the auction catalogue failed to mention the cook, or the original owner, and none of the car's unpleasant past. Once that gavel fell, the sublime Ferrari, freshly painted, waxed, and fitted with gleaming new Borrani wire wheels, disappeared. But the ghosts of its past remained attached, destined to haunt its new owners ever more.

Mike saw the Ferrari accelerating towards him, its high beams flashing, blinding him, its engine getting louder and louder, until he could almost hear the thrash of every piece of its rotating assembly. The noise grew, deafening him, and his vision went black.

He sat bolt upright, sweat pouring from his forehead, and grasped the edge of his bed.

Jesus.

He took a moment, letting his breathing settle, and walked around the room, head in his hands. He couldn't remember where he was, which country, or what he was doing there.

Mike stumbled over to the desk and sluggishly opened his itinerary at an earmarked page. Most of the entries on the page had been crossed off, but one leapt out at him, like a train from a tunnel.

Monaco. Thurs. Ferrari, Cal Spider.

'Just a dream,' he said woozily. 'I hope.'

The first of the Ferraris from the Swiss collection was due to be delivered, as soon as was feasibly possible, to its new owner in Monaco. They hadn't provided an address for a house; instead, the entry Mike found in the sales system had pointed his online map at the Monaco harbour.

Of course it wasn't going to be easy, he thought, as he stared at the dull grey wall of the small interrogation room. *Still, Werner will be pleased. Paid for, delivered, done, just like that.*

The customs officer wandered back into the room, looking bored, and put down a stack of paperwork on the table. Mike could see his passport and insurance, along with a collection of paperwork documenting the Geneva-registered Ferrari 250 GT SWB California Spider he was driving.

Red, with a cream interior. A classic combination, and a metaphysical driving experience.

'All we are trying to ascertain,' said the officer, 'is that you are not smuggling this car into Italy.'

'I'm not sure I'd be so obvious about it,' said Mike jokingly. The official frowned at him and wrote something down.

'So, the car isn't yours?'

'No, as I mentioned, it belongs to a client. We are dealing with the sale for them, and the car is being delivered to Monaco, to its new owner.'

'Surely, something like this, you wouldn't drive?'

Mike nodded in agreement and put his hands on the table.

'Usually, I'd agree with you entirely. But, you see, we had a problem with a car that was transported recently. I don't want the same to happen again, so here I am.'

The officer nodded slowly, spreading all of the paperwork over the desk. Another official marched into the room, carrying presents that had been wrapped by Werner, for both Mike and the new owner. The bigger official tore through the delicate wrapping, inspected the contents of each box, and then dumped them ungraciously on the floor.

Charming, thought Mike. He rolled his eyes and sighed, slowly.

'Where do you drive with this car?' said the officer.

'Down to Monaco.'

'Is the owner Italian?'

'No. It is registered to a Swiss company from Geneva. I'm just delivering it to the harbour. Nothing else.'

The officer leaned back in his chair and studied Mike, staring at him.

'And you are paid for this?'

'No,' said Mike. He laughed briefly, then cleared his throat. 'I'm paying for this, basically, just to make sure it all happens properly.'

'Because you have had problems before.'

'Only once, recently. We had a car that went missing.'

'Stolen?'

'Yes,' said Mike, flatly. 'Another Ferrari.'

'I see,' said the officer, his pen flicking across paper. 'So, you're just doing this out of the good of your heart. Gratuito.'

'Yes. I want it done, and I want it done right.'

The officer looked unimpressed, flipped through the papers casually again, then stepped out of the room. An hour went by, the officer occasionally materialising again with new questions, seemingly intent on nothing but burning up Mike's time. Minutes became an hour, crept towards two. Mike made fists beneath the table, trying to supress the desire to bludgeon his way out of the office and get back on the road.

The older I get, the more I understand these bureaucratic processes, their behaviours. And yet, the less I feel able to say about it.

He sensed that the freedom of European borders, once celebrated for all the reputation they still enjoy today, were in the strictest sense gone and lost forever. The bureaucrats were back. In Italy, France and Germany, certainly, at the very least. Envious and politically small-minded people were taking over. But why were they doing it?

Power over individuals, he realised sadly. And then after that, everything over anyone who looked anything like a capitalist. Otherwise, how could you explain their oft-grotesque misjudgements of situations and people?

The responsibility must be laid at the door of the current politicians. They can't get away with such behaviour. It'll do us no favours in the long run.

Another hour and a half passed. The officer strolled back into the office, handed Mike his documents, and gestured to the door.

'Thanks,' said Mike flatly.

What a fucking waste of time.

Mike marched back to the Ferrari, its paint blazing away in the midday sun, the rich scent of its leather interior welcoming and warm. He gripped its steering wheel, knuckles flashing white for a moment, then paused.

Not a great idea to blaze off in someone else's Ferrari. Take a minute.

The dull drone of cars and trucks idling away at the border crossing was replaced by the staccato shrill of his phone ringing. He dragged it out of his pocket.

An unknown number. Great. Now what?!

'This is Mike,' he said firmly.

'Hi!' said a voice way too cheery for Mike's mood. 'I'm Ralph; I understand you have a Ferrari for sale?'

'Sixteen at the moment,' said Mike, perhaps a little too bluntly.

'The silver one.'

'There are three.'

'Ah, the one with the brown seats.'

Somewhere, a village is missing its idiot.

Mike tipped his head back and rested it on the leather piping of the seat back and hood cover.

'There are none with brown seats,' he said, slowly. 'But we have one, a 275 GTS, in an Argento and Crema combination. Is this the car?'

'Yeah, that's the one,' said Ralph happily. 'How much is it?'

'We generally require a little more before discussing values,' said Mike sternly.

'I'm buying it for a big customer. Real big. Very rich man.'

'Okay. What's their name?'

'No, I'm calling on their behalf, it needs to be private. I will put it in front of them, if we can sort something.'

'Fair enough. Where are they from?'

'Emirates. Very rich.'

At least that has some legs, thought Mike, his fingers tapping the top of the Ferrari's steering column.

'Can you at least give me a family name, so I have some idea of who we're dealing with? It might alter the proceedings.'

'No,' said Ralph. 'I need all the details, and he'll buy when he sees them.'

Mike rolled his eyes.

'I'll be very straightforward. If you introduce me, and the sale goes through, you'll get two-and-a-half percent of the sales price. That's it. But we must talk to the buyer and sell the car. Otherwise, we don't engage.'

'If I can't have any details, you'll lose this deal,' said Ralph, clearly annoyed.

'If you're so concerned, send them to view the car. I can pick them up from Heathrow, or wherever is convenient.'

'That's no good.'

'I thought that might be the case,' said Mike. 'After all, you've not actually got a customer to deal with, or protect, have you?'

'I have sold lots of classic cars in the Emirates, you will see,' said Ralph nervously. 'I am a rich man myself.'

'And my name's Mister Ralph. How about you just cut the bullshit and stop wasting my time?'

The line went very quiet.

'I mean, come on, what is your real business? How do you earn your living? Honestly.'

'I'm a taxi driver,' said Ralph quietly.

'Where?'

'Bangkok.'

Mike smirked, the traffic drifting through the border crossing catching his gaze for a moment.

'I sincerely suggest you stick to your business,' he said. 'And try something smaller, before you jump in at the deep end.'

'Why?'

'You get on the wrong end of one of these people, at this end of the scale, and there can be hell to pay. Save yourself the trouble.'

'Okay. Sorry.'

'You got it.'

Mike hung up, puffed his cheeks, shook his head, and started the Ferrari.

Sharks, he thought, as the Colombo V12 started to sing.

———————— ● ————————

After tackling the usual heavy traffic around Milan, Mike planned to dine on pasta and Moscato d'Asti, somewhere near or in Piedmonte. After, he'd drive the weaving motorway all the way down to Costa Liguria, a relaxing cruise, trying to avoid Genova.

When the Ferrari passed Alessandria, the day's temperature started to rise; Mike sang along to an old Supertramp song on the radio, his fingers lightly guiding the Ferrari's slender wood-rimmed Nardi wheel, the car responding gracefully and naturally to his commands.

A unique balance between sensuality and functionality, he thought. *Perfect.*

The twin exhausts purred as the Ferrari loped down the road, their tone becoming higher pitched and more intense as he wound the V12 out along the sweeping motorway bends on the Autostrada de Fiori. Through tunnels, as the tachometer climbed beyond 4,000rpm, the Ferrari created its own thunderstorm, every combustion stroke sending a melodic bark echoing along the road.

No better car on this trip. Just the thing to have at the Italian Riviera.

Gerry Rafferty's *Baker Street* rippled its way out of the Ferrari's old Becker Radio. He listened to it intently, the song distracting him from the Ferrari's own melody; aside from Baker Street's own famous Sherlock Holmes connection, the saxophone solo always fascinated Mike. It had originally been penned as a guitar part, but Rafferty was struggling to make it work with his people in the studio. Then saxophonist Raphael Ravenscroft came along, who was at the neighbouring studio at the time, and, curious, tried it. After hearing the playback, Rafferty immediately decided to keep it.

A great solo. A favourite. Intense, memorable, creative. Learnt a lot from that one.

A sign for Menton/Roquebrune-Cap-Martin flashed past and Mike nudged the Ferrari from the autoroute, down towards the town. He checked into his room at the Hotel Alexandra, greeted the detailer who would give the Ferrari a once-over before delivery, and sent the Monaco client a text, updating him on their status.

Can't wait, came the response.

'You're going to be over the moon,' said Mike, the sound of the V12 still ringing in his ears.

CHAPTER 21

There was only one man sitting outside the café. He looked to be in his fifties, with a friendly demeanour, and was dressed entirely in casual white marine clothing. He nodded as Mike approached and stood to greet him, moving with grace and ease.

'Mike,' he said quietly. 'Thank you for coming.'

'No trouble at all, Mr Bachmann. It's been a delight. It's around the corner.'

A smile spread across Bachmann's face. Mike escorted him to the Ferrari and Bachmann circled it respectfully, taking it in from every angle.

'You've fine taste,' said Mike, nodding. 'Would you like to hear it?'

Bachmann opened the driver's door and carefully lowered himself into the Ferrari's seat, a pensive yet concerned look on his face.

'First time?' said Mike.

'This is something new,' said Bachmann, laughing a little. 'Most of mine, well, they're fuel injected.'

Mike grinned at him and nodded appreciatively. 'Don't worry, this one's straightforward enough. It's warm; all you need to do is make sure it's in neutral, turn the key all the way, and pull the small switch for the fuel pump. Once that's stopped making a noise, push in the key to start it.'

Bachmann rocked the gear lever from side to side, slipped the Ferrari's svelte key into its ignition, and turned it. He flicked the fuel pump switch and listened until the quiet knock-knock-knock faded away. He looked at Mike, pushed the key inwards, and the V12 turned over, barked, and then settled into a smooth, refined idle.

'Now that,' said Bachmann eagerly, 'is really something.'

'Give it a rev,' said Mike, jutting his thumb upwards a few times. 'And push the fuel pump switch back in.'

Bachmann nervously squeezed the throttle pedal and the Ferrari's V12 responded snappily, with no hint of vibration. He grinned, dipping the pedal a few more times, listening to the Weber carburettors snorting happily.

'This is all part of the experience,' said Mike. 'It's living history, art with life, and driving something such as this is pure emotion. La Dolce Vita, as a sculpture.'

'I am looking forward to experiencing what those who drove this in the past experienced,' said Bachmann. 'My father will live his dreams, I think. And the paperwork?'

'In the glovebox, all of it, and the second key is in a storage box under the driver's seat. The history and Ferrari red book, and some gifts from the previous owner, are in the boot. I've filled the tank, too. Use only high-octane fuel and try to avoid anything with more than, say, five per cent ethanol in it. Less, preferably.'

Bachmann thanked him and waved at a man standing next to an imposing old S-Class.

A W220, and an S600 BiTurbo, thought Mike, looking at it. *That's a piece of machinery, too.*

The man strode over to them, carrying a small gunmetal case.

'This is for you, Mike.'

'Thank you, sir, but I believe the car has all been paid for.'

'This isn't about payment,' said Bachmann, a cordial smile on his face. 'You went to the effort to get the car here today, and that means I can give it to my father on his eighty-seventh birthday, later today.

This was always his dream and now, thanks to you, it will become a reality.'

Mike took the case without opening it, thanked his client very much for his generosity, and strolled over to the harbour elevators, the midday sun shining down on him pleasantly. He wandered back to the Hotel de Paris, ordered a Campari Orange on ice, and opened the box. There were five packages of new Euro notes. He carefully lifted one out and read the tag.

Ten thousand. Fifty thousand all in. Now that's a treat.

He downed the Campari and ordered some champagne.

I could hit the casino over the road. Put it all on red. For Ferrari.

'No, I'm not a casino person,' he said, chiding himself. 'The house always wins, eventually.'

Devil makes work for idle hands.

'But a little fun wouldn't go amiss.'

He pulled his phone from his pocket and picked out a contact.

'Hello Jean, it's Mike.'

'Ah, good to hear from you, Mike. What have you been up to?'

'I'm in Monaco right now. I'd stay and visit in earnest, but I've got to get moving soon.'

'Shame. You should spend a few days here with us in Menton.'

'Thanks. Consider it noted. But what I was wondering was if you've still got that Rolls-Royce I sold you years ago.'

'The 1969 Mulliner Park Ward Drophead?'

'Yes, we've still got it. It's been a great car.'

Mike smiled.

'Consider it sold.'

'I think you might have to pry it from my wife's fingers, if you really want it that badly.'

'I've got to go to Turin this afternoon, then Paris, so I'd need to do it soon. But I can soften the blow.'

'Will my wife like it?'

'It's a beautiful low-mileage 2007 Bentley Continental GTC.

Powder blue, very striking. And a lot more usable and capable. And, yes, still a convertible.'

'A bit more modern, for sure,' said Jean, not sounding convinced.

'It is. It's also in superb condition and finding one like it would be hard to repeat.'

'You want that Rolls-Royce back that badly?'

'I do.'

'And the Bentley?'

'It's in London but it is left-hand drive. Perhaps you can visit me, and I'll get you all sorted in it. You can make it a family trip to London.'

'It's good to hear from you, but this wasn't quite what I was expecting, or planning on,' said Jean. Mike could hear someone moving around in the background, the occasional snippet of French drifting down the line.

'Can you put something on top of that?' said Jean.

'The Bentley, plus, say, twenty thousand Euros.'

'We could do that,' said Jean.

'But I'll need a lift, too,' said Mike. 'Can you bring it to the Hotel de Paris? I'll give you a lift back. Menton is in the right direction for me, anyway.'

'Cover the fuel?'

Mike laughed. 'Sure, fine.'

What was that about free lunches?

'Okay,' said Jean. 'We'll see you in front of the Hotel de Paris in about half an hour, with paperwork.'

———————•———————

The deal was to Mike's taste: uncomplicated and quick. The drive back along the Autoroute de Fleurs, however, was anything but rapid. It had been a long time since he'd been in his trusted 1969 Rolls-Royce drophead, and it felt very different to the Ferrari. But, that said, it was still enjoyable, just in its own way.

Mike had driven the car along the Corniche many times in earlier years, when he was engaged with the Cannes film festival. That was long ago, when the car was called Bluebelle, because of her lovely bright blue colour, and she was everybody's darling around Cannes and Antibes. The smell of the black Connolly leather of the sixties was gorgeous, and it was still there, adding to the positive experience. The engine still ran unbelievably smoothly, and the car still tracked and rode beautifully, just like it always had. As the miles ticked by, he felt a tall wave of happiness sweeping over him.

Driving Bluebelle for over three hours along the coast put Mike in zen mode. He had always liked the long-distance drives across the continent in his much-loved Rolls-Royce, especially through warm Italy and France, and he thought himself happier behind the wheel of this car than with any other car in his life. There were so many good memories lived in this cockpit, and so many good ideas developed in Bluebelle.

All the best thoughts, and the best experiences, he mused, *while driving.*

He watched the Mediterranean landscape sweep past in the sunset light and, enjoying himself, took a new route, after Alessandria, to weave around Milan. The combined sensation of a good deal done, and a fine day's enjoyment, was making him giddy, buoying his spirits.

When he finally arrived at the Hotel Piemonte Palace in the little town of Vercelli, he parked the car in a secure space near the hotel's kitchen. He let the Rolls-Royce idle, cooling off after its long trip, and thumbed through his itinerary.

Tomorrow, France, up to Paris. Some 500 miles, give or take. Ten hours. Maybe I'll meet Marcel Lammers, somewhere in the centre.

———————⬤———————

Mike strolled along the streets of Vercelli, enjoying the hubbub of the evening. The town was ancient and a popular tourist destination, so inviting cafes and restaurants were everywhere. He found one that took his fancy, settled down at the bar, and placed an order with the merry-looking owner.

There was only one seat left in the restaurant, at the tables, and the waiter asked if Mike would be comfortable joining a couple who were already partway through their meal. They waved at him invitingly, so he nodded, and wandered over to join them.

The woman raised a glass to him as he sat down. 'I'm Sofia, this is David.'

'Mike,' he said. 'Where are you from?'

'Zurich,' said David. 'Yourself?'

'England. I'm out here on business.'

'Anything fun?' said Sofia.

Mike accepted a glass of red wine from a waiter and took a long slug of it, savouring its full-bodied nature and rich aftertaste.

Must be a Merlot or, even better, an Amerone from the Veneto region, he thought, nodding approvingly.

'For once, yes,' he said, smiling. 'I just delivered a Ferrari to a collector here, so it's been quite the pleasant trip.'

'Are you a dealer?' said David, as he pushed his pasta around his plate.

'Yes, for my own company. We deal with a lot of Italian classics, among others.'

'That must be interesting,' said Sofia. 'What's it like?'

'Well, you meet a lot of interesting people, and see a lot of interesting places, that's for sure.'

'We're collectors, too,' said David. 'Art, though. There's an auction house here and we're aiming to buy a few pieces tomorrow.'

'Are they like art collectors, car collectors?' said Sofia.

'I would say so, for the most part,' said Mike. 'Plenty of old-school collectors, lots of inherited wealth, lots of hoarders.'

'Sounds like a few people we know,' said David.

'People hoard cars?' said Sofia, surprised.

'Oh, yes. About twenty-eight years ago, for example, I discovered a collection of a hundred and forty-three cars under an old toy factory in Belgium. Bugattis, Alfas, Maybachs, you name it. The owner was ninety-three.'

'That's incredible,' the couple responded simultaneously.

'It was. No one knew about it, either. There was an old Nazi-built facility under his factory, and he'd stashed all his cars in there.'

'You're kidding?' said David, aghast.

'No, and it gets better, too. There was all sorts down there, including an armoured train, a Messerschmidt 262, a record-breaking plane called the Weisse 9, you name it.'

'How fascinating,' said Sofia. 'How did that all come to be?'

'Ah, we only found out later. It transpired that the owner's father had been involved in manufacturing military hardware, namely hugely secretive German acoustic homing torpedoes, and some parts for the V2 rocket motors. There was some underground storage beneath the factory already, but it had been expanded, extended, to accommodate wartime needs.'

'He just upped and casually got involved in making weaponry at some point?' said David, confused.

'They had a lot of experience in sophisticated machining and engineering, from all their small-scale work. Easily and readily transferrable skills, seemingly. Rumour has it that they even made some of the complex wheel cascade decoders, too. Garnette, his name was. Largely forgotten, I think.'

'But how did it all remain hidden?' said Sofia. 'Someone must have got in there before you?'

'We only knew of one access point, and that was this vast iron door, deep inside the factory. But parked in front of it was a 1937 Krauss-Maffei halftrack. Fifteen tonnes, I figure. And it hadn't run, or moved, for decades. No one was getting in without a fight.'

'How did all the cars end up there, then?'

Mike nodded. 'Well, after 1945, Garnette took care of the military equipment of the Allies, and simply started confiscating cars from Germans. He kept the most interesting and sold the others to GIs. It's said that the most famous S-Wagen Kompressor Mercedes ever went through his hands, along with some of the best chain-drive cars, such as the Blitzen Benz Kettenwagen.'

'Beyond me,' said David. 'What's that kind of thing worth?'

'Well, among the pieces he kept were a Mercedes-Benz SSK, and an ultra-rare SSKL. Easily worth, I'd say, forty to fifty million dollars, in today's market. Or more.'

'And the family didn't know a thing?' said Sofia.

'That's right,' said Mike. 'I couldn't talk to them initially.'

'So, what happened to the collection?' said David, intrigued.

'Inevitably, he died. And when it became clear that many of the cars were stolen, like a 1938 Mercedes 540K Cabriolet A from a German industrial family, they were legitimately confiscated.'

'Did anything make it out?' said Sofia, as she poured more wine into Mike's glass.

'The family ended up appointing a lawyer who had been authorised to sell off anything remaining. He was crooked, though, a real scammer. The money disappeared, and a lot of the cars never made it to their new owners.'

'Did you buy anything from it?' said David.

'We got away with the Messerschmitt and a 1937 Maybach SW 38 Cabriolet Transformation by Hebmueller. Both are currently being restored by my friend in Bremen. The 262 might fly, next year, if he gets permission.'

'Let me guess: he's also a collector?' she said, smiling.

'Yes,' said Mike, returning a broad grin. 'He also owns the German Kaiser's motor yacht, which he discovered in a dilapidated condition in an old dry dock in Holland. It was given to him for free, just to clear the docks. He transported it on a shaky World War Two U-Boat pontoon all the way down to Bremen.'

'That doesn't sound easy,' said David.

'It wasn't. I still admire him for taking it on.'

'Best to give these things a shot when they turn up,' said Sofia. 'You never know what might happen.'

'And you're never going to look back and wish you hadn't transported some fine historic automobile home on the back of a ragged pontoon, are you?' said David, confidently. 'That's a once-in-a-lifetime thing.'

'Exactly,' said Mike. 'More wine?'

CHAPTER 22

The Parisian taxi driver's head bobbed back and forth as he repeatedly stabbed the throttle, then the brake pedal, of his battered Peugeot. Mike patted him on the shoulder and pointed at their destination, a cheap hotel on the corner of a road near Porte de Versailles. Time was of the essence. Bluebelle had been left in an underground public car park nearby, and Mike was grateful for not having to tackle the rush-hour snarl-ups in it.

He breathed a sigh of relief as the taxi finished bludgeoning its way through the evening's traffic and deposited him outside a drab-looking building that overlooked the convention centre. He asked the driver to wait, charged through reception, booked a room, dumped his luggage, and rushed back down to the foyer. The taxi was waiting patiently, and Mike leapt back into his still-warm seat and directed the driver to take him to Rue de Faubourg Saint-Denis.

The taxi ground to a halt in traffic a few minutes from the street, so Mike flung some Euros at the driver and hit the pavement. He walked, at a brisk pace, glancing at his Daytona, until he reached Julien Bouillion, a beautiful and once-famous art deco restaurant. An attendant opened the door for him, sweeping his arm in the direction of the restaurant's waiting area gracefully.

An arm shot up from a table near the back of the restaurant and Mike weaved his way through the tables, smiling.

'Just,' he said, catching his breath for a moment. 'Just about made it.'

'Evening, Mike,' said Marcel Lammers. 'Glad you could make it, especially at this notice.'

'Anything to catch up with you. I've heard you have some news,' he said tentatively.

'There is, yes. But first?' said Marcel, opening the menu.

Mike sat down and straightened his jacket. He took a moment to admire his surroundings, his heart still racing a little, and took a deep breath.

'Been a while since I've been here,' he said, raising his eyes to the ceiling. 'Always liked it.'

Marcel nodded at him, and then at a waiter, who dashed over to their table.

'Crabs. Not frozen. Melted butter. White toast, please.'

A wine waiter appeared alongside the other. 'Pommery, Moet? A cocktail, perhaps?'

'Two glasses of pink champagne first,' said Marcel. 'And you, Mike?'

'That's good with me. And I'll have the escargots de Bourgogne, foie gras toast, and oeufs durs mayonnaise.'

Marcel watched the waiters depart, rolled his head around, and then leant towards Mike, his elbows resting on the table.

'I have found a real Bugatti chassis,' he whispered. 'In America.'

'What do you think it is?'

'A Type 41, a Royale prototype. Car number 100.'

'The one crashed by Ettore Bugatti,' said Mike incredulously.

'Yes. It's been repaired but you can see that the front end has been repaired. It's definitely the car Ettore crashed shortly before it reached the French Salon de l'Automobile in Paris, 1930.'

'Is there any other evidence?'

'I've checked it against the pictures from the crash. I'm confident,' he said, and raised his glass to Mike.

Mike clinked his glass against Marcel's, the champagne fizzing merrily.

'That must have been a bad moment,' said Mike. 'Didn't it have a Packard body at the time, for testing?'

Marcel nodded. 'At least four different bodies. Here is what we know. Chassis number 100, which was the first to be registered, has carried not only the Packard prototype body, but also the Coupe Fiacre, the Double Berline, the Weymann, that's the one with the beautiful Hermes trunk in the back, and later maybe another one.'

'No clues on the order of that?'

'Not currently. But Ettore crashed the chassis with the Weymann body on it.'

Mike was shaking his head, impressed.

'There might have been even more bodies made in the series,' said Marcel. 'Six Royales were made in the series, all numbered with the prefix 41, plus the prototype. But we know of at least 11 bodies being mounted.'

'And no one knows about that?'

'Not anyone I've found so far. Some discarded bodies have been reused, too. The Fiacre one, for example, that became the Berline de Voyage.'

'What a mess,' said Mike. 'But a fascinating one. Is it still in America?'

'It is. They want quite a lot of money for it.'

'I dread to think, but how much is it? And who verified it?' said Mike cautiously.

'French Bugatti experts that I know,' said Marcel.

Mike tipped his head and pursed his lips.

'As it's you, I'm going to speak openly,' he said. 'The chassis is a fabulous find but to make it a car, well, there's a lot of other parts you're going to have to find.'

'I'm a few steps ahead,' said Marcel. 'I have a prototype engine with three spark plugs per cylinder, a front axle, and the four brake drums. There are two wheels, the left ones, and a lot of little stuff, that you need to detail the car. The gearbox is not a problem, I have found one in New Zealand. I could rebuild the whole car in three to four years, with your financial help.'

'Have you got original drawings?'

'Yes,' said Marcel. 'Some original, others are copies from the Trust. That's how we found out the prototype chassis is seven centimetres shorter than the later cars.'

'And I'm guessing the prototype engine was derived from the Bugatti airplane, which is why it has three plugs, not two.'

Marcel grinned. 'Correct. It has two ignition systems, including a magneto. But the series production cars only had a conventional ignition system.'

Mike bit his lip. 'Let me mull it over. Another two or three million on top of what you pay for the chassis and the other bits, and you might have a going concern.'

Marcel's chin dipped slightly, then he looked down at his Patek Philippe Calatrava watch.

'But what a car to rebuild,' he said. 'A once-in-a-life-time chance, no?'

Marcel's sensitive eye caught Mike looking at the bubbles in his Champagne glass.

'I'll get to the point,' he said, lifting his own glass. 'We'll need up to 12 million, I figure.'

He looked with big, innocent Bambi eyes at Mike.

'I'm sorry,' said Mike, catching his breath. 'You want us to finance the purchase and rebuild of chassis number 100, if you settle on a body for it.'

'I've got someone in Holland, called Frank, lined up already,' said Marcel excitedly. 'He's a great man with lots of Bugatti knowledge, and the right associates to get the job done.'

'And you're sure it's original?' said Mike hesitantly.

'One hundred per cent. This could be a big deal, Mike. It's worth getting in on. Think of the attention it could bring to you.'

Mike huffed. 'It's tempting. But I'll need a couple of weeks to consider it. We've a lot going on right now, and what happens in that time dictates what we might be willing to spend.'

'I can promise you that time. You are a good friend, after all, and I know you will not mess me around. I will call you in, let's say, three weeks, and we go from there.'

'And here was me, thinking it would just be dinner.'

Marcel laughed heartily and spread his arms.

'And that's on you, right?' he added, hiding a smile.

———————————•———————————

Mike leant back in his chair, his plate clean and the table now empty, as the waiter refilled his glass with ice-cold champagne.

So, he thought, *that just happened.*

A restoration project is rarely straightforward. One involving a Bugatti Royale, however, is on another level altogether. A big challenge, in terms of time, expertise, and resources.

This Bugatti expert he's got lined up, he needs to know what he's doing.

Half an hour later, and feeling the champagne somewhat more significantly, Mike reluctantly paid the bill and wandered outside. The street was filled with activists, all wearing yellow vests and marching along. Mike walked rapidly along the Faubourg without getting noticed or having things thrown at him, to his relief.

Further down, more yellow vests appeared on both sides of the street, smashing in windows of fashion shops and supermarkets. Yellows seemed to appear everywhere, and sprung up at junctions and roundabouts, halting cars and trucks. Taxis, and the police, were conspicuous by their absence, leaving anything parked, or not bolted down, an easy target.

Good thing I'm not in a Rolls-Royce, he thought. *Or the Cadillac.*

Back in his hotel room, peace remained elusive. The television in the room next door was cranked up, footsteps pounded on the floor above, and the heat in the room was brutal. Mike fiddled with the windows, but someone had painted over the frames time and time again, jamming the sliding frames in place. He opened a warm bottle of beer and sighed.

A ruckus kicked off outside and Mike heard breaking glass stabbing through the walls of the hotel. A single yell became a barrage, and other shouts came back at it, growing louder and more numerous.

His phone rang, its rising tone finally making itself audible to Mike over the sound of the chaos below.

'The Austrian Collection's in Buckingham,' said Rick, his voice trouble-free, and loaded with satisfaction. 'We're all good.'

'That's fantastic,' said Mike, sharing his relief. 'All the madness is over here, I think, judging by the madness in the streets.'

'I saw some of that earlier,' said Rick. 'Headline stuff; dustmen, Metro, taxi drivers, all on strike, and all those guys in the yellow vests. Pretty rough, it looks.'

'But what do they actually want?' said Mike, confused. 'There isn't a single shop or car that wasn't smashed up, for one thing. It's a hell of a mess.'

'Don't know,' said Rick. 'Political crap, I guarantee it.'

'Less Europe could be better, sometimes, I think. Maybe, maybe not.'

'I read that story about that Fechtel bloke you mentioned, too,' said Rick. 'The face, that I remembered. He stopped by here once, didn't he, in a Lancia 037?'

'That's the one.'

'When you said he worked on wind farms, I thought you meant he was just a manager, or something like that. Turns out he was involved with the monetary side of things, too. Financing, grants, that kind of stuff.'

'If there's one thing that'll get people riled up, it's money,' said Mike.

'Amen to that.'

Sirens began to pierce the wall of Mike's hotel room, and he heard the hubbub outside diminishing slowly, the people scattering into the alleys, the side streets, into the dark. A vehicle ripped through the street below, its tyres squealing as it lurched to a halt. Mike heard doors popping open, and boots hitting the ground.

'Just take care of yourself,' said Rick.

CHAPTER 23

The wine had set Mike's mind going, memories of France flooding every waking moment. He rested on the edge of his bed, closed his eyes, and reflected on his experiences. Of all the amazing places he had experienced over the years, his most fond memories were of France in the seventies.

He leaned back and exhaled, visions of France's La Nouvelle Vague art films in his head. Although most of the films were produced in the sixties, their full impact was only really felt in the following decade. They opened the door to an inspiring new world for him, one full of surprise and delight. French cinema in those days exuded freedom, romance and beauty, and Paris, with its beautiful cars, wide boulevards, soft street lighting and busy traffic whirling past always-open cafés and restaurants, was its unforgettable backdrop, especially so in the rain.

The soundtrack to this magical scene was relaxing, captivating, soul-stirring jazz. It ebbed from the jukeboxes of countless bars and bistros, the familiar and popular *Take Five* by the Dave Brubeck Quartet rippling out of the more modern and crowded establishments.

Stunning cars, old even back then, could still be easily found on every corner, too. Mike and his friends would sit for hours at Café de Flore, observing the thousands of battered Citroëns, Delahayes, Talbots, Alfas, Simcas, Renaults and Peugeots racing down the Boulevard Saint-Germain. They felt like they were right in the centre of the world, right on the cusp of a brighter, freer future.

For Mike, France in the early seventies felt like the sixties he had always heard about, and every so often he would make his way down there in search of art, adventure, joy and total freedom. He loved the cars, too; every one seemed to be portrayed in French cinema as if it were a character of its own, with its own spirit, while every frame seemed to capture the existential spirit of the time.

French cars' headlights were still yellow back then, as they had been since the late 1930s. They painted the whole country in an enchanting glow, especially on foggy nights. He loved the yellow lights and still lamented their EU-legislated disappearance in 1993. Some things he didn't miss so much, like the old franc notes. They were large, like hand towels, and a pain to deal with. Old and new existed side-by-side, confusingly, which no one really seemed to care about.

Mike rested his head on a pillow and stretched out his arms and fingers, the alcohol coursing through his veins. A pair of Citroën Traction 15CV Sixes and a 1934 Citroën Rosalie sprung into his mind; two cars he had bought for a bundle of old francs in 1976. He found them while filling up his bike at a Total service station just outside Dijon. Behind the pump house was a little scrapyard where cars were just waiting to be taken away to the crushers. While negotiating a price, and struggling to keep control of a huge bundle of old francs, some new francs got mixed in and then quite suddenly he'd struck a deal.

No idea how much I actually paid, he thought. *Was it more than five hundred, or less? Who knows. The owner didn't care, that's for sure. Ça va bien!*

None of the cars drove, which was a bit of a disaster, and entailed digging out a tractor to pull them around, the weather icy and cold. His efforts did not go unnoticed, and he was rewarded with an ancient Peugeot 402 limousine on top for fifty old francs. The price wasn't outrageous, but it was another logistical headache.

None of these things had any value at the time. But they just had to be saved.

Aged only 16, Mike relied on his trusty Zündapp 50cc water-cooled motorbike to rattle back and forth between Germany and France. It helped keep costs down and was an adventure in itself. In the summer, he'd sleep outside; in the winter, he'd relent and pay for youth hostels along the way. He always felt like a homeless wanderer, the proverbial French clochard, but on wheels.

Maybe I still am.

Back at the same garage, he celebrated his new acquisitions with lots of wine and Armagnac, with the suitably cheerful proprietor. Perhaps a bit too much alcohol for a 16-year old, his head woozy as the conversation turned to films. It seemed like everybody talked about cinema back then. They discussed François Truffaut, Éric Rohmer, Claude Chabrol, Louis Malle, Jean-Pierre Melville, and more.

My favourites. The Nouvelle Vague.

There was also a glorious 1946 Buick Roadmaster Convertible parked in the garage below. It was black with a red leather interior and was used daily by Le Patron. The kind of car that you love to see, and desire to own, but it's just too expensive at the time. Sadly, it disappeared, and he never saw one as good as it again.

After sleeping on the garage floor, he was shown other scrapyards around the Dijon area. They took the Roadmaster and the owner drove so fast he scared him half to death. Everybody showed him pretty much all they had, and he saw some huge agricultural buildings and old factories full of pre-war cars; blue race cars, staff cars, a lot of military stuff the Americans had left behind after the war. New engines still in their cradles, boxes full of parts and generators, and even some Sherman tanks and howitzers.

He was acutely conscious then, and the memory still stung him somewhat, that he couldn't identify all the beautiful cars he saw at the time. But he remembered the names: Delaugère et Clayette, Chenard-Walcker, Clément-Bayard, Aérocarène, Amédée Bollée, Brasier, Delamare-Deboutteville, and more. Even Talbot-Lago was new to him, back then.

One steel factory harboured an imposing violet-blue streamlined Delahaye 135 drophead, shaped a bit like a beluga whale, with an odd, almost proboscis-like nose. Unfortunately, it had been too dark to take a picture. It had a beautiful transparent steering wheel and even the switches were all translucent.

And then there was the crazy art deco Panhard et Levassor Dynamic with the steering wheel in the middle. Unsold from new, neglected, and finally scrapped after being left in the open for decades; its engine was the reputedly feeble Knight unit that had long since seized up in the cold.

'Ne roule pas, monsieur. Desolé,' he recalled, the memory of his fingertips tracing down the edge of the Panhard's elegant front wings sharp in his mind. Some of the cars were so strange and bizarre they appeared to have fallen straight from another planet, absolute wonders that would stop anyone in their tracks.

There was one thing they all had in common, though: layers of dust that had built up over the decades, and a distinct lack of recognition or love. Some were totally neglected, sitting outside in the open fields, their metals rusting away, their fluids seeping into the ground.

And that's still the case, for many. Until I find them.

He said to the yard owner that he could very easily imagine Jean Gabin or Lino Ventura sitting behind the wheel of any one of them in a war movie. The owner was so amused that, to the downfall of Mike's liver, he invited him in for red wine and pastis, bolstered by countless Gauloises sans filtre.

One thing from it all: there was a whole world out there, just waiting.

The one that stuck was the Delahaye 135. He made his way back to it, eventually, but it had long since been sold to a US buyer, while the Bugattis had also found a home in France, in a certain Schlumpf collection near Mulhouse.

Wish I had a photo. Maybe it was a Figoni et Falaschi Narval. Maybe.

'Phony and Flashy,' he said to himself, and laughed.

Good times.

CHAPTER 24

The 1969 Rolls-Royce Drophead whispered along pleasantly as Mike pulled into Calais. He made his way to the Hotel Metropole, near the harbour, and made himself comfortable at the bar, and then checked his phone. A few messages came and went, then he felt a hand on his shoulder.

'Mike, glad you could make it,' said a crisp, confident voice.

'A pleasure, Tom. What are you here in today?'

'Ah, a 1946 Alfa Romeo 6C 2500 SS, as you do. And I see you're back in Bluebelle?'

Mike smiled at him. 'Yup. Ended up with some spare change, so took the opportunity.'

'Good. The good ones are hard to come by. Always nice to see a Corniche.'

Mike tutted at him and waggled a finger. 'Come on, Tom, you know it's a pre-Corniche. That only came in in '71, and she's a '69.'

'Fine, fine, okay. Yes, it's always nice to see a Mulliner Park Ward Drophead Coupé. Thank you for reminding me. Anyway, to cut to the chase, I need your help.'

'You? Not what I expected,' said Mike, surprised.

'I've got a truck coming in with five 300SLs on it. From Germany, of course. They've got to go through the stupid Brexit-induced customs loops, and then they're being delivered to another dealer, and then they're going on from there to a client in Asia.'

Tom stopped, ordered a beer, and caught his breath.

'And, really, I could just do with some assistance on the logistics and paperwork front. I thought that might be something Rick could help with, too.'

'Well, we have a fair bit on, but I'm sure there's something we can do to assist. You didn't need to come all this way, though, for that.'

'I didn't. I'm just here to meet the Mercedes but, you know, easier to sound something out in person.'

'Knock the details out in an email and copy Rick in, and we'll go from there,' said Mike. 'You bearing up alright, otherwise?'

'It's not what it used to be. These new regulations are making things more difficult. And the money transfer rules. Everything now has to go through special Government commissions who will examine the big transfers for any sign of money laundering.'

'And, naturally, it ends up taking ages to send money to places such as Asia, and back again.'

'Exactly,' said Tom, shaking his head. 'Customs are another nightmare.'

'Funny how nobody seems to care about the banks transferring vast sums to all and sundry, left right and centre, eh? I wonder how much money flowing out of Moscow today is legitimate, as a case in point.'

'Quite. And then there are the loons who pretend they are buying cars when they don't have the money to actually do so. I've dealt with more than I care to remember this month.'

Mike raised a fist, annoyed, and rapped it on the bar. 'Yup. We've had our fair share of scammers this month. Amazing how big a game some can talk, and the lengths they go to, and for what?'

'Just to tie up your resources, or block a sale, some kind of sick game,' said Tom. 'Or they're trying to weevil their way into your bank accounts, some way or another. It's a shame we don't have more time to track them down. I'm sure they'd not like us burning through their time.'

'Have a look at this,' said Mike, as he slid his phone across the bar. 'It's from Rick; a guy was trying to buy a 1962 Flying Spur from him. He paid a deposit, then pulled the money, and then said it was a mistake. Turns out he did the same to two other dealers, hence this.'

Tom went quiet as he read, a smile breaking out, growing with intensity as he went from line to line.

'Your address is a hovel at the end of some Australian dirt road,' he said, reading a chunk of the message aloud. 'I hope your outhouse has a door on it so people can't see you pleasuring yourself as you get your jollies wasting other people's time. Arsehole.'

'A village missing its idiot, for sure,' said Mike. 'Another?' he added, gesturing at their empty glasses.

Tom nodded and the barman set about recharging them. 'And then there are the fakes.'

Mike's heart stopped for a moment.

'Those knocked-up supposed early Ferraris and Porsches, Jaguars, anything that's supposed to have racing heritage. A proper nightmare, all that copied stuff.'

'Tell me about it,' said Mike, grimacing.

'So many chassis numbers on Porsches and Mercedes 300SLs are wrong. Sometimes, they even exist twice, or even three times. Even more modern GT2 Porsches, same deal. One guy has original paperwork, the other has the original frame but no paperwork.'

'I understand the 300s are similar,' said Mike.

'The SLs? Yeah. I prefer cars without any ifs and buts, like the ones coming in today. Only clean, proven, original history. No stories. Full stop. I don't tolerate a single car with a questionable chassis in our showroom.'

'And you're right to do so. You don't need those shadows hanging over you. You seen any Ferrari replicas in recent history, perchance?'

'Nah, nothing good. The ones that I've seen recently, they're obvious from a mile away. Why, want one?'

'No,' said Mike, laughing. 'But we do have some good Ferraris coming in soon, including a GTO and a 250 LM. Something that could be up your street?'

'If they've got good histories, send me the chassis numbers and one clean shot. I'll do the rest myself.'

'Works for me. I'm heading back to the office soon, so let's keep in touch. They're all in a warehouse, in the UK, so you can come and have a look whenever.'

'Right,' said Tom, firmly. 'And don't forget those chassis numbers, and the paperwork I need for the SLs.'

'Don't worry,' said Mike reassuringly. 'I'll do it when I get into the Tunnel. Don't worry about anything: just leave it to me.'

———————————•———————————

Mike's phone rang and rang as the Rolls-Royce sailed away from Folkstone. He fumbled for his Bluetooth earpiece but the phone stopped ringing before he could answer. And then it rang again, seemingly more loudly and urgently than before.

Sounds like trouble, but then it always does.

He pressed the receive call button and was immediately barraged by an outburst from Rick, his voice strained.

'Harriston, the absolute trotting bastard, has taken our cars from the bonded warehouse!'

'I'm sorry,' said Mike, 'what the hell do you mean?'

'The cars, the Austrian Collection, gone!' shouted Rick.

Mike stamped on the brake pedal and stabbed the Rolls-Royce's hazard warning light switch, and brought the car screeching to a halt at the side of the road, the front brakes locking for a moment and leaving thick, greasy marks on the Tarmac.

'I'm sorry, from the warehouse?'

'Yes, from the bloody warehouse, Mike. Are you even listening?!'

'Well excuse me, for Pete's sake, I just can't even begin to comprehend. How is that possible?'

'I've only managed to raise someone with half of their wits around them, so far. Seems he showed registrations and sales documents, in his name, and presumably a few stacks of cash, too.'

'And the trackers?'

'No joy. They've all been left behind, and they're all still on. But it's a lucky turn, for us. It means no one else knows the cars have moved.'

Fuck. A break.

'Have you called Harriston?' said Mike.

'No, I thought I'd write him a polite bloody letter. Of course I've called him. He might as well not exist, though.'

'We've got to find out what's going on,' said Mike, gritting his teeth. 'Even if the trackers are still showing the cars to be where they should, if the owners find out their cars are gone, they'll go ballistic.'

'What the family thinks about the situation is a moot point to me. We need those cars back, as soon as possible. We've got one missing Ferrari already; we don't need several bloody more.'

'I'll try and raise him,' said Mike. 'Otherwise, it might have to be a politely worded email, at least to get a paper trail going.'

What the hell is he playing at? Why has he taken the cars?!

'I figure we've got a few days,' said Rick starkly. 'After that, it's only a matter of time before someone slips up, asks what's happening with the cars, or any number of things. Either way, we'll be in a whole fucking heap of trouble. If we can't get them back, no one else is going to venture into a deal with us. We might as well shut up shop, at that point.'

'Let's try and get on top of this,' said Mike calmly. 'I'll send an email to Harriston to start proceedings, to try and find out what he is up to, and we'll both work on getting those cars back into that warehouse.'

'Say whatever you have to say to him, Mike,' said Rick slowly. 'I'm not sure it'll have any effect.'

———————————— • ————————————

The Rolls-Royce was pulling a bit to the left, Mike noticed, as he set off back down the road. The sudden deluge of action seemed to have caused one of the calipers a bit of strife, or a drum, and now the car was making its displeasure known. He found himself patting the dashboard, an apologetic gesture to soothe Bluebelle's spirit, and wondered how long it would be until he smelled hot friction material.

He didn't have long to think before his phone rang again, and he resisted the temptation to just throw it out of the window. Fleetingly, he wondered if it would survive the fall, and maybe that the last thing it broadcast would be the sound of an 18-wheeler flattening it, terminating the call with extreme prejudice.

You never know, it could be good news.

He answered and the familiar voice of Chiara slipped into his ear.

'Ciao, Michele. Rick tells me you have a problem.'

'He did?' said Mike, confused.

'Well, hot Italians, maybe I was just the first thing that sprang to mind.'

Mike didn't respond.

'Thinking of Julie?' she said, reading his mind. 'She's talked about you a fair bit, you know. Anyway, Rick and I, well, he knows I have people who might know people, so he spoke to me first. He just wants to protect you, to get it sorted.'

Always has. It's one of the reasons we get on so well, he thought.

'Do you have any insight?' said Mike, grateful for the change of tack.

'Rick tells me that you think it's a Lord Harriston, and whoever else he might be tied up with.'

'That's what it seems like.'

'Syndicates?'

'I don't know. He's sharp, for sure, and not a casual business partner, but he seemed straightforward enough, and reputable.'

'Rick tells me you have problems with another Ferrari, too. Is that Harriston as well?'

'I don't think so. That was before all this and seems a bit more involved. Someone put a lot of effort into it.'

'But all car people, though.'

'Knowing what they've taken, and how they've done it, definitely.

But this new smash 'n' grab, that must have been Harriston. Few knew what we were doing.'

'Do you think it's someone putting him in the obvious spotlight, perhaps?' said Chiara. 'A lot of people have a lot of issues with him.'

'I don't think so. We had a fallout in Salzburg over the acquisition of the cars.'

'We've had a lot of trouble recently with organisations from Shanghai and Hong Kong. They go after our wine collections, in Italy and France. Big heists, utterly fearless, beautifully organised, I must admit.'

'And cars?' said Mike hesitantly.

'Everything, everywhere, for those with the right funding. There are groups out there everywhere, Mike. We've just lost a huge amount to a wind farm scam, of all things, from Denmark. That's over one hundred million Euros we won't see again.'

'Denmark,' said Mike, flatly. 'That's come up a bit, recently.'

You have to wonder what it's all about, don't you, he thought, recalling the American's accent. *Fechtel.*

'Mathias Fechtel. Do you know him?'

'Yes, I know him, vaguely. Pleasant man. He was arranging some of the engineering and financial aspects of our mooted wind farm deal. Pretty far down the chain.'

'He's dead,' said Mike. 'Shot in Peschiera del Garda, the other day. I'd done a little business with him. Read about it in the paper.'

'Mathias is dead?'

'Very,' said Mike. 'But, you know, thinking about it, I introduced him to Harriston, at an auction, many moons ago. Fechtel wanted to meet him, to discuss legislation and business in that field.'

Mike heard voices in the background, footsteps scurrying away.

'You say you introduced the two?'

'Yes. Apparently Harriston was well into power generation, storage, that kind of thing. Fingers in many pies, most of them overseas. A lot of it was tied into electric cars and their market expansion, reputedly.'

'We've just moved him up our list.'

'Who?'

'Harriston. If he knew Fechtel, and Fechtel's now dead, and our entire project is dead, then I want to know exactly what he knows, and why.'

'You really think there's a connection there?'

'You've met Harriston, you've read about Harriston, but you don't know Harriston. He could be anyone,' said Chiara ominously. 'Leave it to me to find out. You shouldn't push, as it might kill your chances of getting your cars back. Me, though, I can push all I want. I will dig in the background.'

'Okay,' said Mike, gruffly. 'But be careful. Harriston presumably has a lot of high-level backers, and lots of government sway. And whoever killed Fechtel, well, they could be dangerous to you, too.'

'No worries,' said Chiara casually. 'We can be dangerous, too.'

CHAPTER 25

Mike paced back and forth across the floor in his tiny hotel room, a single-bed affair in the Kensington Hotel Brompton. He'd made three or four attempts at sleeping, all of them fruitless, and the sunrise was now closer than the sunset. He'd made a few cups of tea to calm his nerves, but all of them had gone cold.

The situation with the Austrian Collection, and the faux Ferrari, was tormenting his mind, a persistent twisting and turning that made him feel like someone was driving a corkscrew through his head. His only consolation was the way Chiara had spoken; it had taken a little of the edge off, and sounded like it would produce an answer, one way or another, to steer them in the right direction.

Just hopefully not into a massive showdown.

'Harriston's got everything he needs, after all,' he said to his room. 'What does he want? Just to steal from other people? To hold power? Is he just a narcissistic psychopath?'

Mike kicked his slippers across the room in annoyance, then put the kettle on again. He watched the cars pass by, beneath his window, under the moonlight, while the water boiled. The clouds were careering over London, in flocks, as if they were fleeing. He suddenly felt utterly isolated and alone, despite his familiar, comfortable surroundings.

Plenty of good memories in this hotel. Let's dwell on those instead.

He reached for his phone and messaged Julie, but the texts went unread. He shrugged his shoulders, refilled his cup, and went back to bed. He was fed up with the Ferrari situation, the Austrian Collection, and Harriston, and whoever else that godforsaken Lord was involved with.

'Maybe they're all connected,' he muttered, as he started to drift off. 'Maybe it's time we pushed back a bit.'

———————————●———————————

The cold shower made Mike feel slightly more alive, but his mind was still mired in darkness. He heard his phone buzz, on the shelf outside, and stuck his arm out to retrieve it. He glanced at its screen through the gap in the shower door, a single update standing out like a sore thumb.

Deposit, he thought. *What?*

He quickly washed off the remainder of the soap, dried himself, and dashed for his laptop. He opened his banking screen and, there, as plain as day, was £40,000. He shook his head, not recognising the sum or the account.

His phone buzzed again. A single text, this time.

We did it. We went ahead. Thanks for the deal. A tip for you. And here's to the next one.

'Thomas,' he said loudly, then clapped. 'So, the deal for the cars with Werner did go through okay. I figured it would.'

Mike felt considerably happier and, to his delight, the weather outside matched his mood: it was bright, warmer, and dry. He carefully manoeuvred the old Rolls-Royce Drophead out of the open-air car park, onto Old Brompton Road, and drove towards Buckingham. He glanced in the mirror occasionally, looking for anything amiss.

It's probably not as bad as you think it is, he thought. *It'll get straightened out.*

He lowered the roof of the Rolls-Royce by pressing a small black button in the centre console, letting the day flood in, and distracted himself by watching the elegant black-and-white instruments, the slow-moving traffic affording him the time to relax and watch their gentle movements. Their soft swaying was mesmeric, and he soon found himself daydreaming, his surroundings transforming into London of old, his mind digging through old car-buying memories.

He could see himself as a young man in the summer of 1983, meandering through countless classic car showrooms in and around Queen's Gate Place Mews, wanting a piece of the promised vintage car land for himself, trying hard to become part of it, anything to do with vintage cars.

Mike was only 23 at that point, but he had been entirely consumed by his love of the classic car world. He thought he was onto something, too; he had recently made some £6,000 by selling his old, trusted Porsche 356 Abarth Coupé, the one with the complicated Fuhrmann engine, to an art dealer in Cranley Gardens. It was a car he bought in Munich, and one which accompanied him faithfully through the snowy European winter, its engine location and traction proving a blessing. The deal he had made was good but his dream purchase, an Aston Martin DB Mark III, was still out of reach.

Walking along Queen's Gate Place Mews, he took in the joyous automotive sights and sounds. The likes of Mercedes-Benz 540K Spezial Roadsters, Alfa 8Cs, and the odd Derby Bentley or Ferrari, could all be seen living and breathing on the streets. To him, it was magic.

However, there was not a single DB Mark III in sight. Only a fascinating one-owner green-green manual DB4 Convertible could have tempted him, but the sign in its window said £10,000, which was totally out of reach.

A horn sounded behind him, and Mike found himself looking down the streets of modern London, over the finely shaped bonnet of the Rolls. But he could still see himself pressing his nose against showroom windows, trawling his way through the auction results, and mentally cataloguing everything he saw, just like it was yesterday.

Always looking for the perfect buy, just like today, he thought, smiling. *Canny management by walking, that's what it is. Never know what you might encounter.*

Mike scrolled back in his mind to the day when he saw a sleek 1965 Aston Martin DB5 peeking around the corner in Petersham Mews. A real old-school gentleman salesman, simply dubbed Mr Ryan, was busy polishing it; Mike had collared him, fascinated by the car, and started quizzing him about it.

It soon transpired that Ryan was the owner of a company called HJM Racing Cars, and that he had a genuine Duncan Hamilton Jaguar C-type sitting in his garage. That, to Mike, signalled immediate competence. It had just been sold, though, and the DB5 had been taken in part-exchange.

Mike's passion for it was evident from a mile away, even to the uninitiated, and Ryan sprang his trap: 'Just £6,000, I'd take for it, for a quick deal.'

Only the most superficial of inspections followed, as Mike quickly took in its gleaming Warwick Blue paintwork and original grey leather, and its embossed HYP 5 number plate. The combination was glorious, the smell of the interior rich and upmarket. It was, as far as he was concerned, fabulous. The engine had been recently refreshed and the car even had a rare five-speed ZF gearbox, too.

He immediately offered £5,000 for it, because you couldn't hit the bullseye if you didn't shoot, and they settled on £5,750 with a handshake. Ryan got his sale, in less than 15 minutes, and Mike got his Aston. It would stay with him for many years and, today, it would command north of £700,000.

Another one I should have kept, he thought regretfully. *But then, well, there are always others.*

'Enough reminiscing,' said Mike, as the traffic started to move again. 'It's time to move on.'

CHAPTER 26

Mike rolled his fingers across the light wood of his table and looked through the French doors at the end of the restaurant. The pavement was busy, as was the road, as everyone weaved their way home for the evening. The busyness of the street would usually irk him but, tonight, he found the hubbub comforting.

'Just you tonight?' said a waitress, offering menus his way.

'No, there should be another,' he said, smiling at her politely. 'But I'll take some water for the table, and a bottle of Mtsvane, if you've got one.'

The waitress nodded and moved on to the next table. Mike checked his Daytona, then his phone, and tutted to himself; the watch had lost a little time. He unscrewed the large crown, carefully dialled the hands to the exact time, and set the crown back in place. Mike tapped its crystal gently, brushed the case off, and shook his wrist.

Probably overdue a service. Seen a lot of action. And there's more to come.

He looked around the Orera, a little Georgian restaurant that was tucked beneath the Hotel Brompton, and then glanced outside again. The screen on his phone remained dark, inactive. He drew air through his teeth.

'I'm sure they'll turn up,' said the waitress, as she placed bottles and glasses on the table.

'I suspect they'll do what they want, when they want,' said Mike, laughing to himself briefly. 'But, yes, I think they will.'

A door clattered angrily in the distance, the rattling of the frame punctuated by intermittent outbursts of Italian. The waitress raised an eyebrow at Mike; he smirked, nodded, and pushed a second wine glass toward her. She filled it, the noise in the corridor outside subsiding slowly.

Julie swept into the room, coat and bags flying around her, her hair whipping up into a tornado. 'Cosi occupati,' she barked as she collapsed in the chair opposite Mike. Almost immediately, she shot back up, leaving everything scattered around her, marched over to him, and planted a full, long kiss on his lips.

'Le mie scuse, scusa, scusa,' she said, each repetition getting slower and slower. 'It's so busy out there, and getting across town was like swimming up the river!'

'That's quite alright, Julie,' said Mike, red flushing from his cheeks. 'I'm not going anywhere. Anyway, I should be thanking you for agreeing to battle through these streets at this time of night.'

'Well,' she said, flipping her head back and tackling her hair, 'I wasn't going to pass up an opportunity to see you. We have much to catch up on, like our Citroën plans!'

Mike beamed at her and raised his glass; a smile spread across her face, from cheek to cheek, and she merrily tapped hers against his, the chime ringing out through the restaurant.

'What are you doing here, anyway?' she said, her eyes flitting up and down the menu.

'I'm just taking a few moments out in London. We've a big problem on our hands but there's nothing I can do about it now, so I'm back to the office tomorrow to catch up with Rick and go from there.'

'I had heard whispers.'

'I thought you might have. But, well, you know what it's like. You can't focus on it all the time.'

'Si. Can't see the wood for the trees?'

'Something like that. Spinning bigger plates than I want to be.'

'Chi non risica non rosica,' she said musically. 'He who does not risk does not get the rose.'

He grinned at her. 'People keep telling me similar. But there's a degree of risk I'm comfortable with, and we're well outside of that.'

'Maybe you're just starting to push in the right directions,' said Julie, her eyes peering over the rim of her glass at him. She winked at him, took a hearty sip of the wine, and then her eyes fell back on the menu. 'You only find out by doing these things, after all.'

'Nothing ventured, I suppose.'

She tapped the top of his hand, then pointed at him. 'Exactly. So, you're laying low here for a bit, and I have you for tonight.'

'If you so please,' said Mike.

'Are you hungry?'

'For this? Not particularly, not yet at least. It's a bit early.'

'You need to shed some of this worry and stress, and you definitely need some fun,' she muttered. 'Pay the bill, Mike, then let's get going. We can always come back later.'

———————•———————

The Sake bar was packed. In the middle of a chequered tiled floor was a rectangular wooden bar, with a dark green glass top, servers in the middle attending to the crowd of clients around them. Julie led him by the hand through the throng, parting the sea with seemingly no effort, and deposited him on a seat by the bar. She disappeared for a moment, then reappeared with another seat.

'Knew there would be one somewhere,' she said, giggling.

Mike watched her as she flagged down a waiter. He still felt exhausted, mentally and physically, but Julie's actions, her activity, her character, her sheer presence alone, was buoying him up, helping him stave off his concerns about what was to come.

'And at least it'll be easy for me to get back to the hotel,' said Mike over the din. 'This place is only five minutes away from mine.'

'Look at you, thinking about the end of the evening already.

Ragazzo sfacciato,' said Julie, chiding him. She smacked him playfully, then turned back to the bar.

Enjoy now, enjoy yourself.

He studied her, capturing the way the light fell across her, across her hair, the delicate nature of her nose, the contrast of her dark eyes, the softness of her skin, and felt a sense of longing. A desire for more time, time to spend with her, to learn all there was about her, to have another half: a partner.

Mike shook his head hastily, an effort to dispel the schoolboy-like feelings of adoration that were swarming through him, but all he could think about was her, her mind, her body. He felt her hand slip around his waist, her fingers digging into him.

'What do you want, Mike?' she said, her head tipping in the direction of the bar staff.

'Ah,' he said, his train of thought thoroughly derailed. 'Have you been here before?'

'Practically a regular,' she responded, smiling.

'What do you recommend, then? I'll defer to your expertise.'

'Let's get some Ginjo-shu. It's a little soft, but it's rather lovely.'

'Just like me, then,' said Mike cheerfully.

Julie laughed loudly and spiralled her fingers at the bar staff. He watched her lean forward, saw her exchanging words with the barman, watched as the glasses and bottle came down. He felt her pressing against his legs, the sensation intensifying as she leant further forward over the bar. He leaned back a little, politely, but a sharp tug on his shirt drew him back. She looked over her shoulder at him, her expression seemingly saying *Where are you going?*

'Alright,' she said. 'Do you know the game that girls in Sicily play, called scissors?'

'No,' said Mike. 'What age are we talking?'

He smirked at her. She raised an eyebrow at him, put her hand on his leg, seemingly processing what he had said, and then laughed.

'Sfacciato, Mike, sfacciato. But, okay, for us, it's an adult game.

Here we go.'

Mike watched her hands darting around as she outlined the rules, her voice only just audible above the din of the bar, the bartender looking on with an amused face as he prepared a small porcelain bottle of hot sake.

'And then the loser of each round must take a cup of sake, drink it fast, and spin on the spot three times.'

Mike bit his bottom lip and laughed. 'I get it. I see.'

'Si, the more you drink, the harder it becomes!'

'And afterwards?'

'Well, the loser has to do whatever the winner wishes to do.'

'And that is?'

'You'll find out at the end!' said Julie, grinning energetically. She slipped off her jumper, revealing a black silk dress beneath, and fanned herself with a drinks menu. 'Ready to play?'

'Si,' said Mike, a mischievous smile spreading across his face.

———————— • ————————

Julie laughed heartily as she pulled Mike out into the street. The security guard standing outside watched them both with a bemused face, Julie giggling, Mike swaying a little on his feet.

'You're not very good at that game, are you, Mike,' said Julie, stooping down to pull off her heels. 'I'd almost think you were losing on purpose.'

Mike ran his hands over the side of his head, took a deep breath of the fresh night air, straightened himself out, and steadied himself against a lamp post.

'At least I know you can be fun now, as well as formal,' said Julie as she tied her shoes to her handbag. 'Just in case,' she added, patting them.

'I could have carried those for you, gladly,' said Mike.

'No, you stay right there,' said Julie. She slipped her phone out of her purse, knelt down on the Tarmac, and pointed her mobile's battery of lenses at Mike.

'Tilt your head to the right a bit,' said Julie. 'That's it. Now look up, towards the buildings.'

Mike obliged, then heard the sound of a camera shutter in action.

'Perfetto. One for my archives,' said Julie.

'Don't I get one of you?' said Mike jokingly.

'Maybe later. But, for now, you may escort me to your hotel.'

He looked at her, an expression of slight confusion on his face.

'Don't jump to conclusions,' said Julie firmly. 'I'm deciding what to do with you.'

Mike cocked his head, nodded at her, and looped his arm through hers.

'This way, then, signora.'

Julie rested her head on his shoulder for a moment, then straightened up.

'Okay. We go.'

The two started to walk, through the London night, only the occasional taxi or passer-by intruding on their peace. Mike breathed slowly, steadily, his head clearing a fraction, and concentrated on the sensation of Julie alongside him, her warmth, her energy, flowing into him.

'What do you want, Mike?' said Julie.

Mike remained quiet, contemplating, and the pair ambled along, arm in arm, just enjoying the company of the other. Julie didn't press him for a response; instead, she just let him think.

I've not done something like this for a long time. And how better I feel for it.

He huffed quietly, then squeezed her arm. 'I'm going to be honest with you.'

'I would expect nothing less.'

'I don't know what I want,' he said starkly.

'I think you do,' responded Julie firmly.

'Well,' said Mike, stumbling for a moment on word and pavement alike. 'Perhaps, but with work, the way the world is changing, and everything else, I'm not sure I'd be much good for someone else.'

'I remember what happened, you know. And Rick told me about it, how it still plays on your mind. But you cannot live in that moment forever. I don't think she would have wanted that.'

Mike looked down the road, at the distant cars, people, places. The world went quiet, and he closed his eyes for a moment. He could see nothing, hear nothing, but he could feel her, right beside him: warmth, safety, companionship.

'I know,' said Mike hesitantly. 'There's been no one else since, you know. It's just been me.'

'You don't have to live like that.'

He felt the sake swimming around in his stomach, felt that rare sensation of heat in his head, and put his hand on Julie's waist.

'I know that too,' he said softly.

'It's not disrespectful, you know. You're too polite, too good, for your own sake sometimes, you know. I'm sure you wouldn't have wanted her to live a celibate, lonely life, if the situation were reversed.'

He nodded a fraction, then drew to a halt in the street.

'And what about you?' said Mike, his thumb unconsciously caressing her waist.

'I want to find out. I don't want any pressure, I don't need any pressure. But I would like time with you, time around you. Company, comfort, support.'

She drew him to her, put her arm around his shoulder, and kissed him gently. The sensation of her lips against his, her body against his, made his mind explode, a din of white noise and blinding light descending.

Julie pulled back and looked at him, admiring his face in the night light, a blissful smile frozen in place.

'We could find out together, you know,' said Julie. 'It could turn out to be nothing, or it you could end up as amore della mia vita, but we will only find out one way.'

Maybe I could have a future with her. Maybe not. But I feel alive.

'I would like to find out,' said Mike confidently.

'Then that settles it.'

'I'm glad you're here.'

'So am I.'

Julie took Mike's hand, squeezed it, and locked her fingers with his. She looked towards the hotel and nudged him towards it. He drew a long breath, nodded at her, and took her cue; they walked, hand in hand, back to his room. He fumbled with the key, popped open the door, and laughed as Julie ushered him hurriedly inside. She pushed him to the edge of his bed, sat him down, and turned around.

'What are you doing?' he said, bemused.

Julie unzipped her dress in one smooth motion, then gently pushed its shoulder straps down her arms, her body swaying left and right slowly. Mike watched on, hypnotised, his eyes picking out every detail, every curve. She looked over her shoulder at him, smiled softly, and let the dress fall, down around her ankles.

'Oh,' said Mike breathlessly.

She grinned at him, walked slowly over to the door, and locked it.

CHAPTER 27

The rain hammered down against the windows and roof of the office at Chapman & Sunderland. It barely registered with Rick and Mike, who were busy trawling through their original documents and details from the Austrian Collection; chassis numbers, engine numbers, all and everything that could be seen and identified, was being carefully detailed for the insurers. They would almost certainly never pay out, as the cars seemed to have been legally extracted from the bonded warehouse, but they felt compelled to complete and send out the required, just on the off chance.

'Chiara says they've quite an interest in Harriston now,' said Rick quietly. 'Well, it was more like "Harriston Bastardo" and "La tua morte e la mia vita."'

Mike exhaled slowly. 'I don't envy him.'

'Me neither. Wind farms, among other things, she was going on about. Chiara thinks he's got one of her cars, too. An 8C Alfa Monza or something, loaned as security for the deal yonks ago. She says it's worth fifteen, twenty million, maybe more, given its history and provenance.'

'At least it's not just us who are losing track of our cars.'

Rick snorted. 'Bit too much of a recurring theme, these days.'

'Un malheur ne vient jamais seul,' responded Mike quietly.

'Come again?'

'A misfortune never arrives alone,' said Mike pensively. He huffed, then his fingers fell back to the keyboard, each click of the keys jarring in the deathly silence of the office.

Neither felt any sense of satisfaction when they finally submitted the paperwork. They just felt grey, miserable, and depressed. Mike collapsed on the sofa, and Rick stomped noisily back and forth across the workshop and office, both lost as what to do next.

Rick marched over to Mike's desk, picked up a pencil, held it in front of his face, and snapped it clean in two between his fingers.

'That's what I'll do to Harriston, that is, if I ever get my bloody hands on him.'

'And there's me, stuck between a rock and a hard case,' said Mike shrewdly.

Rick's eyes narrowed, then a smile flashed across his face. He laughed heartily, some anger washing from his face.

'At least that's one decision made, though. Now all we need is to work out how to find these blasted cars.'

'How about some food,' said Mike. 'We need to get out of this place for a bit, to clear our heads.'

'Right,' said Rick, nodding in the direction of the Rolls-Royce. 'You drive, I'll think. Or drink. Maybe both.'

They found a small Indian restaurant that was still open, and conspicuously empty of clientele. The food was all a uniform shade of red, just with vaguely differing degrees of heat, and little flavour. But, on the upside, the beer was cold, the poppadoms crisp, the lime pickle plentiful.

'Anything from Hadfords or that Benny bloke?' said Rick as he swilled beer around a pint glass. 'We might be without the cars at the moment, but we still need to keep pushing.'

Mike shook his head slowly. 'Not a word. If they're moving, they're doing it too slowly.'

'Shame. Be gratifying to see one of these end up in his hands. From what I read, it sounds like he appreciates vintage things like no other. And Julie?'

'We're… moving along. I'm hoping to see her again soon.'

'Good. It'll do you the world of good. Some might say you're a bit old for her but, hell, maybe that's what she wants. Someone who knows their brain, soul, and the world, a bit more.'

'She's certainly the one in the driving seat, I'll say that much.'

'And Chiara hasn't told you to stop, so I think you're all clear on that front. Not a family I'd want to get on the wrong end of.'

Mike smiled weakly and nodded. The rain continued, relentless, sloughing down the sheet glass at the front of the restaurant. Mike stared into the bottom of his glass, while Rick stared out of the window, watching the odd passing car and truck. There was a figure over the road, standing in the rain, looking back at him.

'Check out that poor sod,' said Rick. 'He must be saturated.'

Mike looked up, across the road, and nodded. 'Looks like they're having as good a day as us.'

Rick laughed coarsely and gestured to the waiter for another pint. Mike looked back across the road; the figure had gone.

The bell at the front of the restaurant rang as the door swung open, the rain and wind cutting into its warm atmosphere for a moment. Rick's head shot up and swivelled, towards the source of the intrusion.

Standing in the doorway was a man, medium build, wearing a waterproof, the rain pouring down onto the floor. He looked at them, eyes scanning over them slowly, and pulled off his weather gear. Rick and Mike watched, cautiously, but he made no sudden movements.

The man approached them, his arms apart slightly, palms spread, and pulled out a chair at their table. He sat down, nodded at the both of them, and snapped a whole poppadom in half. He wolfed it down, then picked up Mike's empty glass, and waved it at them.

'What the bloody hell do you think you're doing?' said Rick, quietly.

'I've come to have a meal,' said the man, 'and discuss a bit of a deal.'

'I don't think you've much that could interest us, son,' said Mike.

'You haven't listened to me yet,' he said, confidently. 'But you're going to.'

'You'll have to try a bit better than that,' said Rick. He laughed at him and waved the waiter away. 'Drinks aren't on us.'

'One word,' he said, cooly. 'Ferraris.'

Absolute silence descended. Rick and Mike leant forwards, their heads cocked.

'What did you say?' said Rick, seething.

'Gentle,' said Mike cautiously. 'Let's hear him out.'

'First,' said the stranger, gesturing at the glass again.

Rick hissed at him, then called the waiter back. He ordered more beers, and more food, and then turned his gaze back to the man.

'Your name, now,' said Rick.

'Peterson.'

'Right, Peterson. What do you know, and what do you want?'

'I understand you're missing some cars.'

'Might be,' said Mike. 'What of it?'

'I know where they are,' he said, gratefully accepting the beer from the waiter.

'And how do you know who we are?'

'We had a fair few of your details, just in case we got asked.'

'In case you got asked?' said Rick, puzzled.

'Yeah. I'm a truck driver.'

'What did you do?' said Mike.

'I drove a truck,' he responded unhelpfully.

'This is a waste of time,' said Rick. 'Spit it out or jog on.'

'A truck with some Ferraris in it. Blokes there didn't seem entirely happy to see them leave, but we had everything we needed.'

Mike stared at Rick and rolled his head a fraction. The two turned to face Peterson.

'It was all pretty hot,' he continued. 'I used to be in the army, so it didn't really faze me at the time, but it all seemed a bit off afterwards.

So, here I am.'

'Trying to do the right thing?' said Mike sarcastically.

'Something like that,' said Peterson. 'It didn't sit well with me.'

Rick looked at Mike, his eyes full of caution. The driver's body language was completely unclear, and neither could fathom what his true intent was. He didn't look as expected; he was of a light build, skinny, wearing half-rim glasses and a long coat.

'Show me some ID,' said Rick, his voice harsh and cold.

Peterson hesitated, then slowly reached into his pocket. He pulled out a battered-looking wallet, flipped it open, and thrust it towards Rick.

'Want to see my passport, too?'

'Yes.'

The only thing Mike could hear was the sound of paper upon fabric as Peterson slid his passport over the thin cloth covering the table.

'And what do you want out of this, exactly?' said Rick, his voice now as cold as ice.

'Money. So I can get out of this, with a clean pair of heels and a clean conscience, or as best as possible.'

'You're going to have to give us some details first,' said Mike. 'We're not going to just dole out cash to someone with a spurious claim.'

'There's another Ferrari being stored with them,' said Peterson, his eyes locked on Mike's. 'They said they got it from you.'

'What kind of Ferrari.'

'GT or something, that's all I got,' said Peterson.

Rick smacked the table, making Mike jump.

'The absolute bastard,' he shouted. A waiter gestured at him, his hand moving from high to low; Rick responded with a stiff middle finger and got an evil glare in return.

'The absolute bastard,' Rick said, more quietly this time. 'The absolute fucking bastard.'

'It's the real one, isn't it?' said Mike. 'That's what they've got. They've got our real 250 GT SWB.'

'And we've got the fake. And they fucking put the whole thing together.'

Mike shook his head. 'Harriston must have made some big promises about delivering these cars, and his back's against the wall.'

'And he had to get them as quickly as possible, by any means possible.'

'And we just happened to be the chumps to take the hit.'

Peterson broke off a piece of poppadom and downed some beer, indifferent to Rick and Mike's increasingly angry tones.

'And you,' said Rick, turning to him, 'you know where everything is.'

'It's fifty grand. That's what I want. Your call,' said Peterson.

'And that gets us what, exactly?' said Rick.

'Location, building, what you've got to contend with. I'm sure it'll be enough to enable you to get them back.'

'Are they even accessible?' said Mike. 'No fucking point to any of this if they're halfway around the world already.'

'They are,' said Peterson. 'But you've not got long. I think they'll be on a boat before long.'

'To?' said Rick, pointedly.

'Shanghai.'

'I fucking knew it,' he spat. 'Harriston's got on the wrong end of something heavy and now we're in the shit as a result.'

'Alright,' said Mike. 'Calm down.'

Rick pulled him to the side, out of earshot. He was vibrating with anger, a massive surge of energy looking for an exit, as on edge and as dangerous as a fire in a ship's magazine.

'We fucking pay this guy,' said Rick angrily. 'I don't like it but let's just do it and find out where our fucking cars are.'

'And then what? It's just us here, Rick.'

'Leave that to me. Let's get this done and I'll fill you in later.'

Rick and Mike marched back to the table and sat down opposite Peterson.

'Deal,' said Rick. 'We'll give you fifty. But you tell us what you know, now.'

'Fair enough,' said Peterson. 'I know where you both live, anyway. The cars are in a hanger in an old airbase in Belgium, near Schilde.'

'That's close to Antwerp, isn't it?' said Mike.

'That's the one. I've got the gate codes and a layout still, if you're interested. I can't imagine they've changed.'

'And the security?' said Rick.

'A stack of mercenaries, but we didn't get involved with them. There's a few dozen, dotted around the base, pretty tooled up.'

'Chinese?'

'Pretty much all of them, I think,' said Peterson. 'They weren't a great fan of Harriston, I can tell you that much.'

'Neither are we,' said Mike, managing a single laugh.

'He'll chew you up if you take on that place, or they will,' said Peterson. 'He's got all sorts of levers to pull on his side, including a stack of politicians. I've seen a few interesting sorts coming and going.'

'Yeah, he's already told us he intends to destroy us.'

'He said that too,' said Peterson, nodding heavily in agreement. 'But before we go any further, can I get another beer?'

CHAPTER 28

Peterson slowly sketched out the layout of the airstrip on a sheet of A3 paper. Mike and Rick watched, their office deathly quiet, as he drew small circles that indicated guard posts and roughed out paths that he thought the guards regularly took. The two leant in, studying his diagram. There were four large hangers, but all their cars were in the second, which was otherwise empty.

'Now, look,' he said slowly, gesturing across the map. 'This place is still live during the day, with the odd flight in and out. And you're not getting a truck in or out during the day.'

'But the runway,' said Rick, the cogs spinning.

'Exactly,' said Peterson. 'Even if you did get a truck in and out, they'd catch up to you in no time. They've got at least two patrol vehicles, and several small foot patrols, protecting the place.'

Peterson pointed at a picture of the Transall that was pinned to a cork board behind them.

'Something like that, that might do the trick.'

'I'm guessing it's not lit, or supported, in any way at night,' said Rick.

'Nope.'

'Of course,' responded Rick sarcastically. 'It wouldn't be easy, would it?'

Mike studied Peterson, who was filling in some smaller details on the map, for a moment.

'I still don't understand why you've come to us, though, supposed morals aside,' said Mike.

Peterson sat down and put his pencil on the table. He rubbed his thighs for a moment, then leant back in the chair. He took a deep breath, exhaled, and dipped his chin.

'Harriston isn't easy to work for. And neither are his, shall we say, associates. I didn't like the way it was all going, so I bailed.'

'You just went AWOL?' said Rick incredulously. 'Fuck.'

'Exactly,' said Peterson, his voice flooded with regret. 'I thought it was the best option left on the table. I didn't want to get any deeper. And I hadn't taken any money at that point, so I thought I'd be okay.'

'But you weren't,' said Mike flatly.

'Nope, apparently. Even though I'd not taken any cash, they've obviously deemed me a hazard. I think they've been after me for a bit, although I've not felt the full force of them yet.'

'Family?' said Rick.

'Wife, two kids, standard setup.'

'And with the cash you're getting from us?' said Mike.

'I'm out of here, with them, and off the grid. Done. I'm out of this kind of stuff. I'll find something a bit gentler overseas.'

'And hope they lose interest in you,' said Rick.

'I think they will. I'm a pretty small fish.'

Rick disappeared into the back of the office and a few dull metallic thunks drifted across the table, followed by a slight scuffling noise, like someone dealing cards. He returned, carrying a small waist pack, and handed it to Peterson.

'Seventy-five grand,' said Rick. 'Right there.'

'I only asked for…'

'You sure about this?' said Mike. 'The idea is to bid down, not up, in my experience.'

'We'd already agreed on a price,' said Rick. 'But he needs it more than we do right now.'

Peterson smiled, a brief flash of relief whipping over his face.

'That's… that's really appreciated,' he said. 'And I'm sorry about the whole motorbike thing.'

'You what?!' said Rick, his voice shattering the quiet.

Mike darted forwards and put his hands firmly on Rick's shoulders, holding him down.

'Okay,' he said, with a stern but composed tone. 'Ooookaaaay.'

'I really am,' said Peterson. 'They asked me to do a few of the tricky jobs. They just wanted to scare you. I didn't know who you were!'

'You bloody well almost killed me,' Rick shouted. 'Fuck, I'm not sure I want to give you any money now!'

'I think you best go now, Peterson' said Mike firmly. 'I'm not sure how long I can hold him off.'

Peterson nodded, turned around, and disappeared into the night.

———————— • ————————

Mike walked into the office, two cardboard trays of food in hand, and sat down at his desk. The minute hand on the clock swept towards twelve, while the big hand crept towards one. He nodded, checked his own Daytona, and rifled through his draws for a clean piece of paper.

Rick marched in, still seething, and strode over to the fridge. He extricated a bottle of white, unscrewed the cap, poured a large glass, and awkwardly dragged his chair over to Mike's desk.

'Here,' said Mike. 'A fry-up. This'll make you feel better.'

'Bastard,' said Rick, snappily. 'Not you, him.'

'Water under the bridge, or something like that. Who knows what we would have done in that situation.'

Rick just grunted at him, then tucked into the takeaway lunch.

'I've been thinking,' he said, between mouthfuls of bacon, 'about this gig. I think we can get the cars out.'

Mike tapped the edge of the cardboard container with his fork expectantly.

'Transalls,' said Rick, inhaling a hash brown. 'We use ours, and I've got a line on another we can, uh, borrow. They'll accommodate all the cars and suit the runway.'

'You're suggesting that we land, load the cars, and then bugger off?'

'Well, they're ours, aren't they? And we need them back.'

'This is a bit *Where Eagles Dare* all of a sudden, isn't it?'

Rick shrugged. 'Pretty run of the mill for me. Guy named Malcolm, in Chester, he flies cargo for Ford, Halewood to Cologne, got a Transall to hand. We could use that, or maybe swap the Boeing for it.'

'You're serious about this?'

'Look, Mike,' said Rick sternly. 'We're in a hole here. We're short a Ferrari already, and now we're short six more. Harriston's taken the lot and we're soon going to have a lot of people looking at us for north of several million. And while there's paperwork, and odds and sods of proof here and there, it'll take years for the lawyers and legal system to sort it out.'

Mike's chest rose, froze, and fell again, after what seemed like minutes.

'And for all that time, we'll be in a box, or unable to do anything, and that'll be it for us. And that's assuming his lawyers and teams simply don't steamroll over us. We've not got that power, or resources.'

'Or finance.'

'Exactly.'

'So, we'd be fucked,' said Mike. 'We're not in control.'

'No. We have to get into the driver's seat of this thing and get our ducks in a row. We've got to step up and, well, get a little ballsy.'

'I'm out of my depth.'

'I'm not,' said Rick confidently. 'We can put this together. A dozen men, two aircraft, a few vehicles, and we'll be set.'

Mike looked around the empty office.

'I'm not sure Simon constitutes eight to ten men. Maybe half, three-quarters at a push.'

Rick grinned at him, then held up a sausage.

'Don't be a silly sausage, Mike. I've got a guy in Essex. He'll hook us up.'

———————— ● ————————

Rick's eyes were lost in the polished surfaces of his flask, as he absentmindedly pushed and pulled it along the top of his desk, his phone crammed between his shoulder and head. Mike hovered nearby, catching snippets of the conversation.

'Right. I see. Yeah, figures, for Tunisia, and Morocco,' said Rick. 'Great.'

He hung up, put his phone on the desk, and downed some wine.

'Malcolm doesn't want the Boeing. He needs tough STOL stuff, for a load of crappy dirt runways he's tackling at the moment.'

'No second Transall for us, then?'

'Oh, no, he's in. He's going to fly it for us. Bit like me, fancies a bit of a brew-up from time to time,' said Rick. 'He's got some textiles to fly in, for some luxury brands that are banging stuff out there, and then he'll make his way over to us. Got a good and willing crew, so no problem there.'

'How much does he want, exactly?'

'Thirty grand, fuel and crew, plus a hit of whatever the final deal is. Let's call it one-fifty, all in.'

'And what about the other men we'll need?'

'We need to speak to a mate of mine, the Colonel, but he's only just back from Afghanistan, and I'm not sure he's resurfaced yet,' said Rick, tapping the desk. 'Anyway, it's not really him I need to speak to.'

'No?'

'No,' said Rick unhappily, his fingers clunkily pressing keys on his phone. 'It's his wife.'

———————— ● ————————

Thirty minutes later, Rick's phone chimed.

'I'd hoped she'd take it,' said Rick. 'She loves the cash.'

'What?!' said Mike.

'She's basically his business manager. I just said I'd give them two hundred grand if they could spare three days for us.'

'Who are these people?'

'Well, the Colonel is ex-military. Same for his boys. They do contract gigs, as and when you need them, no questions asked.'

'And they're happy with the idea of just rocking up to some random airbase, lifting a load of cars, and bugging out again?'

'She says yes,' said Rick, as a smirk spread across his face. 'And you know what, we should call it Operation Wheelbase. I think I like that.'

Mike shook his head in disbelief.

'We can really do this?'

'It wouldn't be the first time I've done something like this with him, let's put it like that.'

Mike rested his elbows on the table and put his chin on his hands.

'Okay. Right, Malcolm and the Colonel will help us get the cars back, we'll be sorted, and Harriston can pick up the pieces and deal with his own problems, and we'll honour our side of the deal anyway.'

'If that was a question, the answer is yes,' said Rick cockily. 'I'm off to meet the Colonel in the Hurricane Pool Hall, near St Pancras, to flesh out the rest. Don't worry about the details.'

———————— ● ————————

The next day, a flurry of activity descended on Chapman & Sunderland. Strange-looking email links materialised in inboxes, containing drone footage and photographs of a decrepit-looking airfield in the middle of nowhere. Rick was glued to his phone, text messages flashing back and forth, a new incoming call erupting every five minutes, or less. Mike just watched, from his chair, as Rick blazed around the office, tackling twenty things at once, and felt a little helpless.

'Is there anything I can do?' he said, leaping on one of the rare quiet moments.

Rick nodded. 'The guys are on their way as we speak. We've nabbed a corner of an old airfield near here, with similar hangers. A couple of old Willys Jeeps and some MoT failures are on the way to them; we're going to rig the Jeeps with foam cushions, so they can practice pushing the cars around. They're going to mock up the place and start planning as soon as they hit the ground.'

'And me?'

'Right,' said Rick, nodding again. 'Get Simon and get him to sort out covering up any markings on Transalls. We don't want to be recognised in Belgium, do we?'

'How long do we have?'

'We're going in on Sunday, bright and early. We'll be on their runway by four in the morning.'

'Bloody hell,' said Mike.

CHAPTER 29

A wave of heavy unease flooded through Mike's body, followed by another of intense fear. But the people surrounding him, and the planning, were curbing his worries a little. The team that had been put together was stout: two Transall C-160s, one very familiar, two dependable and tough crews, and eight reputedly experienced men on the ground. All well motivated by sufficiently high stacks of cash and, in this case at least, acting on behalf of victims. And, of course, there was Rick.

He looked over his shoulder, out of the window, and could see nothing but inky blackness and the occasional shimmer of silver below: the Channel. He glanced to his left and right, at the shadowy faces looming in the dark, the smell of aviation fuel, gun oil, and sweat, hammering its way into his nostrils. The vibrations of the Transall jimmied and jarred every bone in his body, the sweat permeated his clothing.

It must have felt a bit like this, thought Mike, as his foot drummed on the decking of the Transall, *getting in one of those bombers. Crossing the water. Going to war.*

Mike looked up into the cockpit of the Transall. The dim red and green lights of the instrument panels only just illuminated the pilot and copilot, while the Colonel, standing in between them, occasionally blocked out the light as he swayed, watching the skies ahead. Mike could almost sense tracers and flak reaching up towards them, the lead and shrapnel pattering off the Transall's lightweight skin.

The pilot, Malcolm, turned towards him, and gave him a thumbs-up. Mike had only spoken to him for a few minutes, but he'd taken to him like a duck to water; he was a straight-talking guy, honest, affable and amusing.

Thanks for this Wheelbase gig, he'd said. It'll keep the hounds at bay.

He heard Rick's voice in his ear, from the other Transall. Mike looked out of the window and saw the other aircraft roll left and right for a moment, wiggling its wings.

'Malcolm,' he said. 'Don't deviate yet. Keep on my wing, straight and level.'

'Roger,' said Malcolm. 'I keep forgetting that we're legal until Calais.'

'Don't do much above-board work, do you?' said the Colonel, his voice rich and deep.

'Doesn't do much to keep my head above water,' said Malcolm.

Rick's voice came back on the radio. 'After that, we'll go down to FL 100, cancel IFR, and we'll be off the grid.'

'And then we can relax, right?' said Mike, trying to steady his nerves. Someone in the gloom laughed.

'Right,' said Rick. 'Mike, we've a moment; you run them through it again, just to keep everyone on the same page.'

'Okay, Rick, you've got it,' said Mike, grateful for the distraction. 'Alright, you all know this as Operation Wheelbase. Once we're on the ground, the Colonel's men will keep us covered, but keep your eyes open. Crew, get the Jeeps unloaded, and stick to the plan.'

'One pusher, one driver, per each, right?' said someone in the darkness.

'Exactly. The driver gets in the car to be collected, the pusher uses the Jeep to get it into the Transall. Don't get lost, keep your head on a swivel, and just keep loading the cars from the hanger into the plane.'

'And if someone shoots at you,' said the Colonel, 'hit the deck. Just get down, as low as you can, or hide behind something solid, something thick.'

'Like Rick,' said Malcolm. Laughter swept through the Transalls.

'Git,' radioed back Rick, waggling the wings of his Transall in defiance.

'Alright, alright. The sun will be coming up in thirty minutes or so,' said Mike. 'And we'll need to be gone by then, so a little focus, please.'

The Colonel, now sitting in the engineer's seat, made a comment over his shoulder to the co-pilot. It was mostly about the deteriorating weather conditions; heavy rain and a storm was forecast for Belgium. The approach would be bumpy coming in from the north. The other crew were next to the Jeeps, and Mike could sense a little unease arising as the Transall started to bounce around.

'Don't worry about this chop,' said Malcolm. 'This thing's a real man-of-war. It'll take more than a bit of wind to knock this thing out.'

The old battle ships. Like HMS Victory, Nelson's ship. And that's still around.

'Colonel,' said Mike loudly. 'What's the latest on the ground?'

'They're already down there, waiting for us,' he responded. 'We've had that confirmed. We'll serve as a bit of a distraction, then they'll roll up and suppress the guards.'

Suppress. Pretty polite way of putting it.

The Colonel caught a glimpse of the concern on Mike's face.

'Don't worry,' he added, his voice lustrous. 'We're going to try to keep it clean. You boys are pretty tidy, and we don't want to mar that image.'

He pointed downwards. 'Anyway, those guys, on the field, they're all nasty pieces. If they get swept off the board, it'll be good for everyone else.'

Mike clenched his teeth and nodded at him once, a gesture of quiet thanks. He looked down at his phone and swept through the footage of the airfield again; several large square brick military-style buildings, and four large hangers.

Like Bicester. Except less welcoming.

He scrolled through to some pictures, taken from ground level, evidently from some distance away, and looked at the hangers. The third one along, with its huge sliding doors slightly ajar, was where the cars were supposed to be. The picture didn't reveal much but Mike felt in his gut that the cars were in there, just waiting for them. There seemed to be more cameras, newer, dotted around, suggesting whatever was inside was being looked after.

At least they haven't got any tanks. I hope.

'It's a shame we can't just drop something on them,' said Malcolm sarcastically. 'That'd make this a doddle.'

'Wouldn't be much for us to take home then, would there?' said the Colonel. 'Been a while since I've had any fun like that, mind.'

'Something for next time, perhaps,' said Rick, his voice strained. He grunted quietly as he fought to keep his Transall level, the surging wind pushing the plane around aggressively.

Mike closed his eyes but the background noise and thin mechanical whines of the Transall poked and prodded his brain aggressively, keeping him restlessly awake, the aircraft continuing to move, seemingly going nowhere, time frozen, until Rick's voice blazed back over the intercom.

'Batten down the hatches. Three thousand, breaking off radio comms with Brussels in a minute.'

Everyone in the Transall subconsciously tightened their harnesses.

'Malcolm,' said Rick. 'There's some kind of NATO night practice going on south of here, so we should be a bit less obvious amid that clutter.'

'Good by me,' said Malcolm, as he nudged the Transall downwards.

'Mike, you check for any updates from the ground team,' said Rick. 'They're going to pop the lights on, hopefully, so we can get these things in and down. I need to know if that's not going to happen.'

'Alright,' said Mike, trying to sound confident.

Near Antwerp, both pilots were doing circular orbits on different levels, 2,000 feet and 3,000 feet, circling and waiting for the go-ahead from the ground teams. If all went to plan, the guards should be subdued, the security systems deactivated, the lights on, and the hanger doors open.

But there was nothing yet.

'We're eight minutes over,' said Malcolm sternly.

The Colonel shook his head.

'Rick, I'll keep orbiting,' said Malcolm. 'Hopefully, no one decides to come and have a look at what we're doing.'

Chatter erupted over the intercom for a moment.

'This might be our cue,' said Rick firmly. 'Sarajevo approach, Malcolm, sorry. I'll lead.'

Mike could hear Malcolm swallow a lump in his throat, even over the noise of the engines.

'Right,' he said, trying to keep his voice level. 'At least we've got some headwind to help slow us.'

The Transall trembled as it turned towards the runway.

'What's a Sarajevo approach?' said Mike to the crew member across from him.

'Think of a rollercoaster,' he said, 'and then make it ten times worse.'

'It's like a controlled crash,' said another. 'Malcom's not done a combat move like that for a while. Several thousand feet a minute for the descent, and then yanking the thing up at the last possible second.'

'If they're lucky,' responded the other chirpily, 'we can use the Transall again afterwards!'

It was Mike's turn to swallow a lump in his throat. He looked out of the brown-tinted window of the Transall and only saw darkness, interrupted by rain smearing its way over the glass. Then, in the gloom, a weakly lit airfield. In the distance, the lights of Antwerp and the harbours, casting a sickly orange glow into the pitch-black dark.

'And you, you know what you're doing?' said a crew member, his foot tapping Mike's shin.

'Yeah, just keeping everything in check, I hope. And it's not complicated: planes down, Jeeps out, to the hanger, relay the cars back and forth, strap them in, out.'

'As easy as that.'

'As long as no one starts shooting at us,' said Mike.

The Transall shimmied again as Malcolm lined it up to the runway, its engines throttling up and down, the undercarriage graunching as it unfurled.

'Two minutes,' shouted Malcolm.

The guards should have been out ages ago. And the lights are on, so they must have dealt with everything.

Mike realised his foot was now hammering against the deck of the Transall. There was still nothing outside the window. The heat was overwhelming. The engines seemed to be getting louder, like they were now in his ear. The aircraft rose up under him, swaying, and then dropped violently, the hydraulics and turbines whining in protest. He heard someone curse under their breath, and dull, hollow metal clicks in the darkness.

Bloody hell. We're really doing this. We're going for it.

'It's all clear, lights on!' shouted Rick over the intercom. 'They're in the hanger; we're going in!'

CHAPTER 30

Mike yelped as the Transall dived, and the world felt like it had been turned on its head. His heart hammered in his chest as the plane fell away from beneath him, his fingers slipping from the edges of the stamped metal seat. He tried to draw a deep, calming breath, but only caught a ragged mouthful of hot, heady air, and he felt sick to his stomach for a moment.

A terrific *Thud!* tore through the Transall as it slammed into the runway, its engines screaming as Malcolm reversed the propellors' pitch, the brakes glowing red-hot, as he tried to slow the aircraft quickly. He cut the pitch back to normal as the airspeed dropped and speared the Transall directly towards the hanger. Rick's Transall appeared ahead, caught in the glare of the landing lights. The crew member nodded at Mike, hopped up, and started dropping the rear ramp as the Transall slowed further. Another hopped into the Jeep, started the engine, blipping it noisily.

Mike glanced over his shoulder, through the heavily scratched plexiglass of the window behind him, and saw rain, thick, aggressive sheets of it, each frozen momentarily every time the Transall's navigation lights strobed. The water streamed over, under and off the wings, and blasted away from the nacelles, the giant propellers creating hot tornadoes, riddled with aviation fuel, that that tore into anything or anyone unlucky enough to be behind them.

The aircraft nosed over as Malcolm stabbed the brakes, bringing it to a halt, and the Jeep took off, its tyres squealing on the metal ramps, and again as they met the Tarmac of the runway apron. Mike cautiously stuck his head out from the Transall, looking towards the hanger, across the mirror-like surface of the rain-soaked apron beneath, and saw only a few shadowy figures darting around inside. The lights were out.

The Jeep screamed out of the garage, pushing along the first of the Ferraris, a man in dark camouflage behind the wheel. Another Jeep appeared, along with another Ferrari, and shunted it into the back of Rick's Transall.

'Keep it up,' said Mike. 'We're doing it.'

The Transalls' engines were still running, the smell of aviation fuel and fumes saturating the crisp night air. Mike pressed his hands to his head but the din barely subsided, and the nauseating smell made his head ache.

'Mike, Rick, you still on the intercom?' said Rick.

Mike thumbed the button to transmit. 'Yes. All okay, my heart rate aside?'

'A few minutes and we're out of this place. Taken without a shot, apparently. Not so tough, eh?'

Mike smiled, a sense of relief washing over him.

'There are other cars in there but we've no space. There's even a pre-war Alfa Monza.'

Didn't someone mention that Chiara had one of those? thought Mike.

'We got room for that?' he responded quickly.

'Only if we leave the Jeeps behind,' yelled Rick.

'Take it!'

'Yeah. Adding it to the pile now,' said Rick, who then shouted at someone else in the background.

The noise was overwhelming. Mike pressed himself against the hull of the Transall, taking a little solace in its solidity, as the Jeep returned, pushing the real counterpart of the cloned 250 GT SWB. He breathed in as the Ferrari rolled up the ramp, into the fuselage, and the Jeep reversed out again.

Mike watched, his fingers drumming on the side of the Transall at a pace almost matching his heartrate, as the Jeep roared away, its gearbox whining, spray careening from its wheels as it whipped around and sped off towards the hanger again. Mike watched as it disappeared behind hanger doors, its dull green finish making it look like a shadow flitting through the night, then it reappeared, pushing the 1962 Ferrari GTO; the steep Kamm-tailed back of the low-slung grand tourer made the Jeep driver's job easy, the big rubber pads tied to the bumper pressing evenly on the Ferrari's tall, flat rear, causing its lightweight panels no grief.

The Jeep's engine raced as it punted the Ferrari towards the ramp, sweeping across the pad in a graceful arc towards the Transall. The Jeep's rubber pads scrubbed sideways across the Ferrari's rear as the two turned together, one of the GTO's taillights exploding in protest, before lining up on the ramp. The Jeep eased off, then gently shunted the Ferrari up the ramp, into the Transall.

These guys are slick. And the tags on the wheels: Shanghai. Destined for China, after all.

The Ferrari driver bailed out and the crew started throwing straps underneath the car, and over its wheels; the Jeep driver waved at Mike, then made a shrugging gesture. Mike pointed at the Jeep firmly, made a sweeping-away gesture, then a sawing movement across his neck. The driver nodded, looked behind him, put the Jeep in reverse, then hopped out. The Jeep rolled away, into the night, to become someone else's problem.

Eight cars were rapidly strapped down, secured, and ready to go. Malcolm stuck his hand out of the cockpit and made an agitated and amplified circling gesture.

'Let's get out of here,' he shouted over the intercom. 'We're good!'

The Colonel was marching back towards the Transall, towards Mike, his head scanning from left to right quickly.

A deafening crack split the night, cutting clean through the din of the idling engines. Malcolm yelped over the radio, and then screamed.

'Fuck!' he barked. 'I've been hit.'

Mike froze as he watched the Colonel drop to one knee, a pistol materialising in his hand, then flashes of light. A crisp *Pop! Pop! Pop!* echoed through the interior of the Transall.

'Up on the roof,' shouted Rick. 'The second building to the right.'

One of the team flashed by Mike, towards the cockpit.

Fuck! Malcolm! he realised, trying to unfreeze himself.

'It's a bloody mess up here but I think he'll be okay,' shouted the team member. 'Get me a torniquet, someone.'

'Mike, get up here,' shouted Malcolm, pain rippling through his voice.

He grabbed a medical kit from the side of the Transall and darted towards the cockpit, his heart rate sky-high, his breathing short and ragged. Mike could taste metal as he clambered into the cockpit; Malcolm's left leg was a mess of red, his trousers shredded and saturated.

'Some sniper,' he said angrily, as someone snatched the medical kit from Mike's hands. They extricated a torniquet, slipped it around Malcolm's leg, and clamped it down. He moaned and tried to lift himself out of his seat. He punched the co-pilot on the shoulder.

'Aircraft's yours,' said Malcolm. 'Mike, you get in here and take my place, for fuck's sake. You help him get this thing back.'

Another loud *Pop! Pop! Rattle!* ripped through the cabin as Malcom was manhandled back to the seating in the cargo area.

'Time to go,' said Rick.

'Agreed,' shouted the Colonel. 'Everyone, get where you need to be!'

The Transall started to roll forward, the ramp noisily clattering along behind it. The copilot thrust a headset into Mike's hands; he tried to put it on but his fingers were uncooperative, shaking. He forced his fists to clench, flexed his fingers hard and fast, and jammed the headset on, its thick rubber cups scraping down over his ears.

'Ramp's coming up,' came a voice from behind Mike. 'Closed and secured!'

'Got a few stragglers coming,' said the Colonel loudly. 'They'll have to use the side door!'

Mike glanced to his right and saw two shadows darting across the grass, over the runway lights, towards the Transall. He heard the crew wrestling with the small crew door near the cockpit, and shouts from outside, and grimaced at the thought of what it felt like to be moving near the airplane's vast propellors.

In the dark. Eighteen feet of steel, moving at some godforsaken clip. One misstep and lights out, just like that. Pink mist!

A wall of noise, cold and wind washed over him for a second, and then was gone, as the side door slammed shut. Mike felt the nose of the Transall dip and weave as the copilot finished making his way to the end of the runway, and then he felt his hand being guided onto the throttles. 'Up, now,' said the co-pilot. Mike pushed them forward, to their stops, the Transall's nose diving down, the brakes locked on firmly. He looked out of the window and watched the big Ratier Forest-built propellers scything through the rain, white-grey vortices of water spiralling away from each tip, mesmerising him.

The co-pilot's finger was tracing along the gauges in the cockpit, the engines' screams deafening, his other free hand darting across the flap and gear controls.

'We're right behind you,' said Rick. 'Go!'

The co-pilot nodded at Mike and released the brakes. The Transall surged forwards, its propellers tearing through the cool night area, and Mike felt himself automatically resting his hand on the yoke, lightly echoing the copilot's inputs, the gauges climbing upwards as the nose left the runway.

Rotate. We're up.

'Secure that bloody ramp properly will you,' said Rick, over the radio, as his Transall followed them into the sky. 'Everyone accounted for?'

'That sniper might still be up,' said the Colonel. 'We kept his head down, though. Everyone else okay?'

'Piece of piss,' said an unfamiliar voice. 'Wusses,' said another. 'I'll sort this bloke out,' added someone else, their voice moving away from Mike towards Malcolm. 'Looks like in and out, nicked something, but I'll tidy that up for now.'

Mike put his hand on his chest and felt his heart pounding away. *How long did that take? Seconds? Minutes? An hour? Christ.*

The co-pilot busied himself, drawling in a calm fashion to someone in Brussels, requesting an IFR pickup. He was pretending to be a Scottish military airplane, one that had dipped down to sort out a mechanical problem for a bit, one that was now returning home at a steady pace and sensible altitude. The sun was on its way up, the early morning traffic starting to flow in earnest, and the controllers didn't appear to have much interest in them.

Mike tipped his head back towards the hold. 'You alright, Malcolm?'

'Bit lighter than I used to be but this bloke has stopped the worst, and he's got some marvellous morphine.'

How the hell did I end up here? Mike thought. But he's okay; that's good.

'Don't worry,' added Malcolm. 'This isn't unusual!'

The Transalls swept through the sky, away from the Brussels, flying in close formation, and no one paid them any notice. No one came to intercept, no one questioned their flight path, no one so much as raised an eyebrow.

'Gentlemen,' said Rick over the radio, his voice as steady as ever. 'Thank you very much. That was right up to par. Money will be ready, in folding, for you just after landing. Sterling job.'

The rest of the flight went without fuss. They landed at Bournemouth, unloaded the cars into a small, secure hanger, hidden out of sight, and the Colonel set off towards the hospital with Malcolm. He had found an old gun in the loft of his house, and it had gone off when he dropped it, or so they said.

Mike got back into Bluebelle, after his heart had slowed down, and made his way to the Hotel Brompton near South Kensington. Julie joined him again, for another night on the town, raising his spirits even further. Rick stayed in a Travelodge near St Albans.

CHAPTER 31

Mike was still in bed at the Brompton Hotel, the sky outside dark, when his phone rang. He cursed as he rolled awkwardly, his back sore, and grabbed his phone from the bedside table. He didn't notice that the bed was otherwise empty.

Gentle, please, he thought, groggily. *Please be something straightforward.*

'Mike, it's Rick. The driver's dead.'

'What?!' said Mike, his fingers rubbing his forehead as he tried to spark his brain into life. 'Driver? Which series?'

'No. The truck driver. I just saw it on the local news. They found him dead in a pub, poisoned. He had the cash on him.'

'God,' said Mike, restraining himself from smashing his phone into pieces.

'I don't think it'll take long for us to get roped into that story,' said Rick, his voice heavy. 'We'll be on a camera somewhere, talking to him.'

'Got any magic solutions to that problem?'

'I know a few Sergeants, but none locally. Still, I can perhaps nudge them. Either way, we need to find out what's going on.'

'And fast,' said Mike. He sucked air through his teeth for a moment.

'We're not exactly in a position to be going to the authorities, not right now.'

'I doubt they'd be much help anyway,' responded Rick coldly. 'What with Harriston's leverage, and all that's been taking place, it'd be easiest to paint us into the corner.'

Mike let out an anguished sigh.

'We need to get Harriston framed up somehow,' continued Rick. 'Bang to rights. Then this should sort itself out. The rest will just be background noise.'

Mike looked out across the dimly lit South Kensington tube station, its yellowish lights and traffic indicators blinking regularly, casting cautionary light through the gloom.

This is getting nasty, quick. We could be next.

'Harriston needs the GTO, doesn't he,' said Mike, his mind racing. 'It was the only car he really seemed interested in, out of the lot.'

'I'd figure so, probably desperately now,' said Rick. 'It must be promised to someone. You never know, it might be someone in the Communist Party, something like that. A favour to someone that he's yet to deliver on. Maybe someone swung him some of those European deals, he burnt up the cash, who knows, and now he's falling short.'

'He could be under the gun as well.'

'I don't give a fuck about Harriston, to be honest,' said Rick bluntly. 'If he's put himself on that spot, made himself a target, that's his problem.'

The two men were silent for a moment. Mike looked around and realised that he was alone.

'I say we go ahead and just sell the cars,' said Mike. 'And protect ourselves as best we can.'

'We could go to Chiara.'

'Julie did mention they might be able to help, last night,' said Mike.

'Last night, eh? There's a conversation for later,' said Rick inquiringly. 'But we shouldn't get too involved with them. Their vendetta seems very personal. Too emotional. I'd prefer to stick with the Colonel and his lads. No surprises.'

'Fair. But I think Chiara and Julie know more about Harriston than they're letting on. I'm not sure I want to know.'

'Best way, I think,' said Rick. 'Let's keep them out of this, too. Just you watch yourself with that Julie. I think she's a bit too smart for you.'

'Careful, she might hear you.'

'You're with her now? You hound.'

'She's in the bathroom, I think,' said Mike. He looked around the corner; the bathroom door was closed, a few towels dropped on the floor outside.

'You two might make a great combo, you know.'

Mike rolled his eyes and smiled.

'Burlington Arcade, lunch?'

'See you there,' said Rick.

The line went dead.

———————— • ————————

Mike walked through Mayfair, alongside Julie. She would occasionally pull him closer, and he would return the gesture, the soft touch of her body against his comforting him, drawing him in further. She brought him to a stop and disappeared into a shop, leaving him outside, watching her closely through the window, wishing he were alongside her again, longing to talk to her more, to touch her more.

She slipped out of the shop and kissed him softly on the lips, but he remained quiet. He was too afraid that he might disturb the magic of the moment. She remained silent, too, but he knew it was not because she was afraid of him. He was older, more experienced, and had suffered more pain, but she was strong, independent, and knew what she was looking for, what she wanted. A partner, someone to support, to be supported by, someone to grow and to love with.

Julie kissed him again and bid him farewell, promising more time together, the next time. He tried to say something in response but could only muster a mumble and a half-hearted wave.

He didn't want her to leave.

———— ● ————

'Listen, Mike,' said Rick, as he pushed his lunch around his plate, 'to tie this thing up, we're going to do to Harriston what we did to Ratlick.'

'Trap him?' said Mike, his foot tapping the floor nervously.

'Exactly. He wants the GTO. So, let's give it to him.'

'And how will we go about that?'

'What do you see across the road?'

Mike looked out of the restaurant's window, through the passers-by, into the traffic. Between breaks in the cars, buses, and trucks, he caught a glimpse of a showroom, a few cars parked inside.

'A showroom.'

'Ten points. We put the Ferrari somewhere like that, on display, and let everyone know about it. Make it a real scene-stealer. Social media, the works.'

'We might snag a buyer that way, but what about Harriston?' said Mike.

'How badly does he want it?'

'Badly.'

'Exactly. A little smash-and-grab action, that's nothing compared to what he's done so far,' said Rick confidently. 'And we make sure people see it.'

'Cameras, photos, that kind of thing.'

Rick nodded. 'We put it up and out there for a few days, get the Colonel involved, and let whatever happens happen. They get whoever comes, they go to the police, which leads to Harriston, which leads to us getting out of this mess.'

'Operation Wheelbase two-point-oh,' muttered Mike. 'Maybe.'

'There's a place near South Kensington tube station that we could use,' said Rick. 'I've already given it a once-over.'

'How will it play out, do you think?'

'There's a small mews with a little dealership in it, near the Michelin House in Chelsea. Two street entries. An easy place to steal something from, if you wanted to. Not in the public eye.'

'I think I know it,' said Mike. 'And the Colonel will be okay with this?'

'Absolute walk in the park, compared to last time,' said Rick, nodding. 'Once whoever is coming for this thing comes for it, we block the two exits, and that's them done for. We call the police, if the need arises, and sit back and watch.'

'That sounds like we're going to have to be quick, though,' said Mike warily. 'And forceful.'

'Our turf, our terms, this time,' said Rick cheerily. 'Don't fret. One of us should keep our nose relatively clean. I'll get it organised.'

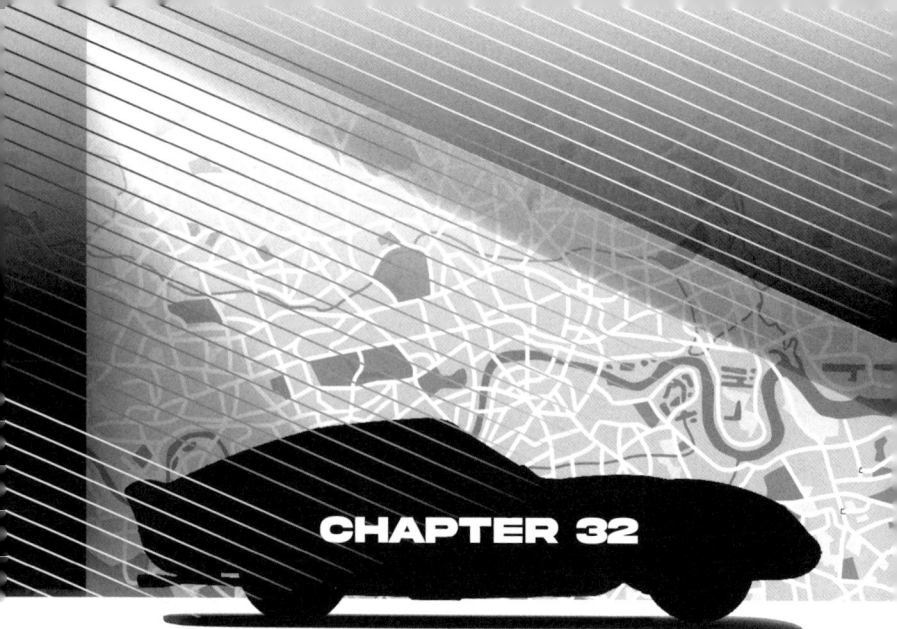

CHAPTER 32

The 1962 Ferrari GTO looked sublime under the soft white lights of the showroom, their hexagonal patterns amplifying the curvature of the 250's sleek body. Its red paint contrasted wildly with the soft amber colour of the walls, and the dark oak flooring. For a moment, it resembled a hot, burning ember, one that had just settled on a piece of freshly cut wood, primed to scorch its surroundings.

Outside, the sun started its lengthy crawl over the horizon, the birds breaking into their melodic dawn chorus. A mechanical howl cut angrily through the morning music, and a loud screeching filled the mews as a BMW screamed into the entrance road. It heaved from left to right, and ploughed through the front of the showroom, smashing the glass entrance and display area, an alarm sounding angrily in response. Its nose dived as it braked hard to a stop, and three men leapt from the car, the driver remaining inside. One jumped into the Ferrari, while the driver reversed the BMW out of the way, while the others dashed around, checking that doors were locked and rooms were empty.

Glass crunched as a Range Rover, a trailer in tow, reversed into the space previously occupied by the BMW. More men jumped out and started to push the GTO up onto the trailer. The alarm droned away as the men busied themselves with loading the Ferrari, none seeming troubled by the din. The door of the Range Rover opened slowly, and a solid-looking boot descended from it, shattering more glass as it drove down to the ground.

Harriston stepped clear of the Range Rover and gestured to the men, hurrying them. The Ferrari was fighting back, its wheels snagging on the side of the trailer, resisting the men pushing it upwards. He shouted at them to sort it out, to get a grip, but they didn't understand English. He yelled at himself in annoyance instead, and stormed back to the Range Rover.

Blinding lights switched on in the courtyard, casting ugly shadows across the paving stones.

'Freeze,' yelled an amplified voice. 'You're on candid camera, mate.'

Vehicles screeched to a halt outside the mews, blocking the path out from it, and footsteps pounding across the cobbles.

'Fuck you,' shouted Harriston. He reached into the Range Rover and pulled out a gun; he waved it towards the lights and shot wildly, stone, splinters and sparks raining down in response, the spent cases clattering across the car's wide bonnet.

Mike and Rick watched, from the floor above, aghast.

'That's a bit much,' said the Colonel. 'We'll have the police here in no time now. I'll go and straighten him out.'

The Colonel reached behind his back and pulled out a pistol, a heavy-looking piece, with worn blueing and wooden grips.

'A word or two from this Hi-Power, I think,' said the Colonel. He darted towards the door, moving gracefully for such a big, powerful man.

'This is getting out of hand,' said Mike. Rick nodded, the ruckus below intensifying as the Colonel burst from a door, his Browning snapping off shot after shot.

An unpleasant silence descended. Whatever was happening, it was out of sight. Mike and Rick craned forward, around, trying to see beyond the view of their window, but there was nothing.

A solitary shot rang out, breaking the peace, and Harriston strolled into view, surrounded by his men. No other noise, no other voice, no return fire. Shadows darted back and forth between cover, hiding, waiting for assistance, or a target.

A dull *bloop* echoed around the mews and something landed in the corner, smoke pluming from it. A thick, acrid cloud began to fill the space, choking everyone. Harriston staggered back towards the Range Rover, his hand over his mouth; some of the men around him split off, seeking refuge from the smoke.

The Range Rover heaved forward, the Ferrari rocking perilously on the trailer, but it kept snagging on one of the showroom's brick pillars.

'He's going to get away,' hollered Mike. 'That bastard's going to get out!'

'Where's the Colonel?' said Rick, hissing through his teeth. 'Where is he?'

The Range Rover surged forward again, the trailer shrieking as it scraped along the pillar, the brickwork teetering alarmingly close to the Ferrari.

'Fuck this!' shouted Mike. He turned and sprinted down the stairs, into the courtyard, towards the Range Rover, his eyes watering from the smoke. The Range Rover's lights flashed over him for a moment, through the gloom, as it reversed and turned, trying to free the entrapped trailer. A shot rang out from somewhere, deafening Mike for a moment, the round embedding itself in the brickwork behind him.

It was hard to make out anything in the thick haze. Torches flashed back and forth, and the sounds of struggles reached Mike's ears as he slammed into the Range Rover's passenger door. He looked up.

Harriston.

The man glared back at him and tried to open the door. Mike heaved back against it, looked up again, and faced a pistol. He ducked, instinctively, as the gun went off, a few pieces of laminated glass raining down on him.

Fuck!

Another gun went off behind him and something hit the floor near him, making a sickly thud. Another shot followed and the Range Rover surged forward again, as a door burst open behind it. Two men charged through, brandishing short, ugly-looking submachine guns.

A volley of shots rang out and the two ducked back into the door as the Range Rover broke free, the trailer popping off the hitch, leaving the Ferrari beached in the shattered showroom. Mike saw Harriston glaring at him as the Range Rover careened away from the mews; the sound of squealing tyres and shattering metal suggested it had pushed through whatever might have trapped it.

'We need to get out of here,' said Rick, as he advanced through the smoke. He had a small revolver in his hands, its barrel pointed towards the ground. 'At least, I do,' he said, nodding at the pistol.

'Leave the rest for the police to sort out?'

'Before they turn up, or anyone else does!' he shouted, drawing a bead on the door.

Mike clambered into the GTO and fished the key from his pocket. The V12 caught quickly, settling to a healthy idle, as Rick snapped off some warning shots towards the door.

'Time to move,' he barked, as he clambered into the Ferrari.

Mike stabbed the Ferrari into reverse and popped the clutch. The car leapt backwards, off the trailer, and clattered to the ground, its bodywork snagging on the ramps. Mike winced and dabbed the brakes.

'Don't be fucking gentle now,' screamed Rick.

'It's priceless!'

'So's being free! Just drive!' he shouted.

Mike shook his head and squeezed the throttle, the Ferrari barking as it accelerated towards the shattered frontage of the showroom, scattering broken glass in its wake. Someone dressed in black darted in front of it, waving a gun. Mike stamped on the throttle and they bounced across its bonnet, up over the windscreen, and tumbled away.

'Keep going!' cried Rick.

The Ferrari's weak headlights flashed over someone curled on the ground, blood thick around their head. The car bounced over flowerbeds and into the middle of the mews, breaking free. Mike twirled the wheel as the tail swept wide, pointing the car in the direction Harriston had gone. A smashed car was beyond the exit to the mews, its hazard lights flashing, someone tucked behind it, fumbling with something. Mike accelerated, sweeping the Ferrari through the gap, out onto the open road.

Each exhaust howled loudly as the Ferrari screamed down the unpopulated streets of South Kensington, right into Stanhope Mews, through the arch onto Cromwell Road.

'Maybe we should slow down,' said Rick. 'I mean, we're in our car, we're not stealing this.'

'Look,' said Mike, his finger darting towards the windscreen. 'That Range Rover!'

He changed down a gear and squeezed the throttle, the needle on the Ferrari's tachometer climbing towards six thousand.

'What are you doing, Mike?!' yelped Rick.

'I don't know,' he shouted back. 'But we can't just let him get away!'

The Range Rover grew larger, the gap closing, the Ferrari's V12 screaming away in anger. They blasted through three sets of red lights, scattering the few early-morning risers away from the kerb, and then Mike saw something, something small, moving next to one of the Range Rover's windows.

The screen in front of him splintered, sending glass everywhere, and something whipped past his face, embedding itself in the rear of the cabin.

Fuck!

He stabbed the brakes, the Ferrari's Dunlop racing tyres squealing in protest, and slowed, one hand carefully checking over his face.

'Best choice,' said Rick. 'This thing would fold up if we got clipped by that Range Rover.'

They watched as the Range Rover drove off into the distance, towards Heathrow, and Mike brought the Ferrari to the kerb.

He let it idle; they did the same, catching their breath and gathering their senses.

'Good thing this has got display plates on it,' said Mike.

'Can't believe fines are on your mind,' said Rick.

'More worried about the police,' said Mike nervously.

'Look, we were doing what we had to. We'll be alright. I'll have a few more words with some people. This is our car, technically; the worst you might get is a slap on the wrist.'

'Jesus,' said Mike, huffing noisily. 'But people got shot.'

'I think that was the Colonel,' said Rick sadly. 'I think Harriston got him, or one of his lackeys.'

'The body on the floor?'

Rick nodded, then stared through the windscreen. His phone rang and, after a few moments' contemplation, he answered it.

'Yeah,' he said calmly. 'Okay.'

He hung up and put the phone on the Ferrari's dash.

'Well?' said Mike expectantly.

'Friend of mine. They've got a helicopter going up and some roadblocks going out. They're at a bit of a loss as to what's going on, so we've got some time.'

'Best get out of here, though, still.'

'Best.'

Mike drove out of London, swiftly and smoothly, fruitlessly trying to keep the Ferrari as quiet and as unnoticed as possible. They scanned the skies and the mirrors cautiously, looking for signs of trouble, but there were none. As the roads opened up, Mike let the Ferrari sing, up to 7,500rpm in third, the gear lever clacking as Mike hit fourth, putting more distance between them and their problems. Their sense of relief grew as London fell further behind, the gauges all looking good, the fuel tank still half-full.

'I think we made it,' said Rick, glancing at Mike. 'For now.'

Rick continued to look in the mirrors, and upwards, his head scanning all around them. They found a hand car wash that was open, with a café next door and a load of industrial units behind it. Rick found one that was happy to store the car for a while, after some cash had changed hands, to keep it away from prying eyes, above and on the ground.

'That was a bloody close call,' said Rick, as they walked away from the unit. 'We got very, very lucky.'

'But Harriston made it out, too,' said Mike. 'None of that went to plan.'

'Not in the slightest. We were only supposed to nab Harriston. Not have a bloody shootout and a car chase.'

'You didn't expect him to be that heavy.'

'I think we may have underestimated the severity of his situation,' said Rick sullenly. 'A cornered animal is as dangerous as a wounded one.'

'And what about the Colonel?' said Mike.

'Not much I, or we, can do about that. Time will tell.'

Rick opened the door of the coffee shop and ushered Mike inside. They sat down, in front of the window, and shook their heads in disbelief.

'Where the bloody hell did that come from, back there?' said Rick. 'You leapt into the mix like a diver who'd seen a pearl!'

'I'm going to chalk that one up to adrenaline,' said Mike uncertainly. 'Well, that and maybe, I think, I'd just had enough.'

'Enough of Harriston?'

'Enough of being pushed around.'

'Remind me to stay on the right side of you. Certainly took back control, I'll say that. And Harriston will be on the ropes now, after all that.'

'GTO's taken a bit of a beating, too,' said Mike. 'The rear end's going to need a lot of work.'

Rick smirked at him.

'Don't worry,' he said casually. 'It's not a real one.'

'What do you mean?' said Mike, aghast. Rick just continued to smirk, a heavy show of satisfaction on his face.

'Oh, you bastard.'

'That's right. It's a replica that I, uh, borrowed for a bit,' said Rick. 'The real deal's in Buckingham, in a storage container.'

'What if you died? I might never have found it.'

'I told Chiara all about it, so don't you worry yourself.'

'Covering the bases, eh?' said Mike, quietly impressed.

'Always, mate.'

'And Chiara, she knows about tonight?'

'Most of it, yeah,' said Rick, sounding a little restless. 'But the fact that Harriston made it out, well, I'm not sure that'll go down particularly well.'

'And I'm sure he's similarly pissed now. I'm not sure there are any limits to this game now.'

'Do you really think the Colonel's dead?' said Rick.

'I don't know. It looks like someone shot him in the head, Rick. I really don't know.'

'I hope not,' said Rick.

CHAPTER 33

The Phantom idled down Mayfair and into an underground car park. Mike and Rick walked out into the street, the clouds overhead hiding the sun, and down to La Traviata, an upmarket Italian restaurant. A woman dressed in a black tuxedo, with a bow tie, greeted them and escorted them to a round table in a quiet area of the restaurant. Chiara was sitting there, a half-drunk glass of wine in front of her, and a heavy-set man to her right. She gestured angrily at Mike and Rick, the man next to her staring blankly at her, and they sat down opposite her.

'You boys must be completely out of your mind,' she hissed. 'Seems you went straight back to your school days, playing cloak and dagger in the streets of South Kensington. The papers are full of it. She slammed a tabloid down on the table; Mike could practically see the smoke and heat rising up from her. Rick picked it up and stared at the text, expressionless.

'Some fifteen people involved, four people injured,' he said, sounding less mechanical with every word. 'Hey, there's no mention of anyone dying or dead in this.'

'You're lucky you're not both dead,' muttered Chiara.

'All we wanted was to catch Harriston red-handed,' said Mike defensively. 'We didn't expect so many to get involved, for it to kick off like that.'

'And do you have him?' she said, livid.

'No,' said Mike. He glanced at Rick, then shrugged.

'He escaped,' said Rick. 'But there's enough on him now to make his life hell.'

'His life was hell already,' responded Chiara. 'Whoever he was tangled up in China with was putting the screws on him.'

'We need to find him,' said Rick. 'Preferably, I think, before he finds us.'

Chiara looked at them, one by one, slowly, studying them. She swirled her wine around, put the glass down, and waited for it to settle.

'Listen, ragazzi, here is some advice. You need to do that kind of thing quietly. Without mayhem. Without anyone taking notice. And without dragging the police into it.'

'Yeah, that might have caused a few problems,' said Rick. 'Lesson learnt.'

'Well, I don't think they'll be troubling you much,' she said knowingly. 'But what were you thinking?'

'It was a good plan,' said Mike defensively. 'It almost worked, too.'

'Almost worked is shit,' snapped Chiara. 'What if you'd got killed? How do you think Julie would feel? Tsk.'

She wagged a finger aggressively at the both of them.

'You should have let my people take care of this.'

'What do you mean?' said Mike, looking confused. Rick didn't look surprised.

'You are the ones playing here, not us,' said Chiara. 'We're used to this.'

'Well,' retorted Mike, 'we almost got him.'

'But you haven't, have you?'

'No,' said Mike, dully.

'But we have!' she responded brightly. 'He wasn't hard to spot or follow. We picked him up after you kicked off that awful kerfuffle.'

'What?!' said Rick loudly.

'We got a lot of his associates, too. They're with the police now. Finding it very hard to explain anything. But Harriston, well, we needed to have a word.'

'I'll be...' said Mike.

'Better than Netflix, I'll tell you that,' she said, smiling. 'He's downstairs, if you'd like to have a word with him. He's not very comfortable, though.'

Rick and Mike stared at each other, then got up.

'Please,' said Rick. He drove his fist into his palm a few times.

'Come with me, then.'

Another guard appeared and escorted the trio towards a door at the back of the restaurant. He opened the door and nodded to other men in the corridor below, who parted, letting them through. Behind them were two iron doors, which the men opened slowly. The group walked through, into a dimly lit storage room. Julie was sitting in one corner, at a wooden table, her face illuminated by a laptop's screen.

'We know you took the money from us,' she said, her voice as cold as ice. 'Your bitcoin wallet, give us the access code now.'

A figure huddled in the corner of the room shifted slightly.

'Bloody hell,' said Mike.

'Seconded,' said Rick. 'What are you doing to him?'

Chiara pulled them out of the room for a moment.

'We've been working on him for a little bit. Nothing too extreme. He's quite soft, really. I don't think he had much left in him, after everything you've put him through.'

'But what for? What's he to you?' said Mike.

'I'll kill you and your whole family,' shouted Harriston from the corner. 'You'll never get a penny out of me!'

Chiara shook her head.

'This can't just be about your Alfa that he took,' said Mike, baffled.

She put a hand on his chest and cut in aggressively. 'No,' she said plaintively. 'Fanculo, for once in your life, this isn't about cars.'

Mike went to speak but Chiara's index finger dug into his chest.

'We go way back,' she continued, her voice haunting. 'You remember my father, Mike?'

'Yes, I do. You said he met a bitter end after that government contract went sideways. His head was chosen to roll, but someone got to him before that.'

'Exactly. It turns out it was Harriston,' she said, then sighed. 'He used my father's credentials to fake army supply contracts, to get the funding, and then ran, leaving my father to deal with the consequences.'

'The government killed your father?' said Rick.

'No. But at some point, amid all of that, Harriston, the prick, signed a contract with the Libyans. They didn't hesitate to chase after who was at fault.'

'I can imagine,' said Rick.

'We are certain he killed Fechtel, or at least had him killed, and that he was involved with the wind farm scam. That cost us tens of millions.'

'Why Fechtel?' said Mike, remembering the newspaper article like it was yesterday.

'I think he had figured out that something didn't stack up. He was going to blow the whistle on Harriston, or his company, at least.'

'Fuck you!' shouted Harriston. A guard put his fist into Harriston's side, and he fell silent.

Chiara shrugged. 'And, of course, he took your cars, too.'

'You fucking Italian bitch,' screeched Harriston. 'You don't know who's involved. They'll get to you next!'

'Are you sure about this?' said Mike, his voice laced with caution.

'We're just talking with him,' she responded curtly. 'We're willing to release him if we get certain things straightened out.'

'I'm surprised, to be honest,' said Rick. He leant against the wall, looking away from Harriston, back up the stairs. 'This guy sounds like he's done you a lot of damage.'

'It's not all his fault,' said Chiara. 'He chose poor business partners. Heavy-hitting partners. He made commitments he couldn't, didn't, keep, like delivering certain assets, funds, contracts. And here we are.'

'Some of those regarding cars?' said Mike.

'Precisamente. Some stolen to order, some to win certain minds, some to sell, some as chips for finance. And some, some as compensation.'

'And the cost of not delivering?' said Rick.

'Worse than this,' said Chiara, tipping her head in the direction of Harriston. 'A lot worse.'

Julie waved another guard into the room. He marched forwards, carrying a chair and a noose. He slung the noose over a hook in the ceiling, set the chair beneath it, and dragged Harriston over to it. He fixed the noose around Harriston's neck and lifted him up, onto the chair, forcing him to stand. The chair was flimsy, and its legs wobbled precariously as Harriston's weight settled on it. He protested weakly.

'For the last time, Harriston,' said Julie. 'Free passage, no grief, if you just send us our money and fifty per cent on top. That's… two-hundred and twenty-five million sterling, today. You can keep the rest.'

No response was forthcoming.

'He has that kind of money to spare?' said Rick in a hushed, doubtfully tone.

Chiara's head bobbed. 'Isolated, illegitimate. That's why it's in crypto, so it can't be tracked or pinned down. We think a lot of it came from certain deals, the rest from corrupt or collapsed crypto exchanges.'

'So, he couldn't just cash it in,' said Mike slowly. 'Because someone might come looking.'

'Precisamente. We think, in time, he would have converted it into other coins, assets, cash, and slowly drawn it down, when the rates were good.'

'I'll stick to the hard stuff,' said Rick. 'At least you know where you stand with that.'

Chiara marched back into the room, leaving Mike and Rick at the doorway, and whispered something in Julie's ear. Harriston shifted around, spinning a little, seemingly uncomfortable at her presence.

'She says you've had your chance,' said Julie. 'We're just going to leave you here and let nature take its course. Well, we might nudge it along a little, but the outcome will be the same.'

Julie nodded at the guard, who flicked open an ugly-looking switchblade.

'Alright,' mewed Harriston. 'Alright.'

Chiara crossed her arms and waited.

'If you let me go, I'll give you what you're looking for, but only if we agree on a deal.'

'I'm listening,' said Chiara quietly.

'I will give you the names of individuals in the government and trade organisations, in Brussels, that are working for us. And the ones in the European Commission, pushing various contracts in an eastern direction. All about generation and storage, batteries, electric car production lines, the works. You keep them going, supported, and we share the profits that come our way. It's millions, maybe more.'

'And what's the endgame in that scenario?'

'We... they are trying to overtake all of the Western manufacturers and OEMs, to push for conventional fuels to be phased out, so they can capitalise on their infrastructure and production facilities.'

'Out with fuel, in with batteries,' said Chiara. 'And anyone who doesn't have what's needed, doesn't have the in, gets crushed.'

'Take the names, do whatever. Just let me go and leave some for me. Deal?'

Chiara waved a hand quickly at the guards. The door closed, thudding shut heavily, leaving Rick and Mike with a solitary guard. He pointed up the stairs, then nodded at them.

'I think it's time we left,' said Rick.

'But what about Harriston? And that deal?'

'I think it's time we left,' repeated Rick.

The Phantom speared towards Chapman & Sunderland Vintage Motors, its engine almost silent, the air rushing by barely audible.

The peace and comfort of its interior was such a stark contrast with anything they had experienced recently, so much so that Mike and Rick felt ominously unsettled. It was almost alien to them.

'We still need to sell these cars, you know,' said Rick, changing the tack of the conversation. 'Let's knock out a combined viewing and sale in Bournemouth, at an airfield, and just get it done.'

'I like the sound of that,' said Mike. 'Something quick, straightforward. We just invite our best customers, so we don't have to vet anyone.'

'Exactly. They know us, we know them, and they'll know what they're getting. We need to generate the money to pay the family, and the quicker we can move, the better.'

'It'll give us more time, I think, in case we need to do anything else.'

'Exactly,' said Rick.

'Twenty people, you reckon?'

'That would be a good number. We've some of the best Ferraris in the world. They shouldn't prove too hard to sell.'

Mike's phone rang. He pressed the answer button and Julie's voice filled the cabin. He smiled. Rick shook his head at him, then made a subtle stabbing gesture, and grinned.

'Julie, it's Mike. We're on the move, Rick's here.'

'Glad to hear it. Hope you get a bit of rest, the both of you.'

'At some point, maybe,' said Rick.

'Just a quick update for you both. We've been compensated by Harriston. We have our money, which concludes our business with him.'

'Is he still breathing?' said Rick.

'He is, at least the last time we saw him,' said Julie. 'Going that far, well, that wouldn't make us any better than him.'

'True,' said Rick. 'And once you're down at that level…'

'That is what we thought,' she said.

Mike's shoulders rose, an immense mental weight sloughing off them.

'I'm very glad to hear that,' he said. 'You both had me wondering.'

'We're dangerous, Mike, but not brutal. We're not like Harriston, or his associates.'

'I suppose,' said Mike, 'it'll catch up with him eventually, anyway.'

'Indeed,' said Julie. 'It's only a shame that we didn't get my mum's Alfa back. Harriston doesn't know where it is any more.'

'Oh, right,' said Mike cheerfully. 'About that…'

───────── ● ─────────

Rick strolled around the office, stretching his legs, wine glass in hand. 'Listen, Mike, this is what we'll do. A silent auction. Closed. Just our bidders.'

Mike nodded at him.

The less fuss, the better, he thought.

'We'll give an option for bidders to deposit sealed bids remotely, too, just in case they can't make it in person.'

'Spread our net a bit wider.'

'Just that,' said Rick. 'And maybe Hadford will materialise and finally stick his fund's oar into the deal, once he sees other people moving on them.'

Mike could sense a positive energy, for once. He was feeling more comfortable, relaxed, back in his domain, back in control. The gears were turning.

'It's not as popular here as it is in Europe,' continued Rick, 'but going the sealed bid route should make some up their stakes, hopefully netting us a bit more cash.'

'And we can state a minimum asking price for each, so offers should be above that.'

'Exactly,' said Rick, his head bouncing up and down in agreement. 'No lowballs, no nonsense.'

'And the bids will all be private, so there will be no speculation, no media attention, no volatility in market prices. These cars are too valuable, too rare, too desirable to be compared to anything else.'

'Six Ferraris, each representing a unique and significant opportunity, from our Austrian Collection.'

'That's going in the email,' said Mike, his pen flicking across a clean sheet of paper.

'Discretion guaranteed. And accessible by air, too. Put that in there as well, just in case.'

'And no commission,' said Mike. 'That'll get their attention.'

'Let's get the invites out.'

CHAPTER 34

The first Ferrari flashed up on the screen and the lights in the warehouse dimmed, leaving only the car in question illuminated. The silence was broken only by the odd word slipped between the bidders and their family, assistants, or investors. Mike recognised many of them; Edward Hadford, Joseph Groniger, Thomas Saganer, and even Dr Bayerwald, were all present. There were seventeen registered bidders in total, but perhaps thirty or so people in the room.

Chiara caught his eye and winked at him. She had a small piece of white paper in her hand; she wrote something on it, tucked it into an envelope, and walked over to the auctioneer. He took it from her, inspected it, and slipped it into a stack of similar envelopes.

So much money in play, so casually, thought Mike, as he watched the auction from the back of the room. Other bidders approached the auctioneer, and handed over their envelopes, then retreated to their seats. The process didn't take long: five cars were sold within 30 minutes, contracts signed, some written agreements fleshed out, deposits deposited, and transfers organised. But not for the GTO. It remained unsold, despite sitting front and centre, despite its pedigree.

But it'll find a buyer, in the end.

Rick appeared alongside him, holding two glasses of champagne. He handed one to Mike, then downed half of his own.

'I've just had word back from Malcolm's crew,' said Rick quietly. 'The original 250's back with its owner in Malta now.'

'It's coming together, then,' said Mike. 'We've done it.'

'And it's been a good night so far, too. The payments are starting to come in as well, which is good. We've a pretty tight schedule.'

'Let's hope we can move the GTO on after the fact,' said Mike warily, as his phone started chirruping away in his pocket. He pulled it out, glanced at the screen, shrugged, and answered it.

'Benny,' said Mike cheerfully, his elbow digging into Rick's side. 'What a surprise! I didn't know you had my number.'

'Hadford gave it to me,' said Benny, his voice dulcet and refined. 'Said you were selling some toys.'

'We are, or were,' said Mike. 'It's a Ferrari collection.'

'Were?'

'Yes, the auction is taking place as we speak.'

It was Rick's turn to elbow Mike.

'Ah, but there is one car left, and it's the best one.'

'Oh, what is it?' said Benny. 'A Short Wheelbase?'

'No, better in my eyes,' said Mike. 'It's an original 250 GTO. One of only 36. Certified to the nines, all documented.'

'Listen Mike, I've been out of the loop for a bit. I'm in Rome now, just picking up some things for my sisters. Hadford sent me the location. I'll be there in, say, three hours.'

'From Rome? In what? The Enterprise?' said Mike, his voice thick with disbelief.

'No. I'm knocking around in an F-15C. It's getting on a bit, but aren't we all?'

Mike gawped. Rick watched on, his expression a mixture of confusion and amusement.

'You'll be telling me you've a tanker somewhere to keep you up next,' said Mike, still not entirely convinced Benny wasn't pulling his leg.

'Something like that. Over Verona, out of Treviso. Anyway, how much is the GTO?'

'For you, it'd be forty-five million, US. Shipped to your location of choice, of course.'

'See you soon, then,' he said, 'and thanks.'

'Same to you, Benny,' said Mike. 'Same to you.'

The call ended and he leant back against the wall, desperately trying not to yell with delight. Rick poked him, eliciting no response, so he did it again, but harder.

'Ouch,' responded Mike, stifling a laugh. 'What?!'

'Well?' said Rick. 'What was that all about? You look like you've just won the lottery.'

'You'll see,' he said, cheerfully. 'Give it three hours or so. You'll see.'

———————— • ————————

Mike and Rick listened to the howl of Pratt and Whitney turbofans in the clouds above the hanger. The noise intensified and a white dart flashed between breaks in the cloud, then began to subside, the noise of the birds twittering away in the trees filling in the gaps.

'Friend of yours?' said Rick, pointing to the skies.

'Friend of mine,' said Mike. 'It's Benny, one of the potential buyers I told you about a long while back. Like you said, he's in the Royal Saudi Air Force.'

A gleaming white F-15C speared out of a cloudbank and settled into an approach, touching down neatly just past the threshold. It taxied smoothly towards them, one engine winding down, and came to a halt just outside the hanger. Silence descended as the canopy started to rise, the big jet whistling and humming in ever-decreasing pitches as switches were flipped and breakers were pulled.

Benny waved from the cockpit, helmet in hand. 'Hello, Mike,' he shouted. 'Got a ladder, or some steps?'

Rick looked at Mike disbelievingly, then scurried over to the hanger, returning with a tall aluminium step ladder.

'That'll do, friend,' said Benny, as Rick erected the ladder next to the F15's cockpit. 'You must be Rick?'

'That's me. You sure know how to make an entrance, I'll say that much.'

'Thanks. I only wish it was a D variant, then I'd have two seats, and a bit of space for luggage!'

Benny turned to Mike, then slowly wrapped his arms around him. 'It's been a while,' he said. 'It's good to see you.'

'And you,' said Mike. 'It wasn't that long ago that Rick and I were talking about that Submariner I gave you.'

'Yeah,' said Rick. 'This guy complains about not getting free lunches, but he'll happily give away a top-end watch. Go figure.'

Benny nodded happily. 'Well, that's Mike. Always generous. And I've still got that watch, you know.'

'You're joking?!' said Mike.

'Not at all. Front and centre in my collection, just as a reminder. Reference number 6538, with a rare tropical dial. It's a bit smarter than it was back then, though.'

'Wish I could say the same about myself,' mused Rick.

Benny grinned and gestured towards the hanger, where some of the auctioned cars were carefully being loaded into covered transporters, destined for their new homes. 'I don't know, it looks like you're doing quite well for yourselves.'

Mike grinned at Rick, then at Benny, then slowly put his hands together. 'Now, about this Ferrari.'

———————•———————

The bottles of beer Mike was carrying rattled and clinked as he collapsed on the leather sofa, next to Rick, in their office. Rick was silent, staring at the ceiling. Mike joined him and proffered a beer in his direction, saying nothing. He felt Rick take it from him, heard the pop of its cap coming off, heard the bubbles, heard a hefty swig being taken.

'Well,' said Mike, exhaling heavily. 'Let's not do that again.'

Rick clinked the top of his bottle against Mike's, then laughed quietly to himself.

'I'm just glad he liked the car. I wasn't expecting him to buy the 737 as well, though.'

'I'd say it was cheaper than shipping it, but…'

'It was cheaper than the Ferrari, at least.'

Rick looked at him, the humour and relief flushing from his face.

'Seriously, though, we've done well here. We've made a substantial profit, the decks are cleared, we've more cars lined up, and everything's in order. What do we do now?'

'How about a holiday?' said Mike, laughing.

'I don't know about you, but somewhere hot would suit me to a T right about now. Maybe a break from cars and planes, who knows?'

'I'd give it about ten minutes before you were looking at the classifieds again.'

'Yeah, and you'd be nosing around the nearest local auction or yard before the breakfast buffet had shut.'

'Maybe I'll spend some time fiddling with that cloned Ferrari we've still got kicking around. It doesn't seem like anyone wants to lay any claim to it.'

'Let's see if the police stake a claim to it first,' said Rick. 'I've not heard anything yet, though. I can't really see why it'd be of interest to them.'

'Maybe we can use it to scam some scammers out of some cash.'

'Don't you go getting all brash now,' said Rick, his finger wagging. 'Let's rest on our laurels for a bit.'

'And what do you think Chiara will do, now the dust is starting to settle?'

'Ah, she'll carry on, doing the usual. She'll always be one of those types pulling the strings in the background. Maybe we'll give her a slightly wider berth. And Julie?'

Mike shrugged, trying to look nonchalant.

'We're just going to play that one by ear,' he said quietly. 'But I'd like to think there's some mileage in it.'

'Perfection takes time,' said Rick. 'But you look happy. A lot happier than I've seen you in a long time.'

'There's a lot to be said for that.'

Simon appeared in the doorway, holding a hot cup of tea and a torn piece of paper from a notepad. He pushed his glasses up his nose, then looked at the scribbles he'd made.

'Gents,' he said buoyantly. 'Just had a call about a find. Sounds pretty super. Some twenty-one cars, apparently, in a basement in Italy.'

Rick looked at Mike, sighed, and shook his head.

'Twenty-one cars?' said Mike, ignoring Rick. 'That sounds like a job that'll need at least four trucks.'

Rick sighed loudly again, sat up, and put his hands on his knees.

'Best make it five,' he said, eyes rolling. 'Just in case there's something else we want to come back with. There's always bloody something else, I guarantee it.'

'Just in case,' said Mike, smiling at him. 'You never know, after all.'

Michael Kliebenstein is an award-winning author and classic car specialist. Leveraging over 45 years of automotive experience, he travels the world to find the ultimate in historic cars for collectors, museums, and other car-related companies.

Many of his experiences and discoveries serve as the basis for his articles and books, including the outstanding SuperFinds (published by Porter Press International), a truly unique work that explores significant and remarkable car finds from the 1960s and 1970s. Kliebenstein, who has been involved with cars since he was old enough to hold a Matchbox model, is also a collector, restorer, racer, photographer, advisor, and marketing expert. Above all, he is a true classic car enthusiast and has a driving passion for collectors' cars in their untouched original condition and form.

michael-kliebenstein.de